Bhima
Lone Warrior

MADATH THEKKEPPAT VASUDEVAN NAIR was born in 1933 in the village of Kudallur in Kerala's Palakkad district.

Possibly the most loved and widely read writer in Malayalam, MT, as he is affectionately known to friends and readers, started life as a teacher. He moved on to journalism in 1957, and retired as the editor of the *Mathrubhumi Weekly* in 1997. He is now president of the Thunchan Memorial Trust.

MT's literary oeuvre is as varied as they come: novels, short stories, screenplays, travelogues, literary criticism and books for children. The short story is, by his own admission, MT's favourite literary form – it's certainly one he excels at. He has over twenty collections of short stories to his credit, ranging from *Kutti Edathi* in the fifties to *Sherlock* in the late nineties. Much of his fiction chronicles the disintegration of the matriarchal joint family system of the nairs of Kerala and the conflicts associated with this process, which is the world he grew up in.

Unusually for a literary giant, MT is intimately associated with cinema. Apart from being a prolific screenplay writer – he has written over fifty screenplays – MT has directed or been otherwise associated with the films based on his screenplays or stories. *Nirmalyam*, his first screenplay and the first film he produced and directed, based on his short story 'Sacred Sword and Anklets', won the President's Gold Medal in 1973. *Oru Vadakkan Veeragatha* (1989), *Sadayam* (1990), *Kadavu* (1991), *Parinayam* (1994) and *Oru Cheru Punchiri* (2000) all won national awards. Twenty-two of his screenplays have won Kerala state awards.

He was awarded the Jnanpith in 1996 and the Padma Bhushan in 2005. His award-winning novels include *Nalukettu* (1954), which won the Kerala Sahitya Akademi Award; *Kalam* (1969), which won the Central Sahitya Akademi Award; and *Randamoozham* (1984), which won the Vayalar and Muttathu Varkey Awards.

GITA KRISHNANKUTTY has translated the novels and short stories of several Malayalam writers, including M.T. Vasudevan Nair, Lalithambika Antharjanam, N.P. Mohammed, Paul Zachariah, Anand and M. Mukundan.

Bhima
Lone Warrior

M.T. VASUDEVAN NAIR

Translated by
GITA KRISHNANKUTTY

HARPER PERENNIAL

NEW YORK • LONDON • TORONTO • SYDNEY • NEW DELHI

First published in English in 2013 by Harper Perennial
An imprint of HarperCollins *Publishers*

HarperCollins Publishers India, Cyber City, Building 10-A, Gurugram,
Haryana-122002, India

www.harpercollins.co.in

11th Impression 2018

Copyright for the original text in Malayalam © M.T. Vasudevan Nair 1984
Translation copyright © Gita Krishnankutty
Illustrations copyright © Namboodiri 2013

P-ISBN: 978-93-5029-759-9
E-ISBN: 978-93-5029-760-5

This is a work of fiction and all characters and incidents described in this book
are the product of the author's imagination. Any resemblance to actual persons,
living or dead, is entirely coincidental.

M.T. Vasudevan Nair asserts the moral right to be identified
as the author of this work.

All rights reserved. No part of this publication may be reproduced,
stored in a retrieval system, or transmitted, in any form or by any means,
electronic, mechanical, photocopying, recording or otherwise,
without the prior permission of the publishers.

Without limiting the exclusive rights of any author, contributor or the publisher of
this publication, any unauthorized use of this publication to train generative artificial
intelligence (AI) technologies is expressly prohibited. HarperCollins also exercise
their rights under Article 4(3) of the Digital Single Market Directive 2019/790 and
expressly reserve this publication from the text and data-mining exception.

Typeset in 10.5/14 Adobe Thai 13/14
Jojy Philip New Delhi 110 015

Printed and bound at
MicroPrints India, New Delhi

HarperCollins Publishers, Macken House, 39/40 Mayor Street
Upper, Dublin 1, D01 C9W8, Ireland

*S*ootas and magadhas, let us sing ballads about the Kuru race once more. Let us salute Kuru and his son, Pradeepa. Let us salute Pradeepa's son, Shantanu. Let us salute Ganga – she who sprang from Vishnu's sacred feet, who witnessed birth, love, sin and death. Let us salute the great Bhishma, the renowned son Shantanu had by Ganga, who amazed even the gods with the harshness of his vow. Let us salute Vichitravirya, the son the fisherwoman had by Shantanu. Let us salute Dhritarashtra and Pandu, begot by Krishnadvaipayana-Vyasa upon Vichitravirya's wives. Let us salute Vidura, the equal of Lord Dharma, whom Krishnadvaipayana had by a servant woman.

Then let us salute Yudhishtira.

Let us salute Kuru, whom Samvarana of the race of the Moon had by the daughter of the Sun, Tapati.

Friends, let us sing once more of the greatness of the races of the Sun and the Moon.

PART 1

The Journey

The sea was black in colour. The waves dashed against the shore, screaming, as if devouring the palace and the great city of Dwaraka had not sated their hunger.

The five of them stood on the rocks, gazing at the scene below in amazement, in disbelief. In the distance, at a spot that must have marked the crest of the victory pavilion of the old palace, the water was now still. In front of it, the slanting head of a tall, majestic pillar rose high. The small stone structures of the ramparts dotted the shore beneath as far as the eye could reach. A lone chariot that had escaped being shattered when the waves flung it down lay leaning on its side, its yoke sunk in the sand.

Vestiges of Dwaraka's old splendour, which the deluge had masticated and spat out, lay scattered on the wet sand of the shore like the lifeless bodies of thousands of animals lying on a sacrificial site.

Yudhishtira whispered a warning to calm his now faltering heart: 'Remember, all beginnings have an end. Oh heart, remember everything your grandfather, Krishnadvaipayana, said to you before the great journey.'

Arjuna, who had been compelled to witness the destruction of Dwaraka earlier than the others, moved back, reluctant to go down to the seashore.

Dwaraka had been trembling with fear. When they saw Gandeevi, everyone, including the women, had crowded around him, relieved that a protector had arrived at last. The women's quarters in the palace had been terrorized by the nightmare of a female form with a black body and a face that grinned, showing huge white teeth. Wearing black clothes, she had prowled through the darkness of the corridors. Old mothers spoke of how they had begun to see evil omens much earlier. Jackals had come out of their dark lairs in the daytime in search of prey and howled in the middle of the city at high noon. The people of Dwaraka were relieved to see Arjuna, who had come to save them from danger. The women crowded around him, placing their trust in the speed of his hands, in the strength of his Gandeeva bow. It was a futile task to try to console them, saying that it had all been a bad dream. When the wicked dacoits had gathered up the women before his eyes and dissolved into the forests, Arjuna, the great archer, had wept within, knowing his strength had ebbed away. The modesty and good name of the women of Krishna's palace had been torn to shreds among the wild thickets in front of him, and the echoes of their wails still rang in his heart. Meanwhile, the rough hands of the deluge-waves and the famished wind had already begun to attack the body of the now naked, shelterless city. In the sound of the waves dashing on the shore, Arjuna continued to hear a laugh filled with the arrogance of having erased the history of the Yadava race.

When he had walked through the emptiness of the battlefield of Kurukshetra earlier, after the great war had ended, weaving his way among carcasses and over rivers of dried blood, Arjuna had felt no sorrow. War was the dharma of the kshatriya race and death lay on the other side of victory. Krishna had walked with him there, reminding him wordlessly that everything that had happened so far had been a move in a chess game played by destiny.

Had Krishna, who died when a hunter's arrow pierced him, foreseen his end? Krishna, who wielded the strength of his weapons and of his soul? Sighing, Arjuna thought that of the duo Nara–Narayana, man and God, that he and Krishna had been, only Nara remained.

Arjuna had taken a firm decision not to turn and look back when he started the great journey – not only at the road behind, but at any of the paths he had trod in life. Standing apart, away from the vague clamour of the waves, he warned himself once again: do not turn and look back.

Draupadi, Subhadra, Chitrangada, Uloopi, all the countless women whose names he could not even remember, had been nothing to him in life. As the brahmin who taught him the scriptures when he was young used to say, they had been no more than sacrificial flames set alight to offer his seed to the gods. Or mere ornaments for an archer to lift up and display at his moments of victory.

But Krishna, who had been nurtured by this little country and clan that the sea had swallowed and was now licking its lips over – that man had poured his love over him. For the first time, and for the last, he was aware of the vastness of a love that had no limits.

When he was young, Arjuna had tried to see all aspects of love in the teacher who had singled him out proudly in front of a multitude, declaring that this disciple was dearer to him than his own son – the ideal of love that a young man cherishes.

Dronacharya had needed at that time to nurture self-confidence in the soul of his young disciple, knowing that the burden of the gurudakshina that he would demand from him later would be extremely heavy. The emotion felt for a sacrificial horse as it is led out to graze is also love.

Had Krishna not mastered the strategies of a charioteer, Arjuna was aware that he himself would never have become the leader the world now knew. Krishna was the friend who had always arrived to rescue him from the traps he kept falling into because of his pride, who had never found fault with him. Arjuna had faced many dilemmas in life, even contemplated suicide. He hoped the world would never learn that his heroic tale ended as it did, that Arjuna failed Krishna on the simple mission entrusted to him: the safety of Dwaraka. The ever-victorious Arjuna had watched, defeated, as the Kirata dacoits seized the women of the city. He now thanked his elder brother, Yudhishtira, silently in his heart for having finally taken the wise decision to lay down the burden of life, say goodbye and start on this great journey.

News of the calamities in Dwaraka had reached Hastinapura earlier. But when Sahadeva went to the palace to tell the women what he had heard, he had not realized that the destruction was so terrible.

Sahadeva looked at Nakula, who was staring at a particular point in the sea and realized that the years had not taken a toll on his brother's physique. Older than him by a few seconds, Nakula's face still had the liveliness of youth. His form was radiant even when clothed in bark. Nakula stood, walked, talked with the awareness that the eyes of beautiful women followed him through the little openings set into the doors. He had not given up the habit of standing with his head tilted slightly back and his right fist firmly planted on his waist.

Sahadeva gazed at the distant spot on the sea where Nakula's eyes were riveted. The tip of the majestic pillar that had been visible earlier had sunk deeper and was continuing to sink. If he wanted, he would now be able to calculate how many seconds more it would take to become invisible. Mental exercises were always a delight to him. Sahadeva remembered that it was no longer necessary to astonish or amuse anyone. The great journey had begun.

When the pillar was finally submerged, Bhima suppressed the smile of simple delight that had risen to his lips and looked at Yudhishtira, who stood with his eyes closed and his head bowed. Bhima remembered what he wanted to say to Draupadi, who stood behind his elder brother, her head also bowed: that withered garlands had been lying on the seashore, in a narrow channel between the chariot sunk in the sand and a broken lion-pillar. Between the garlands, he had glimpsed a huge ruby, obviously part of some ornament, glowing like an eye of fire in the sunlight.

No, Draupadi would not have seen anything. Gazing only at her feet, she was trying not to see that Dwaraka had been destroyed. Bhima remembered that it had always been a habit of Draupadi's to stand immobile, letting her mind wander over distant places.

Bhima suddenly thought of the short time he had spent in Dwaraka as a guest and student. The day he arrived, he had not felt the happiness of having come to an uncle's house. Balarama, his cousin, had treated him distantly, emphasizing the difference in their ages. In the mornings, anxious not to waste time when the messenger came to call him, Bhima used to rise early and get ready – remove his ornaments, knot his hair over his head, wind his upper cloth tightly around his waist and smear boar's fat over his body. He was always worried: would the guru teach him the secret strategies used when waging war with the mace, the ones he taught Duryodhana? It seemed to him that his guru often forgot that he had asked him to come for a lesson in the mornings. In the evenings, while the guru spoke through a haze of liquor, Bhima would sit at his feet, listening to everything he said. When would he reveal the secret of the strategies that Shukacharya had told him about earlier and that only Balarama knew? Bhima was uneasy at night, wondering what he should do or say so that the guru would show the same interest in him that he showed in Duryodhana. Whenever he took leave of the guru, he took care not to betray his disappointment at having learnt nothing new.

Krishna had been away at that time. And Bhima had met his uncle, Vasudevar, only twice: as soon as he arrived and when he said goodbye to him on the twenty-second day. All that had lingered awhile in his memory was the astonishment he felt when he encountered the wealth and prosperity of Dwaraka.

Yudhishtira began to walk forward. Bhima's turn came next. He walked past Arjuna, who was trying to conceal his grief, climbed down the rocks and reached the seashore again. Yudhishtira had already gone far ahead. The others must be following, thought Bhima – Arjuna just behind and after him, Nakula. Behind Nakula would be Sahadeva, in front of Draupadi, who had to be the last.

So they walked through nights that knew no difference from days. As the miles fell behind them, Bhima felt that they were in the vicinity of regions they had wandered through earlier as pilgrims, during the period of their exile in the forest. Do not think of that, he rebuked himself. His teachers and his elder brother had said at the beginning of their journey: the mind that seeks the path of salvation should not engage in such activities.

The past no longer exists for us.

When memories and hopes are wiped out, the mind becomes still and unwavering, as pure as crystal.

Was not the sacred rivulet of Sira somewhere here?

Even if you see it, you must walk on as if you have not; that is the rule.

As the peaks of Himavan became visible in the distance, it seemed as if Yudhishtira's pace quickened. Bhima walked on at his own pace, listening to the footsteps behind him, the swift intakes of breath.

The slopes of Himavan! On which side was Shatasringa, which caressed me when I was a child, Bhima asked himself. Was the hermitage of the sages who had given him his name and conducted his thread ceremony still there? Shatasringa, our foster-mother, do you see Bhimasena, do you see the Pandavas as they go on their final journey?

Bhima recalled a forest on the banks of the Ganga, on the western slope of glowing Himavan. A shrivelled forest. The fragrance of the madhuka flowers that had fallen during the last monsoon still lingered beneath the trees. Forest streams licked the bitumen off the rock surfaces in its valleys. There was a gleam in the eyes of the black-skinned beauty who ran through the forest, bearing the scent of the flowering kutakappala trees in her hair. Shadows stole shyly over the ground, screaming silently at the festive boisterousness of youth. Where, where were those forests whose names he did not know, the forests that had laughed, covering their eyes partially as they looked on his naked manhood?

Once they crossed the heights and descents and reached the other side, a thorny desert terrain stretched out before them. They had to continue their journey until they crossed the distant peak of Meru. After that, everything would end peacefully in yoganidra, where the mind lies between sleep and meditation. Bhima stopped when he heard a sob and a subdued lament in a voice that he could recognize in the midst of any chaos.

He called out in a voice loud enough for Yudhishtira to hear, 'Wait, Elder Brother, Draupadi has fallen down!'

Without slowing down or turning back to look, Yudhishtira said, 'I am not surprised. She lost the strength of mind she needs to find her way alive to the feet of the gods long ago.'

Bhima was taken aback. Was Yudhishtira speaking of his noble wife?

He heard Yudhishtira's words, wafted to him on the wind, clearly, 'She loved only Arjuna. Even when she was seated beside me for the Rajasooya sacrifice, her eyes were on him. Continue to walk, do not wait for those who fall down on the way.'

Yudhishtira kept walking.

Bhima heard the footsteps behind him come closer. His eyes steadily gazing at the peak of the great Meru mountain, Arjuna skirted Bhima who stood blocking his way, taking care not to touch him.

Bhima said to him, 'Draupadi fell down.'

Arjuna did not seem to hear. Bhima wondered: had the wind, which blew so fiercely through the thorny bushes, making them tremble, deadened his tired voice? But he could find no more words to say.

A little later, as Nakula's form of molten gold, perspiring with the effort of movement, passed him on his left, Bhima heard him murmur: 'There is no time to wait for anyone.'

Bhima waited for the moment when the youngest one, Madri's son, the one he always thought of as a child, would gather Draupadi up in his arms and go past him. Sahadeva would never leave her on the ground and go on. She was not just the wife for whom he had been fifth in line as a husband, she had also unstintingly poured a mother's love over him.

But, in the end, when Sahadeva too went past him, looking neither left nor right, his eyes riveted on the footsteps of those who had gone ahead of him, his lips quivering in concentration, Bhimasena forgot the rules of the great journey. He turned around. And in that one moment when he forgot all the scriptures, all the rules, the peak of Meru that had invoked him with its invisible power, lay behind him.

Dragging his exhausted feet, Bhima retraced his path.

He stood by Draupadi, who had lost her balance and fallen on the scorched earth, among the thorny bushes. Her shoulder-bones twitched as she lay with her lips pressed to the earth, her breath faint. He knelt down beside her. Withdrawing the hand that had shot forward to touch her shoulder, he called: 'Draupadi!'

Draupadi's exhausted form stirred. She sat up with an effort. Bhima saw with relief that her eyes, which had first wandered all around as if seeing nothing, were gradually becoming clearer.

But he saw only disappointment reflected in them. Yudhishtira and Arjuna had not waited for her. No one had waited.

He repeated, 'I am here.'

Her eyes became hard, then grew moist. They followed those who had gone ahead, into the emptiness of the desert. She saw no one. The wind had erased even the footprints of those who had gone that way in search of eternal peace.

She looked at Bhima, who stood bewildered, not knowing what to do for her. He saw the silent questions that crowded her eyes.

Her lips moved. But he could not make out the words she managed to speak. He longed to know whether they expressed gratitude, or were a prayer, or whether they asked for forgiveness. Or were they a curse on those who had gone away?

He waited for her lips to move again.

A prayer took shape in his mind: say something, for the last time, say something. Just once.

Once again, Draupadi's tired head slipped down.

Somewhere in front of them, could he hear the sound of the wheels of the heavenly chariot approaching to welcome Yudhishtira? Somewhere very far away?

What he actually heard, however, was from the distant past. Chariot wheels rolling over palace courtyards, forest paths, the battlefield …

Bhima sat down sorrowfully, waiting for her eyes to open, gazing steadily at her.

Then he smiled.

PART 2

THE MURMURS OF A CYCLONE

1

I remember the journey from Shatasringa to Hastinapura only vaguely. I had climbed into the chariot because I wanted to see the sights on the way. But I slept most of the time. I would wake up when we reached resting places on the wayside, then go back to sleep.

While waiting at the fortress gates of the capital city, I could see the mansions in the distance. On either side of the doorway, below statues of lions, stood four guards with swords at their waists and long spears in their right hands. The spear-points glittered brightly above their red head-dresses.

What fascinated me were the huge drums that hung outside the doorway, on either side of the flagpole. I turned around to ask a question and noticed that Mother looked uneasy. A thought arose in my five-year-old mind when I saw her face as she stood there with Sahadeva on her hip and Nakula pressed close to her knees: Mother was afraid! I realized it was not the moment to ask questions.

Among the ascetics who had accompanied us from Shatasringa was one who was very old. He went with the other brahmins who had come with us to meet the guards and came back alone.

Mother asked, in a voice tinged with anger, 'How long are we to wait?'

The old ascetic said, 'A messenger has gone to the royal court. Pandu was the king of Hastinapura. Therefore, his wife and children have to be received with all due ceremony.'

My elder brother, Yudhishtira, stood quietly behind Mother. My younger brother, four-year-old Arjuna, who was running to and fro among the stationary chariots, came up to me and asked, 'Is this our kingdom?'

I did not reply.

Before we started on our journey, when the servant maids were getting us ready, Mother had said to us, 'We are going back to the capital.'

I had often wondered why we had been living in tents in the forest when a kingdom and all the comforts of life were waiting for us. The servant maids had told us of the obsession the kings of the Kuru race had for hunting. I had asked myself repeatedly: at the time when, after performing the Ashvamedha sacrifice successfully, my father should have been ruling over the country, wielding power and prestige, why had he chosen to go and live in the forest with Mother and our younger mother, Madri? It was difficult for me to understand a passion for hunting that lasted six years. Besides, kings who set out to enjoy the pleasure of the hunt did not usually take their queens with them.

I knew, as we waited at the gates of the fortress, that we were the princes of Hastinapura, where our father's elder brother, Dhritarashtra and his children lived. Aunt Gandhari had sent messengers bearing gifts and pearl-studded jewels to the forest. And we had heard much about Bhishmacharya, whom we had been taught to revere like a grandfather. It was he who had brought up my father and his elder brother. Our real grandfather, Krishnadvaipayana, they said, was always away, wandering around the sacred forests.

Aunt Gandhari had given birth to a son at the same time as I was born. I had heard the servant maids whisper to one another that if my uncle had not been blind, and had not therefore entrusted the kingdom to my father who was his younger brother, it was that child of Gandhari's who would have become the crown prince. My elder brother, Yudhishtira, now had the right to the throne of Hastinapura. It was he who had been told to light my father's pyre in the forest, seventeen days earlier.

I looked at my elder brother, who stood half-hidden behind Mother. I thought he too was afraid. This brother, who made a fuss if we even touched him while playing, saying we had hurt him: was it about him the sootas and magadhas sang songs of praise? The songs said he would conquer fourteen kingdoms and earn the title of Emperor.

Suddenly, conches sounded and drums thudded from within.

Groups of people had started to gather, perhaps because they had heard we were waiting at the fortress gates. Many of them were women. People were pointing at us and saying something to those behind them. As the crowd swelled, those in front came closer. Watchful, Mother rebuked Arjuna softly for straying away from our group.

The palace guards moved to either side and the bodyguards came out. In the group of people following them, I noticed a man walking rapidly towards us. His grey hair was knotted above his head like a crown. His beard was white. Taking long strides, he overtook all the others.

Mother said, 'Walk on, walk on …'

She set Sahadeva down and greeted the man respectfully, her palms joined above her head. Then she knelt down before him.

He touched her head and said, 'All the boys have come, that is good.'

Mother looked at my elder brother and said, 'Prostrate yourself before your grandfather.'

We prostrated ourselves before him one by one, in order of our age. As Nakula and Sahadeva waited for Mother to indicate their turn, he swept them up together in his arms.

By that time, a noisy crowd of men and women had gathered around us.

I looked at the grandmothers who were embracing Mother. We greeted them one by one, according to the instructions of the sages.

A man stood at a distance from all of us, watching and smiling. He was one of the group who had accompanied Grandfather Bhishma. He wore no upper cloth, no ornaments. I thought the eyes that peered through the wavy hair that fell over his forehead had a smile in them. He was thin and tall. He was not a brahmin, nor did he wear the decorations of a kshatriya.

Mother noticed him when she broke free of the group of women. She quickly prostrated herself before him. He smiled and said something to her but I did not hear what he said.

Mother's eyes were searching for us.

'Prostrate yourselves before your younger uncle, Vidura.'

Someone pushed Yudhishtira from behind so that he stood in front of us.

After Yudhishtira had made his obeisance, Uncle embraced him and said, 'You look even more radiant than I had imagined, child.'

When the courtesies were over, Uncle gripped my shoulder in a caress and said to someone who stood near him, 'Bhima has grown bigger than Duryodhana!'

People washed our feet with water. The crowd that was pushing itself closer to us began to sound vociferous. Bhishmacharya called Vidura and said something to him. Vidura spoke to the old ascetic, who was part of the group which had come with us from Shatasringa: 'The brahmins, the noblemen and all the families who are gathered here have come to meet the sons of Pandu. Please introduce them.'

The old man came up to us and then turned to the crowd. The royal group at the fortress gates and the crowd around us fell silent, waiting to hear him speak.

'The great and benevolent monarch Pandu, king of the Kauravas, is no more. You all know that.'

He paused.

His voice grew louder as he started to speak again.

'Noble people of Hastinapura, extend your welcome to the brave sons that Pandu had by his wives through divine boons while he was in Shatasringa!' Taking Yudhishtira's hand, he led him forward. 'This is Yudhishtira, the son of Kunti, Pandu's eldest son, born through the blessing of Lord Dharma. The prince who will one day be famed by the name of Dharmaputra, Dharma's son.'

My elder brother smiled. He was always careful to display the exact degree of humility each occasion demanded. He was being very attentive to Mother's instruction that all eyes would be upon us and that we must therefore conduct ourselves with the dignity proper to princes.

Someone moved me forward.

'The second Pandava, born from the blessing of Vayu, the Wind God, Lord of one of the eight directions. Bhimasena is destined to become extremely strong.'

Thinking that my uncle's son, Duryodhana, might be somewhere among the group of women and would hear this, I held my head high and looked for him. Did these people not believe the ascetic? They were laughing. Were they laughing at Vayu's son, destined to become the mightiest of the mighty?

The ascetic lifted up Arjuna, then set him down and said, 'Arjuna, the middle Pandava. The young warrior born of the God of Gods, Indra. Celestial voices proclaimed at his birth that he will subdue all archers.'

He then pointed to Nakula and Sahadeva, one of whom straddled Mother's hip while the other clung to her hand, 'Nakula and Sahadeva, twin sons of Madri, who fell upon her husband's funeral pyre, choosing to follow him. When they grow up, no prince on the face of this earth will be able to challenge these boys, born from the blessing of the Ashwini Devas, in intelligence and beauty.'

The smiles on people's faces had vanished. They looked stunned: it must have been at that moment that they remembered the deaths in the forest. I too felt sad when I recalled my younger mother, Madri, who had flung herself into Father's pyre and died. The servant maids had comforted us, saying that many kshatriya women had done the same thing.

One of the ascetics said, 'Let us get ready to conduct the funeral rites for Pandu and Madri, who performed many good deeds, lived in the forest and earned wealth in the form of sons so that the Kuru race could grow and flourish. Once the mourning period is over, let all the noble brahmins and lords conduct prayers and sacrificial rituals to honour the gods who conferred this wealth in the form of sons upon them.'

Vidura said to Mother, 'Come with me, the king is waiting for you in the court.'

Mother went in with all the old women. Yudhishtira followed, holding Vidura's hand. Arjuna and I walked behind Grandfather Bhishma. The women had hoisted Nakula and Sahadeva on their hips. Fascinated by everything they saw in Hastinapura, the little ones laughed delightedly.

A woman whose face was entirely concealed by a black cloth wrapped around her head waited alone at the entrance to the main hall of the court. Mother ran up to her and fell at her feet in obeisance. She lifted Mother up and said, 'Forgive me for not coming out to welcome you. You know I never go out.'

We did not need to be told who she was – our aunt Gandhari, who always covered her face and never went out. Her messenger used to bring us gifts. I longed to see the face behind that black mask. We prostrated ourselves before her in turn, then stood within the circle of her long, slender arms on which the blue veins stood out clearly. She said to each of us softly, in a voice that was almost a murmur, 'May you prosper.'

Mother wiped the tears from her eyes.

My aunt placed her hand on Mother's shoulder and said, 'Walk on. He is waiting.'

My blind uncle. When she had learnt he was blind, my aunt had decided to cover her face, live within the confines of the palace and never go out.

He was alone, his presence filling the couch placed in the centre of a space surrounded by intricately carved wooden pillars. A forest of hair rose above a golden band, in the centre of which glittered a jewel. Devoid of pupils, his eyes were like white circles. His heavy jaws moved constantly, as if he were chewing. I was frightened when I looked into his rolling eyes, and stopped some distance from him. Was he chewing on something, or muttering to himself?

Mother said, 'I am Kunti, who has become a widow. My sons and I bow before you in obeisance.'

He placed his hand on my head when I prostrated myself before him. Standing afterwards within his embrace, I was suddenly struck by the size of his massive arms.

He said, 'These five boys are also my sons from now on.'

Mother wiped tears from her eyes once more.

I felt that his feeble voice did not suit his massive frame.

One of the songs I had heard the sootas sing in the forest had been about this uncle. It said that King Dhritarashtra had the strength to subdue 10,000 elephants in rut. While Nakula and Sahadeva were prostrating themselves before him, I avoided looking at his eyes and gazed instead at his huge hands and broad chest. How small the devachhanda necklace with its hundred strands looked, lying on the expanse of his wide chest! The singers were right. His hands were as massive as sala trees. If he had had eyes, he could have defeated all the kings with just those huge arms.

Maybe the sootas and magadhas who wrote the songs had exaggerated a bit. But it was clear that this uncle had the strength of at least one rogue elephant.

I suddenly noticed three boys who had entered the hall and

were standing behind Uncle. The one who stood on his right, running his fingernail over the golden bubbles on the corner-piece of the couch kept staring at me. Long earrings hung from his ears and a rashmikalapam necklace with fifty-four strands lay over his breast like armour. I said to myself, it looks ugly on him. I was probably jealous, since I wore only an ekavali chain with a single strand.

Having sent away the people who had come from Shatasringa with gifts, Grandfather Bhishma joined us in the court.

He saw us children standing at a wary distance from one another and smiled. 'Come, Duryodhana and Dussasana. You are all going to be together now. Chitrasena, child, come here.'

Uncle was speaking to Vidura, 'You must perform the funeral rites for Pandu and Madri. Make sure the brahmins are given all the usual gifts.'

It was Chandrasena, the youngest of them, who came up to us first.

Duryodhana had been born on the same day as I. Not moving from where he stood behind the couch, he continued to stare at us. I tried to smile at him. He pretended not to notice. He looked bigger than me.

As we walked towards the palace kept ready for us, I laughed.

Yudhishtira looked at me warningly. Pretending I had not seen him, I said to Arjuna, 'Did you see, Uncle's sons are wearing flowers in their hair!'

My elder brother said, in a tone that implied there was nothing strange about this, 'Blockhead, princes usually wear flowers in their hair. There were not enough servant maids in the forest to bring us flowers, that's why we didn't wear them.'

I had been about to say something else, but I kept quiet, since he had called me a blockhead. When Grandfather Bhishma had called them to meet us, Dussasana had looked at his elder brother, as if asking him what to do. I had wanted to ask Duryodhana, isn't it difficult to wear a burdensome necklace with fifty-four strands? Dussasana, the younger brother, wore only a manavakam chain with sixteen strands around his neck.

When we were at Shatasringa, I had once listened with great interest as Mother set out all of Father's jewels to teach my elder brother about the different kinds of ornaments and their names. I had secretly decided at that moment that, when I grew up, I would wear a star-necklace with twenty-seven huge pearls. I had heard that it was the necklace that best suited intrepid warriors with massive bodies.

Why had Duryodhana looked at us with such resentment? Even when I smiled, he had continued to look grave.

Preparations were still underway in the palace that had been set apart for us.

One of the older servant maids came up to me and said, 'Let me look at you properly.' The maids caressed us, one by one, telling us stories as they did so. There had been a cyclone here in Hastinapura the night I was born in the forest. Vultures and owls had screeched. Jackals had come into the palace grounds and howled. Astrologers had observed the positions of the stars and predicted that I had been born in order to annihilate my race. The old woman reminded us that this prediction was equally applicable to Duryodhana.

Many people came to see us, most were palace attendants. They stood respectfully before Yudhishtira, who was only a year older than I, their palms joined. Yudhishtira would be a king in the future. Therefore he remained serious most of the time, smiling only when necessary as he accepted these courtesies.

Nakula and Sahadeva were in the hall inside, with Mother. The visitors paid their respects to Arjuna as well, since he was going to be the greatest of archers. Before they left, they recalled the story of the strange child who had fallen down from someone's arms as soon as he was born and, instead of being injured, had shattered the rock on which he fell. So they came and looked at me with amazement. Pretending to hold me close and caress me, they pressed various spots on my body, testing its strength.

I was surprised to learn that stories had reached the palace about me as well. I had heard, while we were in the forest, of how I had fallen once from my mother's arms and how, when she picked me up, terrified, she had been very relieved to find that nothing had happened to me. But the story had gathered strength as it made its way here.

I hid my embarrassment. Was my build so different from that of other children?

On our first night in the palace, we were served abundant quantities of food and there was a variety of dishes. I made the discovery that food could be made in so many varied forms and with such a multitude of flavours. In the forest, anything we could find to fill our stomachs when we were hungry had been considered food. Those who served us smiled as they refilled my empty plate. Yudhishtira looked at me warningly, as if to say this was not suitable behaviour for a prince, but I pretended not to notice.

At night, an old soota came and sang ballads that narrated stories from the past. When he began to sing the tale of how

King Shantanu had seen Ganga and desired her, Yudhishtira asked him to stop. We had heard it so many times. So he sang the story of the serpents, Kadru and Vinata, instead.

Feeling sleepy, I went away. When I lay down, I thought about Father's death. All of us had to perform the funeral rites the next day. But if we were to believe what the ascetics had said, was it really my father who had died? The father whom I, who was going to become so mighty, must venerate, was the God of the Wind – and he was immortal.

From the time I could remember, we had been taught to pray to three forces: to Indra of the thousand eyes, Fire with seven flames and Rudra who had been born as the blazing light of Brahma's fury. I looked at Arjuna, asleep next to me. At least one of the prayers he recited daily must reach out to his father, Indra.

Did my father, who was the Lord of the Hurricanes, ever think of me?

I had a dream that night: a mighty elephant in rut lunged forward to attack me, tossing its tusks. When I tried to climb a tree to escape from it, a watchman brandishing an axe barred my way.

I woke up with a start and found my elder and younger brothers sleeping on either side of me.

It seemed to me that I had seen the face of the axe-wielding watchman who guarded the tree somewhere. It resembled the face of Uncle's son, Duryodhana.

Half asleep, I closed my eyes and prayed silently. 'O God who chains the stormy winds, I, your son, a child five years old, am here.'

The god who was my father did give ear once to my heartfelt prayer. Many years later.

2

Our youthful years in Hastinapura were filled with very busy days.

Before day broke, we would begin to hear music in which strains of the conch, the mridangam, the veena and the flute mingled. Reluctant to get up, I would lie in bed. In a little while there would be the sounds of brahmins performing their rituals of purification. The intermittent thudding of drums would follow; then the trumpeting of one of the less obedient elephants from the distant sheds and the clatter of horses' hooves keeping time with the rolling of chariot wheels. During that period in my life, I thought that the most beautiful music in the world was the sound of rolling chariots.

The five of us had begun to sleep in separate rooms and each of us had a charioteer to serve us, as well as shudra women as servant maids. In the morning, once we were ready, we had to go to a class where we learnt the Vedas. I was always the last to arrive. Our uncle's sons were taught in another place. We had heard that Vidura's sons would study with us, but they did not come. I asked why, and Yudhishtira said, 'It's just as well if they do not come. They are shudras.'

Grandfather Bhishma and Vidura would sometimes stand at the door and observe us. Our teacher stood up to pay obeisance only when Grandfather came. Signing to our teacher that he should continue, Grandfather would walk away hurriedly.

After this class, we would practise with weapons in the courtyard of Shukacharya's residence. We were by ourselves there as well. A year later, when Kripacharya began to teach us,

Uncle's sons came to train with us. Three of our teacher's senior disciples came to assist him.

Princes are required to learn four kinds of warfare, waged with chariots, elephants, horses and foot soldiers. One could become a rathaveeran, a warrior who had mastered fighting from a chariot, only after becoming adept at waging war from a chariot drawn by a single horse. The soota ballads included heroic stories of how Bhishma had waged war against the kingdom of Kashi in a chariot drawn by a single horse and brought back our grandmothers, Ambika and Ambalika, as brides for Vichitravirya.

After we received instruction in the use of weapons, we had to bathe and then eat. Before we went to the inner hall for a meal, we had to go and see Mother. She now lived alone in a palace. Its southern wing was empty. Our grandmothers and our great grandmother, Satyavati, used to live there. On the day when the last rites for our father were over, they had all left with our grandfather Krishnadvaipayana for the forest. I had heard it said at the time in the palace that they were going to perform penance in order to attain a very special Heaven known as Devapadam.

Later, however, I learnt that Grandfather Krishnadvaipayana had advised the women to leave Hastinapura quickly, rather than stay and witness the many riots and quarrels that were going to break out there.

Krishnadvaipayana had watched from a distance while the brahmins performed our father's funeral rites. It was then that I saw him properly. I had heard that he used to come sometimes to Shatasringa at night. His dark-skinned, slender body was completely smeared with ash. Matted hair carelessly bundled up in a knot; a yellowish beard that had grown so long, it completely concealed his neck; a length of coarse bark wound around his waist. His light red eyes glowed bright. I observed him while the rituals were being performed. We had heard that he was immortal. No one knew the Vedas and Shastras as well as he did. It was because our grandmother, Ambika, had been terrified at the sight of him and closed her eyes that her son, our uncle Dhritarashtra, had been born blind. And our grandmother Ambalika had turned pale with fear and given birth to my father Pandu, a baby devoid of physical strength. The next time, my uncle's mother had sent her servant maid. The woman had not been afraid of him and he had therefore given her the boon of a son who had no deformities at all. I did not know whether that fearless servant woman was still in the palace. I had not heard anyone speak about her. It was said that, thanks to Krishnadvaipayana's blessing, her son, Vidura, grew up to be so intelligent that even the greatest teachers revered him.

I saw nothing in Krishnadvaipayana that was frightening. But he stayed at a distance from everyone and no one went up to speak to him.

When he set out for the forest with his mother, Satyavati, who was bent double with age, and my grandmothers, Ambika and Ambalika, he had given orders that there were to be no followers, no mourning.

My mother was alone now.

I had assumed that Mother did not know how we were faring in our studies under Shukacharya and Kripacharya, for she never came anywhere near the weapon house.

But one day Mother sent for me.

'Are your studies going well?'

'Yes.'

'And what are you most interested in?'

Kripacharya had started lessons on various types of combat strategies. It was war with the mace that really interested me.

But I said, 'Bahuyuddham, fighting with my bare hands!'

Mother's face darkened. 'Bahuyuddham is for low-caste people. Kshatriyas should learn it, of course, but ...'

Mother was silent for a while, as if thinking of something. 'I was told that you've been harassing your uncle's sons.'

'Who, me? I ...' I was distressed, not quite knowing what to say.

Mother said, 'Remember, it is always us they will find fault with. Do not allow yourself to become known as one who brings evil to his clan.'

It was not I who had been born to destroy his clan, it was Duryodhana. I had heard the sootas muttering among themselves that Grandfather Krishnadvaipayana himself had predicted that calamities were going to take place soon. I was afraid that Duryodhana was spreading false rumours about me.

I often went to the elephant sheds when I had no lessons. There was an old hunchback among the mahouts. He looked as if he would be blown away if an elephant trumpeted, but even the wildest rogue elephant would obey him when he spoke. He had learnt from the great sages all the texts that dealt with elephants and the treatment of the diseases that they were susceptible to. He used to allow me into the sheds with him.

King Dhritarashtra's elephant was as big as a little mountain. Many of the elephants were named after old kings of the Kuru race. Since I was so interested in the animals, the old man granted me certain small privileges. I could touch their trunks and offer them bits of sugarcane. One day, he was showing me the spot on the forehead from which fluid would begin to ooze when an elephant was in rut when we noticed three people standing at a distance, gazing at the elephant shed – Duryodhana, Dussasana and Yudhishtira.

When I came out of the shed, however, I was taken aback. The third one was not Yudhishtira, it was Karna.

I did not even know his name at that time. He was just one of the boys who came with the Kauravas to Kripacharya's classes.

I knew what their stance and their expressions meant. The three of them had evidently planned a united effort to knock me down. I was not afraid of facing them one by one. But I did not want to be defeated in front of the servants who worked in the elephant sheds. I avoided them and went out through the door on the opposite side, saying to the old mahout, 'It's getting late, let me go and have a bath.'

As I walked on without looking back, I heard footsteps rapidly approaching from behind. My legs trembled with fear. What if I ran away? But my cousins and their friend would turn that into a story: Bhima is not only a blockhead, he's a coward too. Tales of how Duryodhana had taught many people obedience were popular amongst the children. Abruptly, I turned around.

Duryodhana was smiling. It was the first time I was seeing him smile. Like a reflection, Dussasana smiled as well. This younger brother always followed Duryodhana like a shadow, obeying everything he said. He looked as big as I was. And strong.

'Take a good look at him, Duryodhana. Look at Vrikodara, who was born to kill all the Kauravas.'

It was Karna who spoke.

When I was a small child, my mother, noting my fondness for food, had said in jest to the senior-most of the servant women: 'My second son is a real vrikodara, he has the stomach of a wolf! Whatever he eats, he's still hungry!'

The name Mother had given me with such affection became a nickname that people in the kitchen area called me scornfully. And once it reached the outer halls and courtyard, it became a synonym for Bhimasena. Every time I heard it, anger would course through me.

I stood there like an idiot.

'Blockhead! Are you the one who's going to kill the Kauravas?'

Duryodhana stood in front of me, laughing contemptuously. In what was probably a pre-planned move, Dussasana slowly closed in behind me. The third one stood apart, ready to enjoy the game.

Even as I wondered how to escape defeat, I couldn't help thinking that this Karna, some charioteer's son who went around in Duryodhana's gang, had an uncanny resemblance to Yudhishtira. Except that the supercilious smile on Karna's face would never be seen on Yudhishtira's.

I knew at once that Shukacharya's rules for Dhanurveda, the science of archery, would have no relevance to my present situation. Duryodhana stood in the vyshakha stance: legs wide apart, balancing on his little toes, his knees firm. And Dussasana, on my left, was in the ardhamandala stance, his knees bent. The charioteer's son stood apart, laughing softly.

Fury, not fear, blazed inside me.

The outer courtyard of the elephant shed was empty. I had

to get this over with before any guards or servant women came that way.

In Shatasringa, as a child, seated on my mother's lap, I had watched tribal people from the forests bring honey and bitumen as gifts and then stage fights to entertain us before they left. Those who fell down from the rocks would not give up, they would fight their way back to the top. Once, I saw a boy who still looked like a child grab a gigantic figure, lift him up and then fling him down. At the end of the fight, when he bowed before Mother, his dirt-smeared face wreathed in a broad smile, she threw him a gold bangle as a prize.

I realized that it was the rules of the forest that would serve me best here.

'Poor blockhead, he's trembling with fear. Spare him. Make him cross his hands, touch his ears and bend down low a hundred and one times, then let him go,' said Karna.

I sprang forward before I could be attacked, a trick I had learnt. Dussasana had assumed that Duryodhana was my target, so he did not expect me to spin left suddenly, hold my chest in and hit him hard with my elbow. He was flung to the ground. I was unsteady on my legs for an instant, and Duryodhana threw himself at me before I found my balance. I was thrown so far that I fell against the wooden frame of the outer shed. I heard Karna laugh again.

But Duryodhana had fallen down as well. He had no idea how quick I, who had grown up running and playing in the forest, could be. Before he could get up, I fell on his back, wound my arms around his neck and pounded his ribs with my fists. Dussasana came running up to help, but I lunged at him and caught his hair with my right hand. Both of them were twisting and turning, trying to shake themselves free. I knew that if they succeeded, they would hit me till I was helpless. So I grabbed both their heads and dashed them against each other. Dussasana's cry of pain spurred me on. I dashed their heads together again, and Duryodhana cried out as well. There was more anger than pain in his voice. Let me reduce these two to a state where they cannot get up, I thought, then I'll deal with the charioteer's son who had been enjoying the spectacle.

'Let go of them, let go!'

People were shouting. My topknot had come loose and someone tugged at my hair authoritatively. I saw that it was Kripacharya.

It was clear that Karna had fetched him, although he was still standing at a discreet distance as if he had no part in anything.

Angry and tearful, the brothers babbled incoherently, unable to express what they wanted to say.

'He's always like this. We weren't doing anything and he …'

I longed to say that it was not I who had begun it. I looked at Karna, standing apart from us. I wanted to let him know that I did not mind if he came at me, a third opponent. I would teach him a lesson when I got him alone, and use a whip to do so.

Kripacharya told us sternly that games like this had to be restricted to the weapon house.

Duryodhana's eyes had reddened. He turned and looked at me as if to say, it's not over yet, and walked away quickly.

Kripacharya tried to control his anger. 'You are brothers. Have you already begun to fight?'

I did not say anything. He walked away, muttering to himself.

When I went to the river that day, my brothers had already had their baths and were on their way back.

'Where were you?' asked Yudhishtira.

I did not give him a clear reply. Nor did I tell anyone about how I had hurt Duryodhana. Surely Kripacharya would not think it a serious matter.

However, Mother asked me after a few days, 'Son, did you spring out from hiding and knock Duryodhana down?'

Yudhishtira was standing beside her. He must have heard what happened and reported it to Mother at once.

I answered, 'No.'

Yudhishtira reminded me, 'You must not tell a lie.'

I looked at Mother and said, 'I was not in hiding. The two of them together ...'

Mother signed to me not to continue.

Yudhishtira came out with me and said, 'All the children in Uncle's palace are going to get together and teach you a lesson.'

'Who said so?'

'I heard.'

I described what had happened in detail only to Arjuna. He advised me to be very careful.

Arjuna used to go late in the afternoon to study archery with Kripacharya. Whenever we were together, all he talked about was archery. One must be able to challenge all the kings, he said, from a chariot drawn by a single horse. Every day, he meditated on his father, Indra. He was sure that his father would come one day to give him divine weapons.

Arjuna told me that the bow and arrow were not suitable weapons for me, and advised me to learn how to wage war with the mace from Shukacharya.

That day, after my evening prayers, I stood alone on the riverbank and meditated on the God of the Wind who had fathered me. Give me your blessing and make me exceedingly strong. Let your son, Bhimasena, be the first in rank in the use of all weapons.

What could I do to please the god who was my father? Who would be able to tell me? Maybe my father's intelligent younger brother, Vidura, would know. But I did not have the courage to ask him. Although he was always somewhere near us, he seemed very distant and usually spoke only to Yudhishtira.

War fought from chariots for Yudhishtira, war with the bow and arrow for Arjuna: the teachers had already decided on who was to learn what. Yudhishtira was to be king – and kings had to be expert at waging war from chariots. Celestial voices had predicted much earlier that Arjuna, being Indra's son, would be an invincible archer. Therefore he had to be given special lessons in archery.

Mother still fondled Nakula and Sahadeva in front of the servant maids in the women's quarters and the kshatriya women who came to visit her. 'These twins, Madri's sons, are dearer to me than the sons I bore myself.'

Nakula and Sahadeva had no great aspirations.

Everyone knew that Mother had a very special affection for Arjuna, though she never said so openly. All the women in the palace loved Arjuna with his beautiful, dark skin. I had seen it in their eyes when we stood together.

The magadha nomads sang about Arjuna when they came to the palace. These singers were supposed to know the future. They sang of how, riding in his chariot drawn by white horses, he would subdue the world with a divine bow and a quiver that would never be empty of arrows. Beautiful apsara women would feel restless, consumed by desire for his dark-skinned body. Even Agni and Varuna would obey the commands of his sharp arrows.

Mother wiped her eyes, which had filled with tears of joy. When they finished singing, she poured gold coins into their hands.

I looked at the northwest and meditated upon the God of the Wind who kept watch there. Was my divine father, who was somewhere in the distance, listening to my prayers?

At that moment, a thousand ripples moved over the surface of the water, like the gathers of a dress unfolding. A gentle breeze suddenly wafted in from somewhere and tousled my hair. Invisible hands that had the moist feel of little drops of water embraced me.

Someone whispered in my ear: I hear you, I hear you.

3

I knew that Duryodhana would rely on the support of his gang to take revenge on me. So I was very wary.

My aunt Gandhari had many children, and I did not know the names of many of them. Besides, her husband, my uncle, had had children by soota and shudra women. All of these children went around together.

On days when we had no classes, we went hunting. Sometimes the chariots went as far as the boundary of the forest. The hunters would organize guarded camps. Soldiers would go on elephants and agitate the forest, so that all the animals came out of their lairs. Archers would then shoot down the fleeing animals with their arrows. These were part of the lessons that kshatriya youths had to learn.

One of Kripacharya's older disciples, Nirbheekara, led these expeditions. We – that is, the older children – spent our time with the archers in the camps. While the rest of the group waited for the game to be cooked, we were allowed to wander as far as we liked in the forest, provided we stayed within earshot. I was sure Duryodhana would take his revenge on me during one of these expeditions.

I was delighted every time a hunting expedition was organized. I looked forward to the moment when an animal fell down, pierced by an arrow that had been released after the hunter had carefully calculated how swiftly the prey could run. Holding my breath, I would wait for the instant that directly followed the twanging of the bow, thinking, there, now the animal is leaping high into the air. And then, when it lay on the ground, immobile, I would look at the archer and see a smile of victory on his face. Whether he was a soota or a shudra, I would want to embrace him.

When we met each other during Kripacharya's lessons on weapons, Duryodhana always turned his face away, while Dussasana's look held a warning: your day is coming.

In the forest, I was very careful never to wander too far from the crowd.

One day, as we were setting out on an expedition, Arjuna said, 'Watch me shoot an arrow and bring down an animal today.'

We had not yet been given our own bows and arrows. These expeditions were meant for us to study the forest and the way animals moved. The older boys carried spears and hung hunting knives in leather sheaths at their waists. Both were just ornaments.

That day, the forest had been agitated, but not a single animal had come near our camp. I was with an archer from Ahichhatra, one who had just joined the army. Suddenly, we heard cries from the camp on the other side. An animal had fallen. Hunters often cried out to announce danger, but these were the rarer cries of celebration.

We joined the hunters as they assembled in a clearing. A huge buck had fallen. Smiling broadly, full of happiness, Arjuna received the felicitations of the hunters. He was ten years old at that time, and I was eleven. I felt proud of my younger brother's triumph. I gripped his shoulders and pulled him towards me.

Yudhishtira said to him, 'Don't forget, a kshatriya has to offer a sacrifice to give thanks to the gods when he shoots down an animal for the first time.'

I looked at Duryodhana. He was standing with his back to us, casually conversing with someone, as if what had taken place was a trivial thing.

On the way back, I was right at the end of the group. Duryodhana and his gang had left earlier, so I ambled along slowly, listening to the calls of the forest birds. I could let my guard down.

And then I heard the cries. These were cries of warning.

A wild boar had jumped down from among the rocks, and now stood, confused, in front of the hunters. It was still for a moment, sniffing. Even from a distance, I could see its tusks, covered with red clay. I was wondering whether to move out of its way when I heard the cries again.

The hunters used to say that a wild boar was more dangerous

than a tiger. And this one was leaping at me now like an arrow just released from a bow. I was standing on a grassy ledge that lay on a forest trail stamped out by the feet of hunters. There was not even a tree nearby that I could hide behind. Terrified, I realized that the infuriated beast had caught my scent and was coming straight at me. It was pointless for the hunters to cry and shout and try to divert its attention. It was flying towards me like a sharp arrow fitted with tusks.

Maybe this was the end. Impaled on the tusks of a wild boar, he who was destined to become the mightiest of the mighty would die, not even giving the sootas a chance to weave a heroic tale of the death of a warrior. This animal certainly did not know what the hunters had taught me – that a wild boar attacks with not a look at the ground, not knowing what obstacles bar its way. It was coming at me with its head raised, its tusks flared and its mouth wide open. Some power beyond my own strength forced my spear into the beast's mouth, and I felt one half of the three-foot-long weapon penetrate it.

As I was flung down, I remembered not to let go of the spear. The clay-smeared tusks were right in front of me, next to my chest. In the animal's final thrust towards me, the spear-point pierced it even deeper. Confident that it would no longer be able to defeat me with its strength, I arched my body and drew myself up. The exhausted animal suddenly writhed in agony.

As the frightened hunters came up, I planted my foot on the lifeless beast and drew out the spear. A stream of blood spurted out and sprayed my body.

I felt I was on the verge of collapse. Arjuna placed his hand on my shoulder. I wound my arms around his neck and waited until I could breathe normally again. Then I smiled.

'When we heard your screams, we feared it was all over,' said the hunters.

Had I screamed then? I did not remember. All my attention had been on the clay-smeared tusks. When had I screamed?

Yudhishtira said gravely, 'You blockhead, what a foolish thing to have done! Don't let Mother know.'

There were no cries of jubilation, no celebration to mark the occasion when I had first killed an animal. Nor did my elder brother mention the sacrifice I should offer the gods in order to please them.

We walked away. But I had decided that I would offer my thanks to the gods anyway. I was certain that someone had lent my hands greater strength at the moment when danger had come so close to me.

I was now fully aware of the strength I possessed. Maybe I was still a blockhead to my elder brother. And Vrikodara to the Kauravas. But Bhima had grown up and become mighty, I said to myself joyfully.

I went to the river well before the hour for evening prayer and swam and played in the water. Then I immersed myself, climbed out and said my prayers. And that day too, the messenger came in the form of a gentle breeze, bearing a message meant only for my ears.

Duryodhana and his companions arrived at that moment. They must have known I had come to the river earlier than usual.

I knew there was no point in being afraid. Many hands stretched out and took hold of me. I kicked down some of the attackers. Curled fists pounded at me, but I felt no pain. Morons! They did not know that if they crowded around me, their own arms and legs would become useless. Pretending that I was overcome, I waited until I could imprison Duryodhana and Dussasana, who were both lunging at me, in my arms. Once I had caught them by their necks, I dragged both of them along and jumped into the river. They twisted and turned, making strange and horrible sounds, as I pushed their heads deep into the water. When it became certain that they would die if I held their heads down anymore, I let go of them. They climbed out with great difficulty, vomited water and sat down on the stone steps.

I stood in front of them, holding my head high. Terrified, the other members of the gang had withdrawn to a distance.

'If you come to attack me again – look at me, fellow!'

Duryodhana raised his head slowly.

'I'll kill you,' I said. 'I'll kill all of you!'

The next day, I was summoned to Aunt Gandhari's palace. All of us were summoned, so I was relieved, thinking it could have nothing to do with the fight on the riverbank.

We filed in, Yudhishtira taking the lead. When we entered the small hall, we saw Mother standing there, with our aunt. The black cloth lying over her head covered only half of Aunt Gandhari's face. Was it me that her eyes were searching for?

Duryodhana and his younger brothers came in. They lined up to the left of us, in front of our aunt.

Aunt Gandhari called me. 'Son, Bhimasena, come here.'

I moved forward slowly. She signed to Duryodhana to come forward as well. Could the eyes behind the black veil see me?

Our aunt asked softly, 'Have you already begun to fight with each other?'

I did not answer. Duryodhana made an attempt to say something, but no words came out.

Aunt Gandhari addressed all of us, 'Let me know if you have begun to fight. Then I too will go to the forest, the same way our mothers and grandmothers went, and you can amuse yourselves fighting one another.'

I had heard people speak of how our aunt had come as a bride from Gandhara to the city of Hastinapura, accompanied by her brother, Shakuni, a hundred bodyguards and a hundred servant maids. People had crowded at the gates of the fort to see the beautiful bride. The grandmothers received her, washed her feet, gave her innumerable gifts and led her inside. It was while the wedding celebrations were in progress that our aunt had learnt that the Kaurava prince, Dhritarashtra, was blind.

When Grandfather Bhishma discussed the wedding with King Subala, her father, he had told him the truth, but the father had not told the daughter. Her brother, Shakuni, wanted to take her back at once to Gandhara, but our aunt consoled him. Subala had accepted the gifts that Bhishma sent, and consented to give his daughter in marriage. Honouring her father's word, our aunt became Hastinapura's bride. After she was married, she never left the palace. Even within it, she walked around with her face covered.

It was this lady, our aunt, who was talking to us.

I wondered whether Aunt Gandhari had forgotten that those who were listening to her were just young boys.

'All the men of the Kuru race have enjoyed seeing their women weep. I know this …'

Her head bowed, Mother whispered something that Aunt did not hear.

'I grieve now for the brides who will come to each of you. The sighs of the princesses who were offered as sacrifices to blind and impotent men still float within these palace walls …' Her voice faltered. 'If you stand together, there will not be a single king in this world who will not pay tribute to Hastinapura and bend his knee before you. Do any of your teachers teach you this?'

No one said anything. Only Yudhishtira bowed his head.

Her slender fingers touched my arm. They were trembling.

'Evil spirits wander in and out of this palace, disguised as astrologers and sages, waiting to see people fall dead. You should learn to live together; none of you is anyone else's enemy. This is something they will never teach you …' She took her hand off me and said, with her head bowed, 'If I hear that any of you has been fighting outside the area where you are being trained to use weapons, I will leave this palace at once. You boys can celebrate after that, killing one another and dying.'

All of us were silent. Our aunt got up and went in, Mother holding her arm. An arm the colour of gold, on which her blue veins showed clearly. She is even more beautiful than our younger mother Madri was, I thought.

We went our separate ways. I more or less understood that what our aunt had said was meant not just for us rivals, Duryodhana and me. But it took me many years to fully comprehend what she said that day.

Although Aunt Gandhari had not made any of us take an oath in front of her, there was a manifest change in our attitudes. We no longer ignored one another when we met in the weapon house. Shukacharya once brought a Yadava who had been trained by Balarama to wage war with the mace. This man made me confront both Duryodhana and Dussasana and later Chitrasena as well. Sahadeva began learning how to use the sword. Whenever we sustained minor injuries, our opponent came to console us. All this time, Karna stayed apart from us, practising with the bow and arrow. He had a special teacher for archery, so for days together, he would not be seen in Duryodhana's company. We forgot our old quarrels.

One day, when we had no lessons, Chitrasena came and called me. 'Come, everyone is ready.'

I was in the elephant shed. A batch of elephants, newly arrived from Kamaroopa, were being trained, and I was riveted.

'Where to?' I asked.

'To the water festival in Pramanakoti. All of us are going. Come on, everyone is ready to go.'

Pramanakoti was a promontory on the banks of the calm Ganga. Bathing houses had been built there for members of royal families. Stone platforms and halls had been constructed for people to sit and watch the competitions that were part of the water festival. But strangely, even the night before, no one had mentioned this festival.

'Who all are going?'

'All of us, just us.'

Duryodhana and his companions had gathered in the courtyard of the palace. The pleasure chariots used when going for festivals stood ready, horses harnessed to them.

I went up to where Arjuna stood with Nakula and Sahadeva.

'Isn't our eldest brother going with us?'

'I don't think so.'

Smiling, Duryodhana came towards me.

'Come. The cooks have already left. Don't worry, the food will not be disappointing!'

He patted me on my back.

I went looking for my elder brother and found him playing dice with one of Uncle's ministers, using vibheetika seeds as counters.

'You haven't yet left?'

I had a feeling that he was not pleased at my having turned up at a time when he was learning to play the game.

I wanted to say to him, if you are not coming, none of us is going. That was what I had been taught: whether we were going to fight a war, or perform funeral rites or celebrate a festival, my place was behind him.

My elder brother was reluctant to stop playing a game he had begun to enjoy. But seeing me standing obstinately at the door, he muttered something and got up.

Duryodhana had kept places for me, Yudhishtira and Arjuna in the first chariot. Nakula and Sahadeva were in the second chariot with Dussasana and Chitrasena.

The Ganga curves inward in a semicircle at Pramanakoti over the spot where the water runs deepest. The water festival takes place in autumn. As we went down to the bathing ghat, Duryodhana said, 'Let the chariots return. We'll walk back along the riverbank in the evening.'

Yudhishtira grunted assent. The disappointment of having lost a day he could have spent playing dice, his new passion, still showed on his face.

As the chariots swung around to leave, I walked to the small garden just outside the bathing houses. There was a strong aroma of food. The cooks had built hearths on which many preparations simmered in huge metal cauldrons. One of the cooks from the big palace was supervising. Knowing how much

I loved food, he said, 'Wild goat and black deer are cooking. You can taste some pigeon flesh right away if you want.'

There was a delicious aroma of cooking meats. I opened some of the packages that were ready. Country beans dipped in sugarcane juice and then fried, large ball-shaped modakams made of jaggery and powdered grains that had been fried in ghee.

I ate just one modakam ball and left.

I climbed a tall pillar, stood on top of it on one leg, arched my body and earned the admiration of the small boys who were standing below. I leapt into the water and swam, first lying flat on my back, then prone. Then I dived deep into the water, caught the unwary by their feet, frightened them and laughed. I made Chitrasena lie flat on my back and swam from one end of the bathing ghat to the other, astonishing the onlookers.

Duryodhana was equally enthusiastic, and even after all the others had climbed out of the water, he and I continued to play in it. It amazed me to think we had been enemies once. When we finally went ashore, Duryodhana said, 'Take your time.' The servants came and took away our wet clothes. Duryodhana said to me, 'We'll eat last. I have a secret for you.'

Everyone had crowded in to eat. Duryodhana called one of the servants and said to him, 'Serve us in the place I told you about.'

Duryodhana's grand preparations at the beginning of the water festival made me feel very humble.

The servants spread a sheet beneath the jamoon trees. As soon as the food had been set out on silver plates, Duryodhana signalled to them to leave. He picked up a piece of fried meat, chewed it and said, 'I have something special just for you and me.'

He opened a leather pot, sniffed it and nodded his head. 'Liquor.'

My first reaction was fear. We were not old enough to drink.

'Fine liquor distilled from madhuka flowers. Only the lower classes drink liquor distilled from barley. This is very special and said to be fit for princes. Try it.'

I took the leather pot from him and sniffed it. It had the smell of withered flowers. I gave it back to him and said, 'No, we are not old enough to drink.'

Duryodhana smiled. 'You became a man the day you brought down a wild boar with your spear.'

I knew that, although I was only eleven, my body was as developed as that of a boy of sixteen. I had begun to feel embarrassed at my nakedness when servant maids came to change the water in the bathing rooms.

No one in the palace had commented on my killing the wild boar. Nor had I heard a single word of congratulation. Vidura had conducted a sacrifice in honour of Arjuna's first kill and Bhishmacharya had given him an arrow fitted with golden wings as a prize.

Duryodhana, whom I had considered my enemy, had been the first to praise me. My heart filled with love for this son of Dhritarashtra.

He raised the pot to his lips, drank a mouthful and said, 'The first animal he shoots down, the first enemy he kills, the first woman he enjoys: these are occasions every man remembers.'

He was speaking in the grave voice of an adult.

'The day he first drinks liquor is important as well.' He smiled and drank again. Then he placed the pot on the ground and brushed back the hair that had fallen over his forehead. His face had grown flushed.

'Your elder brother, Yudhishtira – he's a clumsy idiot who has neither courage nor might. What will he do when he grows up?'

What he had said about my brother did not please me. I had often thought that, though my brother excelled at learning the scriptures and could repeat anything he heard without making a single mistake, he was worse than Nakula in the weapon house. However, Duryodhana had no business saying so.

Yudhishtira was being trained solely to govern the kingdom. Nakula would manage the affairs of the palace and care for the cows. Sahadeva would collect the taxes and control the finances. Arjuna would wage war and so would I. Although no one had described them clearly, all of us knew even then what tasks we would have to take up.

Fortunately, Duryodhana did not pursue the subject. He looked at the pot of liquor I had pushed away and said, smiling gently, 'If you're afraid, don't drink. Liquor is for grown-ups.'

I stretched out my hand at once.

It tasted both acrid and sweet. If I was to drink like an adult, I could not betray my dislike. Determined not to let him defeat me, I drank another mouthful. And then bit into the thigh-piece of a wild goat.

Duryodhana told me that he would soon be going to Balarama to learn how to wage war with the mace. I was envious. Balarama was my mother's eldest brother's son. And yet, neither Mother nor Yudhishtira had considered sending me to him.

'Do you know who the strongest king is?'

I pondered the question. Not Balarama. Jarasandha had defeated him. I had heard about Jarasandha's might in many ballads. So I answered: 'Jarasandha.'

Duryodhana smiled. 'No, my father, Dhritarashtra, is the strongest. Jarasandha has only the second place. But my father will never wage war. Remember, he abdicated his kingdom long ago.'

Duryodhana told me that his father's strength, which equalled the might of 10,000 elephants in rut, was a boon from the gods.

'I too will receive that boon after some time.' He moved his clothes aside and pounded his left thigh with his fist.

'The God of the Wind plucked mountains and juggled them like balls. He will give me that strength.' Inadvertently, I had spoken aloud the prayer in my heart.

Duryodhana's laugh had a tinge of mockery.

'Don't laugh. I am Bhimasena, the son of the Wind.'

Duryodhana burst into loud laughter.

'Yudhishtira from Dharma, Bhima from Vayu, Arjuna from Indra. You are all absolute idiots, as Uncle Subala says. Couldn't your mother have thought of better tales to tell?'

I felt numbed. The import of what he said sank slowly into my mind. Anger made my throat go dry. Duryodhana extended the second pot towards me like a challenge and I took it. I gulped down half the contents in a single mouthful, then tossed the pot away.

'First a convenient hunting expedition, then a long sojourn in the forest, all meant to hide the identities of the fathers of her children. Simple people will believe anything the sages say. But why repeat these things to me, Vrikodara?'

I got up and his loud laughter echoed again: 'The Wind God's son, mightiest of the mighty!'

My legs were unsteady. I lunged forward to grab him and fell down. I tried to scramble up, using my hands for support, but my hands would not obey me and, before they could find a hold, my head hit the ground.

Just as I lost consciousness, I thought I heard more laughter and other voices approaching us, one of which was Dussasana's.

Then someone shouted, 'Where's the rope? Where's the rope, to tie him up?'

The voice of Karna, the charioteer's son.

4

As I drifted back to consciousness, I thought at first that I was caught between the skulls of two rogue elephants fighting each other, their tusks interlocked. The cage of my chest was being pressed inwards. If only I could find something to hoist myself up with, a creeper I could hold on to ... but no, I could not move my hands. It was only when I sank down into the depths of the river that I knew I was drowning.

I tried to move up and realized that my hands were tied together behind me and so were my legs. This was certainly the end.

My skeleton, all that would be left after the crocodiles ate me, would surface on some far bank of the Ganga. No one would ever know it was Bhimasena, the son of Kunti. Oh, God of the Hurricane, is this the end of your son, I screamed in my head, weeping. Muddy water gushed into my mouth and nose.

In a final attempt to escape, I kicked wildly. My prayer reached someone at last, for it bore fruit – the knots on my legs moved. I twisted my feet and did what I could to free myself. The gods were with me, the rope slid off my ankles. I leapt upwards.

I thought the little air trapped in my water-logged lungs would shatter my ribcage and gush out. However high I lunged, there was water above my head. I didn't think I would be able to survive. All the strength in my legs had ebbed away. Just as I was convinced that death was very close, my head broke the water. I breathed. I vomited water, then breathed deeply again.

My hands still lay uselessly trapped in the knots, but I had trained myself long ago to float in water without paddling or using my hands.

It was pitch dark all around. Where was the riverbank? As I floated along, breathing, I found I could move my hands slightly. I willed my body to relax and go with the current, paddling slowly with my feet at intervals. Above, the sky, empty even of stars, enveloped me like a black deerskin.

As I moved along with the current, I wondered who all had been involved in that joint ambush. Duryodhana, who had arranged the feast and the special 'secret' for me must have planned everything ahead. If he told my brothers that I left as soon as I had my meal, they would have believed him and gone back themselves. It was Duryodhana, Dussasana and the charioteer's son, Karna, who had tied me up and pushed me into the river. What about the other Kauravas? It would be hard to find out if Duryodhana had included them in the conspiracy. Chitrasena and the others must certainly have known that something was going to happen under cover of the water festival. If I escaped from this danger …

I felt something beneath my feet. There were alligators in many parts of the Ganga. I had heard that most of them were sinners whom great sages had cursed and turned into alligators. I quickly withdrew my feet and started to paddle again, then realized with delight that what my feet had encountered was the riverbank.

I trudged up the slippery mud with difficulty. What a relief it was to feel the firm ground of the bank beneath my feet! I made out black thickets in the darkness. I took four or five steps forward and fell down. As I lay there, exhausted, my eyes closed, the cold pierced my body like the sharp twigs of a prickly plant.

I heard someone whistle and opened my eyes. The darkness was no longer so dense. I heard sounds in a language I did not understand, but they were certainly in a human tongue.

Soon, some people surrounded me and began to chatter loudly. The dialect they spoke was not Prakrit. Someone untied the knots on my hands. Many hands attempted to lift me, and I tried to help, hoisting myself up with considerable difficulty. Around me were men with yellow skins, short bodies, small eyes and hairless faces and chests. Behind them were women with large metal rings in their ears, wearing animal skins dipped in coloured dyes. When I turned towards them, the shortest of them laughed with a tinkling sound like a toy rattle. At some point, I had lost my clothes in the river.

A man wearing a head-dress decorated with red-and-black feathers wove his way through them and came up to me. A leather quiver filled with arrows hung from his shoulder and in his right hand was a bow made of bamboo, with its bowstring loosened. Everyone made way for him. At first, the small round eyes that stared at me seemed full of cruelty. Gradually, I saw a softness flood them.

He asked me in a language I understood, 'Who are you?'

I told him my name and said I was from Hastinapura. He signalled that I should follow him. He walked ahead, parting the bushes to make way, and I followed. The others came along as well. As we reached the thickest part of the forest, the air filled with the radiance of sunrise.

In a clearing where the trees had been felled and the ground levelled, I saw dwellings made of rounded logs. I realized these folk were nagas. I had heard that they lived in the forests on the banks of the Yamuna. The servant women used to narrate stories about the nagas to frighten children. That they gave up their human forms at night and turned into serpents. That they came out of the forests solely to take revenge on those who had treated them badly. That they hunted with small arrows tipped with poison.

One of them gave me an animal skin that had not been dipped in dye to wear. I was not sure exactly what animal it was. Then they gave me a wooden bowl of cooked ground grains to drink. It was hot. Faint from cold and hunger, I drank greedily. When I held out the bowl a second and then a third time, the women smiled. One of them took a pot off the fire and put it down near me and they all laughed in unison.

My hunger appeased, I closed my eyes and leant my head against the wooden wall. Someone covered me with a huge deerskin. Its warmth enveloped me inside and outside. The man with the feathered head-dress muttered something and everyone left. I slept peacefully.

The first two days, I was completely idle. I felt the women were competing with one another to feed me. Their main pastime was watching me eat.

On the third day, I went to hunt with the men at night. I learnt from them that it was much easier to hunt at night. The eyes of birds and animals were visible even from a distance in the forest and, with a little practice, easily identified. When these hunters heard a lone animal calling out to its mate, they could figure out its location.

I took leave of the naga who was the headman of the tribe on the seventh day, at the edge of the forest. I held out my arms to embrace him and he lifted his arms high and saluted me.

'May all auspicious things be with you, Pandava prince!'

I was distressed, not knowing how to express my gratitude.

He had taught me many things over the past few days, prefacing everything he said with: 'This is the law of our forest.' The necklace made of tigers' claws hanging on his chest and the head-dress onto which feathers had been sewn were the marks of the headman of the tribe. He had wanted to know who had tied me up and thrown me into the water and all I had answered was: 'An enemy'.

He then counselled me, 'You must never show an enemy kindness. He will acquire greater strength from your kindness and become invincible. This is our law: you can let an animal escape, but you must never give a human being a second chance.'

I did not believe him though when he said that it was better to have faith in one's own strength than in divine weapons. The heroes of all the war stories that I had heard had been victorious only because they possessed divine weapons.

The naga asked, 'What if the enemy performs penance to procure a weapon that is stronger than yours and the gods give him one? Of what use would the first weapon be?'

I found that a difficult question to answer.

At dawn on the eighth day, the palace guards were taken aback when they saw me enter the courtyard wearing a deerskin. It did not take long for the news to spread. Bhima, who was thought to have left the country, had come back. I went straight to Mother.

She first looked at me and heaved a sigh of relief, then her face grew flushed and she asked gravely, 'So you think you can go wandering around without telling anyone?'

She could barely control her tears.

Yudhishtira and Arjuna came in just then.

'Where were you?'

Making sure no one else could hear us, I told them what had happened. That Duryodhana and Dussasana had thrown me into the river at Pramanakoti. 'The two of them and that lowdown charioteer's son, Karna.'

Careful not to let me see how shocked she was, Mother gazed steadily at one of the sacred Sri Chakras drawn on the paved wooden floor. I did not tell her that Duryodhana had mocked me as well, saying that the stories Mother had told us about our birth were lies.

'All of us believed him when he said that you had gone back earlier. We must tell Grandfather Bhishma at once about what happened. Come, Bhimasena,' Yudhishtira said.

Mother said, 'Don't tell anyone. Just be careful. Be wary all the time.'

Arjuna argued, 'But Aunt Gandhari told us that we should

all live together like sons born of one mother. We have to tell her about this.'

Mother shook her head to say no.

Yudhishtira was very upset. How could we go on living here, he kept asking. He turned to Mother. 'We could go and stay in Uncle Vasudevar's palace.'

I was quite enthusiastic about this suggestion. I could learn how to wage war with the mace from Balarama. And Krishna, who was the same age as I – no, a year younger, actually – would be there for company.

Mother said, 'That's exactly what the Kauravas want. It will suit them admirably if those who have a right to the throne go away quietly. Are these the principles of statecraft you are learning, Son?'

Confused, Yudhishtira did not know what to say.

'Is that all you need, a place to live, in some kingdom or other?' Mother asked.

A servant maid came in and said that Vidura was waiting outside.

Mother stood up as Vidura entered, saluting her. She bowed hurriedly to him and walked up to us.

Yudhishtira said, 'Uncle, at least you must know – that our uncle Dhritarashtra's sons and the charioteer's son, Karna, gave Bhima poison to drug him and threw him into the depths of the river to kill him. What shall we do?'

Vidura glanced at Mother who stood with her head bent, gazing at her feet.

'All five of you must be very cautious. Especially Bhima and Arjuna.'

Yudhishtira went out and we followed. I turned back and

saw Vidura seated on a stool near Mother. She did not seem to be paying him any attention. Obviously, the attempt to kill me at Pramanakoti had upset Mother very much. What if she were to hear the scandalous stories Duryodhana had told me?

I went to Shukacharya to pay my respects, but did not tell him the whole truth. I said that I fell into the river and lost my way in the forest when I reached the bank. He did not ask me any questions. I met the Kauravas in the courtyard as I was going back. They circled me, pretending to be overjoyed that I, whom they had given up for lost, had returned.

I thought to myself, what shall I tell them about these past few days? But I did not have to tell them anything. An event infinitely more interesting than my return had occurred and become a subject of discussion. A brahmin with a great reputation as a teacher of archery had come to teach us – Kripacharya's sister's husband.

On his way to see Kripacharya, he had stopped to amuse the children playing outside the palace with some bow and arrow marvels. Hearing about this, Grandfather Bhishma came out and the next thing the children saw was the venerable old man prostrating himself before the brahmin. Declaring that it was great good fortune for the Kauravas and the Pandavas, he appointed that brahmin as our teacher. Dronacharya.

After that, endless stories were told about Drona in the elephant sheds and among the horse trainers. People said he had divine weapons that Parashurama had given him.

However, an old mahout who was listening to all this with an air of indifference, remarked: 'Once a brahmin, whose duties are to perform sacrifices and teach the Vedas, acquires the skills of a kshatriya, all is finished.'

The soota who had told us the story of how Parashurama and Drona had met was displeased.

'So what? What's wrong if a brahmin learns kshatriya skills?'

'There's nothing wrong. But they will become the ones to be feared. In the end, they will master the art of cruelty and the kshatriyas will have to learn it from them, that's all.'

The old man did not pursue the argument. He got up and went into the shed to give the elephant named Dhritarashtra palm leaves to eat.

If what the naga had said was right, if Drona had enemies, the first thing they would have done was to obtain from Parashurama weapons that were more powerful than the ones he had given Drona.

Every night I had horrible dreams about sinking steadily into bottomless depths, my chest torn asunder with excruciating pain. And every time I woke up with a start, I would say to myself, 'No, no one deserves kindness.'

5

A date had been fixed for the display of our various skills. So these days whenever young people got together, all discussion centred on this event.

The arena was chosen and a sacrifice performed to purify the space. Viewing galleries were put up everywhere.

It was Arjuna who came and told me that the day and date had been decided. From his ardour and enthusiasm, you would have thought that all the grand preparations were meant solely for his debut performance.

As he grew up, his black skin had acquired a bluish tinge and he had grown taller. Anyone who caught sight of him standing in a group would look at him a second time. The light down of manhood had begun to show on Arjuna's face. But he never paid attention to his clothes or ornaments. Nakula and Sahadeva were the most handsome of us. Nakula was inordinately proud of his good looks. If he was anywhere near a pool of clear water or a metal mirror, he loved gazing at himself.

Hearing of Dronacharya's arrival, princes began to come from neighbouring countries to stay in Hastinapura and be taught by him. People openly praised Arjuna as his best student. When Arjuna went down to the courtyard of the weapon house with his bow and arrow, even the servants would stop working and look at him with admiration.

Apart from the kings who had been invited, the city folk too would come to witness the spectacle that was soon to take place. Messengers went up and down the city on elephants, blowing trumpets and announcing the arrangements.

Everyone was busy honing and polishing weapons.

Astonished to see me seated idle, Arjuna asked, 'Have you completed your preparations?'

I grunted indifferently. Seeing his enthusiasm brim over, I was tempted to be impudent: 'Will Ekalavya come?'

Arjuna's face darkened. The archer Ekalavya, the son of a nishada chief, had claimed that he was Drona's disciple. Drona and Arjuna had been amazed at his prowess when they came across him during a hunting expedition. He had gone to Drona once, seeking to become his disciple, but Drona had turned him down because he was from the nishada tribe. It was said that, training on his own in the forest, his arms had acquired a strength and speed that would shame Arjuna.

'Let him come.' Arjuna tried to look as if he didn't care.

'Can one shoot an arrow, I wonder, if one loses a thumb …,' I said, as if I were dim-witted.

The servant in the elephant shed had told us the story of how a group of people had attacked Ekalavya while he was asleep. They had cut off the thumb of his right hand, then fled into the darkness. A soldier-spy had brought this news to the shed.

The next day, when we were all standing in the yard of the weapon house, an old man had appeared at the door. We could make out from his clothes that he was a tribal from the forest. Arjuna was training with Ashvathama at this time.

The old man looked like a nishada, and appeared to be the headman of a tribe. So Kripacharya went to ask him what he wanted. We did not hear what they said to each other. Kripacharya took the packet that the old man held out, came back and gave it to Drona. A packet made from an erikku leaf.

Drona took the packet and looked inquiringly at Kripacharya.

'He said that the nishada Ekalavya sent it to you as gurudakshina, his gift to his teacher.'

Drona's face grew pale. We were all curious when we heard Ekalavya's name. Arjuna pushed his way forward to stand right next to Drona, who opened the packet with a casual air. We heard him draw his breath in with a gasp.

We craned our necks to see what gift the disciple in the forest had sent the teacher he had chosen in his mind.

In the leaf packet was a thumb on which the blood had clotted.

Since that day, I had not heard anyone talk about Ekalavya.

Arjuna turned to walk away, and I said, 'I hear the nishada is dexterous with his left hand as well.'

Arjuna faced me and replied, 'The display of skills in Hastinapura is not meant for nishadas.'

When Arjuna had gone, I could not help laughing. I was sure he had had no knowledge of the attack on Ekalavya. But why was this beloved younger brother of mine agitated every time he heard about some expert archer somewhere?

He was jealous even of Drona's son, Ashvathama, afraid that the teacher would teach his son lessons and strategies that he himself would never learn. Bhishmacharya had arranged a mansion for Drona, evicting a minister from it, and Arjuna spent all his time there, explaining to us that he was attending to his teacher's welfare.

Dronacharya fascinated me. It seemed as if he had decided even before he came to Hastinapura exactly how far each of his disciples would advance. I was certain that Ashvathama was ahead of Arjuna. Karna was allowed to come and learn with Duryodhana. But if Karna approached his teacher to attend on him, he was always ordered to stand at a distance because he was the son of a charioteer.

While I was studying chariots, my teacher realized that I had overtaken Yudhishtira in this field, although he had started earlier than me. Each time I leapt out of a chariot as the charioteer increased the speed and jumped back in again without waiting for him to reduce the speed, Yudhishtira's disappointment was evident. I was given a clever charioteer, Vishoka, a few years older than I. He encouraged me to get in and out of the chariot from both the left and right sides. In war, the charioteer has to sit on the left while the warrior sits on the right. When going for a marriage, the charioteer sits on the right and the warrior on the left.

'Among princes, it's quite common for a marriage to turn into a war,' Vishoka reminded me, laughing.

Instead of letting me go on with my training in the use of chariots, Dronacharya moved me away from it. Maybe because he assumed I would never make a name as an archer, he sent me to join Arjuna and Ashvathama. Let the blockhead suffer in the background!

Determined to surprise Arjuna, however, I practised secretly all night, with Vishoka to help me.

Drona must have decided that, being heavy-built, I would be slow at pulling out an arrow and placing it in the bow. He could then say, 'Blockhead, a mace is best for you.'

As it turned out, Dronacharya was even more surprised than Arjuna. When I sent five arrows one after the other, and all of them hit the wooden tiger-face hanging at a distance on a flagpole, he congratulated me softly.

Then he praised Kripacharya's teaching skills loudly and advised me, 'Waging war with the mace is as important to the kshatriya as learning the strategy of chariots and the science of archery. The mace is the weapon great warriors use. Concentrate on it, Bhimasena, once you finish the basic lessons.'

He had already decided the limits to which each of his disciples would exploit their skills.

Even more amazing was the way Dronacharya deliberately ignored certain facts. Anyone who observed with care could tell that Karna had greater speed of movement than Arjuna. And yet Drona pretended not to notice this. If the renown his best disciple earned was to be the mark of his own success as a teacher, the challenge to it would come not from Ekalavya the nishada, but from the charioteer's son, Karna.

Nakula was the next to come and talk to me about the performance of skills. He had chosen a blue silk waist cloth, a pale yellow upper cloth and a gold belt encrusted with a large amethyst to wear on that day. He thought an ardhaharam necklace would be adequate. This was only a show of skills after all, wasn't it, he asked rather doubtfully. I smiled as if to say yes.

I had not thought about the clothes or ornaments I was going to wear. Whatever I wore, people would look only at my massive body. I had no illusions that a hair ornament or a pearl necklace would make me handsome.

Although my body had grown to the size of a young man's, I did not have a moustache as Arjuna did. I had just a few stray coppery strands on my chin. I felt that as my body grew bigger, my neck was becoming smaller.

I got up when Vishoka asked me, 'Aren't you going to get ready?' So the time for the great festival had come.

A sacrifice and a purification ceremony were performed at the invocation and after that the drums began to thud. From the gallery that was reserved for us participants, we could see Dronacharya and Ashvathama standing in the area where the sacrifice had been performed. My brothers and I were by ourselves. All the young men who had come to study in Hastinapura were with the Kauravas. The space meant for them was to our right. The women were just beyond and Mother was among them. The highest viewing gallery, built above the steps where the women were seated, was meant for Uncle Dhritarashtra and the two ministers who would explain to him what was taking place at every moment. As Duryodhana and his group came from behind the sacrificial site into the arena, trumpets sounded, probably in response to a pre-arranged signal. All of them were dressed as if going to the venue of a swayamvara, in gleaming silk clothes and ornaments that glowed brightly. Nakula and Sahadeva began to assess the worth of their garments.

My eyes sought Mother in the group of women and finally found her. She was in the first row all right. Parshavati, Vidura's wife, was on one side of her and on the other, Yuyutsu's mother, a shudra woman, one of the servants who had looked after our aunt during her pregnancy. When my uncle had a child by her, he gave her a house for herself and granted the child the right to call the king 'father'.

Yuyutsu was right at the back of the Kaurava section, wearing ordinary clothes.

The drums thudded again. The sound of the trumpets merged with the fanfare of conches and drums as our uncle placed his hands on the shoulders of Sanjaya and Vidura, who were on either side of him, and began to climb the steps of the viewing gallery.

It was time to begin the display of skills. Kripacharya, who was in charge of the events, would call out the names in order of age. Grandfather Bhishma and Dronacharya would stand at one end of the arena and supervise the proceedings.

Yudhishtira demonstrated how fast he could ride a chariot and how well he could control it. The arrows he aimed at a metal boar fixed on top of a distant pillar and at a bull's horn hanging from a great height found their mark. He shot arrows from a chariot while seated in it, lying down in it and standing with his back turned to the target. The charioteer had harnessed the light brown horses that had just arrived from Kambojam so low that it looked like they were flying and not touching the ground. The rhythms of the silver bells tied to the pin of the axle kept changing rapidly. Finally, after having demonstrated the highest speed at which the chariot could move, the horses came to a halt below the king's viewing gallery and Yudhishtira alighted. The exhibition of his skills had been far more impressive than I expected.

There was light applause for my brother from the spectators.

My turn came next. I had not decided what to do even when I went down to the arena. I made my salutations and climbed into the chariot. Vishoka held out my bow and quiver to me.

As I fastened the quiver, he said, 'If you want to amuse the children, you can demonstrate how fast a chariot can go, but you don't have to. Three arrows, right into the mouth of the metal boar.'

I shot the three arrows. When all three found their mark, the spectators stirred in their seats. Yudhishtira had shot only one.

Vishoka whispered, as he usually did during our training sessions at night, 'Now seven on the bull's horn.'

This was a chance to display the speed of my hands. Seven arrows flew, one after the other. I remembered what the naga had told me: it is within your mind that you must see the target, not with your eyes. After all seven arrows had left the bow, I lowered it and looked, to make sure.

'They did not miss the target.' Vishoka spoke without turning his head.

The spectators manifested their astonishment louder this time.

Dronacharya came hurrying towards me. 'Show them how you wage war with a mace. There are many others after you to demonstrate skills in archery. Combat with the mace, the mace!'

I looked at him. Soaked in perspiration, his sacred thread clung to his dark-skinned body. Drops of perspiration hung from his grey beard, ready to drip down.

I had already noticed kites circling in the sky, drawn by the odour of the blood on the sacrificial site. I had decided that, if one of them flew down to a height at which I could aim an arrow, I would shoot it down. I also intended to make a formal salutation on my own to Mother when I climbed the steps after all the events were over.

'Blockhead, you're wasting time.'

I gave my bow and arrow back to Vishoka and, seething with anger, picked up the mace from the floor of the chariot. I twirled the iron-studded mace in the air and asked Dronacharya, careful not to let my anger show, 'Against whom shall I display my skill?'

I was not really waiting for an adversary, but I heard cries and shouts from the Kauravas, and saw Duryodhana standing up. Eager cries rose from the spectators, who had already guessed at the deadly rivalry between the eldest of the Kauravas and the second of the Pandavas. Taking off his upper cloth and ornaments, Duryodhana gave them to Dussasana and vaulted into the arena.

Three attendants lined up in front of him with maces. Duryodhana picked one, threw it up to test its weight, rejected it and accepted the second one. Then he walked slowly towards me. Drona and the attendants withdrew. I had no preparations to make, wore no ornaments that might prove obstacles.

Duryodhana came right up to me. He said, 'The spectators must not be disappointed.'

Duryodhana was taller than I was by a finger and a half, so his body looked a little less bulky than mine. I knew that his strength was not to be underestimated. He would do his utmost to defeat me and declare himself the victor before all these spectators. But there was a secret he did not know. This was not just a competition for me. I wanted to make sure I would never experience again the nightmare of sinking helplessly into the depths at Pramanakoti. Here, before me, lay an arena where I could avenge myself in broad daylight, before tens of thousands of people.

Standing in the jataka stance, Duryodhana repeated, 'Blockhead, the onlookers must not be disappointed.'

I took my stance casually, the valita. He swung his mace, changed his position and took up a new stance, the pratyaleeda. Instead of parrying his blow, I arched backwards and his mace skimmed over my body, almost touching it.

The silence of the crowd roared in my ears. I staved off the second blow. Having judged the strength of his arms, I attacked. He discovered that all the assumptions he had made during our training sessions, concerning the swiftness with which the blockhead Bhima could swing a mace, were wrong. He was completely taken aback. The faster he retreated, the faster I advanced, still attacking him. Sparks flew as our iron-studded maces clashed.

And I found words to insult his arrogance as he retreated further, 'Coward! This is a battle, not a dance!'

I knew his strength was ebbing, albeit slowly. As he continued to fight, trying to shake the perspiration off him, he muttered something, his voice sounding distorted and horrible. My moment of vengeance was increasingly closer. In the intervals between withdrawing his mace and raising it again, he kept forgetting to protect the left side of his rib-cage. It occurred to me that if I changed the pattern of my foot movements abruptly, I might be able to bring my mace down on a vulnerable spot between his ribs. I had to wait till he grew weaker. I kept fighting, convinced that my chance would soon come.

Occasionally, at moments when he became aware that his prestige was waning in front of the spectators, he attacked me with renewed ferocity. If I kept Pramanakoti steadily in mind, I was certain I could fight without weakening until sunset. The speed of his hands was slackening. The mace whirled in my hands like a living entity, greedily looking for that crevice in time when it could strike and kill.

The delight in my heart must have shown on my face, for I saw the shadow of fear creeping into his eyes.

'This is in memory of Pramanakoti.'

'Stop!' Many voices cried out.

At the instant when victory was close to me, I had to pull my hands back.

'Stop, stop!' I was surrounded by voices.

Ashvathama sprang in front of me, covered Duryodhana and roared, 'Bhimasena, stop!'

I lowered my mace slowly.

By this time, Dronacharya and Kripacharya were in front of me. 'This is not a battle, it is an exhibition of skills.'

The elderly Shukacharya who arrived last smiled and said, 'Enough. That's more than enough.'

I could not believe my eyes when I turned around. All the spectators were on their feet.

I started to walk back to our seats and heard the sounds of the crowd vaguely. Like the murmur of reeds that bend, then straighten again after a wind sweeps through them.

6

Arjuna was coming down the steps as I climbed up. Even though he looked very serious, he smiled and murmured: 'How stupid our brahmin teachers are!'

I went back to my seat, near Yudhishtira. I could see from his face that he had a number of questions for me. The drums and trumpets stopped and we heard Dronacharya's voice. He was presenting a participant to the spectators, hinting to them that a much greater performance was to follow. 'Here is my beloved disciple, dearer to me than my son – Arjuna, who has learnt how to wield all weapons with equal skill.'

Wearing leather gloves and a breastplate studded with golden stars, Arjuna walked to the centre of the arena. It seemed as if the eyes of all the young girls showered blue flowers on his path at every step he took. The four of us looked at one another. Pride filled my mind, which had until then been clouded with anger, and it grew clear again.

Yudhishtira contented himself with remarking that I had taken more time than was necessary.

Once the salutations were over, Arjuna demonstrated the power of his arrows and the distance they could travel at an astonishing speed. Proving to us that he could use both left and right hands with equal dexterity, he shot five arrows into the mouth of the metal boar and twenty-one at the bull's horn.

Each newly released arrow brushed the tip of the previous one, scattering sparks. The spectators were wonderstruck.

Another archer entered the arena at that point. The charioteer's son, Karna.

'Enough of your arrogance, Arjuna!'

No one introduced the newcomer. Arjuna, the great archer, watched helplessly as Karna split the arrows in the boar's mouth, one by one. After that he drew a swastika on the ground with arrows. Taking aim at arrows that were falling down vertically after being sent up into the air, he directed them upwards again. He made arrows dance in the air, not allowing them to touch the ground.

The crowd roared in amazement.

Duryodhana, who seemed to have taken leave of his senses, shouted: 'Karna, the Kuru kingdom and I bow before you!'

Yudhishtira asked angrily, 'Who gave the charioteer permission to compete?'

Karna addressed the teachers loudly, so that all the people could hear, 'Grant me the opportunity to fight a duel with Arjuna.'

I went down to the arena, realizing that the situation was becoming awkward.

Arjuna said something about the fate of uninvited participants. Going closer to him, I saw that his courage was waning.

Duryodhana and his companions ran up, embraced Karna and helped him fasten his breastplate.

Aware that he had no justification for withdrawing, Arjuna glanced at me. Tightening his breastplate from behind, I said to him, 'The charioteer's son does not merit any kindness.'

Bhishmacharya, Dronacharya and Kripacharya came up to us. They looked at Karna, who stood ready, and at Arjuna, who seemed to be waiting for me to get him ready.

Craning my neck over Arjuna's left shoulder, I asked Kripacharya, 'Ask him whether any of Kunti's sons will do. I have a score of my own to settle.'

Arjuna said, 'No, I will dispatch him where he deserves to go.'

I pleaded, 'Let me go. He can choose whatever weapons he wants.'

Kripacharya, who had been looking troubled because he could find no reason to postpone this confrontation, suddenly came forward as if he had found a way out.

'Arjuna, Kunti's youngest son and the son of Pandu, is a prince born in the Kuru clan.'

Karna turned towards the teacher, his eyes blazing.

Kripacharya raised his voice. 'We therefore need to know his opponent's clan and the name of his father before a duel is started. Kshatriya youths do not fight with those whose clans do not equal theirs in prestige.'

Karna's face, which had been burning with valour, suddenly grew ashen.

I spoke again, 'I do not need to know all these things. Just the weapons he chooses ...'

Duryodhana rushed towards Kripacharya, furious. 'Is there not a rule, my teacher, that the clan of a warrior does not have to be checked?' Raising his voice, he then proclaimed, for all to hear, 'From this moment, Karna is a king. I gift the kingdom of Anga, which I received from my father, to Karna.' He screamed, 'Where are the priests? I am sure not one of them has come, since alms are not being given here today. Is anyone here?'

A few old priests rushed up with pots of water.

Duryodhana placed his hand on Karna's shoulder and said, 'The celebrations will take place according to tradition later. This is enough for now.'

The brahmins chanted mantras, poured three pots of water over Karna's head and performed a coronation. Karna embraced Duryodhana.

Duryodhana cried out arrogantly for all the teachers to hear, 'King of Anga, you have my unending friendship.'

Derisive laughter arose suddenly from among the spectators. An old man was walking into the arena. All of us thought he was a spectator who was not quite right in the head.

Soaked in perspiration, his loosened clothes bunched up in his hands, the old man limped in and cried out, 'Where is my Karna?'

Karna, who had been standing as tall as the sky until then, seemed to shrink. He hurried up to the old man. 'Father, what are you doing here?'

So this was the charioteer, Adhiratha.

Karna stood before him with his head bent. The old charioteer, gripping his shoulders just below the rings that circled them, was saying something to him.

I no longer felt angry or anxious. I could not help pitying Karna. Adhiratha must have heard from someone that his son was in danger and come running to look for him. I am not sure why I suddenly felt a great sympathy for the charioteer's son, rendered helpless at the very instant that he was crowned king. However, I heard the naga's voice from faraway: if the enemy is shown kindness, he grows stronger.

The law of the forest is to finish off the prey at the spot where it falls. A wounded animal should not be allowed to escape. Laughing, I shouted for everyone to hear, 'Weapons do not become you. You should wield the whip that's the mark of your family profession.'

I knew I was demeaning myself in everyone's eyes. It had not been to earn applause from the spectators that the three of them, including this fellow, had laid a trap for me that day in Pramanakoti, had it? I was no god, to grant boons even to an enemy.

Karna came towards me, hissing, trembling from top to toe.

I repeated, 'I will fight with anyone, even if he is low-caste. If I will do for you, welcome!'

Duryodhana pointed his index finger at me and shouted, 'Can you look at Karna and say you are convinced that this radiant youth was born to a charioteer? Bhima, no one seeks the source of warriors and rivers.' He looked at the teachers as if expecting them to say he was right. Then he moved nearer me and said, 'Nor do people ask the secret of how the impotent Pandu had children.'

I cursed Drona's son, who caught hold of the arm I had raised, aiming it at Duryodhana's left sixth rib.

The drums thudded again. Dronacharya looked at the light dimming over the Asthagiri mountain and said, 'The exhibition of skills is over. The sun has set.'

There was still enough light in the arena for fighting a duel. Duryodhana, who had been standing aggressively, like an elephant in rut, placed his hand on Karna's shoulder and walked towards the stone steps.

Everyone began to move away, but I stood still. Nakula went

away with Arjuna. Sahadeva came running up to me and said, 'Mother has fallen down in a faint.'

Mother must have been convinced that danger was going to overtake Arjuna.

When had she fainted? What Duryodhana had insinuated to me about our paternity could not have been heard in the women's gallery.

'Never mind, she's recovered now.'

Instead of going back to the palace, I walked slowly to the Ganga. I said my evening prayers and stayed there, listening to the secret murmurs of the flowing water. The wind arrived, trampling the waves. There had been the intoxicating fragrance of pollen in the breeze that the Lord of the Wind had sent to make Menaka's clothes flutter wildly and reveal the nakedness that the sage would desire. I felt that those evenings of my childhood, when I used to come at dusk to this deserted riverbank to hear the wind murmur a message in my ears, were very distant now.

The God of the Hurricanes, Dharmaraja, Indra – they must have all heard what Duryodhana said. I wondered why none of those fathers had protested. The hurricane had not roared. Lightning and thunder had not flashed their swords in the night clouds. Lord Dharma's invisible hand had not placed weapons in Yudhishtira's arms to strike Karna down.

Trying to comfort myself with the thought that the gods were waiting for another chance to take their revenge, I walked back to the palace in the darkness.

No celebrations were carried over into the night to mark the day's events.

Vishoka, my charioteer, came to attend on me and remarked,

while I was changing my clothes, 'Everything went well. No one was defeated. And no one was victorious either.'

As he was leaving, I asked him to send me some liquor.

The servants brought my food and left. I thought Vishoka had forgotten my unusual request. Then I heard the tinkle of anklets outside the door. A servant maid entered with a silver platter. She bent down respectfully to place a pot in front of me and the fragrance of sesame oil scented with the manjishtam herb rose from her hair.

I looked at her as she turned to go. Silver anklets, a single garment of pale coppery silk. Below the chain encircling her waist, her hips moved gracefully to the rhythm of her footsteps. At the door, she turned around. There was a smile filled with humility on her round face.

Contrary to habit, I drank a great deal but had no appetite for food. I lay down, but sleep eluded me.

I got up and went out. Walking through the corridor, I saw light outside Yudhishtira's room. I went up to the door and heard voices talking softly inside. I thought it might be some shudra woman he had sent for before he went to bed. But just as I was about to go away, my elder brother grunted and a male voice murmured something, so I went in. It was Vidura.

I saluted him with joined palms and turned to go.

He said, 'We were just telling each other old tales. Sit down, son.'

He went out. I sat on a stool in the circle of shadow beneath the small metal oil lamp fixed to the wall.

My brother got up and raised the wicks. Then he asked, 'Will you play a hand with me?'

Before I could reply, he picked up a platter on which there were silver dice and sat down cross-legged on the floor.

'I don't know the game,' I said, trying to avoid playing.

'I'll teach you.'

To please him, I sat down. Silver dice with four, three, two and one marked on them. If you threw a double number, you could play twice. He began to explain the various moves and how gains and losses were calculated.

To prove that the rest of the rules were very easy, he started to play. I played as well, in order to please him.

He won every game he played. Smiling, he said, 'Expertise in the game lies in making the dice obey you.'

I thought that he probably needed trivial victories like these to dispel his gloom.

'I must travel up and down the country, mingle with lords and noble people. Uncle Vidura tells me that the demand to make me king should come from the people themselves.'

I grunted as if in agreement. Then I remembered to ask, 'How is Mother? I didn't see her.'

'She fainted, that's all. Once she knew no harm had come to Arjuna, she was all right.'

I had another question for him. Had his father, Lord Dharma, ever reached out to him, at least at a moment when he was entirely alone? But I was not sure whether the time had come to ask this question, so I kept quiet and went on with the task of letting myself be beaten by him in the game.

'You're a real blockhead. You've lost again!' he said and stopped playing.

I went out. I walked through the corridor and went into the

courtyard through the door at which stone lamps smoked and flickered.

All the palaces were asleep. The sounds of elephants tearing up palm leaves could be heard from the elephant sheds. I could dimly make out the Saptarishis and Arundhati in the northern curve of the sky. It was a cold night with no wind.

I sat down on a platform made of rough stone, then lay flat on it. A shadow-like form approached me and I sprang up, afraid that it was an enemy.

'Who is it?'

It was a woman – the servant maid, who had taken off her anklets and come up to me soundlessly. The same one who had brought me liquor earlier.

I had not been able to celebrate the killing of my first enemy today. And this woman did not know that she was the first one I would experience. I caught hold of her hand and drew her close, as if I was used to doing these things.

'What is your name?'

She gave me a name, an ordinary one that I was never to remember again. The first woman who came looking for me. When the initial touches of welcome were over, she seemed to change. The waves and clefts of her nakedness circled me and she wound herself around me like a wild creeper. She guided my rough hands and untrained fingers into the valleys and mounds of her body.

But I was not aroused. She finally drew away from the cold granite statue that I was with a faint gasp, a suppressed shudder. She glanced at me, then turned and walked away, melting into the darkness beyond the open door.

Gazing at the smoking stone lamps in the distance, I asked myself, 'Has the tradition of Pandu continued into this generation as well and given birth to a giant without virility?'

I went back to my lodging and finished the liquor that was left in the pot. An acrid taste spread through me. I lay down on the paved wooden floor, beyond the mattress of darbha grass the servants had laid out for me.

The liquor had begun to act. The scent of the servant maid's hair seemed to be clinging to my chest. Even as I slid into sleep, the scenes played out that day at the performance of skills were clearly etched in my mind.

I remembered what Vishoka had said. No one was defeated. No one was victorious either.

PART 3

Forest Trails

1

Harvested barley fields stretched all the way to the mountain slopes. It was the month of Phalguna, so the heat had abated. Once Hastinapura lay behind us, my mind grew lighter.

I felt increasingly enthusiastic as we reached Varanavata, a small town on the slope of a mountain. In Hastinapura, I had nursed a constant fear that enemies lurked everywhere. I had no need to be afraid here. Vaishya traders laden with gifts came to the tents that had been erected for us near the festival ground. Shudras arrived to perform menial tasks. And brahmins to give us their blessings and receive alms.

Yudhishtira gave the brahmins the gifts that were their due: gold coins heaped over ghee and grains on trays made of fig wood. Uncle Dhritarashtra had instructed him, 'Give them all the gifts they should receive. Enjoy the festival. I will send attendants ahead with money and grain.'

The farmers usually gathered here once a year to celebrate a festival. As people began to crowd around our tents, I felt that our arrival was a bigger event than this Indra festival, which was not as grand as I had expected. Farmers came to sell or exchange mules and horses. There were not many elephants and the few there were did not have the marks of aristocracy.

People who had come from the villages pitched their tents and stayed for ten days, buying and selling. Groups of musicians came to entertain them. A number of prostitutes had come from the Madra region. The Vaishya markets contained mainly tools, clothes and medicinal plants from the mountains.

Wandering around the festival area, I was really surprised – was this the great celebration that Uncle had described as a spectacle people were fortunate to see even once in a lifetime? The sole event I found enjoyable was an elephant race that took place on the second day.

On the first day, I saw an old brahmin seated in a group of people receiving alms from the prostitutes. He took what they gave and blessed them. I asked Yudhishtira, 'Are brahmins allowed to receive gifts from prostitutes?'

'Yes, they are. The twice-born give blessings to whoever gives them gifts. These women who are giving gifts here must have made a vow to conduct a ritual to please Kama, the God of Love.'

I had heard about the prostitutes of the Madra region. They drank heavily, shouted obscenities. But the women lined up here, carrying platters filled with flowers, grain and money to give as gifts, clearly had a kind of rough beauty.

Uncle had sent an attendant named Purochana from the palace, solely to take us around the festival ground.

My brothers were all disappointed when they discovered that the festival was so mediocre, and Sahadeva said as much. It was Yudhishtira who had first expressed a wish to come to Varanavata after listening to Uncle's descriptions of it.

Nakula said to Mother, 'I've had enough. We are not farmers. Let's go back to the capital.'

Mother asked gently, as if it was a trivial matter, 'How can those who have been exiled go back to the palace?'

Astonished, Arjuna thought Mother was joking, 'Exiled! What are you saying? No one has exiled us.'

'When the Kauravas kept talking about the beauty and grandeur of Varanavata from every angle they could think of, did any of you stop to wonder why they were praising it so eloquently? They wanted to hear you say, "Uncle, we want to go there." That way, no one would be able to blame them later, accuse them of having sent us here. When you were so enthusiastic, my son, about coming here, Uncle's task was made easy.'

My elder brother shrank before Mother's look. 'But what was wrong in that? Didn't you see, Mother, how they even gave us enough money to give as gifts to the brahmins?'

Mother smiled gently. 'Yes, they did. Who controls the treasury and the ministers now? Do you realize how little they have spent?'

Yudhishtira saw that we were all looking questioningly at him. Muttering to himself, he walked hastily out of the tent.

We saw Purochana standing with his palms joined respectfully at the door. He told us that an old palace that had been built long ago for hunters had been repaired and made comfortable for us. We could move into it whenever we wanted.

Yudhishtira came in, rubbing his eyes. Mother's words had made all of us uneasy. She was right. Uncle and his ministers had no particular reason to suddenly show Pandu's sons so much affection and send them to attend a festival. We had been stupid not to realize it earlier. Our mother, who had never stepped out of the women's quarters, had been really perceptive. I looked at her with respect as she sat huddled on the ground, her white upper cloth hiding the parting of her hair. No one who saw her in a crowd would have known she was a queen. How soon her face had grown wrinkled …

We arrived at the house that stood isolated on the hill slope only when the carpenters and masons had left after renovating and polishing it. The little palace was built on a plate-like clearing levelled out of the forest right in the middle of the mountain range. We caught the scents of new wood and lac as we entered.

There were no attendants, no servant maids. No wonder Mother had hinted that this was an exile. But the middle-aged, light-complexioned Purochana, who had the scar of a burn extending midway down his forehead, ran around busily, his manner clearly saying: here I am, to do everything you need. He listened to our instructions with an air of humility.

I sensed danger lurking in the air, felt vague suggestions of it in my bones and nerves and hinted as much to Arjuna.

'Look, we've come armed with our bows and arrows and other weapons. There are five of us, we have nothing to fear,' he replied.

Yudhishtira too tried to set our minds at rest, saying that Mother was imagining things. At night, Purochana slept outside the main door, to keep guard. Surely, no enemies would come looking for us at the foothills of distant Varanavata.

I examined the back door. Copper sheets had been nailed down on it outside in such a way that it could not be opened. That was not surprising – the house was situated on a mountain slope and was best secured from outside at the back since there were no servants to guard it.

We could not sleep that night. We sat together and spent the time talking. Yudhishtira remarked that he had not forgotten to bring dice, but no one was interested in playing. Nakula spoke to Sahadeva about the horses he had seen at the festival. He knew quite a bit about the qualities of horses and how to train them.

Yudhishtira murmured to himself, 'I wonder whether Purochana would be interested in a game …'

None of us volunteered to find out.

Mother, who we had thought was asleep, came in very quietly. 'Don't stand up. I can't sleep either.' She sat down next to Sahadeva. 'What did Uncle Vidura tell you when you took leave of him?'

Uncle had been with us until we climbed into the chariots that had been brought to the entrance of the palace. The rituals of farewell had been conducted according to custom, since Yudhishtira, who was a crown prince, was starting on a journey. Our attendants, the charioteers and the ministers and lords at Dhritarashtra's court had all been present. Vidura had been amongst them.

'He didn't say anything particular. He gave us his blessing and said, like everyone else, 'come back safely'.

'He said nothing else? Try and remember, he must have said something more …'

Yudhishtira said, rather gruffly, 'Yes, as usual, he had something philosophical to say.'

Mother's voice was harsh. 'Tell me exactly what he said. He's not a person who scatters philosophy around carelessly. I want to hear the words he used.'

Yudhishtira pressed a hand to his forehead and thought for a while. Then he raised his head triumphantly, remembering. 'He said weapons are made not only of metal.'

'Then?' Mother looked at him steadily and repeated, 'Then?'

'He added, sometimes the same people who provide protection from the cold set fire to the forest.'

Mother looked triumphant. 'What more? What more?'

'He also said that those who live in the forest must learn even from a porcupine. He didn't say anything more.'

Mother sighed and got up. 'Pay obeisance in your minds, all of you, to that great man, Vidura.'

Mother went up to the wooden walls, ran her fingers over them and said, 'Fire is our enemy here. We should have realized that the moment we smelt the odours of lac and ghee. This house has been readied for burning us alive.'

Mother paced around the room thoughtfully, looking at each one of us in turn. 'With Dhritarashtra's ministers and attendants around us, what more could he have said to intelligent people?'

My elder brother shrank before Mother's gaze. Before she went in, Mother looked at me and said, 'Be careful of Purochana. It is you who must think of a way of escape.'

We hurried to examine the walls. All the crevices had been filled with lac. We laid our noses to the floor, it smelt of ghee. The interstices between the wooden planks that paved the floor had been soaked in ghee. Wood that would catch fire easily had been used for all the joints.

I paid obeisance first to Mother in my mind, then to the great and magnanimous Vidura.

Yudhishtira said, 'Let's kill Purochana at once. We can go back then. We're not prisoners.'

My blood had begun to boil as soon as I realized the extent of the treachery we had been exposed to. How cleverly they had prepared a place they could roast us alive in and brought us to it, ostensibly by our own wish! Who all had played a part in this plan, apart from Dhritarashtra, Duryodhana and his companions? Grandfather Bhishma would not have known. Nor our teachers. Karna was sure to have been told of the conspiracy. And Shakuni, the sight of whom disgusted me. Duryodhana himself was not astute enough to have conceived such a devious plan. Karna and Shakuni, it had to be the two of them. Then I wondered – could it have been the blind monarch who had suggested the device of setting fire to us while we were asleep? After all, it had been he who encouraged us to come to Varanavata. Mean, lowdown scoundrels, lowest of the low.

When day broke, my younger brothers and I pretended we were going out to hunt and made a note of the mountain pathways around our dwelling. When we got back, Purochana feigned sympathy for the fact that we had not caught anything.

I knew that if I gave his head a blow with my left hand, this man who pretended to be our humble servant and was a spy for our enemy would fall down dead. I found it unbearable to stand before him smiling, as if I knew nothing.

Yudhishtira could be remarkably astute sometimes, and it was at one such moment that he warned me, 'Even if we run away from here, the Kaurava spies can waylay us somewhere and kill us. The house must burn. And we must make our escape from it.'

Arjuna agreed, 'We must stay in hiding and find out what will happen when they think the Pandavas are dead.'

I said to Yudhishtira, 'Let's talk it over with Mother.'

'I've already spoken with her. She says it's not yet time.'

The next day a passer-by from Hastinapura came that way. He said someone had told him at the festival that we were here and he had come to pay homage to the crown prince. Purochana stopped him in the courtyard and questioned him for a long time before he told Mother that we had a visitor.

Mother ordered that the man be fed. He ate with the greed of someone who had not seen food for days. Satisfied that the man was only a wanderer in search of food, Purochana went out. The man's pathetic manner changed abruptly.

Waiting until Purochana was completely out of sight, he said, 'They plan to set fire to the house in the last quarter of the night of the next new moon. We must set fire to the place that day, before midnight, and get out. Note the spot where the queen stands now carefully. The tunnel that my helpers and I are digging will end there.'

He pointed to Mother's feet and sketched a circle around them with his finger. Picking up the crumbs he had spilt, he got up and murmured softly, 'I am one of the men sent by my master, Vidura, to dig the tunnel.'

We heard him laugh at some witticism of Purochana's as he went out through the courtyard.

The five of us stared at each other. Once again, our Uncle Vidura had amazed us.

There were six days more until the new moon day when we must set fire to the house. There were so many questions I had wanted to ask the tunnel-digger.

I laid my ear to the spot he had indicated to us, but could hear nothing.

Purochana went out only once a day, to buy foodstuff.

Arjuna wandered around the deserted areas outside, shooting down birds with his bow and arrow. Yudhishtira began to teach Nakula how to play dice to overcome the boredom of this period of waiting. Sahadeva helped Mother in the kitchen.

One night, as I lay listening on the floor paved with wood, I distinctly heard the sound of an axe falling on rock from underneath.

The night of the new moon arrived.

We had asked Purochana the previous day to fetch brahmins, and he had enquired curiously why we needed them.

'It's new moon, the day kshatriyas offer a sacrifice to their forefathers.'

Purochana seemed satisfied with Yudhishtira's explanation.

Mother insisted that all the prescribed rituals for the sacrifice be performed. But we were not sure that this guest-house in Varanavata had the necessary facilities.

Mother said, 'This is the palace of the Pandavas now. Sacrificial rites must be conducted accordingly.'

Sahadeva was still doubtful, and Mother said to him, 'We must make sure our forefathers and the gods are with us to protect us from this great danger.'

The sacrificial site was made ready in the courtyard. All of us helped hang streamers around and decorate it.

The brahmins arranged by Purochana arrived. There were twelve of them: four priests to conduct the sacrifice, four to recite prayers and another four to chant the Sama Veda.

As the fire began to burn, we studied the flames for good and ill omens. We offered sesame seeds and grain a 108 times to the sacrificial fire. Then we offered ghee a 108 times, and the flames turned golden.

The brahmins sprinkled water over the young bull that had been tied to the sacrificial stake, to purify it. They adorned its forehead, shoulders and waist with flowers and sandalwood paste. They spread kusha grass over the ground.

The priests began to chant mantras.

'May your breath take on the life-breath of the world.'

Once the animal had been purified, the brahmins turned their backs on it. The chief priest ordered that the animal be silenced. Three people who had come from a slaughter-house silenced the animal by suffocating it. A sacrificial animal is never killed, it is silenced.

The brahmins sprinkled water over it again to purify it, then Yudhishtira sliced off the animal's head and threw it into the fire. The blood-stained grass on the ground was meant to please the demons.

The flames blazed contentedly, knowing that no smoke or ashes had defiled them as they received the sacrifice. We could see the relief on Mother's face as she watched from a distance.

All twelve brahmins and their assistants left after receiving gifts. As the remains of the sacrificial offerings were first smelt and then gathered to be taken to the kitchen, we heard beggars calling from outside – a tribal woman and her five sons.

Mother looked at them for a while, then said, 'Give them as much food as they want.'

Purochana's manner made it clear that he did not like the idea of a tribal woman entering the house with her children.

'There is so much food,' said Mother. 'It is good that we can give alms to so many people before we ourselves sit down to eat.'

Purochana stopped muttering.

Sahadeva served the beggars large helpings of meat.

Mother said, 'I saw some leather pots in the store room. Go and have a look.'

We brought the pots of liquor and Mother signed to us to serve them. The newcomers thoroughly enjoyed the hospitality they received so unexpectedly. After a while, they forgot to be quiet and meek, and began to laugh, squabble and make a great deal of noise. I looked at Mother enquiringly to find out whether I should chase them out. But Mother was actually enjoying the commotion they were making.

The woman said it had grown dark and they had to reach some place very far away. Mother said, 'It doesn't matter, you can sleep here. We have so much room.'

I had not thought Mother's generosity would go that far. I darted a look at Arjuna. We had many tasks to do that night. Mother seemed to have forgotten this in her excessive hospitality. I wondered if she had entirely forgotten Vidura's message when she saw the old woman and her five sons, all between the ages of ten and seventeen.

Yudhishtira glanced outside and said, 'It's not yet dark.' He smiled at Mother and said, as if to let her know that he had not forgotten the courtesies that guests were entitled to, 'These people know the forest trails, after all.'

Ignoring him, Mother invited them again, 'There's plenty of place. You can sleep in the outer room or in that hall, wherever you like.'

The woman smiled in relief. Grabbing the leather pot from her eldest son, she drank deeply again.

Mother came towards us as we stood helplessly, astonished at her insistent hospitality.

Yudhishtira started to speak, 'Today's …'

'I know. They have come today as a blessing from the gods. Let them sleep here.'

I was taken aback.

Mother lowered her voice, 'Spies will come here to look for our dead bodies tomorrow and they will find six skeletons. What made a mother with five sons come here seeking alms? You have the blessing of your forefathers!'

Mother looked at the woman of the forest and her sons, smiled and went in. We were stunned.

We heard all of them singing loudly in the outer hall.

I was distressed.

Yudhishtira noticed this and said, 'They're just tribals, after all. You needn't think of it as a sin.'

Our guests grew quiet after a long time. They were probably feeling drowsy after having eaten and drunk so heavily. I thought, poor sacrificial animals, they came seeking alms and were going to be silenced that night. I tried to find comfort in the thought that six forest dwellers were not of such great value. Then I immersed myself in preparations for the night.

I stood outside Purochana's room, listening. He had gone to bed, but was not asleep. I knew he would not be able to sleep.

All five of us strapped clothes and weapons to our backs. Mother came out, ready to leave.

We removed the planks of wood at the spot the tunnel-digger had indicated and saw only soil at first. Moving it aside to a depth of about six fingers, we heard the murmur of voices beneath us, then glimpsed a light. Someone standing there removed clumps of soil from below and made enough space for one person to go down. Yudhishtira went down first, then Sahadeva. I lowered

Mother slowly into his arms. After Nakula went down, I said to Arjuna, 'Go ahead. I have a task to finish.'

I ran silently towards the front door. I picked up the small oil lamp burning in the room, took out the wick and poured the oil on the door. No sooner did I set it alight than I realized how skilful the Kaurava architects were – the walls and pillars caught fire even before the tongues of flame touched them. The wick in my hand had burnt out, so I fashioned a torch from the leg of a chair that had collapsed.

I moved to the central hall and came upon Purochana, coughing and struggling to say something. I saw his face in the glow of the flames. It no longer had the humble expression of a servant. What I saw was the cruel glare of a wicked hunter cheated of its prey. He looked around wildly, searching for a weapon, and I brought my fists down on his bare head.

He moaned when I grabbed his neck and clothes to lift him up from where he lay. I threw him like an empty leather liquor pot into Mother's old bedroom, which had become a pit of fire.

I went back to the kitchen, but could see nothing because of the smoke. I heard the tribals from the forest screaming in unison from the outer hall.

I did not have to climb down, I toppled headlong into a crevice where a red light glowed. Sahadeva groaned softly as I landed, trampling his legs.

We all moved forward, keeping our eyes on the red glow at the end of the darkness, each of us gripping the shoulder of the person in front.

On the way out, Arjuna asked, 'Have all of them been silenced?'

I said, 'They are peacefully asleep. Or rather, in a yoga sleep gifted them by the blessing of the God of Fire.'

Sahadeva smiled.

I heard Yudhishtira's voice from somewhere in front, 'We don't need any witticisms, blockhead.'

The tunnel ended just beneath the rocks. We had to climb up to the path that led out of Varanavata. Yudhishtira started to go up the steep trail cut into the cliff, lost his balance and fell back. I overtook my younger brothers and examined the path. We would have to dig our fingers into the small crevices on the cliff-face and pull ourselves up carefully.

'This is even more dangerous than the house of lac!' Yudhishtira cursed the path.

As a test, I hoisted Sahadeva on my shoulders and carried him up. Feeling more confident, I took Mother up next. Yudhishtira insisted that he could not climb and began to search for other paths, and I finally had to take him up on my shoulders as well. Nakula came behind me and Arjuna in front. Every now and then, Nakula held on to my waist to lever himself up.

When we finally came out, I was exhausted. I smiled and said to Nakula, 'It would have been better to carry you as well.'

'I prayed for you today, brother, for the first time in my life – that you wouldn't fall back on top of me!'

Thanks to the relief of having escaped, everyone felt light-hearted. Following Yudhishtira's example, I scolded Nakula jestingly, 'Don't you know this is no time to be witty?'

We turned to look at the pleasure house we had left behind. The dark night seemed to have caught fire. As we reached the valley again, we caught the glint of water in the darkness. The tunnel-digger who was our guide said, 'If you cross the river, you'll reach the forest. My master, Vidura, said that would be the safest place for you.'

The river was a tributary of the Ganga. We did not have to worry about how to cross it. We could clearly hear the sound of a boat rowing towards us.

'The boat is here.' The guide joined his palms in an obeisance to Mother and all of us. 'Grant me permission to leave. Do you have a message for my master?'

Mother said, 'Tell him we have begun our journey.'

2

The forest was dry and scorched. Shorn of leaves, the pale trees waited for rain. My brothers slept next to one another on makeshift mattresses of dried leaves. Mother was already up. Noticing that I was lying awake on the bed of dried grass I had made under a tree, she said, 'There's no water anywhere.'

I got up and walked around, trampling the dry leaves. I did not find water anywhere. When Vidura had decided this forest was a safe place for us, he had obviously not remembered to check if there was water. There had been enough food and weapons for everyone in the boat that had come for us during the third quarter of the night. It had always seemed to us that Vidura spent most of his time wandering around the palace grounds like a stranger, dispensing advice on how to follow dharma, and yet he had attended to the most minute details of our escape. In spite of that, we would have to find some other forest with running water and move our refuge there.

Once we had crossed the river, our journey was difficult.

Mother was so tired that I carried her on my shoulders. After going quite a distance, Yudhishtira had sat down, saying he could walk no further. Sahadeva then suggested that we sleep at the spot where we were camped now.

A wild rabbit sprang out of the thickets and raced past me. There had to be water in a forest that had animals. I saw footprints on the dry grass and, at one spot, the moist excreta of a jackal. I sniffed, trying to catch the scent of water. Only forest tribals and animals could trace water by its scent. I suddenly heard the sound of water birds nearby – music my ears welcomed at this early morning hour in my parched state. I quickened my pace.

I came upon a small pond shaped like a water-lily leaf, filled with clear water. There were bright green bushes around, standing proudly amidst the dryness.

I drank some water. Mud and the odour of smoke clung to my body. I climbed down into the pond, which was deeper than I had thought. I swam for a bit, bathed, came back ashore and wrung out my clothes, then wondered how I could take some water back. I tried to fill some in my upper cloth, but it dripped out before I took ten steps forward. As I stood there, distressed, not knowing what to do, I heard a soft laugh from the bushes. A young tribal woman emerged from them, wearing only a deerskin around her waist. I wondered whether she had been watching me. I looked angrily at her as she came up fearlessly to me.

She wore bracelets carved from boar's tusks on her hands, a necklace of tiger-claws and a chain with a single strand, its links shaped in half-squares. Standing next to me, she seemed almost as tall as I was. She was the colour of the heartwood of a blackwood tree. There was a sound of snapping twigs at her ankles as she walked. Her tiger-claw necklace tinkled as she walked around me. Springing from her body, her breasts looked like the swollen glands of rogue tuskers from the Kamaroopa forests.

Signalling to me to wait, she ran into the thickets and came back carrying a heap of large leaves. She stood next to me, stitching the leaves together with thorns, and I caught an unpleasant odour of animal fat from her dishevelled knot of hair. Grabbing my upper cloth, she placed the stitched leaves on it. How easily she had made a container for me to carry water! As I walked back after filling it, I knew she was following me. I turned back just as I reached our camp. She was nowhere I could see her.

My mother and brothers, all of them wrung out and exhausted, got up and drank water. Yudhishtira, the man who the sages of Shatasringa had predicted would rule from Gandhara to Magadha and from Vahleeka to Vidarbha, lay drained of strength on a bed of dried leaves. And my mother, who had once been waited upon by eighteen servant women, was seated on the bare grass, her head bent. I felt very unhappy.

Mother had sent Vidura a message, saying the journey had begun. Where were we going?

The forest woman appeared suddenly, bearing wild fruit and a bamboo stem filled with honey. We had not even heard her footsteps. She spread everything before Mother, knelt down, bowed her head to the ground and paid her obeisance.

Mother, surprised, looked at me for some reason.

'Who are you? What is your name?' she asked.

The woman looked at me, withdrew her eyes and said softly, 'Hidimbi.'

'I think there are a lot of tribals in the forest,' said Yudhishtira, trying to assume the authority of a crown prince. 'I wonder whether she will wait upon Mother. Tell her we'll give her gifts.' He asked me, 'Does this woman know our language?'

Hidimbi hid a smile.

Mother asked, 'Do you have a family?'

She replied in a dialect in which Prakrit was heavily mingled with Paisachi: 'I'm alone most of the time. I have a brother. He hunts all over this forest, through Kamyaka to Gandhamadana. He comes here very rarely.'

'Where is your house?'

She pointed to the forest.

Yudhishtira remarked, 'People like her don't have houses – the forest is their home.'

Hidimbi laughed softly again.

She went away, saying she would come back.

Yudhishtira warned me, 'Be careful. These people know sorcery. Don't let her come near you, especially at night.'

Why was he saying this to me? When she stood before us, had he noted something in my expression beyond the interest everyone had felt at seeing her?

I dozed until the sun went down. Then I set out, telling the others I was going to find out what kind of animals there were in the area. I took with me a small spear, about the length of three arms. Arjuna had already set up a target on a tree some distance away and was practising archery.

I walked in the direction opposite to the pond I had found in the morning. Once again, a rabbit sprang out of the bushes, passing so near me that I could have aimed my spear at it. I suddenly heard a cry and saw her running behind the fleeing rabbit that had got far ahead of her. The chase seemed futile. She flew through the thickets like an arrow with a vulture's feather tied to it. I could no longer see the rabbit. I saw her fall down.

I walked towards her, thinking that she had tripped over the roots on the path. Before I could get to her, she got up and turned around. She lifted her hand to show me a huge rabbit she had caught by the ears. It was struggling to free itself. She laughed and I laughed with her. Then she let it go. The rabbit stood trembling for a moment, as if in disbelief, then ran for its life, terrified.

I leant my spear against a rock nearby and sat down. She came up to me and ran her fingers over the spear, testing the sharpness of its pointed end. She sat down, picked up a cluster of withered palasha flowers that had fallen in the wind and chewed on it. A reddish wetness spread over her pale blue lips.

I reached out for her, and she wound herself around me like a black serpent. Her hair with its odour of animal fat came loose from its knot and spread darkness over my face. The night I had remained frozen with the servant woman in my arms seemed like some foolish dream. I now felt that my teachers should have taught me the subtleties of a woman's body. The fire within me had seventy flames, not seven. No, not seventy, ten thousand. It was as if the one who performed the sacrifice desired to be offering, fire and ashes all at once …

We walked close to each other as we went back. I stopped when I heard Nakula's and Sahadeva's voices, and she went ahead.

I wandered around the forest until it grew dark. I watched the pushya star rise between the branches of an udumbara tree that looked like a hefty tribal lifting his hands towards the sky. Then I went back.

Yudhishtira scolded me for having stayed out so late in the dark forest. We sat down to eat and Sahadeva served me liquor. There had been no liquor among the foodstuff Vidura had sent us.

Nakula said, 'Hidimbi brought us more gifts.'

I woke up late the next morning to the sound of Yudhishtira shouting, and went to find out what had happened. The packets of grain we had brought with us, the leather bags meant for giving gifts to the brahmins, the small gold pots we used for pujas, had all disappeared.

Yudhishtira was convinced, 'It's her, the tribal woman. She's a demoness. She walks around in human form in the daytime, then comes at night as a sorceress and steals. We're lucky she wasn't greedy for human flesh, or she'd have eaten us.'

I walked around our camp. I could identify animal footprints on any rock surface. I saw huge footprints clearly, made by a man walking barefoot. I went towards the pond. As I approached it, a thicket murmured, 'Don't, it's dangerous.'

I stretched my hand out and it closed over her hair. I pulled her out. She stood before me, trembling.

'Do you want gold? Or grain? Who robbed us?' I asked, not letting go of her.

I suddenly heard a sound like the grunt of a wild boar. The footsteps that approached me seemed to make the earth quake. A tribal as tall and erect as a palm tree appeared, carrying a huge branch in his hand. I knew that none of the lessons I had learnt of war would be of any use here. Words would be as futile.

I escaped the first blow he dealt me with the branch only because I moved away very quickly. Luck was with me as well. The tip of the branch seared my chest as it swept by. I felt the wetness of blood form a stinging line over my chest and realized I had to confront this fellow not with strength, but with the speed of my feet and the suppleness of my body. He aimed a second blow at me. I escaped. Before he could regain his balance, I sprang on him and hit him hard, letting my fists sink deep into his ribs. He knew he could no longer deal me a blow with the branch, so he started to fight with his fists. This was what I wanted. He aimed his fists at my chest and stomach. I sprang into the circle of his arms and hit him, aiming at his nose and lips. The scream he tried to stifle escaped from his throat with a spurt of blood.

He was extremely strong. Few in the forest would dare confront him. But Shukacharya had taught me how to identify the most vulnerable spots on the body, and between the blows he dealt me, I took aim carefully at every spot I had learnt about.

The fight convinced me that I was in no way inferior to him in physical strength. When he wrapped his arms around me like a wrestler, I dealt him a sharp blow on the vital nerve at his throat. He trembled like a giant palm caught in a hurricane. Stretching his huge hand towards the ground for balance, he toppled down slowly. I could have stopped there. But I knew well that only an animal could be spared, a human opponent could not be given a second chance. I lunged backwards, aimed a blow at his neck and felled him.

I heard Arjuna's voice, 'Move, I'll finish him with an arrow.'

Mustering the last vestiges of his strength, the man tried to grab me as he scrambled up, winding his arms under my armpits, but I sprang away. I dug my knees into his waist and pressed his shoulders down. I caught his hair and distinctly heard his vertebrae snap like tanni seeds.

The twisted body suddenly became still.

I got up slowly. Bhimasena had killed for the first time.

I was Bhimasena, the mighty son of the Wind God. I wanted to shout loud enough for the whole forest to hear.

I looked at Hidimbi who was standing there, stunned. 'Where are the others? If there's anyone else, let him come. Bhimasena is ready.'

She covered her face with her hands and wept.

'Who is this?'

She said, between sobs, 'My brother.'

As we walked back, Arjuna said, 'I could not find a single spot where I could have aimed an arrow.'

The salty taste of the blood on my lips seeped into my mouth. I said, 'He was very strong.'

What was important in a fight was who first felled the other. Kshatriyas did not have to decide whether the kill was just or unjust. The dharma of battle was to kill. The victim who died was blest as well. Somehow, I did not feel the pride of a victorious warrior as I washed off the bloodstains of my first kill. A vague uneasiness crept through me, like the buzz of a bee inside a fig.

I went walking by myself again and came to the rock where the rabbit-chase had taken place the day before. Wild goats raced out from the clearing in the middle of the high peak behind me, their hooves clattering, and disappeared.

I sat down. Noon shadows began to gather around the trees. I continued to sit there, doing nothing. She came, after a while. There were no tearstains on her face, nor she did find fault with me. She sat down next to me and gently stroked the wound that stretched like a sword-thrust over my breastbone. Her heels brushed against my body.

'He was a cruel man. But he was the only blood relation I had.' There was no sorrow in her voice. Her lips trembled.

I put my arm around her, drew her down to my chest and said, 'I am here for you.'

Her fingers, gentler than the touch of a feather, wandered over the blood clotted on my body. We forgot war and death.

I made her walk in front of me when we returned to the camp at dusk.

I asked her to stand in front of Mother and said, 'From now on, she will serve you, Mother. She is my bride.'

Only I noted the startled look in Mother's eyes. Hidimbi prostrated herself. Mother laid her hand on her head and said, 'May all auspicious things be yours.'

I said to Hidimbi, 'My elder brother, crown prince Yudhishtira. Prostrate yourself before him.'

Yudhishtira gave her his blessing, moved aside hastily and said, 'I should give you a gift, but I have nothing with me. It's a bad time for me.'

She smiled gently. 'You don't have to give me anything. I will be content if you always show me kindness.'

I introduced my younger brothers to her, then walked away to the forest, leaving the women to get to know each other. Sahadeva, who came along with me, congratulated me. Yudhishtira was just behind us.

He asked me to step aside, so that the others would not hear, and said softly, 'Her people know sorcery. Don't seek pleasure with her at night. You must stay with us.'

In my childhood, I had heard stories about demons who practised magic. The servant women had told us how a demon disguised as a deer came to tempt Sita, how the demon-king,

Ravana, disguised himself as an ascetic and abducted her. Had the tribal I killed been a sorcerer, the day would certainly not have ended as it did. However, I listened to Yudhishtira's advice gravely, my head bent.

A change came over Hidimbi after three days of mourning. She began to wear flowers in her hair and around her neck. She showed me all the hidden beauties of the forest. Trees that flowered even in high summer, plants whose stems were filled with sweet liquid, regions where forest goddesses dwelt, hidden streams, lakes where only blue lotuses bloomed …

I forgot the enemies in Hastinapura and the hardships of life in the forest. The days were never long enough and I longed for the nights to go on, for the sun to never rise.

One evening when I came back from the forest at dusk, Mother said, 'It's time for us to continue our journey.'

Arjuna said, 'A special messenger came with a message from our Uncle Vidura. We have to move to Ekachakra.'

Yudhishtira explained, 'Ekachakra is a small place, a brahmin village. If we live there meditating like brahmins and seeking alms, no one will recognize us. I cannot endure the hardships of the forest any longer.'

What was happening in Hastinapura? We had heard that Uncle Dhritarashtra had lamented the fact that the mansion in Varanavata had burnt down. Who else had wept? The messenger had not said.

Had Bhishma wept? Or Dronacharya? Or my charioteer Vishoka?

Mother hurried us. We did not have many preparations to make for the journey. Hidimbi was getting ready to go out and search for the fruits and roots we needed to take with us.

Mother glanced at me. 'It would not be right for Hidimbi to come with us.'

Yudhishtira placed his hand on my shoulder. 'We have to live amongst them like brahmins. So ...'

Hidimbi was tying something up in a packet. She stopped and looked at Mother. Then gazed at me. Unable to meet her eyes, I turned away.

Sahadeva came up to me.

I said softly to him, 'She is with child.'

'Mother knows.'

Mother got up, went to Hidimbi and laid her hand on her head. 'You are my first daughter-in-law. May you have a good son. I will always remember your love and care.'

My brothers, who were ready for the journey, followed Yudhishtira. Mother looked warningly at me and began to walk forward. I fastened my bow and arrows to my shoulder and continued to stand where I was.

Mother hesitated, then came back.

'Send your son to see me when he grows up. He will be the eldest son to all my five sons.' She walked away.

I stood before Hidimbi.

Bhimasena was a pauper who had nothing valuable, not even something that would serve as a sign, to give her or the child who was going to be born to him.

She had prostrated herself at my feet. I raised her, pressed my lips to her head and stood helpless, unable to find the words to say goodbye to her.

Then I hurried to catch up with the forms that were growing distant in the faint darkness.

3

The stories the sootas made up later about my second duel used to make me laugh. The truth was that Baka was not as strong as Hidimba.

We had just begun to eke out a livelihood by begging, staying in one half of a brahmin house in Ekachakra. The very next day after we arrived, we learnt that King Vetrakiya was going to conduct the Purushamedha ritual, in which human beings had to be offered as sacrifice.

Yudhishtira, who had heard about the Purushamedha sacrifice from learned brahmin teachers, knew its intricacies. I too had once heard an old tale about a greedy brahmin, Richeeka, who had sold his son Shunashepha as a sacrificial victim in exchange for a hundred cows.

My elder brother said the Purushamedha extended over forty days. All castes were offered in sacrifice – a brahmin, so that the person offering the sacrifice could become a great scholar of the Vedas, a kshatriya in order to achieve everything a king should possess, a vaishya to appease the winds, a shudra for the rites of penitence, a thief to placate the dark forces, a murderer for Hell, an impotent man for sins, and then a barber, a player of dice, a lame man and a veena player. Yudhishtira described the qualities of the sacrificial victims. Eleven men each would be given in sacrifice on fifteen occasions over these forty days.

In the old days, there were people who made the Purushamedha a Sarvamedha: if the person who conducted the ceremony offered himself in the end as a sacrifice, it became a Sarvamedha. There was no point asking why, an answer did not exist. 'Give me all, as I give you all' – that was the assumption. If the principle of the sacrifice was an appeal for a blessing, then what did the sarvamedhi, the victim who offered himself as the final sacrifice, attain? Yudhishtira had no answer.

A nishada named Baka had undertaken to fetch the men King Vetrakiya needed to offer in sacrifice.

Mother overheard the father, mother, daughter and the little boy in our house arguing with one another. Baka's messengers had ordered them to send a brahmin subject from the house.

Baka collected the men who were to be sacrificial offerings in a huge cave in a forest just beyond the village. None of the villagers were strong enough to oppose him. Besides, Baka combed the countryside to catch people on behalf of the only person they could have appealed to, their king.

As the commotion grew louder, Mother said to the family, 'If only one person need be sent, I have a son who is very strong. He will go.'

When Mother told us that she had given them her word, I said nothing. Sometimes, the physical strength I had been granted as a boon could be a curse as well.

'When I saw how they grieved, I couldn't help saying what I did,' said Mother.

Yudhishtira was furious. 'What a stupid thing to say, Mother! We sleep in peace only because we rely on Bhimasena's strength. Don't you know that?'

Mother had heard the brahmin and his wife arguing about who would go. The son said he would. Then his younger brother plucked a blade of grass and declared he would kill Baka with it. Mother's heart had melted at that point and she had said: 'I will send my son.'

Sahadeva voiced a doubt. 'But we are kshatriyas, aren't we? Isn't it a brahmin subject that Vetrakiya wants?'

All of us pretended to ignore this childish question.

Yudhishtira was deeply distressed. 'If we lose Bhimasena …' He looked at me sadly. 'Every time I consider ways to establish my right to the throne, it is the thought of his might that gives me comfort.'

Arjuna said, 'My elder brother will not lose. He will not be defeated – let the people of Ekachakra be saved from Baka.'

Yudhishtira nodded and added, 'And we will earn the blessings of the brahmins as well.'

I paid my elder brother a silent obeisance in my heart for having said that all four of them basked in the shade of my strength. And if I did not come back alive, there was something they would still attain: the blessings of the brahmins.

Baka was bigger built than Hidimba. But he had neither the strength nor the speed of Hidimba, who was used to running around the dense forests, hunting and fighting battles.

As I waited outside Baka's cave, I was overwhelmed by the stench of liquor. Three of his followers stood around me, the sacrificial offering who had arrived, and argued about my good qualities and defects.

They invited me in respectfully.

Baka had a copper-coloured beard. He was perspiring profusely and the huge round eyes in a face flushed with liquor looked at me with a mocking smile. When he got up, the waves of flesh on his body heaved. His breasts were as full-grown as a woman's and folds of fat covered his ribs. The flesh that hung from his double chin flowed over his neck and coppery beard to his chest. The stench of liquor and sweat made me retch.

I do not remember the details of that fight clearly. I know I began with words.

'Have you heard of Hidimba? He fell like a mountain; the vultures and jackals have not yet finished eating him up. You can go and look at him if you want. I am the one who killed that sorcerer, Hidimba, in a duel.'

This was a strategy mentioned in the science of war – an attack with words, to render the enemy helpless. Once he realized that I had not come prepared to lay my head on a stake on Vetrakiya's sacrificial site, the nishada's manner changed. He roared, and I replied with a murderous bellow.

I knew that if his arms succeeded in trapping me, they would crush the life out of me. I noticed a copper cauldron of ghee simmering over the fire. The pieces of a bison that had been skinned and cut up lay scattered on the floor. Baka did not expect the boiling ghee and the copper cauldron to fall on him as he swung his arms and prepared for battle. He roared like a wild boar in pain and anger, and moved towards me, his footsteps unsteady. I pretended to fall down. He was not prepared for the kick I aimed at the slender ankles that were completely out of proportion with his enormous body.

'You first, then Vetrakiya.'

I trampled on the mountain of flesh that had fallen on the ground and evaded the hands that were groping in the air to catch me. Locking my knees, I pressed them on a vital nerve. I held his head down with my right hand, gripped his leather belt, lifted up his waist and pulled him upwards, using all my strength. I felt many parts giving way inside his rolls of flesh. Baka screamed. I moved my knees to his neck, raised his head abruptly and snapped it. He stopped twitching.

As I got up, I could not believe what had happened. Was this all the opposition that Baka, who had terrified the people of Ekachakra, could offer me?

His followers waited, uncertain what to do. I said to them, 'Remove the corpse to some faraway spot. And take care you are never seen in Ekachakra again.'

Trembling with fear, they stood with their palms joined respectfully. I walked back light-heartedly, as if I had just finished taking some exercise. Mother looked unconcerned, as if I'd come back from a forest stream where I'd gone to get water. Nakula and Sahadeva were impatient to hear about the duel. Yudhishtira embraced me with relief.

Arjuna asked, 'Did you kill him?'

'Yes.'

Once he and I were alone, I told him about the strategy I had used.

I tired of our stay in the brahmin household very quickly. Yudhishtira had instructed us not to go out. Kaurava spies were sure to be around. Vidura had made it clear that Duryodhana was not entirely convinced we had all died in Varanavata.

When the brahmins overwhelmed us with gratitude, joy and gifts for having killed Baka, Mother said to them, 'My son was able to accomplish this only because of the power he has attained through chanting mantras. So it is the gods you must thank.' The master of our household offered a goat to the gods to express his gratitude.

It was difficult to disguise myself when I went out – I could not conceal my enormous body behind a sacred thread and stripes of holy ash. Nor would a moustache or beard grow on my face as they did on Yudhishtira's and Arjuna's.

Yudhishtira tried to make a dice player of our brahmin host, but did not succeed. He took to holding forth on the Vedas and Shastras and this became a pastime for him.

The villagers thought we were members of some noble family, reduced to begging because of unfortunate circumstances. According to them, the evil destiny was not our fault – the region where we were born and bred was to blame. When kshatriyas who have the capacity to bestow alms fall on evil days, the twice-born brahmins have to go out and beg for alms.

Mother got in touch with some brahmin priests through our host. Some of them came to see her from time to time, and she always talked to them privately.

Sahadeva said to me, 'They are looking for a bride for our elder brother. I heard only bits and pieces of what they said.'

How could Mother think of arranging a marriage at a time when we were wandering around the country, begging for a living? I hinted as much to her once or twice, and she said, 'It is through marriage alliances that you must muster strength now. If we have no friends, we must acquire relatives.'

How long were we going to continue here? When would Vidura's messenger come again? The instructions that directed our movements here and our journeys to other places had to come from a little house just outside the palace in Hastinapura.

Yudhishtira confided a secret to me. 'Vidura's spies are working for us. Our older uncle, Dhritarashtra, is not willing to believe that we perished in the fire. He does not yet know that Hidimba was killed. Duryodhana might guess that we are alive if he hears of the death of Vetrakiya's henchman, Baka. Let our uncle decide for us.'

He meant Vidura. But I was not ready to accept that living

like wild rats in a lair was strategy. Why not return and challenge the Kaurava chieftains to a duel, one by one? That was kshatriya law, after all.

Meanwhile, we lingered in Ekachakra, a village where the wooden roofs of brahmin houses dotted the landscape and the air was filled with the chant of Vedic mantras. The days were scorching. Instead of game we had hunted, we ate the grains we were given as alms.

One evening, I went out and walked around the thatched houses outside the village. What if I walked all night, never stopping to rest, towards the forest? The forest that would give me everything I needed, where champaka flowers would have started to bloom now. Where the forest maiden whose body had the tenderness of neermatala flowers ...

What would our enemies think when they heard that the second Pandava, the mighty one, had deserted?

I returned only after dark. No one was asleep. I knew they had been waiting for me. They were trying to control the impatience that was evident on their faces.

Yudhishtira said, 'King Drupada's daughter's swayamvara is going to take place, she is going to choose a bridegroom.'

This was not a matter that concerned me, so I showed absolutely no interest.

Arjuna and I had seen Drupada's palace. Panchala, Drupada's kingdom, was a prosperous one and their king was stronger than the Kurus.

Soon after we finished our studies, Dronacharya wanted all of us, the Kauravas and the Pandavas, to gather an army and confront Drupada. Drona and King Drupada had been friends as children, but had fallen out with each other at some point and parted company. Drona wanted to seek revenge with the help of his best disciples and the Kaurava army. His aim was to capture at least half the Panchala kingdom.

I had wondered why a brahmin like him desired a kingdom and wealth. Vishoka had told me why, as a secret. Pure brahmins did not desire wealth. But Drona, although he had been born a brahmin, had grown up as a kshatriya, which was probably why he gave such importance to the value of the Panchalas' cows and of the gold in their treasury.

Arjuna and I had visited Drupada as Drona's mediators. Drupada had, at any cost, to ask pardon of our teacher for the wrong done to him. If he did not, Drona would arrive with the Kauravas, the Pandavas and the army of Hastinapura.

King Drupada had aged, but his radiance had not dimmed. He received us with a warm smile and told us that if his son, Dhrishtadyumna, had been there, he would have insisted we stayed awhile. He promised to send gifts and a message of affection to the brahmin teacher. After a moment's thought, he decided to accompany us.

The image of Drupada, who had smilingly extended such warm hospitality to us when we arrived at his place threatening to wage war, still lingered in my mind.

Dhrishtadyumna, who was younger than us, was away in some distant place at that time, studying archery. I later heard people say that he was acquiring great expertise in waging war from a chariot. I knew he had an elder brother as well, Shikhandi. This was the first time I had heard of Drupada's daughter.

Draupadi, Dhrishtadyumna's twin sister, was said to be dark-skinned. There were kings who were ready to pay any bride price, however high, to marry Draupadi. However, her father decided to choose a warrior who would prove victorious in a contest with a weapon.

'You must go and have a try. We have nothing to lose. And if you win ...' Our elder brother went on to say that we could declare the Pandavas were alive the moment we acquired Drupada as our relative.

We talked about the wedding hall in Drupada's palace when we went to bed that night – all of us except Yudhishtira. He was silent, although he was awake.

Nakula and Sahadeva knew nothing beyond the fact that something had happened between Drupada and Drona after they finished their studies.

Nakula asked me, 'What happened between our teacher and Drupada? The two of you were mediators.'

Arjuna replied, 'Drupada committed a grave crime against our guru. In their youth, when they were companions, he made Drona an empty promise: "When I become king, you can use my treasury as you wish." But once he became king, he grew fed up with Drona, that's all.' Arjuna laughed.

Yudhishtira said gravely, 'Are you mocking our brahmin guru?'

'Am I not right? Didn't Drupada get irritated with him and send him away because his needs were insatiable, no matter how much he was given?'

Yudhishtira was silent.

Sahadeva asked, 'Why did our teacher want wealth?'

No one answered him. Assuming that everyone had fallen asleep, I closed my eyes. Arjuna moved close to me.

'You didn't hear what the brahmin messenger said about Draupadi, who is also called Krishnaa, did you?'

'No.'

'He said she is ravishingly beautiful.'

I was not surprised. She had been born as the fruit of many prayers and rituals. I recalled the people I had met during the journey to Panchala. They had been good-looking men and women.

'The brahmin told us something else …'

I turned and looked at Arjuna's face.

'Ravishingly beautiful … and her perspiration has the fragrance of lotus flowers.'

I knew Arjuna was thinking about the competition. We did not know who all were coming. If Karna, who had challenged Arjuna in public at the time of the display of skills, was going to be there …

No. I corrected myself. Charioteers could not compete in a kshatriya wedding hall. But then, Karna now had the title of the king of Anga. I would have to ask Yudhishtira about the rules.

I knew that an unclear image filled the smile in Arjuna's eyes, an image that wafted the scent of lotus flowers.

For some reason, that night I did not dream as I usually did of the black beauty whose sweat had an ordinary human odour.

4

There were as many suitors crowding the wedding hall as there were guests. The brahmins sat at the back, next to the sacrificial fire. Rather than invite attention by entering as a group of five, each of us went in separately. Arjuna came in last and, looking for a place to sit, found one near me. The people around us were trying to identify the kings who were present.

Duryodhana was in the forefront of a group that entered just after us. Arjuna nudged my foot gently to let me know, but I had seen him already. Among the suitors were old men, grandfathers and men with three and four wives.

There was a huge pillar in the centre of the hall. The target was fixed to the top of it.

In the old days, a warrior's dharma was either to fight a war and win a bride, or be chosen by a bride in the swayamvara hall. Wealthy kings paid a bride price to the fathers of young daughters and bought them for meek sons, or sons who were past their youth. The young men of our time despised this custom.

The sootas sang continuously, accompanied melodiously by the veena, the flute and the mridangam. They praised Krishnaa, the maiden who had taken shape from the radiance that arose from the fire of a ritual performed for Drupada by a virtuous priest and his assistant. The fragrance of burning sandalwood and akil wood wafted through the hall along with the music.

There was a sudden silence as Drupada walked to the centre of the hall. People thronging the space beyond the great pillars pushed forward as far as they could.

Drupada welcomed the guests who had been invited, as well as all the others who had come, hearing of the event. 'I am blest,' he said over and over again.

Everyone's eyes turned to the inner door of the hall. I saw Dhrishtadyumna first: he looked very young, but strong and handsome. A golden crown studded with pearls kept the wavy hair falling over his forehead in place. The bracelet on his upper arm was encrusted with beryls, and an ardhaguchham necklace with twenty strands hung over his chest. Gems glittered on the belt above his yellow waist-cloth. Then I saw the young girl standing behind the prince. This was Draupadi! What first struck me were her black eyes, which gleamed brighter beneath the arrow-like collyrium-tipped eyelashes than the sapphire glowing in the centre of her necklace. She was dressed in white silk and held a golden wedding garland in her hand. The hall grew completely silent.

I heard Arjuna murmur, 'O God of Gods!'

I thought, if Indra, the God of Gods, was my younger brother's protector, it was at this moment that he should come to him. Arjuna was faint with desire for the young girl.

The brahmin messenger had not exaggerated at all. I looked at Draupadi again through the flames of the sacrificial fire. Radiating loveliness, she was like a blue lotus that had just been touched awake by the rays of the rising sun.

Dhrishtadyumna explained what the suitors had to do. The wooden bird in the mechanical cage spinning on top of the pillar had to be shot down. The bars of the cage were very slender and placed close together. The archer had to string the huge bow placed in the hall and take aim with it.

An attendant removed the silk cloth covering the great bow. It was embossed with brass sheets, each the length of at least six arms.

It would require an extraordinary expertise to hit the target inside the spinning cage. And, more importantly, the blessing of good fortune as well. But I knew it was the great bow Drupada had got ready that was going to give the archers greater cause for worry. The nishadas used bamboo bows that were the length of seven and nine arms. However, this bow was not made of bamboo. The secret of Drupada's metal bow must lie in its craftsmanship.

What if the bow broke as it was being strung? I had heard a story about Rama breaking the bow in Janaka's hall before he split the target. If Rama of Ayodhya could win the contest even after breaking his bow, I certainly had a chance to test my skills here.

The attention of the spectators turned to two people who had entered. Drupada ran towards them, saluting them with joined palms. I recognized Balarama at once. The other one had to be Krishna. Balarama had come to Hastinapura once, soon after Father's funeral rites had been completed. He was middle-aged now. Mother had told me that Krishna was a year younger than me. We had heard a while ago that they were going to move from Mathura to their new palace in Dwaraka.

Balarama and Krishna were not going to join the contestants. King Drupada led them respectfully to the raised seats in the hall.

'Krishna! Krishna has arrived,' said Arjuna.

'Softly,' I whispered. 'I saw him.'

Krishna gazed at the spectators and guests. The first king who came forward for the contest was the middle-aged son of the king of Kalinga. The magadhas called out his attributes. When he took up the bow and raised it, I realized how heavy it was. In a vain attempt to hold it straight, the contestant lost his balance and fell on his knees. A wave of laughter broke out from the spectators.

I pondered over what the secret of the bow might be and was able to roughly guess what it was. It had obviously been fashioned with the intent to mock the marksmen who used it – molten metal had been poured into it indiscriminately to deliberately upset the balance. Even an archer who succeeded in holding it straight and stringing it was certain to miss the target by the time he positioned the arrow and took aim.

We watched several archers make an attempt, one by one, fail and withdraw from the contest. Arjuna watched closely as the bow twisted and turned in the strangest way, like a living being, in one pair of hands after another. He had eyes for nothing except the bow, which behaved differently in the hands of each archer.

Yudhishtira caught my eye. He looked extremely disappointed. Duryodhana was the next contestant. He managed to lift the bow up to his waist, then abandoned the attempt.

Catching sight of someone who had got up from the group of suitors and was walking towards the bow, Arjuna caught his breath.

The magadhas and the sootas called out: 'Karna, the king of Anga.'

No other qualifications were mentioned, nor were any astonishing feats described.

Although he was my greatest enemy, I could not help admiring his air of nonchalance. As he strode forward, holding himself straight, his head almost brushed against the streamers in the hall.

I thought Karna had realized that the balance of the bow had been tampered with. Careful not to let people see the twitching in the muscles of his arms, he managed to finally string the bow. So he had won the first round. The spectators held their breath and waited hopefully, admiringly.

Dhrishtadyumna lowered his head towards his sister and murmured something to her. I thought her lips moved.

Dhrishtadyumna moved three steps forward and said, 'Stop! Only kshatriyas can take part in the contest.'

Slowly turning the bow he had strung, Karna looked at Dhrishtadyumna. The entire audience could see fury blazing in him like a forest fire in summer.

Dhrishtadyumna continued smilingly, 'My sister will not accept anyone whose clan is lower than hers. If you wish to go on with it simply as a form of exercise, you may do so.'

I watched Karna's body, which had been as taut and firm as the drawn bowstring, dwindle and shrink.

Arjuna heaved a sigh of relief.

This was the second time I had felt sorry for my enemy. He looked even weaker and more defenceless now than when he had stood exhausted in Adhiratha's arms.

With a greater expertise than he had shown earlier, he unstrung the bow and let it fall from his hands. It fell on the stone floor of the hall, clattering and echoing its protest. Karna walked with his head bent to the back door. The murmurs of the crowd grew louder.

The rulers of Chedi, Vidarbha, Vanga, Kekaya and Kamaroopa had all finished their turn. No one else came forward. The magadha said: 'If the kings have decided to take a respite, the brahmins can take their turn.'

The announcement was a formality, they did not expect anyone to come forward. The only brahmin archer who might have done so was Ashvathama and he had not come.

We looked at one another. Yudhishtira must have been aware of my stare, for he made ready to get up, then sat down again.

Arjuna whispered to me, 'Our eldest brother is not participating, so it is the second one's turn.'

I patted his thigh and said, 'I'm not going. May good fortune be with you.'

Arjuna stood up. The spectators must have thought he was some silly brahmin boy. No one who had seen him in Hastinapura would have recognized this black-skinned brahmin youth, with dishevelled hair covering his neck, and a face and body entirely smeared with sacred ash. My heart filled with doubts and prayers as I watched my younger brother dragging his feet, walking towards the bow with his head bent. It was so unlike him not to move with the firm, measured tread of a practised athlete.

I could not see Draupadi's face clearly because the pillars behind the sacrificial fire screened it from view. All I caught sight of was one foot, adorned with golden toe-rings. I drew a deep breath. Was there a fragrance of lotus flowers mingled with the perfume of incense? Was Draupadi perspiring?

The voices of the old men seated around us sounded cheerful – they were obviously relieved that at least one brahmin youth had come forward to compete.

Arjuna stood at the centre of the hall and lifted the bow high, holding it well away from him. I realized that he had made specific calculations about the weight of the bow the balance of which had been so cleverly jeopardized. He seemed to find it more difficult to string the bow than Karna did. Once the bow settled into his left hand and over his shoulder, well under his control and perfectly steady, I grew feverish with eagerness. An attendant ran up to him with a quiver and he took an arrow out of it. After examining its tip and base, he looked at the target, making silent calculations in his mind. Some brahmins in front of me suddenly stood up and blocked my view. By the time I scrambled up, the hall was resounding with shouts. What a nuisance, I had not been able to witness the instant of victory. Arjuna's arrow had found the target! The audience had fallen utterly silent with amazement. Draupadi glanced at her brother and her father, then walked with them towards Arjuna, who stood waiting with a half-smile. He bent his head when she was before him and, standing on tiptoe, she garlanded him.

Everything happened very fast. I had expected that mantras would be chanted and the customary rituals performed after the contest. I remembered then that this was the first time I had seen a swayamvara ceremony.

The brahmins shattered the silence with cries of joy. Then a riot broke out. The kshatriyas crowded around Drupada, who had been dragged away to a distant spot. Voices were raised in argument. If the contest had been meant for kshatriyas, it was wrong of the brahmins to have taken part. Someone remarked loudly that the kings who had come to compete were in no way inferior to the Panchalas in wealth and military strength. Duryodhana stood before Drupada, gesturing angrily and shouting.

A group of people rushed towards Arjuna, thinking, no doubt, that it was wiser to confront the brahmins than attack Drupada and Dhrishtadyumna.

Retaining his composure, Dhrishtadyumna gave orders to the commanders of his army to prepare themselves. A roll of drums echoed at once from outside the palace.

I pushed aside the people who were in front of me and the man who had initially blocked my view fell down. I leapt over the group of singers and landed near Arjuna. I pulled down a long pole to which streamers had been tied. This was not a battle, it was a riot, and a pole was the weapon best suited to it.

'Let those who are unwilling to accept the victor talk to me first.' I lifted the wooden pole high as I voiced my threat. Arjuna told me later that I had shouted.

Amongst the crowd of people that rushed at me furiously, I saw a twisted face, one that I would have recognized anywhere, at any moment of time. Shakuni. I could not resist the impulse to stretch out my left hand and give him a blow. He reeled away and fell somewhere.

I said, 'Come. Come one by one, or all together.'

Who is that? Who is he? Who? I heard many voices ask questions at the same time.

I introduced myself. 'Another brahmin who has learnt the science of weaponry.'

The attackers halted, uncertain.

Someone asked, 'Is it right to behave like this in a wedding hall?' I was not sure who it was, maybe one of the kings.

Guarding Arjuna from the rear, I said, 'Then let's move to the courtyard of the palace.'

The rioters quietened down. An old king's counsel proved opportune: 'If Drupada is happy to give his daughter to a wandering brahmin, we have nothing to say.'

The protesters withdrew and I glanced at Draupadi. How wrong I was to have assumed that the poor girl would be terrified. Her veiled smile seemed to suggest that she had enjoyed watching the spreading riot; she wanted more of it!

The army was getting ready outside. Dhrishtadyumna had left the hall. I said to the troubled Drupada, 'Do not be afraid,

King. If only these people I see here are going to fight, there is no need for your army to get ready. We can handle them.'

The king looked astonished, as if he did not believe me.

I thought it unwise to linger here while threats and weapons bided their time around us. I said to Arjuna, 'Take your bride and go. I will be with you.'

Arjuna paid obeisance to Drupada, 'Grant me permission to leave. I had vowed to offer a sacrifice and a puja if I won. I will come back with the maiden after I perform them.'

I said to the king, 'A chariot. Let a chariot be waiting outside.'

Where were Nakula and Sahadeva? I had not seen Yudhishtira either. I wished they had been with us to guard us on both sides and at the rear if there was an attack outside.

The chariot was ready. Arjuna got in first, then helped Draupadi up, gripping her hand. I leapt in and sat to the left of the charioteer. Four or five stray arrows flew towards us and fell near the wheels of the chariot. I grabbed the whip from the charioteer, twirled it and spurred the horses to fly through the ranks of the monarchs who had come from outside Panchala and were now preparing to muster their armies.

I asked the charioteer to stop when we came to the outskirts of the city. We alighted. Draupadi hesitated. Arjuna said, 'Get down. Our people are here, nearby.'

He asked the charioteer to return to the palace.

We began to walk. We could see the potters' village where we had stayed the night before in the distance. As we turned into the lane, Arjuna stopped. 'Do not be afraid, Princess. We ...'

He looked at me as if asking my permission to speak.

'I think my father guessed right,' said Draupadi softly.

We did not understand what she meant.

'We … we are …'

Draupadi smiled. 'I guessed as much. Arjuna, the son of Kunti.' She looked at me. 'It is not right for brahmins to pull out pillars and fight. The younger brother played his role better than his elder brother.'

I could not help laughing.

Walking between us, Draupadi said, 'I heard my father say when they were making preparations for the contest: if the Pandavas get to know, they are sure to come. Particularly the greatest of all archers, Arjuna.'

Attempting to maintain the role of a brahmin, I asked, 'But weren't the Pandavas burnt to death in a forest fire in Varanavata or somewhere like that?'

'Not even the Kauravas believe that.'

We stopped in front of the potter's hut where we had stayed the previous night. At the door, I said, 'Wait, let's give Mother a surprise. This is our palace.'

In Panchala, Draupadi had smiled even at the sight of bloodshed, as she stood amidst the kings ranged to wage war. Now she looked at the potter's hut calmly, completely unperturbed.

I knocked on the closed door and called out, 'Mother, open the door. Don't you want to see the alms we received today?'

Mother did not reply. I called out again.

Mother said from inside, 'Share it, all of you.'

Draupadi suppressed a smile. Mother opened the door and Arjuna and I entered, laughing loudly. Mother's eyes brightened as she saw Draupadi, and a smile tinged with wonder touched her lips.

'Look at the alms we received: the daughter of King Drupada. The bride Arjuna won by his skill in archery.'

Draupadi knelt down and touched Mother's feet in obeisance. Mother blessed her. By this time, Yudhishtira arrived with the sons of Madri.

I said in jest, 'Look, when I told Mother about the alms we received today, do you know what she said, not aware of what I meant? That we should all share the alms!'

Nakula and Sahadeva burst out laughing. Mother and Draupadi had gone in already.

Yudhishtira said very gravely, 'What a blunder Mother made, saying that. However lightly she said it, a mother's command remains a command. The law of dharma ordains that it cannot be disobeyed.'

Draupadi heard this as she came back. She had been smiling at something, but a sudden cloud darkened her face.

All of us fell silent. The moments when we should have celebrated victory froze.

Yes, this should have been an instant of celebration. Not only because of the triumph in King Drupada's capital. The Pandavas, orphaned until now, had become strong because they had acquired powerful relatives. Many people in Hastinapura would shudder when they knew that the Panchalas would back us now with their great army and their wealth. They would even wonder whether those who had survived the depths of the Ganga and the house of lac were immortal. The elders would declare that we had the blessing of the Gods. The blind king and his sons would no longer sleep in peace.

We had reached a crossroads that marked the end of our

misfortunes. And then, this childish argument about the law of dharma! Saying nothing, I walked out.

Yudhishtira called out, 'Wait, Bhimasena. Krishna said he would come. Our elder brother, Balarama, and Krishna are both coming. Wait!'

I did not wait.

5

I stood by the deserted stone pond near the cowsheds. I could hear dogs barking in the distance and the cries of calves that had strayed from the herd.

Hearing footsteps approaching me from behind, I thought it was Sahadeva or Arjuna. But it was my elder brother. We stood for a while in silence.

Balarama had left very quickly. When I saw Krishna and Arjuna looking for liquor to celebrate, I had come away. The water of the pond was choked by weeds. A fish came up through a gap in the weeds, drank some water and sank down again. Yudhishtira walked around the pond. Then he said, looking at the cowsheds, 'They say the king of Panchala has 20,000 cows.'

I did not reply. My elder brother came nearer. 'Arjuna is fortunate. A good match for Draupadi.' He smiled. 'It was not until I saw Draupadi that I realized that blue-black could be so beautiful.'

I attempted a smile.

'Arjuna must marry Draupadi. Isn't that the right thing to do?'

'What a meaningless question!'

'And yet Mother is upset because she made that foolish statement.'

I moved and sat down on a piece of the wall that had not crumbled.

He said, 'I have heard of many wives in the epics who had more than one husband. Don't you know about Jatila?'

I did not know. I was not as familiar with these old tales as my elder brother was.

'Jatila was the wife of the Seven Sages, the Saptarshis. There are so many examples like her. But Draupadi is Arjuna's by right, I am quite certain of that. Mother is troubled about what she said.'

Fully aware of my elder brother's train of thought, I kept resolutely silent.

'If Grandfather Krishnadvaipayana or our Uncle Vidura or someone well versed in the laws of dharma had been somewhere nearby, we could have asked them for advice.'

'What advice?' My voice had grown harsh. 'Draupadi is meant for Arjuna. If you insist that she should have more than one husband, you can share her with him. But only after you make sure of his opinion, he who won this victory by his bravery and strength. As for Draupadi – we've never had the custom of consulting the likes and dislikes of women, have we?'

Yudhishtira latched onto that question for his next argument. 'Who says so? The Kuru clan has always revered women.'

'Our aunt Gandhari was bought for the blind king. Shalya sold Madri to Pandu in exchange for gold nuggets and gems, though he knew Pandu could never have children.'

'To our father!'

'Yes, to our father. I wonder if anyone consulted Mother Madri's wishes.'

I tried not to lose my temper. No matter how great a scholar he was of the Vedas and sacred texts, I thought this man, who was clinging to a straw, Mother's words, deserved only contempt.

He got up with a sigh. If he continued to argue, maybe even this blockhead of a younger brother would find the right words to retaliate. He must have realized this, so he started to walk away, saying no more.

I had no intention of letting him go that easily. 'Wait.' I caught up with him. 'Leave me out of this. There's a woman waiting for me in the forest. She carries my seed. I am content with her, even though she may not be worthy of living with those of the Kuru clan. And leave Madri's sons out of it too, they are too young for marriage. May Jatila have companions in our era as well.'

A bitterness consumed me after he went away. And later, a relief that a burden had been lifted from my heart. Imagine, he was saying that we had to share Draupadi, a young girl in whose eyes the curiosity of childhood had not dimmed.

I walked on aimlessly. I realized I was approaching the next village when I heard the sound of blacksmiths striking metal pots from the huts around me. I went back. As I approached our potter's hut in the darkness, I heard a sound from the bushes. A footstep, the sound of a twig snapping. So a new enemy had found us. I clearly made out a human form creeping through the darkness and moving towards the window. I followed without making any noise. If it was not an enemy, it had to be the enemy's spy. I swept him into the circle of my arms as he crept forward, trying to insinuate himself into the hut and he turned and twisted in my grasp. My adversary was stronger than I had expected, but he was not able to shake himself free. It would have been easy to kill him, but I had to first know who he was.

'Who are you? Whose spy?'

'I'm not a spy. Nor an enemy.'

I had a feeling I knew the face, even in the darkness.

I let him go and he said, 'I am the crown prince, Dhrishtadyumna. Which is the hut where the brahmins who came to Panchala live?'

I smiled. 'One of those brahmins stands in front of you. Welcome.'

The Prince recognized me. 'Father sent me to find out who you are.'

'There are five of us. We were called the Pandavas in our better days.'

'We heard many rumours. Father grew uneasy and I offered to play the spy.'

'I am Bhimasena. The archer who won Draupadi in the contest is Arjuna. My elder brother, Yudhishtira, and Madri's sons, Nakula and Sahadeva, are with us.'

'Just as we guessed. What a relief! We heard that it was a brahmin who killed Vetrakiya's henchman as well. They say he put an end to the ritual of human sacrifice.'

I smiled. 'Yes, it was a brahmin.'

'And the one who killed Hidimba, who was roaming the eastern forests, shattering the abodes of the sages …?'

'A wayfarer, before he played the role of a brahmin.'

Laughing, Dhristadyumna saluted, then embraced me. "Tell

us what we must do. We know how biased Dhritarashtra is. I am with you in whatever you do.'

'We will need you. We will certainly come to you, asking for help. Very soon.'

He gripped my hand. 'You are welcome. Always.'

I tried to persuade him to come in and meet the others, see his sister.

'Not now. Let the wedding be over. Let me go and tell my father the news.'

I entered the hut after he left. Draupadi was sleeping peacefully at Mother's feet. I sat down in front of the food that had been set apart for me. Mother got up and raised the wick in a small earthen lamp.

'We must have a grand wedding.'

I grunted.

Today, at dusk, I had performed a sacrificial ritual and given gifts to a brahmin, then sent the same brahmin to Vidura.

Mother told me about Krishna's and Balarama's visit. The construction of the palace in Dwaraka was not complete, but the Yadavas had moved there. Mother gave me a bit of news: Balarama had stayed in Hastinapura quite some time to teach Duryodhana how to wage war with the mace.

'The priests and scholars say that it is in no way sinful for a woman to have many husbands.'

What was Mother trying to tell me? Had Yudhishtira prevailed upon her to speak to me again about Draupadi's wedding?

I reminded her gently that we had to establish Yudhishtira's right to the throne of Hastinapura with the support of our Panchala relatives; that we could not afford to displease Drupada in any way. 'That is what we need most, that's the problem the

Pandavas have to deal with now – a more serious one than this matter of polyandry.'

'Yes, that's right. Only if all five of you stand together without any discord amongst you will the Pandavas be a strong force. And for that to happen, we must follow this custom of having many husbands, which you speak of so contemptuously. It is good if the scriptures support it, but even if they do not ...'

'But ...' I fumbled for words. I, who had been so garrulous with Yudhishtira, found it difficult to speak.

'All the eyes that looked at Draupadi had passion in them, even Sahadeva's, though he is still a child. I saw it. Only I could see, being a woman.'

I sat with my head bowed, looking at my food and feigning indifference, as if what she said did not apply to me.

Had Mother seen the flames of desire in my eyes as well? Somehow, I could not bring myself to challenge her.

I sighed. Was a tender beauty wafting towards me on the night air that was delicately tinged with cold? And the fragrance of lotus flowers?

Mother kept talking in a very soft voice. The force of the Pandavas lay in the five of us standing united. We would be stronger then than five great armies equipped with chariots, elephants, horses and foot soldiers. 'I want my sons to rule a vast kingdom.'

'We will. Even without all this, we will stand united and win.'

Mother smiled. Time could bring about so many changes in human beings. She did not want Nakula and Sahadeva to ever be distanced from us because they were Madri's sons. She wanted no differences of opinion between Yudhishtira and me.

She had considered all this when she decided that Draupadi would be wife to all five of us.

I went out to throw away the leftovers. She was still seated in the same spot when I came back.

'Yudhishtira said you spoke rudely to him.'

I did not defend myself, nor did I deny it.

'Look and me and tell me the truth. Do you not want to be the second in line to possess Draupadi?'

I was afraid to look at Mother. A heap of unclear images tumbled through my mind: arrows of antimony, the petals of blue lotuses, sesame flowers, mandara buds, the swelling on the forehead of elephants in rut …

I did not look at Mother. I raised my head only when I was sure she was getting up to go. She turned towards me with a faint smile on her face.

'Blockhead, when I asked all of you to share the alms, I knew it was Draupadi!'

I felt sorry for having been such a weakling before Mother. Then a laugh suddenly broke out of me.

Women have been described in so many ways: as wombs that receive seed, fields meant only for sowing and so on. You who described them thus, you have not seen this woman, my mother!

Part 4

The Lure of the Dice

1

I kept count of the days and the months. The architects and our attendants thought I was irritated by the slow pace at which the construction of the mansions was proceeding.

The stone masons and carpenters worked day and night. The forest of Khandavaprastha that no one had wanted was turning into a city. When it was allotted to us as our share and we arrived there, the vaishyas saw its possibilities for trade and quickly set up dwellings. Eighteen shudra families, to which some of Mother's old servants belonged, moved there and a number of their relatives and acquaintances followed them. Trees provided such plentiful timber that houses rose like magic. We first stayed in four mansions that had been built in the forest a long time ago. Yudhishtira occupied a huge palace that had been built for kings when they came sometimes to hunt. Mother stayed with Nakula and Sahadeva in the second big mansion. The third was given to Arjuna, and I took the smallest house, meant for the guards, situated at the edge of the forest.

We had returned to Hastinapura in full splendour, like princes. While we were in Drupada's palace, Dhrishtadyumna had suffocated me with his hospitality. Drupada had overwhelmed all five of us with gifts.

Duryodhana and Karna had made an unexpected attack on us stealthily, careful not to let Grandfather Bhishma or Vidura know about it. Shakuni, Bhurishrava and Jayadratha had been with them. Since it took place during our visit to him, Dhrishtadyumna had not considered the attack dangerous. He dismissed it as a mere bit of entertainment. But it was my first battle. None of Arjuna's arrows missed its mark that day. The Panchala prince, Dhrishtadyumna, had fought splendidly from his chariot.

We had confronted them at a spot that was quite a distance from the gates of the fort.

War always intoxicated the Panchala army. Duryodhana and Karna had been in the front ranks of the Kauravas. The action lasted barely three hours. We counted the corpses of forty servants who had come with the Kauravas and six horses. Two of our men had been injured and one soldier died.

Arjuna said he saw Karna fall down on the floor of his chariot. The charioteer had turned his chariot around and withdrawn so skilfully that Arjuna had not been able to make out how badly Karna was injured.

Only after this incident had the blind king realized the need to live peacefully, in friendship.

Vidura came with a message, but Dhrishtadyumna ridiculed him. I had to bring the situation under control, reminding Dhrishtadyumna that Vidura was an envoy and that we were deeply indebted to him. Although we were being given only a forest as our share, Vidura urged us to accept it. He said we could build a capital there and that when people from Hastinapura moved in, the place would turn into a city.

We arrived in Khandavaprastha as wealthy people. Architects

came from Panchala. Drupada sent money and grain in carts drawn by donkeys. Krishna sent innumerable gifts as wedding presents. He gifted Draupadi and all of us gold and pearls in Drupada's presence, and Mother's eyes filled with tears of joy. She had not expected so much from her brother's son.

Yudhishtira had begun his honeymoon in the old palace and seldom came out. I had thought he would come with Draupadi now and then to look at the new city that was coming up, but that did not happen.

Draupadi was to spend a year with each of us in turn. Mother laid down a rule that none of the others could even enter whichever house she was in during that period. We did not know whether it was Yudhishtira or Mother who had framed this rule. Yudhishtira summoned the four of us, prefaced the conditions that were laid down with the words 'The sages have said …' and summed them up with 'Everything is for our good.'

One day, Yudhishtira came up to me as I was watching some elephants being made to drag logs of wood. These days, his face always wore a dissatisfied expression.

'Is there a message from Arjuna?' I asked.

He did not reply. He asked, as if the thought had just occurred to him, 'Has Arjuna gone on a pilgrimage or on adventures in search of women?'

I did not quite understand him, but I made a guess.

'I heard talk about a naga girl. The nagas are good people. I've told you that before. When I was on the banks of the river in Pramanakoti …'

'Yes, yes. But I heard about another girl, Chitravahana's daughter. I wonder whether they are kshatriyas.'

He walked away as if he was displeased.

It had not surprised me that Arjuna had encountered beautiful girls while he was on a pilgrimage.

This pilgrimage was a torture my younger brother had inflicted upon himself unnecessarily. We had all tried to dissuade him, but he stood firm. Maybe he thought a pilgrimage would be more amusing than life in Khandavaprastha.

One night, we had been talking about clearing the forest towards the north. A brahmin ran up to us suddenly, gasping for breath, one of those who had come and settled here earlier with a number of cows. His cows were missing. People had seen a band of forest thieves herding them away.

Arjuna rushed off at once, while the brahmin waited. He said to us, 'You must make them realize that there is a ruler here now to administer this place.'

Arjuna took a long time to come back. He had filled his quiver and was tucking extra arrows into his waist as well. He said, with a foolish smile, 'I made a blunder. The weapons were in the big palace. I forgot the rules and ran in. And then – it was wrong of me, I put her to shame.'

I reminded him that the brahmin was waiting, and said, 'All right, we'll see what to do after you come back.'

I expected Yudhishtira to come out, but he didn't. Arjuna caught the band of thieves who had stolen the cows, made them surrender and promise to behave themselves. By the time he came back, the news that he had transgressed the rules had reached Mother.

Yudhishtira said, 'Don't worry about it. According to the scriptures, if he comes upon his elder brother's wife scantily dressed …'

Mother was present.

Arjuna did not give Yudhishtira a chance to discuss the topic further. 'According to the rules, I have to go on a pilgrimage lasting twelve months. That's all, right? I deserve punishment for the wrong I did.'

While getting ready for the journey, he remarked, 'I've been wanting for a while to wander around. This is a blessing in disguise.'

He left the same night.

We soon heard that he had married Uloopi and, a little later, Chitrangada. About four months after this, Mother and the three of us were invited to our elder brother's palace. We waited in the outer hall and he came in, looking happy and excited.

'A messenger has come from Dwaraka with a request from Arjuna. He asks for permission to marry Krishna's sister, Subhadra.'

Mother wanted to know whether Balarama and Krishna had given their consent.

'Krishna gives his full consent and is very happy. Balarama had to agree. Subhadra was prepared to elope with Arjuna, so he had no alternative.' Unusually for him, Yudhishtira spoke louder than he needed to.

Was a fragrance of lotus flowers wafting in from somewhere beyond the inner door?

Yudhishtira paced up and down and murmured, partly to himself and partly to us, 'Krishna is a good friend and our uncle's son. There are no warriors today who can defeat him in war with the discus. If Krishna and the Yadavas are with us – Mother, what is your decision?'

Mother asked, 'Where is the messenger? We must give him

gifts. Tell them that all of us send our blessings to him and to the peerless beauty Subhadra as well.'

Arjuna had married three beautiful girls in one year. Meanwhile, the honeymoon of the first bride he had won through his astonishing skill in archery was still not over. The first anniversary of her marriage was approaching. I had been counting the months and the days, starting from the wedding celebrations conducted in Drupada's capital city.

Four days before the day of the anniversary, I completed the preparations I had made in my house without letting anyone know that they were intended to please Draupadi. The plants in the back courtyard had already flowered. A swing-cot made of red devadaru wood had been suspended from the ceiling with forest creepers, and I had obtained the softest kusha grass to spread over it as a mattress.

The sculptors had decorated the interior according to Vishoka's instructions. My sudden interest in planning the garden and decorating the house had not surprised Vishoka in any way.

'The day is approaching, isn't it?' he asked casually.

I answered in the same manner, 'Yes, I think so.'

I thought brahmins would be summoned when the fourth day dawned and that rituals of some kind would be performed. I hung around Mother, to remind her that I was in the vicinity.

New elephant sheds were being built, and Draupadi came up to me most unexpectedly while I was standing next to them.

Over the last year, I had seen her only three times and always from a distance.

She looked a little fleshier. She seemed to still like wearing white. A single strand of jasmine was coiled through her hair. Seeing her from so close, I thought the girl I had seen in Drupada's capital had grown into a young woman. A smile gleamed in the large blue-black eyes, which seemed moist. The vestiges of a pandanus garland she had worn earlier clung to the single strand of pearls around her neck.

Her eyes wandered over my half-naked form, enveloped in the dust of the workplace. I invited her to see how the elephants brought from Panchala were being trained.

'One of my maids told me that you can fight single-handed with a rogue elephant. Is that true?'

I smiled. 'I've never had to until now.'

'I heard that Baka used to eat a whole cartful of food every day, as well as the two buffaloes that drew the cart. Was he really so gruesome?'

'Baka grew bigger with the words that were used to describe him. That was a very trivial fight.'

'The story goes that the whole country was terrified by his dying scream, that his blood flowed until it reached the Ganga. Tell me exactly how it happened.'

I was embarrassed. One is only half-conscious during a fight. What is important is who snatches the opportunity to kill first. Tribals who live in the forest and nishadas do not know the rules; they only know how to kill. Fights waged with them are not suitable stories for sootas and magadhas to sing about. Nor would they amuse a beautiful girl.

I said, 'Good fortune was on my side, that is all.'

'I thought I would see a real fight in the wedding hall. But all that happened was that the warriors fenced with words and then ran away, right?' She laughed. 'Blood flowing into the Ganga, that's what I'd like to see!'

To get away from descriptions of fights and killings, I asked, 'When is Arjuna coming back?'

She made an effort to control herself, but a bright red flush spread over her blue-black cheeks.

'I don't know,' she said softly.

She walked towards a building that was nearly completed and I followed.

This young woman, whose figure was so much slighter than Hidimbi's, could throw me into utter confusion. I rebuked myself. I was not a servant, waiting upon her wishes – I was her master, her husband. I stopped when we reached a spot from where my garden was visible.

Paying no attention to it, she asked, 'Is Subhadra dark-skinned?'

'I don't know.'

'I've never heard songs in praise of Yadava women.'

We walked through the garden and passed by the swing-cot, but she took no notice of it. Suddenly, she stopped walking and laughed.

'I can play a good game of dice now. I'm still learning.'

I laughed as well. The forest was just before us.

Draupadi looked at the trees and asked, 'What is it like, the language the women of the forest speak?'

Did not Draupadi realize that the house behind her, maintained so well by Vishoka, the garden around it and this swing-cot were all waiting for her? I pretended I had not heard her question.

'A sacrificial ritual has to be performed today. The brahmins would have arrived. I must go.'

She had begun to perspire. As I stepped forward to lay my hand on her shoulder and breathe the sweet scent of her perspiration, she moved away.

'Today's ritual is to ensure that a son is conceived. Don't you know that the year Arjuna lost has been added to the crown prince's turn?'

She walked away, then turned and smiled. Did her eyes hold relief or a promise? Or just compassion?

I was alone. I heard a chariot approaching. Three chariots stopped near the big palace. Balarama got down first, then Krishna.

Arjuna alighted from the second chariot, which was decorated with flowers, then Subhadra, holding the hand he held out to her. The emeralds on the chain lying over the auspicious line of the parting of her hair glittered beneath the cloth that half covered her head. Her skin had a pale reddish tinge. As Mother had said, you could tell even from a distance that Subhadra was a beauty who had no equal.

A warm breath touched me. Draupadi was standing next to me, watching the scene.

'The women servants shouldn't grow anxious, searching for me. I'd better go.'

She turned to me as she was going, 'Arjuna escaped from Drupada's hall only because of the strength of Bhimasena's hands. I will always remember that.'

She disappeared behind the palace.

I touched Balarama's feet in obeisance. Krishna greeted me respectfully. I accepted Arjuna's salutations. He had grown even darker.

The reception for Subhadra and Arjuna and the ritual Yudhishtira was conducting for the begetting of a son took place simultaneously, at two different spots.

Pots of liquor were ranged before the Yadavas. Sahadeva was appointed to look after their needs. I moved from one spot to the other to see that all was going well in both places. The celebrations lasted almost until dawn.

I finally went home. Knowing that busy with looking after the guests, I would have eaten nothing myself, Vishoka had kept liquor and food ready for me. Liquor with a strong odour, distilled from sprouted barley.

'Both rituals went well,' said Vishoka.

'Get a chariot ready for me at dawn.' Charioteers did not need to be told the destination.

'Can't you wait till the Yadavas leave to start your journey?' asked Vishoka hesitantly.

'Three horses and all the weapons I need. We have to start at dawn.'

Vishoka left. I finished the liquor, but did not go to bed. I went out and stood in the faint darkness. The second phase of the honeymoon was beginning in the palace where today's ritual had been performed. The lamps in Arjuna's mansion had not been put out. A new bride was beginning her first night there. I watched as the lamps were extinguished one by one. The chariot horses had been unharnessed and I heard the clatter of their hooves as they wandered around the yard.

I walked to the back of the house. Darkness had descended from the forest into the garden. In the darkness, the swing-cot hung like the corpse of a forest-dweller lying on a scaffold.

Seated on the soft kusha grass that covered it, I searched

above the dense trees for the asvamukha stars. Suddenly, the forest grew as high as the sky and the sky descended on the earth. Stars exploded and broke into fragments somewhere inside my head.

2

I halted near the pond shaped like a water-lily leaf and waited in vain for footsteps to approach, trampling over the moist blades of tender grass. Then I turned back and reached the spot below the rocks where wild goats grazed.

The monsoon had spent its passion and the forest lay quiet. A mouse deer arrived in front of me, panting wildly, and stood confused. I let it go, lowered the spear I had raised and flung it towards a fig tree. I watched its brass-studded tip quiver as it pierced the tree to a depth of six fingers and then grow still. Then I walked to the boundary of the forest.

Vishoka had given the horses grass and water, then hitched them again to the chariot and was waiting for me.

Where to next?

Eastwards.

An aimless journey. Vishoka smiled when I told him there were no animals in the forest. There was no need for my charioteer to know that his kshatriya master had gone in search of a woman. Women appear, receive a man's seed and go away. It was not worthy of a man's prestige to even think of them after that.

I slept in wayside lodgings in regions I did not know. I hunted only when all the food I had was over.

The hilly terrain became level once more and I saw a river. Which one was it?

'The Ganga again. We are near Kashi.'

It was a small city. The first thing that caught my eye was a lane where washermen were hanging out silks dipped in dyes to dry. At the crossroads, flags and streamers were fluttering as if to welcome someone. Vishoka spoke to the people of the city to find out what was happening. It was the svayamvara of the sister of King Senesha. Another svayamvara?

A contest had come my way unexpectedly in the middle of this dreary journey.

I had intended to walk through Kashi like a mendicant, wander down the banks of the Gandaki river till I reached Kamaroopa and then go back.

I bathed in the Ganga. Since I was entering a capital city, I took Vishoka's advice on what to wear and how to do my hair. He brought a barber and I had him shave off my ragged beard and trim my nails.

The palace in Kashi was only half the size of the one in Hastinapura. We were amazed by its walls, built of bricks baked in a kiln. We generally used wood. Of course, the people of Kashi had always been known for their craftsmanship. The silks they wove had reached as far as Kekaya and Gandhara.

Chariots to which three and five horses could be harnessed waited in the outer courtyard of the palace. Vishoka looked at the flags on them and said, 'Most of them are kings of small countries.'

Ancient Kashi, where my grandmother was born. It had now been divided in three. A kingdom here was only the size of one of our bigger villages.

The attendant who took our chariot and horses was of a medium complexion, thin and tall. I noticed that everyone here shaved regularly. Those who wore beards had trimmed them neatly to a triangular shape.

Vishoka said to a bearded man who took over our horses: 'Bhimasena, the young prince of Khandavaprastha.' If Vishoka had expected a change of manner in him and great humility, he must have been sorely disappointed.

Serving women carrying platters filled with turmeric and unhusked rice were lined up to receive us. All of them had the auspicious mark of married women in the parting of their hair.

Assuming that the men standing outside the hall were ministers, Vishoka greeted them respectfully and said, 'We are from Khandavaprastha. This is Bhimasena.'

A young man who was biting on the pearl chain around his neck scrutinized me and came forward.

'Khandavaprastha? Where is that?'

Vishoka saluted him again. 'Near Hastinapura.'

The young man saluted me indifferently and said, 'Bhimasena? I've heard of a Bhimasena who is Yudhishtira's younger brother.'

Vishoka said quickly, 'This is Yudhishtira's brother. Arjuna's older brother, Bhimasena.'

The young man's manner changed. He saluted me again. Since we were the same age, he embraced me.

'I am Senesha. This kingdom is blest.' He said to himself incredulously, 'Arjuna's elder brother, Bhimasena ...'

Their reception became so respectful, I was embarrassed.

People flocked towards me to catch a glimpse of Arjuna's older brother. I realized that none of us in Khandavaprastha had realized the extent of Arjuna's prestige. By this time, the palace attendants had crowded around Vishoka, to learn about my heroic exploits. I found it strange – people from all castes were singing songs of praise here – not just sootas and magadhas, but even shudras!

An old minister invited me to join the group of suitors as I walked towards the seats for the spectators. Several heads turned to find out who was being accorded such great respect.

Conches were blown. The rituals began. The brahmin priest sprinkled ghee and sesame seeds over the sacrificial fire to consecrate it. Senesha removed his upper cloth, put on his crown, gave gifts to the brahmins and prostrated himself before them.

I was only interested in observing how different the rituals in Kashi were from those in Panchala. This was a simple svayamvara, a contest was not part of it. The singers sang praises of all the kings who had come. Just as they started the story of a victory Senesha's father had won in a war, the women entered the rear of the hall. I saw the head of a woman who towered above the group, covered so completely with flowers that her face was invisible. Senesha walked towards her, took her hand and led her to the centre of the hall. She gave the gifts that the attendants had arranged at that spot to the brahmins. I had not seen this custom in Panchala.

I was astonished when I saw the bride. At first sight, I thought it was Hidimbi, dressed and adorned like a princess. The same tall figure. But she was not as dark. Her skin was the colour of clear wild honey. She had the same long eyelashes that Hidimbi had. And large brownish eyes.

'My sister, Balandhara, daughter of the late King Devesha.'

As Senesha spoke, the bards sang two lines about the

maiden, a gift granted to the king by the generous blessing of the Gods.

The bride paused before each of the kings who were seated in a semicircle as the bards sang of his qualities and victories. Their words turned unknown regions into great kingdoms. Battles I had never heard about and riotous escapades to snatch cattle became wars between gods and demons.

Seated next to the last king in the row, I watched the spectacle indifferently, as if it was a piece of entertainment like a display of physical skills meant to amuse an audience at a festival. I had sat among the brahmins in Drupada's hall with a heart that beat fast. Here I was a mere spectator.

The bride approached me and a singer with a quavering voice began to introduce me. I stood up, as custom demanded. The younger brother of Yudhishtira, the son of Dharma. The elder brother of Arjuna, the equal of Indra, he who stood alone on the bare ground, waged war against the entire Yadava army, defeated them and carried away Subhadra, Krishna's sister. Pandu's son, a jewel of the Kuru race, the mighty one who set out to conquer all the kingdoms in a chariot drawn by a single horse!

I squirmed in embarrassment, praying for the bard to end the verse in which I killed Hidimba, Baka and several other demons whose names I had never heard, all as formidable as Ravana. Evidently, Vishoka had not been idle!

And then something unexpected happened. Balandhara's eyes wandered uncertainly over my face as I struggled to hide my embarrassment. Raising her head higher, she flung the wedding garland around my neck.

The spectators shouted their congratulations, the blowing

of conches and the thudding of drums resounded through the air.

Another bride entered my life.

Balandhara had to perform a sacrifice for her ancestors. The assembly sat down to the feast without indulging in arguments or idle boasts. Attendants dragged in copper cauldrons filled with venison cooked in ghee-rice, fish fried in mustard oil, roasted mouse deer. There was sweet payasam flavoured with honey and liquor distilled from the nine special grains and perfumed with flowers.

Vishoka waited for a moment to catch me alone and whispered, 'Good. Kashi and the Kuru dynasty have always been close, even in olden times. We must take artisans from here to Khandavaprastha. They are excellent craftsmen.'

Vishoka had received a generous share of gifts.

I waited during the first quarter of the night in the bedroom where a ghee-lamp burnt bright. Accompanied by handmaids, Balandhara came in, her head bowed. As the maids withdrew, one of them closed the door softly. The sound of their suppressed giggles and gentle footsteps died away. Balandhara's face glowed like the cinders of burnt akil wood There was no embarrassment in her eyes, only curiosity.

'Come.'

I was aroused, the heat that lay suppressed in my loins blazed through me. I gathered her in the circle of my arms. When I pulled off her upper cloth, the perfume of musk assailed my nostrils. Her nipples twisted between my fingers like tiny perungal fish. I tasted the sweetness of the honey-mango on her lips.

At some point that night, I woke up and looked at Balandhara sleeping beside me. Recalling the day's unexpected events with wonder, I lay supporting my head on my elbow, filled with a pleasant sense of fatigue.

She opened her eyes and asked with a faint smile, 'What will Draupadi think when you return to the capital with another wife?'

'It is customary for kshatriyas to marry more than one wife,' I answered casually.

'And the forester's sister?'

I was suddenly angry. 'She must be busy raising my child now.'

Balandhara laughed loudly. 'At dusk today, my maids joked about Panchali's conjugal schedule. One of them even said that according to her calculations, I would get four consecutive years!'

The ghee-lamp flickered and paled, as if to let us know that the chariot of the sun had begun its journey.

I got up. 'It's time for me to leave.'

'Three chariots, including yours, would have been standing ready in the fourth quarter of the night.' She got up as well.

Four women servants accompanied Balandhara in her woman's chariot, pulled by mares. Senesha's gifts were piled into my chariot – carved silver platters, golden goblets, chests made of ivory. Water, liquor and food were loaded in the third chariot. Five bodyguards and an uncle of Balandhara's also got into it.

Senesha and his ministers saw us off.

The day we reached Khandavaprastha, dusk had fallen. Amazed, Vishoka pointed out areas that had been turned from forest land into open spaces. As we passed through, we saw the remains of huts that had been burnt down.

Sahadeva was the first to run up to us when we arrived in the courtyard. He chided us for not having sent a messenger with news at any point during our journey.

All the new mansions had been completed. More people had moved in from Hastinapura – potters, chariot-makers, jewellers.

Sahadeva saw me staring at the clearings in the forest and said, 'Arjuna and Krishna cleared those areas. They conducted the work like a festival, with innumerable servants and warriors and plenty of food and liquor.' He made it sound as if I had missed a grand celebration.

'And the nagas?'

'Those forest tribals? They resisted for a while, then began to complain. When the houses were set on fire, they ran away.'

I asked Vishoka to arrange lodgings for the people who had come from Kashi, and told Sahadeva to take care of Balandhara's uncle.

Mother had moved into a new mansion. She did not scold or embarrass me. She welcomed Balandhara affectionately, blessed her and told her that she would be spending her days with her in this mansion. 'From now on, these are the women's quarters. I moved here because it is so much more convenient.'

Looking at me, she added, 'We do not know when more brides will come, after all.'

I learnt that a son had been born to Arjuna and hurried to his palace. Krishna had gone back to Dwaraka. Arjuna introduced me to a short, slender, slightly built man who was with him. 'Mayan. He's an architect from the south. He is building an audience hall for us.'

I mentioned having seen walls built with earthen bricks

in Kashi and Mayan said: 'They are not strong enough.' He explained a way to make beautiful bricks with coloured clay that had been baked and strengthened. He was going to pave the floor of the hall with blue tiles. He knew how to make new colours from resins. His workers could carve stones into sections thinner than wooden planks.

I went in to see the newborn child and Arjuna accompanied me.

Subhadra took the child from the maid who was carrying him and held him out to me. He was asleep. He had Arjuna's complexion and Subhadra's facial features.

'Krishna named him. Abhimanyu.'

I kissed the sleeping child's head gently and went out.

I had not yet visited Yudhishtira, although, according to the rules, I should have seen him first. Sending a message through an attendant, I waited in the inner hall of his palace. He appeared at the door, and I prostrated myself before him.

'Come, come in.'

As I followed him, he said with great happiness, 'Draupadi is with her attendants, she is pregnant.' He continued: 'I met Balandhara's uncle. He is coming here tonight for a game of dice. The kings of Kashi are very noble. I've heard of Senesha.'

Later, Mother took Balandhara to Yudhishtira to pay him obeisance and receive his blessing. I was with Mayan at that time, looking at the mansions that had been completed and the audience hall that was being built.

At night, Balandhara said to me, 'I saw Draupadi.'

What would Draupadi have asked her? What would have happened during their first meeting? I wanted to know, but I feigned indifference.

When she remarked, 'It doesn't astonish me …' I looked at her, puzzled.

'Any man would wait four years for her. She is much more beautiful than I imagined.'

'So what did she say to you?'

Balandhara smiled. 'I am not even sure she saw me properly. I had the feeling she thought of me only as a speck of dust that obscured her vision. Subhadra spoke to me at length.'

I pulled her into bed, so that we could stop talking about Draupadi.

Next morning, I saw the weapon house that had been renovated recently. The construction of a huge chariot to which seven horses could be harnessed was just being completed. I swung a mace in the air. Then I fenced with Nakula for a while, with short and long swords. A number of young men who had just joined the foot soldiers gathered around to watch my exploits.

Mayan examined my maces and said, 'I will make you an excellent mace. It will be completely of metal, but you will not find it too heavy.'

With his index finger, he sketched on the ground the designs of several military devices that he was going to make. His knowledge of weapons astounded me. He spoke of new weapons used in other regions – spears that could be thrown only once, arrows tipped with tiny crescents that could slice a head off a body. An old servant woman came up to us and told me that Draupadi wished to see me.

I walked to Yudhishtira's palace. My elder brother was playing dice with Balandhara's uncle and did not even raise his head.

I went through the hall and a corridor and another servant woman took me to a second door. Draupadi was seated inside.

I spoke the customary blessing given to a pregnant woman: may you bear a heroic child.

The tiredness of pregnancy only enhanced the loveliness of her face.

I rebuked myself: 'She is the wife of your elder brother.'

'What have you decided about the Rajasooya sacrifice?'

I had heard about it vaguely, but knew no details. Nakula or Sahadeva had mentioned it, that was all I knew.

'Krishna said we do not have the right to conduct the Rajasooya unless we defeat Jarasandha. The king agrees. Once we perform it, we can avoid unnecessary wars.'

She got up, went in and came back holding a chain threaded with pearls and emeralds. 'A wedding gift.'

I took it from her and ran my fingers through the strands, separating them. I waited, not knowing what to say.

She said, 'Neither the Kurus nor the Panchalas have a grievance against Jarasandha. However, the truth is that it would be meaningless to perform the Rajasooya without defeating him.'

These were matters of state that we men had to discuss. What was Draupadi trying to tell me?

'You know there is a person in Khandavaprastha who will leap forward to do anything Krishna tells him to do. When the time comes, you must advise your younger brother not to involve himself in the Yadava family's schemes of revenge. It is to make this request that I sent for you.'

So I had to take care that Arjuna did not court danger of any kind. I stood up.

'If Jarasandha proposes a duel and *you* accept, it might be a different story. I think it will be wise not to take up the remnants of Krishna's war. I may be right or wrong.'

'Let me think about it.' What else could I say?

As I was about to leave, Draupadi said very softly, 'I move house next on full moon day in the month of Kartika.'

I hurried out.

Why had Draupadi sent for me? To give me a wedding gift? To make sure we avoided a war with Jarasandha? Or to remind me that it would be my turn in four months?

I lay beside Balandhara that night, cold and empty of emotion. I pondered, my eyes open, and the picture grew steadily clearer. It was imperative to declare war on Jarasandha. But Yudhishtira would be exempted from the test of strength for the Rajasooya. Draupadi would become queen. I, not Arjuna, had to be the one to confront the mighty Jarasandha. She had forgiven me for marrying Balandhara. The full moon night in the month of Kartika and the nights that followed would wait for me as a reward for killing Jarasandha ... it was all crystal clear.

I thought resentfully of a night when I would pull off her clothes with blood-stained hands, tear them up, fling them away and enjoy her with the power of a tribal from the forest.

What if Draupadi was dreaming of the same thing now? I would not be surprised if she was.

I looked compassionately at Balandhara as she slept peacefully, proudly wearing one more new ornament.

3

'He took off his crown, knotted his hair and swung his mighty arms. Slapping his chest and thighs, Jarasandha stood up, ready to fight. War was celebration for him. I admired him, wanted to salute him in my mind.'

'Tell me, I'm listening. Tell me everything in detail.' Draupadi had been lying in bed, exhausted, but the indolence slid away from her like one more upper cloth as I began to talk.

From the first night she came to my house, Draupadi had looked tired and weak. Whenever I caught her in my rough hands, she looked at me pleadingly, pitiably and drew away. Her eyes seemed to beg me not to hurt her. I tried to make my fingers lighter than butterflies. Gently, I warned myself, be patient. I commanded the wild tribal in my heart: be as tender, as kind, as delicate as the fingers of beautiful girls plucking santana flowers in Heaven.

She pushed my hands away and said again, tiredly, 'Don't. Tell me the story of the duel first.'

I began, 'Jarasandha's country, Magadha, lies in the middle of five mountains – Vaihara, Varaha, Vrisha, Rishi and Chaityaka. Outside the palace walls is a forest of pachotti trees. As soon as you enter the fort, there is a market selling everything from food to flower garlands and perfumes.'

I paused.

The lamp had gone out because I had forgotten to fill it with ghee. The radiance of the full moon poured in through the small window set high in the wall: the full moon of the month of Kartika that had arrived after twenty-four months.

She had prefaced the obeisance she made to me as she

entered my bedroom with the words, 'I am a fortunate woman.' As soon as the maids left, she said, 'Tonight is meant for talking and setting our minds at rest. Tell me how you escaped from the house of lac.'

When I finished the story of Varanavata, she seemed even more fatigued. But she said, 'Tell me the stories of the wars you waged with your mace.' She kept encouraging me to go on.

I continued the story of Jarasandha.

'Three large drums made of elephant hide were hung at the door of the fort. We beat them noisily as we entered, as Krishna had instructed us to. Jarasandha always extended a cordial welcome to those who went to him demanding to fight a duel.

'Duels were an everyday amusement for Jarasandha. The kings he defeated in war were dispatched to caves that had been converted to prisons, then given in sacrifice.

'The people in the marketplace looked at us as if we had come begging for death. When the guards approached us, Krishna said to them: "We hear the fellow who reigns here is a lowdown scoundrel, an upper-caste man who gives people of his own caste in sacrifice. We have come to fight a duel with him."

'The guards looked at us contemptuously and led us to the hall where sacrifices were performed. There were seats for guests of honour. When plates were set out for a meal, Arjuna was angry. Krishna reminded the attendants again: "We have come to fight."

'An old minister who was supervising the function in the hall said: "Those who come to fight a duel are usually given their last meal here."

'The attendants concealed their smiles. Jarasandha came to us at midnight, while we were resting. He looked as huge as our

Uncle Dhritarashtra. His arms were as massive as the shafts of a yoke. He saluted us, we saluted him back.

"'I am always happy to engage in duels." He looked at us smilingly. "But none of you is an enemy. Nor do I remember having harmed any of you."

"'You deserve to be killed because you offer kshatriyas in sacrifice," said Krishna.

'Although Jarasandha performed human sacrifice, he followed certain rules. He never imprisoned those who came to fight duels with him without reason.

'I looked at Jarasandha's calm demeanour with respect. He could afford to stay calm and extend all the customary courtesies to his opponents because he had complete confidence in the extraordinary strength of his hands.

"'Who are you? The first custom we follow is to get to know each other, after all."

'Krishna introduced Arjuna first. Then he spoke of the victories I had won. He described the challenge I had thrown in Drupada's court as if it had been a great war that I won single-handed. He said I had fought from a chariot drawn by a single horse, conquered Senesha and his huge army and carried away the bride. He did not mention the killing of Hidimba, I'm not sure why.

'Krishna ended by introducing himself: I am Krishna, brother of Balarama of the Yadava clan …

'Jarasandha burst out laughing. "Forgive me for not having remembered. You were very young at the time. And then, since you ran away, defeated, I saw you only from behind …"

'The king's calm manner suddenly changed. He said to his minister, "Make preparations for the duel – arrange for all the pujas and sacrificial rituals. Beat the drums and announce the news to the people of the city.

'He looked at us and asked, "Who will fight first?"

'"You can choose."

'Jarasandha smiled and, once again, what Krishna had predicted happened.

'"The spectators will be disappointed if my opponent lacks strength. This young man has the body of a wrestler. So let it be Bhimasena."

'A duel was as pure and sacred to Jarasandha as the Soma sacrifice. With each moment, his moral stature grew in my mind.

'At dawn, the scene was set. Jarasandha was seated before the sacrificial fire, adorned with flowers, his body smeared with medicinal paste. The brahmin priest conducted a ritual that requested fame for the performer of the sacrifice. Attendants lined up with medicines for wounds and loss of consciousness. Jarasandha took off his crown, knotted his hair and got up.'

Draupadi was no longer tired. Her eyes gleamed like turquoises. She moved very close to me. Her slender fingers moved over my hands and neck, caressing them, then ran through my knot of hair, grabbed a handful and twisted it playfully. They moved back over my shoulder to my hands.

A feverish excitement tugged at the chains of my body like a dog that has scented its prey.

'Wait. Finish the story first. I will narrate it to the chief of the sootas, have him compose the finest song about it and give him a pair of gold bangles to go singing it throughout the country. And then …?'

I continued.

'First, we held each others' hands. Then we saluted each other. We raised and lowered each others' hands, looking for gaps where we could attack. Jarasandha lunged at me without warning and I faced him, holding my head down. He retreated and slipped away when I tried to capture him in my arms. Then, unexpectedly, he gave me a kick. I was flung off my feet and, as I tried to regain my balance, he deployed a tactic we use in wrestling which crushes the windpipe. I gave him a blow on the stomach to free myself. Then I tried standing close to him and fighting, but he countered me with his fists. I attacked him, digging my elbows into his waist and ribs. He roared and I roared louder. I was told later that the spectators drew back, terrified.

'I realized that he was going to encircle me tightly with his arms and suffocate me to death. Keeping outside his reach, I attacked him. He could not match me in speed. My blows fell on the vulnerable spots of his body before his fists could parry them and, gradually, his movements slowed down. Arjuna and Krishna kept shouting to encourage me. Every now and then, he rushed at me like a whirlwind in an effort to capture me in his arms, but each time, I managed to evade him. I guessed that he wanted to somehow make me move to the front of the stone pillar. Hours passed, and Jarasandha began to realise that this duel was not an event at a festival. All I believe is that the Kuru gods of the kshatriya heroes who died in sacrificial arenas made my arms stronger.

'The strength of this mighty man, who was at least four times my age, astonished me. At every moment when I felt I was on the verge of collapse, some force gave me strength. He still wanted to get me to the front of the stone pillar. He came at me, yelling, and I guessed that he would use all his might to gather me up in his arms and dash me against the pillar. As he lifted himself up and rushed at me like a flying mountain, I fell on my left arm. Or rather, I sank down quickly, as if I was falling. Swerving to protect his head from the pillar, Jarasandha stretched out his hand to steady himself and stood balanced on one leg. I caught both his knees, and, using all the strength of my right shoulder, flung him down. He fell on his face with a bellow. I leapt on his back, making sure my knees landed on his vertebrae and heard their links snap with a cracking sound. I grabbed his hair and turned his face around. A potful of blood gushed out of his mouth. After that, I remember nothing. It's the truth, I remember nothing. I was told that I roared. His hands twisted and turned helplessly as his neck broke. I brought my hands down again on his spine and he stopped moving …

'Arjuna said I roared again. I scrambled up, half-conscious. Arjuna rushed up to support me, but I brushed him aside and went out. My body was soaked in blood, Jarasandha's blood … my …'

Draupadi was before me, gasping. I felt she was not fully in her senses. Sharp teeth sank into my uneven beard. Where was the Draupadi who had been lying here, tired and indifferent? Her body circled me like a whirlwind. Her nails and teeth tore hurtfully into me at many spots. But what I felt was not pain, it was desire. Not desire, but the languor of desire. The rest of the night, I flew on the peaks of this emotion like the Manthara mountain had flown, suspended from Garuda's claws after he plucked it from the earth.

4

It was said that Mayan's craftsmanship was so exquisite that the hall he had constructed could compete with the halls of the gods. The areas paved with blue tiles looked like spaces of water. This was the hall where Duryodhana was humiliated. People used to say that the sthalabali, the sacrifice performed to consecrate a site, was completed when the white marble stones were spattered with blood at the time the Rajasooya rituals were performed. The fame of this hall spread in all eight directions in a very short time.

I stood there by myself, while the others were getting ready to go to Hastinapura. The scenes that had been played out at the spot came back to me.

Concealing his envy, Duryodhana had come to have a look at the hall with his attendants and been utterly confused because he could not distinguish between the spaces with water and the solid floor. Those who were watching found this reason enough to laugh at him. People had told us that he still carried the resentment of that occasion within him.

The kings who had come for the Rajasooya sacrifice assembled here for the celebration that would mark the crowning of the king of kings. Draupadi took part in all the rituals. Pots containing water brought from the Ganga, the Yamuna and the Saraswati rivers were lined up. The pots that were going to be used for the anointing ceremony were filled with water of many kinds, from seawater to dewdrops. Brahmins mixed honey, milk and ghee into the water, and then added fluid taken from the womb of a cow.

The anointing ceremony has greater importance in the

Rajasooya than the rituals performed around the sacrificial fire. First of all, the master of the ceremony has to be chosen and ritually welcomed. Most of us were surprised when Bhishma chose Krishna for this. Several faces registered protest, but Sishupala of Chedi was the only one to stand up and demand, 'How does Krishna the Yadava have that right?'

Many spectators enjoyed this. I wondered whether the king of Chedi would claim the right himself. Actually, there were a number of people in the assembly who merited the honour more than Krishna.

Sishupala said to Bhishma, 'Several people in this gathering are more deserving. I propose you, Great One!'

Everyone was in favour of this suggestion. But our grandfather began to extol Krishna's good qualities. Sishupala's fury turned against Grandfather in a short while.

'You've shamed yourself often enough, interfering unnecessarily in other people's affairs and displaying chivalry towards those who do not deserve it. All of you will remember Amba, who had given her word to marry someone else and whom you brought by force to Vichitravirya, who was dying of consumption. Everyone knows that she was deprived of a home both in the place where she was born as well as the palace she was brought to as a bride, and that she committed suicide. All that this heroic act achieved was that two widows survived the victim of consumption!'

Bhishmacharya fell silent. The audience was stunned. I knew what Sishupala had said was true. But I was not sure whether he should have said it before that great gathering.

But Sishupala was not ready to stop. 'Then you performed another good deed, never before carried out in good kshatriya families. You brought in an outsider to impregnate the widows!'

Sishupala's blow struck at the roots of our clan.

Arjuna hurried up to me and said, 'The argument is no longer whether Krishna or Bhishmacharya should be the master. All Sishupala wants to do is wreak havoc on the Rajasooya.'

I had not anticipated a threat of war.

Sahadeva, who had still not shed the obstinacy and hot-headedness of youth, got up and went down to the hall. 'I am the youngest son. It is I who have to wash the master's feet and welcome him. I am going to perform this ritual for Krishna. If there are people here who do not approve, let them come with their weapons. I am ready!'

Until that day, Sahadeva had never had occasion to employ a weapon. All he had ever done was receive gifts and attend receptions in the kingdoms to which Yudhishtira had sent him as a messenger, asking their kings to accept his right to perform the Rajasooya ritual. I began to feel uneasy.

Duryodhana and his followers, who were waiting for an opportunity, were sure to side with Sishupala. Grandfather Bhishma was trying unsuccessfully to restore order.

Sishupala turned on Yudhishtira, 'You earned the right to conduct the Rajasooya because Jarasandha is dead, isn't it? All these cowards surrendered without protest in the name of that victory and now you consider yourself an emperor! Can you deny it if I say that all of you disguised yourselves as brahmin priests, managed to win Jarasandha's confidence and then killed him treacherously?'

My blood boiled. Bhishma had gone up to Sishupala again with conciliatory words.

I pushed Sahadeva aside and said, 'Leave him to me. It was I who waged war with Jarasandha.' I knew I had to be the one to confront him.

Krishna, who had been watching indifferently, got up at that moment. He seemed completely unaffected by the challenges and accusations thrown at him. I saw him pick up his discus. All I saw after that was blood spattering the king of Chedi's neck like tiny red cheti flowers. Krishna's discus had flown at a speed that no eye could follow.

I was amazed at Krishna's expression, calm and serious, as if suggesting that anyone who objected to what he had done could attack him with whatever argument he wished to use. A few people left, but no more challenges were thrown. While the bodyguards from Chedi removed the body, the priests began to chant the mantras for the anointing ceremony.

It was to be the first and the last ceremony conducted in that great hall.

Vidura came with a message from Uncle Dhritarashtra, inviting us to visit Hastinapura. He said that our uncle wanted to see Yudhishtira and give him his blessing for having performed the Rajasooya sacrifice. While there, Yudhishtira and Duryodhana could play a few games of dice. A new hall had just been built in Hastinapura for gambling sessions.

Vidura visited Mother and spent a long time talking to her. He came out, went up to Yudhishtira and warned him, 'It is good to know they will receive you warmly and extend their hospitality to you. But you must be careful to avoid playing dice.'

Yudhishtira laughed. 'Aren't gambling and war equally important to kshatriyas? Is it not against dharma to refuse if they come and ask me to play a game?'

Vidura, who understood the connotations of dharma very well, tried to be amiable, 'I brought this message myself so that I would find an opportunity to warn you to be careful.'

'I will not suggest a game myself. But if someone asks me to play, I will not refuse.' To console Vidura, he added, 'Duryodhana will never be able to defeat me if he plays high stakes, though I do not say this because I think playing dice is good.'

I knew Yudhishtira was secretly delighted at knowing that he would have an opportunity to play dice. I could not help imagining a scene where he had gambled away most of the gifts the kings had given him and was returning home glumly, throwing out a few philosophical maxims from time to time ...

Vishoka arrived to tell me that everyone was ready.

Mother and Sahadeva were watching our things being loaded in the chariot. Nakula arrived and I asked him whether we needed such elaborate preparations for the journey. He smiled and said softly, 'Mother is not sure whether we will come back here.'

Arjuna and I had told the charioteers earlier that we would not need any weapons. The Kauravas would take care not to attack us directly for fear of criticism from the people. Now that everyone had begun to talk endlessly about the hall Mayan had built, Khandavaprastha had become Indraprastha. The Yadavas, the Panchalas and several petty kings had become either close relatives or friends. Indraprastha could claim equality with Hastinapura.

Would Duryodhana retaliate in some way for having lost face in Mayan's hall? When he had lifted his clothes high, thinking that the blue tiles were water, it had been Draupadi who laughed the longest. In any case, I had decided that, once we reached Hastinapura, I would keep one eye open while the other slept.

The chariots were ready. Yudhishtira came out and Draupadi followed. I looked at her while she climbed into the chariot – Draupadi, who had come seven years ago as a bride. She had not changed at all. No one would have said, looking at her, that she had borne five children. She still glowed bright, like a ghee lamp lighted at dusk. They say that in the time frame of the gods, a human year is only a day. Maybe this daughter of Panchala had been born on earth with that divine attribute.

Vidura and Sanjaya were waiting to receive us in Hastinapura. We first paid obeisance to our grandfather, Bhishma, then prostrated ourselves before Uncle Dhritarashtra in order of age. He ran his hands over each of us and remarked on how much each had grown. Gripping my forearm and the bracelet on it tightly, he congratulated me on having grown so mighty. I noted that Uncle's hands were longer and harder than Jarasandha's.

I walked to the weapon house. Dronacharya and Kripacharya were resting. I did not want to disturb them, so I went to meet Shukacharya. He had moved. His room was next to the elephant sheds and smelt of elephant dung. He had grown old and weak.

He was so delighted to see me, he could not find words to speak. He got up with difficulty, curled an emaciated fist and pounded me affectionately on my chest.

He said, 'I get all the news from old disciples who come now and then to see me.'

I invited him to Indraprastha.

'No, this is enough for me. How much longer? I've even begun to like the smell of elephant droppings.'

When I took leave of him, he asked, 'Did you go to Duryodhana's palace?'

'No.'

He smiled. 'Duryodhana had a sculptor from the Pandya kingdom make him a huge metal statue of a man. An attendant turns wheels from behind it and its arms and legs move very quickly in combat postures. Duryodhana's principal pastime these days is waging war with that statue.' The old man laughed softly and added, 'I hear the statue looks like you, Bhimasena.'

I laughed as well. I saluted my guru and left. The mahout who used to work in the old elephant sheds had died. Other people whom I had known gathered around, full of affection and respect.

I ate, then rested. An attendant came with a summons to go to the new gambling hall. I first went in search of Arjuna, but could not find him. When I reached the hall, I found that the gambling session was not intended as mere entertainment, but as a royal celebration. Many guests had been invited and were in their appointed seats. Bhishma, Kripa and Drona were seated on either side of Dhritarashtra. Sanjaya, who functioned as Dhritarasthra's eyes, was seated immediately behind them to tell the king what was happening at each moment.

The game was about to begin. I could clearly see the look of eagerness on my elder brother's face. Gently shaking the ivory box that contained the dice, he waited expectantly. So he had not meant it seriously when he had said, even while resting on the way here, that he would try to avoid playing as far as possible.

Soubala's son, Shakuni, and Duryodhana were standing on the opposite side. It was a setting designed for the occasion.

There were comfortable couches to sit on, on both sides. I saw Karna, seated next to Dussasana, among the Kaurava brothers.

'They are playing the game with high stakes,' Arjuna, standing next to me, remarked. This meant that very expensive objects would be wagered.

Duryodhana said, 'I will place the wager, and my uncle, Shakuni, will play. All gains and losses will be settled between you and me.'

So Shakuni was going to play for Duryodhana. It did not seem right to me. I knew nothing about gambling, but I had always feared and detested Shakuni.

'It is not right for one person to play for another,' said Yudhishtira, smiling. 'But I will play, all the same.'

It seemed as if Yudhishtira had been waiting for this chance for years. He looked so confident, I thought that perhaps he would defeat Duryodhana and shame him. Maybe he was using this occasion to prove to us that the countless days he had spent playing the game were not going to be a waste. He looked around to check that all four of us had come to watch and smiled when he saw us.

I had heard that, apart from the wagers the players themselves made, spectators who had a passion for the game would make wagers among themselves as well.

Both threw the dice to see who would start the game. Yudhishtira threw doubles, six and six; Shakuni threw four and one. So Yudhishtira had to start the game, since he had thrown the higher number.

He rolled the dice in the palm of his right hand. Then he raised the gem in the centre of his necklace of precious stones with the fingers of his left hand and said: 'This gem, set in gold, is priceless. I wager this necklace.'

Duryodhana said, 'I have many precious gems. I will be happy to see you win.'

Yudhishtira played.

Duryodhana called out, 'Three …!'

When Shakuni rolled the dice, Arjuna murmured, 'Hmm … I wonder …'

Shakuni smiled, looking at the dice he had thrown, 'Look, I won!'

Still smiling, Yudhishtira took off his necklace and put it on the ground.

When Yudhishtira shook the dice again, Duryodhana said, 'You did not say what your wager is.'

'A hundred chests of gold!'

The spectators grew noisy. Arjuna glanced at me. I began to feel uneasy.

After making sure that Duryodhana had accepted the wager, Shakuni played. Twelve again! Before the minister who was calculating the gains and losses could call out the result, I knew from Yudhishtira's face that he had lost.

A hundred chests of gold! It was the entire wealth we had collected from several kingdoms for the Rajasooya sacrifice. He had wagered all the gold in the treasury of Indraprastha.

I got up, unable to watch what was happening. Everyone's eyes were riveted on the game. I left the hall, climbed down the steps and walked into the courtyard.

I heard the roar of the spectators. Who had won?

From time to time, I heard the shouts of those who had laid

bets. Who was winning, who was losing? I could not accept that victory and defeat could be decided by the throw of dice.

I heard a sound as if the entire assembly had exploded.

Sahadeva came running up. The fury in his voice was broken by faint sobs, 'Please come and see. Our brother, Yudhishtira, is insane. We've lost everything, including Indraprastha, in twelve games. Even the gems in his crown are gone. He has just wagered Nakula.'

I realized that danger had closed around us in an entirely unexpected way. The word a kshatriya gives in a gambling hall is sacred. As a child, I had heard the story of a king who had been cheated in a game and lost. He had had to work as a cook for another king in exchange for food and lodging.

There was no point running away. Since he had begun with Nakula, it would not be long before this madman turned me too into an object to wager. I had heard it said that there were people who had mastered all the secrets of the game of dice – maybe Shakuni was one of them. Duryodhana would surely have had good reason to make his uncle play on his behalf.

I went back with Sahadeva to the hall, only to hear that he had been wagered as well.

'I have a suspicion that you are using deceit to win. There is something wrong with the dice,' said Yudhishtira.

Shakuni smiled and looked at Duryodhana, who said loudly, for the entire gathering to hear, 'We will not insist that you continue. If you will accept, King, that you have lost, we can go our ways.'

Shakuni said, 'Let's stop playing anyway. You have nothing left to wager, after all.'

Yudhishtira's voice rose, 'My wealth is unlimited. My

younger brother, Arjuna, whose heroic deeds have astonished everyone – he is the next wager.'

I looked at Dhritarashtra. The lifeless eyes of the blind king, who was being told about the gains and losses from moment to moment, were full of laughter.

Shakuni won again. We suddenly heard Vidura addressing Dhritarashtra, 'King, the Kuru dynasty is going to be ruined by this game of dice.'

Shakuni's eyes sought me out. He said to Yudhishtira, 'You have one younger brother left, the mighty Bhima.'

We did not actually hear our elder brother say 'yes', but we saw the game had started again.

Shakuni, who I believe knew all the secrets of the game, won that round too. 'We won. Do you have anything else to wager?'

Distressed, his face pale and drawn, Yudhishtira looked around. He was aware that he was a figure of ridicule to the spectators. But anger had rendered him oblivious to everything.

'I am next. If I win, I will take back everything I lost. If I lose, I become your slave.'

He lost that game as well. He sank back on the couch, looking like a heap of ashes at the tip of a burnt-out torch.

The silence in the hall was more frightening than the cries and shouts had been.

So it was my unhappy destiny to live out the rest of my days in Hastinapura as a servant, a slave. I had to bow my head and accept. There was no way I could raise a hand in protest. I was the second brother.

I saw Shakuni and Duryodhana whisper to each other.

Shakuni asked, 'Don't you have one more piece of wealth, King? Panchali, the wife of the Pandavas?'

Murmurs of protest arose from the spectators who had been silent so far. I heard voices say, 'Unfair, unjust …!'

Unperturbed, Yudhishtira said, 'I do not withdraw. I wager my beloved Draupadi, who equals the great goddess Lakshmi herself. My turn, Soubala!'

Even the rattling of the dice could be heard in the deep silence that followed.

I closed my eyes. The silence roared in my ears.

I opened my eyes when I heard Duryodhana's voice. 'Let Draupadi be brought here. Vidura, the son of the servant woman, can go and fetch her. Let the Pandavas' wife do household work in my palace.'

I stood up.

5

Vidura went up to Dhritarashtra. It was the first time I had ever heard him raise his voice. His body trembling violently, Vidura pointed at Duryodhana and said, 'Don't you remember? Jackals came into the palace courtyard and howled when this son was born. Hastinapura will turn into a burning ground because of him. The Kuru dynasty will perish!'

Ignoring him, Duryodhana spoke to an attendant standing nearby, 'Pratikami, go and fetch Draupadi.'

I looked at the gathering around me as they waited for Draupadi. I thought that deep within them, every one of them wanted to see her being brought to the hall, although they pretended that what was happening was unjust.

Duryodhana walked up and down, ignoring Yudhishtira,

who lay exhausted. Karna and Dussasana came down to join him. Karna murmured something in Duryodhana's ear. Duryodhana smiled and nodded in agreement.

Pratikami came back alone and waited in front of Duryodhana with his palms joined.

Karna asked, 'Where is Draupadi?'

So this was Karna's day, I told myself, his chance to settle old scores with Draupadi.

'The queen wishes to know whom the king offered as a wager first, himself or the queen. She also wants to know whether the great and noble men in this assembly who know the laws of dharma approve of this.'

Yudhishtira said, 'Let Draupadi come. All of us became slaves because these people cheated while playing. Let the assembly note that injustice and condemn these people.'

Duryodhana shouted, 'Let Draupadi come!'

Pratikami waited, trembling. He ran his eyes over the spectators, caught sight of me and turned away, terrified.

Duryodhana said, 'The servant is frightened. Dussasana, go and bring her.'

Dussasana went in eagerly, happy to be entrusted with such a pleasant duty. I, usually so arrogant about my strength in secret, felt helpless as I waited, rubbing my curled fists together. The sight and scent of blood had never perturbed me, but I shuddered now.

Then a sob heaved through me. Gripping her long hair in his hands, Dussasana dragged Draupadi into the hall like a sacrificial cow is dragged to the stake. Clutching her loosening waistcloth to prevent it from falling, Draupadi looked around.

I saw drops of blood between her trembling feet, like rubies scattered over the white marble floor. She was pulling at the single piece of cloth she wore, trying to cover her breasts with it. She was obviously having her period. A thousand eyes tore like vultures at her half-naked form.

Controlling her sobs, Draupadi asked, 'Is it right to have dragged me to this assembly in this condition? Let this gathering, which includes our Grandfather Bhishma and the wise Vidura, say: am I a slave?'

She looked around, holding her head high like a queen. Her eyes searched the faces in the gathering, looking for someone to speak in her favour. Finally, they rested on me.

We have to endure it, there is no way out. Yudhishtira, the son of Dharma, values his word above all other things. So we are all slaves.

I took a few paces forward, looked at Yudhishtira and said, 'There are gamblers with homes in streets full of whorehouses. Even those wastrels do not wager their women.' No longer able to control my fury, I shouted, 'Sahadeva! Bring me fire, before I do something terrible. Let me burn my hands. All I can do now is punish myself.'

Arjuna caught my shoulder and said, 'Don't, don't …'

Vikarna, one of the Kauravas I had never paid much attention to, said, 'No one has answered Draupadi's question, which is: how can someone who has wagered himself and lost, wager another person? I say that Draupadi is not a slave.'

Apart from defying Duryodhana, he had thrown to the gathering an argument that had not occurred to me at all. The question Draupadi had asked, whether she was a slave or not, was no trivial one.

Taking no notice of Duryodhana, who was looking at him

angrily, Vikarna went on: 'Hunting, drinking, gambling and womanizing – if one becomes addicted to any of these, one abandons the path of righteousness. Dharma was destroyed when a noble woman was brought from the inner court to this hall, clad only in a single piece of cloth.'

Furious, Karna pointed an arrow-like finger at Vikarna. 'Hey you! We could have brought her here naked. What nobility does a woman who lives as the wife of five husbands have?' Giving Draupadi a look of contempt, Karna turned to Duryodhana, 'Make the slaves remove all their clothes and jewels and give them to you.'

Yudhishtira took off his upper cloth. He had removed his ornaments earlier. Taking the hint, Arjuna, Nakula and Sahadeva took off their ornaments.

In response to a signal Karna gave with his eyes, Dussasana let go of Draupadi's hair and placed his hand at the spot where her cloth was knotted at her waist.

I lunged forward and made a sound. Dussasana looked at me without taking his hand off. He was probably afraid I would break the rules and attack him.

I screamed for everyone in the hall, for the whole palace, to hear: 'I make a vow before all who are gathered here. If I do not kill Dussasana one day, tear his chest apart and drink his blood, I am not Bhimasena. I do not wish for the peace and happiness my ancestors earned through their good deeds!'

One of the spectators remarked, 'No one has answered Draupadi's question: is she a slave? Bhishma and Vidura, who are so learned, are here, after all.'

Everyone looked at Vidura.

'There is something in what Vikarna said. This problem

has two sides. Once, when Prahlada and Kashyapa had an argument …'

The gathering intervened impatiently. 'Let Bhishmacharya speak.'

Bhishma, who had been seated unmoving all this while, spoke. 'Yudhishtira must say whether Draupadi is free or a slave.'

Duryodhana seemed to be enjoying these arguments. Karna was obviously impatient and kept muttering something. Duryodhana tapped him on the shoulder and said, 'Let Bhimasena, his younger brothers and Draupadi tell us that Yudhishtira has no right over them. I will then let all of them go free.'

Was it from Duryodhana's brain or Karna's that this question had taken shape? It was I who was caught in a dilemma now. All eyes were on me. I did not hesitate.

'Yudhishtira is our elder brother. He is our king and our guru. When he was defeated, so were we. If he says we have become slaves, we are slaves. But …' No old stories, no sayings from the scriptures, came to my aid. I clenched my right fist and held it out. 'You see my hands? One day, you will see me crush all the Kauravas with my bare hands. I am ready to do so even now, all I need is a word of permission from Yudhishtira.'

The hall fell silent again. Suppressing his anger, Karna said mockingly to Draupadi, 'The wealth and women that belong to slaves are their master's property. You can begin work in your master's house now. There will be good-looking men there as well, so you will have no cause for regret.'

Duryodhana pointed at Yudhishtira and said, 'Can you say that you did not wager Draupadi? Then the argument will end. No citing of the texts, no old tales. Just the matter in hand. Yes or no?' He looked at Draupadi, moved his waistcloth to expose his left thigh, patted it and said to her: 'Or *you* must say Yudhishtira is not your husband, that will do.'

Draupadi pushed Dussasana's hand aside, ran up to Dhritarashtra and fell at his feet. Only at that moment did many of us remember that the king, who had been absolutely silent, was in the gathering. In the commotion that Duryodhana had created, I had completely forgotten his presence.

None of us heard what she said to him. He spoke, 'This woman is as dear to me as a daughter-in-law. I grant her the boon she craves from me. I set her free.'

Draupadi said something to him again. 'I declare the Pandavas free as well, for her sake. Those who won the game will keep the kingdom and its wealth.'

No one protested; the announcement had been so unexpected. The gathering became vociferous again, from sheer relief.

Karna was much angrier and far more disappointed than Duryodhana. He cried loudly, 'So the Pandavas have escaped for the time being, thanks to a woman's tears. What valiant heroes!'

By the command of the king, we were free. Yudhishtira came up to me looking exhausted, and I said to him, 'I am not putting off either of my vows, since I am free now to fulfil them.'

I knew I had the strength to confront all of them single-handed. What I longed for was to avenge myself against at least three of them at once, if not all: Karna, Duryodhana and Dussasana.

Yudhishtira stood before me and begged me in a tone that was almost a prayer, 'Don't, you must not!'

The charioteers had made ready the chariots for our return journey. Everyone had got in when I arrived. Draupadi sat next to Mother, her head bowed. Looking at Mother's tired face, I thought she seemed to have suddenly grown very old.

One of the charioteers said, 'A messenger is coming this way.'

I saw Pratikami running up to us from the palace.

He saluted Yudhishtira. 'You are invited to another game of dice, if you are ready to play.'

'Who invites us?'

'The great king, Dhritarashtra.'

I glanced at Mother. She sighed deeply and closed her eyes. All of us looked at our elder brother. We watched the gambler in him tugging him this way and that. He obviously saw before him a chance to recover everything he had lost.

Arjuna said, 'Don't accept.'

Yudhishtira hesitated. Pratikami waited. He was, after all, only a helpless messenger.

'What does he want as a wager now? Didn't Shakuni tell you? Our severed heads?' asked Sahadeva.

He turned to Draupadi, his expression appealing, as if asking her to say something, anything ... Draupadi sat immobile, gazing steadily into the distance.

Arjuna said, 'Let the chariot leave ...'

'Wait!' Yudhishtira.

Nakula went up to him. 'Let all we have lost go. You are not going to recover anything, playing against Shakuni.'

Yudhishtira looked questioningly at Nakula. Then he alighted from the chariot. On his instructions, the charioteers began to unharness the horses. We followed him back again to the palace.

When word came to me that Yudhishtira was winning game after game, I felt no emotion. Nakula and Sahadeva took turns to come running to me with news of the gains and losses.

I had started to drink the moment I entered the guest house.

Then news came that he was losing. I remained indifferent. When Nakula came instead of Sahadeva a second time, I said to him, 'Tell me whether it's time to give him our heads. I am ready.'

He sank down exhausted in front of me, gasping for breath. He was silent for a while, then he said, 'That might have been better. Twelve years in the forest. Then one year in some country, incognito. If someone recognizes us during that year, another twelve years in the forest. Good, isn't it?'

I didn't care anymore.

Sahadeva said, 'I have a request to make of you, Elder Brother. Some day, when we have an opportunity to kill the Kauravas, you must leave one of them to me. That lowdown scoundrel, Shakuni!'

My younger brother was trembling with grief and anger. Pulling him to me with my left hand and holding him close, I comforted him, 'We will certainly have an opportunity. Do not grieve. The forest is not such a bad place to live in.'

I drank the remaining liquor and stood up.

PART 5

The Flowers in Kubera's Garden

1

It rained in the month of Phalguna as well. Rainwater stagnated for days inside the huts we had built of leaves and branches. We spent most of our time in the kitchen hut, where a fire burnt constantly. From time to time, flowers fell like showers of gold coins from the konna trees, making a mockery of our precincts, tempting us into believing we were still living in a palace.

Fortunately, Mother had chosen to stay with Vidura. Draupadi could have gone with our children when they were sent to Drupada's palace, since only we brothers had to endure the punishment of exile in the forest, but she chose to stay with us. She no longer had ornaments or serving women. And yet, watching her going in the morning and at dusk for a bath in the forest stream, like a maiden in a hermitage, I felt she had adapted herself to our evil destiny faster than any of us.

This place was much more beautiful than the Kamyaka forest, where we had stayed earlier. It was filled with flowering trees. Small animals that were edible were plentiful. However, Yudhishtira had found it easier to cling to the appendages of royalty in the camp in Kamyaka. The attendants and maids who had come there with us had waited as of old upon his commands. Relatives and friends had come to visit us and offer sympathy. Having fallen out with Dhritarashtra, Vidura had stayed with us for a few days, spending his time imparting bits of philosophical counsel to us, or telling us stories about the dispensation of justice. He had returned to Hastinapura when Sanjaya came to tell him that the king was no longer displeased with him, and had commanded him to return.

Draupadi's high spirits had dulled and it was only when Dhrishtadyumna and Krishna came to visit her that she grew lively again. Until then, she had never found fault with us, but she said to them, 'I expect nothing more from these five men. My sole comfort is knowing that my father, my brother and my relative, Krishna, are still around.'

Krishna had come to know of the game of dice, Yudhishtira's defeat and Draupadi's humiliation long after it had happened. The Yadavas had been engaged in a war with Shalya at the time.

Glancing at Yudhishtira who was seated with his head bowed, Krishna said, 'Had I been around, I would not have allowed the game of dice to take place.'

Draupadi often spoke of the insults she had endured and the hardships that she, who had grown up in the Panchala kingdom, waited upon by 500 maids, had to suffer now.

Krishna comforted her, 'Draupadi, the Kauravas will be completely wiped out as the result of their evil deeds, I will see it happen before my own eyes. It is I who tell you this, I who can see the past, the present and the future.'

Draupadi listened to him indifferently, as if she did not believe him.

He declared with conviction, 'The sky may fall, the Himavan mountain crumble and the seas dry up. But Krishna's words will never prove a lie, they have never proved so until now.'

A brightness touched Draupadi's sad face. Krishna certainly knew how to use words as skilfully as he wielded the discus.

Vishoka, who had accompanied Balandhara when Senesha had taken her to Kashi, came back. But I had no need of a charioteer in the forest. He said he would hang around doing odd jobs, but I insisted that he return to Kashi.

When the rains began in Kamyaka, we moved to the Dwaitava forest. I suggested that all the attendants be sent away and Yudhishtira did not raise too many objections. Indraprastha became a half-forgotten daydream.

We met at meal times, then went our separate ways. The occasions on which we spoke to one another grew rarer.

A bit of news I had heard while we were in Kamyaka had made me uneasy: that Hidimbi had been waiting for me to go and fetch her, or send a servant to bring her. Kirmeera told me this – Kirmeera, whose life I had spared, although I defeated him in a duel.

The site we had chosen for our camp was Kirmeera's hunting ground. One day, when I returned from a hunting expedition, I was told that a forest dweller had claimed that he was the overlord of the Kamyaka and Dwaitava forests and accused Yudhishtira of taking them over. He had commanded us to leave before dawn the next day and asked his followers to set fire to our huts.

Yudhishtira gave orders: 'He must be killed. Even sages have been forced to leave the forest because they could not bear his atrocities. We have reached a point where we cannot even get priests to conduct our pujas and rituals. This tribal certainly deserves to die.'

Killing was always my job. However, when I met Kirmeera,

I came to know that he belonged to the nishada tribe and that Baka was his brother. He had heard of my duel with his brother. The attendants who had witnessed it had told him that I had confronted Baka directly and defeated him. Kirmeera bore me no ill will for this. The reason he wanted to fight me was not because of Baka, but because he thought I had abandoned Hidimbi.

I was astonished. Hidimbi!

Kirmeera and Hidimba had been companions and had hunted together. Around the time I met her in the forest, Kirmeera had even wanted to marry Hidimbi. He accused me of having used sorcery to seduce her.

Kirmeera heard of Hidimba's death only seven months after he had been killed, when he returned from hunting elephants in the eastern forests. He rushed to Hidimbi, confident that she would accept him since she no longer had anyone in the world. But she sent him away, saying, 'The husband I love came for me. I carry his child in my womb.'

Kirmeera went away, but continued to visit her. He told me that the son she bore was growing up strong and courageous. His name was Ghatotkacha. I repeated the name silently, Ghatotkacha, telling myself I must not forget it.

Kirmeera and I had met as enemies, challenging each other to a duel, but we became friends. He invited me for a meal – pork cooked in rice, liquor distilled from the stems of sugarcane. As I was about to leave, he gifted me a hunting knife with a handle carved from the horn of a wild buffalo.

When I went back, I saw from Draupadi's face that she was impatient to hear me describe the fight with Kirmeera. Yudhishtira wanted to know all about it as well.

All I said was, 'You will not have any more trouble from him.'

Yudhishtira assumed that I had been defeated and had escaped with my life.

Once we were by ourselves, Draupadi asked, 'What happened?'

'We did not have to fight each other. We parted as friends.'

'Ah, a friendship between tribals. Yes, I see …' She did not say anything more.

Her expression annoyed me and, for no reason, my annoyance was aggravated as the days passed.

Eventually, it exploded for no particular reason against Yudhishtira, when I heard him discuss ways to get hold of a brahmin priest. He was full of complaints: no brahmins were available in the forest, it was not possible to conduct pujas and rituals. Sacrifices that had to be performed regularly had not been done. Destiny was the cause of all these evils. His expression showed that he was surprised no one sympathized with him. His voice was full of self-pity.

I asked him, 'So have you decided to wander around for the twelve and one, thirteen, years in order to keep your word?'

Startled, he looked at me. 'What else can I do?'

'We have a number of relatives and kings who are our friends. We should fight and destroy the Kauravas.'

Hearing my voice, Draupadi came out. She surveyed the scene and said, with a faint smile, 'Once again, a dinner of wild root-vegetables. In the old days, I used to eat only after I had fed all the guests and people who came seeking alms on golden platters. Our evil destiny, what else can I say?'

The veiled mockery in her words escaped Yudhishtira. He

said, 'Our younger brother suggests we do not wait twelve years but wage war now. I think we should wait patiently.'

Draupadi's gentleness vanished. 'Five husbands, all great warriors! A brother who equals a thousand men! A father who has mighty armies, splendidly equipped. And yet, look at my plight!'

Yudhishtira sighed. 'Time punishes those who stray from the path of dharma. Console yourself with the belief that this is the will of God.'

'Prosperity for those who dragged me to the gambling hall and threatened to disrobe me. Exile in the forest for the wife of the Pandavas. If that be the will of the gods, I revile those gods. The god who decreed such things is avaricious, unjust, cruel!'

Yudhishtira smiled at Draupadi as she stood before him with her eyes blazing and her hair undone. Then he began to speak to me about concepts of righteousness and injustice, Heaven and Hell ...

After a while, I said, 'Brother, I have heard you say that there is no virtue a king can have higher than that of safeguarding his own people, the principles of his family and his subjects.'

Arjuna came back from hunting at that moment and looked at both of us in turn, trying to find out what had happened.

'I was talking about the trivial sufferings we have to undergo here. We reach the celestial feet of the gods only after our life on Earth.' Yudhishtira hoped to find an ally in Arjuna. 'I cannot renounce righteousness and truth. I am Yudhishtira, the son of Dharma. No matter what agonies I have to endure, I cannot go against dharma.'

Arjuna said, 'One command from you, just one word is enough. My brother Bhimasena and I will turn the Kauravas to ashes, just like fire and wind wipe out a forest.'

Draupadi intervened, 'But the king's unshakable decision is that we must hold ourselves in patience for thirteen years!'

Nakula and Sahadeva arrived. The arguments went on – dharma, justice, law, until Sahadeva could stand no more. 'I would be obliged if you could tell me what dharma there is in a game of dice. Let these twilight discussions in the forest help us to increase our knowledge as well.'

I thought, maybe Sahadeva should not have bared the sword-edge of contempt so sharply, so openly.

Yudhishtira was furious. 'Could you not have obeyed when I asked you to bring me fire to burn my hands? I …'

I corrected him. 'Wrong! It was I who wanted to burn my hands.'

'Why couldn't you have attacked the Kauravas and destroyed them then, without my permission? I would not have hindered you. Now all of you turn against me …' Yudhishtira was so angry, he could not find words.

'And why did you go back when they invited you again for a game, knowing full well that Shakuni would cheat?' There was no answer to Nakula's question.

Arjuna said, 'Elder Brother, you mentioned the gamblers in the red-light districts. I know how the minds of gamblers work. Those who have been defeated in a game, Nakula, go back to play in the belief that they will retrieve everything they lost in one second. Whether they live in brothels or in palaces, the minds of gamblers work the same way.'

Arjuna started to walk away, then stopped and turned to me. 'Brother, Bhimasena, you vowed you would kill the Kauravas. No matter when we fight that war, all four of you must spare the charioteer's son. Karna will die only by my hand, that's for sure.'

As he walked off, he took an arrow out of his quiver and shot it upwards. A wild pigeon fell amongst us, an arrow pierced right through its body. A cluster of wildflowers followed, shaken out of the trembling branches, as if celestial bodies had showered flowers over us.

At night, Arjuna approached me. 'I'm going away.'

'Where?'

'Somewhere far away. I'm fed up of this place, it's unbearable.'

I waited uncertainly.

Arjuna said, 'I've been hearing about all kinds of new weapons. People have begun to try out weapons that are not mentioned in the texts dealing with archery. I can use this time to learn more about them.'

'Shouldn't you consult our elder brother …?'

'Tell him I've left. These are not royal precincts. So why observe formalities?'

'Tell him before you leave.'

I was distressed that Arjuna was going away. Having him nearby always strengthened my self-confidence. Then I quelled the impulse of sudden delight I felt at knowing that Draupadi would be more aware of me in Arjuna's absence.

Arjuna left before sunrise. When I came back from the forest stream after my morning ablutions, I saw that Yudhishtira looked anxious.

I said, 'Arjuna has gone to visit centres that have a reputation for the knowledge of archery. I gave him my blessing.'

'It is always a relief to have Arjuna close by. Anyway, I am glad he has gone to achieve something worthy.'

I thought I would follow the spoor of an animal I had seen that morning, and set out with my bow and arrow and my spear.

I was right, it was a stag. I crept up, trying to get close enough to throw my spear at it. Suddenly, a twig snapped underfoot. The stag fled. I aimed an arrow at the nerve in its ear and was about to hurriedly aim a second one lest the first miss its target when the animal fell.

It was huge. Since the arrow had pierced it only behind its ear, the skin was intact – it was lustrous and beautiful. I could dry it and make Draupadi a garment. Even though it would not be as beautiful as the fine woven silks she had worn in the palace, it would look attractive enough if I dyed its inner surface with the juice of kasumbha flowers.

I slung the animal over my shoulders and walked back. Drops of its blood dripped over my chest from the wound I had made when I pulled out the arrow. I saw Draupadi standing on the path, trying to pluck a cluster of bakula flowers. She did not notice me until I was very close to her. She looked at the animal lying across my shoulders.

'When will Arjuna be back?'

'I don't know. He had told me he would send a messenger from time to time with news.'

'I used to sleep peacefully in this forest because I knew he would be lying outside with his bow at his head.'

I adjusted the animal across my shoulders and its blood gushed out and flowed in a stream over my body. Draupadi looked at it for a little while, then broke off a branch and mopped up the blood with leaves, standing very close to me. The odour of smoke wafted from her hair. The deerskin she wore did not cover her shoulders. Below her navel, that looked like a shrivelled ashoka bud and across the skin of her firm, unblemished lower abdomen, a muscle twitched like the string of a crossbow.

I put the animal down and said, 'I never sleep. Not a single night have I slept deeply since I made the vow in the gambling hall. I am here to keep watch, you can sleep in peace.'

A mace fight with Duryodhana, a wrestling match with Dussasana, the tactics they were likely to employ, the strategies I would use to counter them by surprise: these were what I thought of when I lay down at night. At first, this had been a pleasant pastime, then it became a habit.

The dragonflies fluttering around the wild flowers were humming in my ears now. Flames arose in my loins.

She chided me. 'Have you forgotten? It is the king's turn now.'

She walked away and I picked up the animal lying on the ground.

Rules … rules governing each one's turn. I thought, none of this had existed in the past.

All the sages who performed penance had broken rules, even the great ones who had framed them. Most of them had been so weak-willed that semen had dripped from them when they glimpsed the loveliness of a naked woman's body. Sharadvan had forgotten to chant his prayers when he caught sight of the woman, Kripi, who was the mother of Kripacharya and Drona's wife, without her clothes. The sage Bharadvaja, Drona's father, had desired Ghritachi when he saw her having a bath. I had heard the sootas sing of how, seeing that same woman, our grandfather Krishnadvaipayana's 'shrivelled body had trembled, his mind had grown confused …' Krishnadvaipayana, who had approached Vichitravirya's widows unwillingly, with revulsion, had had a son by Ghritachi. No one ever spoke of him. But the truth is that we had another uncle somewhere.

And now we abided by the rules of chastity these men had framed.

I took the animal to our camp, then went to the forest stream and immersed myself in it. I recalled one of the lessons priests had to learn, it seemed like a joke to me: if lust awakened their bodies, they had to go and stand in cold water to make sure they did not break the rules of abstinence.

When I returned, I found Yudhishtira in a very happy mood. He had at last got hold of a person to conduct our pujas and rituals – an old brahmin, Dhoumya, a man who had travelled a great deal. The old man was describing the sacred spots he had seen.

'Why don't we travel and visit holy places instead of staying here?' asked Yudhishtira. I agreed. It was better to wander around and see new countries than live here quietly. Dhoumya said he would come with us. Yudhishtira said we should consider it fortunate that we had with us a great sage who would conduct the prescribed rituals for our ancestors at all the sacred water sources. Madri's sons were more enthusiastic than I was about the journey.

Our next camp was at Brahmashiras. We spent seven days there, then crossed the Kaushiki river and reached Rishabakoota. While we were there, I listened to a sage narrate the story of Rishyasringa. The king of a neighbouring country had sent a courtesan to seduce Rishyasringa, who had been raised by his father, Vibhandaka, so austerely that the boy had never known even the scent of a woman. The young man saw the courtesan as a playmate and brushed against her accidentally. When we reached the point where Rishyashringa described to his father the wonder he felt when he discovered that his new friend had soft fruits hidden in her chest, we really began to enjoy the story. In order to ensure an abundant harvest, the neighbouring kingdom of Lomapada, from where the courtesan had come, used to celebrate a huge festival on the first night a pure young man slept with a virgin. Rishyasringa had drunk liquor without knowing what it was, and his descriptions of the festival delighted Sahadeva. Draupadi was amused by the marvels the young man discovered in the playmate who had come to visit him, marvels he did not possess himself. Some sages could narrate stories much better than the sootas could. The stay in Brahmashiras dispelled our gloom.

Next, we camped in the valley of the Mahendra mountain. Another old man joined Dhoumya there, a priest named Lomesha. Both of them suggested that we do the rituals for our ancestors in Vytharani.

The Vytharani was a huge waterfall, we heard its roar from a distance. Lomesha narrated the legend of the place to us. It was said that when Bhoomi Devi, the Goddess of the Earth, was a young virgin, Brahma tried to persuade her into a marriage she did not like, and that, in protest, she sank down to the nether world at this spot. The bridegroom, Kashyapa, and Brahma pleaded with her until she came out. Shiva's bull, Nandi, had sprung into the cave earlier in search of the young girl.

We performed the rituals in order of age. The priest chanted mantras evoking the memory of our ancestors in Jambudweepa, which includes the land of Bharata, where all of us live, and we repeated them. After that, we invoked the souls of each ancestor into the tip of a blade of kusha grass.

When my turn came, I had doubts. Whom should I

meditate upon when I invoked my ancestors? Pandu, who was not my blood relative, or the immortal Lord of the Wind? Like Yudhishtira, I meditated on the great King Pandu, then Vichitravirya. But once again, I had doubts. Surely there was no need to make a funeral offering of rice and sesame seeds to Krishnadvaipayana, who was still alive, and pay him obeisance …? Then to Shantanu, Pradeepa, Kuru, Yayati …

When the rituals were over and we came up from Vytharani, I asked the priest, 'If we must invoke the memory of ancestors according to lineage, should we go back to King Shantanu or to the brahmin, Parashara?'

As always, Yudhishtira said, 'Blockhead, don't talk nonsense!'

When I lay down that night listening to the roar of Vytharani, I did not think as I usually did of wrestling bouts, but of my great-grandmother, Satyavati, whom I had seen only once when I was a small child. I tried to capture the image of a beautiful young woman rowing a boat. If the songs I had heard were true, Parashara, the brahmin who conquered the young girl smelling of fish, as she steered her boat through the middle of the great river, must have been an extraordinary man. I imagined the scene: an oarless boat drifting along a swirling, rushing river. The fisher-girl resisting him and being flung down to the floor of the boat, choked with muddy water and reeking of fish. The soul of the brahmin who subdued her with the might of his hands merited a funeral offering of at least three rice-and-sesame balls laid on tips of kusha grass. But no one had recalled him when we did the rituals.

The night on the mountain slope was bitterly cold and the wind blew tiny droplets from the waterfall on us. I could not sleep. Surely, no one would perspire on such a night. And yet the icy wind wafted the scent of lotus flowers to me.

2

I had ceased to keep track of time as we journeyed. All I could remember was that we had left Hastinapura a very long time ago.

Eventually we received a message from Arjuna, brought to us by a sage who had met him. We were asked to wait at a spot beyond Gandhamadana, where Arjuna would join us.

But before we received that message, Balarama, Krishna and their close friend Satyaki, who belonged to the Vrishni clan, came one day to the sacred spot of Prabhasatirtha. Krishna gave us news of Mother. She was comfortable in Vidura's home. Krishna had been sending messengers regularly for news of her, and had gone there himself once. Subhadra and Abhimanyu were doing well in Dwaraka.

'Let Arjuna come back, then we'll decide what we should do.'

Once we began to speak about war with the Kauravas, Balarama fell silent. He did not want to take sides, since he had friends in both factions. All the same, he felt that it was wrong of the Kauravas to have appropriated the kingdom by winning a game of dice.

We grew close to Satyaki very quickly. He said, 'The longer we delay, the stronger our enemy will grow.' His body was as massive as mine, and we were alike in our appetite for food.

It was a fortnight after our friends left that the sage met Arjuna, and it took him still longer to bring us his message.

The sage explained to us the route to Gandhamadana. We arrived at the foot of a mountain covered by a dense forest and realized it would not be easy to scale it and get to the other side. Just where the mountain path began, we found a cave that some hermit had lived in. Since it was already dusk, we decided to stay in it that night. It was a fortunate decision, for a great gale blew that night and heavy rain lashed the mountainside.

We started to climb in the morning. At first, it was not too hard to follow the path trod by the ascetics and pilgrims who had come that way. After a distance, trees that had fallen in the storm the previous day blocked our way. We looked for another path, but the one we found was so narrow, we could hardly place our feet on it. Somehow, we managed to climb another lap. When we looked up, the mountain still towered before us, obscuring the sky.

I walked ahead of the others, clearing the branches with my hunting knife. Nakula was behind me, then Sahadeva. Draupadi followed them and Yudhishtira was last of all.

Yudhishtira cried out suddenly and I stopped. Draupadi had fallen down. I found it difficult to go down to the spot where they were. Yudhishtira had helped her sit up. Draupadi looked at me as if to say, 'It's too hard …'

Suddenly, a group of young forest tribals appeared, carrying axes, with ropes wound around their shoulders. I signalled to them to stop and asked them to show us the way to the top. The older ones among them smiled, but looked bewildered, as if they could not follow what I was saying. The one who seemed to be the youngest said, 'This is no time to climb Gandhamadana. More gales and storms are expected.'

His face was like a child's, but muscles rippled over his dark, firm body. I thought the young men probably belonged to one of the nishada tribes.

'But we have to go on.'

The young man looked at Draupadi, who was seated on the ground, exhausted, reluctant to get up. Although younger than the others, he obviously wielded authority over them. He said something hurriedly in the Paisachi dialect. His expression suggested that he was scolding them. The older men began to run in all directions. By this time, Nakula had come up to me.

The men came back carrying branches and creepers. They trimmed the branches, fastened them to each other with creepers and fashioned a cot. Nakula and I glanced at each other, admiring their craftsmanship. The young man signed to the others to bring the cot forward.

'The woman who cannot walk can sit on this, and we will carry her up.'

At first, Draupadi protested, saying she would walk up herself. Finally, when Yudhishtira also insisted, she climbed onto the cot. The boy went ahead, clearing the path and Draupadi followed in the makeshift palanquin the tribals had made for her. Once she overcame her initial embarrassment, she seemed to enjoy the ride in the rustic palanquin. She even smiled at me.

When we had covered quite a distance, the boy told us that just off our path was a spring with clear water, beside which we could halt if we wanted to. But we wanted to go on to the top. We knew there were well-known hermitages there that existed from the olden times, and that there were people living in them.

Four men carried the cot. I watched them tread surely

and firmly on sharp stones. The guide who walked ahead cut footholds with his axe at spots where it was difficult to make one's way. The forest, which was so dense that it was dark even in the daytime, gradually grew thinner. Isolated flowering trees replaced the dense forest vegetation. It was nearly sunset when we arrived at the top.

The cot was lowered, and Draupadi got down and smiled gratefully at the tribals.

In the distance, we saw smoke rising from the huts in the hermitages and heard the Bhagirathi river roaring down the slope. Everywhere, there were trees filled with flowers and fruit. It was more beautiful than the sage had described. A small branch of the Bhagirathi, having decided not to travel further, had curled itself into a pond. Beyond it lay the snow-covered peak of the Hiranya mountain. The fatigue of the day's climb through the great forest disappeared as we looked around us in delight.

The tribals had walked away. Remembering that we had not even said a word of thanks to them, I ran and caught up with them.

'You did us a great service. We do not even have anything to gift you.'

They smiled. The guide said, 'We do not expect anything.'

'We are the princes of Indraprastha. If you ever hear that good fortune has come our way, one of you must come and visit us. We would like to give you gifts.'

They smiled, knowing the words were only a formality.

'I am Bhimasena. We are the younger brothers of King Yudhishtira.'

The older ones among them looked at one another doubtfully,

as if they did not understand. I pounded my chest with my fists and said, 'I am Bhimasena, son of the great King Pandu.'

The boy who was their guide said in a gentle voice, 'I am Ghatotkacha of the nishada tribe from the Hidimba forest, the son of Hidimbi.'

Goose pimples broke out on my body. I thought the face that was smiling at me was somehow at odds with his physique. My arms almost swung out to embrace him, but I controlled myself.

'I ... I am your father.'

'I thought so, when I heard the name.'

He knelt down and touched my feet in obeisance. I bent down, held his face in my hands and lifted him up.

Smiling, Ghatotkacha said, 'My companions and I will be in this area. Is there anything else you want us to do?'

I saw Draupadi watching us from a distance.

'I will need your help when you are older. In a war.'

He saluted me again, ran down to catch up with his friends and disappeared from sight. I thought, I had not asked him about his mother, about Hidimbi ...

When I went back, Yudhishtira asked, 'Did you have anything with you to give them as a gift?'

'No. And if I had, they would not have taken it. The boy who was our guide is my son. Hidimbi's son, Ghatotkacha.'

'Good. He is a radiant child.'

At night, people from the hermitages came to visit us. They vacated some huts thatched with kusha grass for us to stay in. After days, we ate cooked food.

Yudhishtira was very happy. The soft moonlight of the month of Chaitra shone pale yellow. The fragrance of akil wood and sandalwood wafted in the air from the abodes of the sages. After her evening prayers, Draupadi smeared her forehead with sandal paste and wound flowers in her unbound hair. Small clay oil lamps burnt bright. I noticed in Draupadi's eyes a tenderness that would melt alabaster and felt as if wild birds were fluttering their wings in my ankles. I saw Yudhishtira's eyes wander over her body with desire and quickly made my calculations. No, I had to await my turn, it was still far away.

It was the next day that I set out on the journey in search of a flower that the imagination of the storytelling bards later transformed into a heroic tale. Their songs said I met Hanuman, who had lived much earlier, in the Treta yuga, on the way, and that I fought Kubera's huge army single-handed. The maids in the women's quarters added several jokes to the story to entertain the children.

It all started when the wind blew a flower into the courtyard of our thatched hut. I did not notice Draupadi pick it up and walk around the hermitages, sniffing its fragrance. When she came my way after some time, I was still gazing at the silvery gleam of the Bhagirathi flowing into the valley.

'Here, this is a sougandhika flower,' said Draupadi, holding out a small blue lotus. 'It looks ordinary, but has a beautiful, an extraordinary, fragrance. They say there is a lake below the Kadali forest where only this flower and nothing else grows.'

I did not think that was a marvel. I had seen an area in the Hidimba forest where only blue lotuses grew. But it was true, this flower did have a very unusual scent. The lake she spoke of was in Kubera's country and no one was allowed to pluck the flowers there. The sages told me that guards had been appointed to watch over the spot.

I knew that the wealthy Kubera's gardens and orchards were near Gandhamadana.

'If only I could get some of these flowers, I could use them for my puja and also …'

I understood what she wanted, but showed no great interest.

'The guards will not let anyone in. Otherwise I could have sent Nakula or Sahadeva.'

'So you want *me* to go …?'

'It's just a wish I have. Since Arjuna is not here, who else can I ask?'

I knew it was not a ruse to get rid of me. None of us ever disturbed Yudhishtira and Draupadi when they were together. And if it was a spot rich in natural beauty that she wished for on this, their fourth, honeymoon, this region was full of them.

I realized that it would probably be a journey in search of a woman's crazy dream. Still, I said, 'All right, I'll see what I can do.'

I set out, assuming that the Kadali forest was nearby, but did not come upon it until I had travelled a great distance. As I entered, guards came up to me, clamouring loudly. I told them I was just a pilgrim going to see the lake where the sougandhika flowers grew, so they did not attack me. They must have thought I was a madman, to come so far from Gandhamadana for that. Anyway, they pointed me the right way and I continued my journey.

When I finally saw the lake, I felt that I had not walked all this way in vain. The beautiful green water was filled with thousands of dark blue flowers. A fragrance so heavy hung in the air that it made me dizzy. I thought I would first have a swim, then pluck a few flowers and go back. I went down to the water and found it lukewarm. As I began to swim, something whizzed past between my legs. It wasn't a fish. I realized it was a spear that someone had thrown at me, and swam back.

I turned, careful to make no sound, surfaced above a cluster of leaves at another spot and breathed freely. There were three guards, all brown-skinned, short mountain tribals. They had the physique of the nagas, but were certainly not nagas. All of them carried long lances as weapons. I was unarmed. They were arguing about where I was likely to surface after having sunk below the water. I did not think it necessary to fight mere guards, so I swam towards the spot where they stood and went ashore. They raised their weapons threateningly.

I pretended ignorance and asked them who owned the place. They answered that the entire region, as far as the eye could reach, belonged to the wealthy Kubera, and that it was forbidden to touch even a flower growing there.

Holding myself ready for a surprise attack at any moment, I argued that the water sources on the mountain were part of nature and no one could claim them as their private wealth. I planned to grab a weapon from one of them if I had to. Before the second man raised his lance, I would plant my right foot on his navel … According to the rules, a warrior has to always be prepared.

Instead of attacking me, they began to argue noisily among themselves and with me in turn. Another man ran up and joined the group. He was taller than me and unarmed, with coppery hair that swept his neck. The other three gathered around him and continued their mutual recriminations and murmurs of protest.

The newcomer turned to me. Who was I? From where had I come and for what?

I said I was one of the pilgrims staying near the Naranarayana hermitage, and that I was a Pandava.

'Of the Pandavas of Hastinapura?' he asked, surprised.

I nodded in assent. I added truthfully that the woman with us had heard of the blue lotuses in the lake and wanted them, that I had come to pluck some. He ordered me to wait, instructed the guards to keep an eye on me and went back the way he had come.

He did not return. I had to spend the whole night shivering, seated between the lances of the guards. It would certainly not have been difficult for me to strike them down and leave the place. But the man had asked me to wait. What if ... what if Kubera himself were to come back with him? Orchards, forests filled with medicinal plants and fragrant herbs, mines – an incredibly wealthy king who lent money to other kings. A hope that I might catch a glimpse of him lurked in my mind. So I decided not to be rash.

The guards made a fire. In its glow, I could clearly make out on their faces what they thought of me for having compelled them to keep watch here. I knew they were waiting for the slightest provocation to plunge their lances into me.

Yudhishtira was safe in the precincts of a hermitage, so he had nothing to fear.

When it was daylight, I saw the tall, hefty man I had met the previous day coming back. I was astounded when I saw the people following him: Yudhishtira, Nakula, Sahadeva, Draupadi and Ghatotkacha.

Kubera's servant brought them to me and watched their reaction.

Yudhishtira said, 'Yes, this is my brother, Bhima.'

There was a rest house belonging to Kubera a short distance from the lake. The man invited us to wait there, and said he would send messengers with the news to the capital before dusk that day. Yudhishtira thanked him for his courtesy.

I remembered that I had not accomplished the task for which I had come. How had Ghatotkacha joined the group? Yudhishtira had sent Nakula and Sahadeva to search for me in all directions when I had not returned. In the forest, Sahadeva had met Ghatotkacha, who knew where Kubera's gardens and this lake were situated. Just as they were setting out with my son as their guide, the man who had left me with the guards had arrived, to find out whether the person they had caught was really a Pandava pilgrim or an enemy.

Ignoring Nakula's mocking expression, I plucked a handful of flowers and held them out to Draupadi. I thought the beauty of the lake would enchant her, that she would say something about it. But she gave Yudhishtira the flowers without so much as sniffing them. As for him, he murmured something about having had to tramp miles needlessly, just because some people were so stupid, and walked on. Ghatotkacha stayed back as if waiting for my orders.

We walked on as well. By the wayside, I saw a handful of sougandhika flowers on their stems lying abandoned on the ground.

3

I came back one day from a hunting expedition to the sound of loud laments and wails. Since our neighbours were sages, I had not expected any danger to assail us in Gandhamadana. What could this calamity be?

As I ran towards the camp, I saw that a tribal from the forest had flung Draupadi over his shoulders and my three brothers were trying to prevent him from carrying her away. The fellow kicked Sahadeva, who had fallen on the ground, and kicked him again where he had fallen.

Yudhishtira was standing in front of him, shouting, 'You rascal! If you have the guts, give me a weapon, fight and defeat me. Then you can take the woman away. That is dharma.'

Had the circumstances been different, I would have laughed. The tribal knocked down Nakula, who was looking for a chance to attack him from behind. The man was unarmed, but certainly strong.

I was excited. Here, in the middle of our long journey, was a good excuse for a duel and a suitable opponent. The fellow seemed to have realized that he had met his match in me. He let go of Draupadi and she freed herself.

Yudhishtira cursed him, 'May you be destroyed for having touched Draupadi!'

He put out his long tongue, licked his lower-lip and looked at me aggressively. He was appraising me, figuring out what I was going to do, and showing no trace of fear. I had a hunting spear about three arms long. It would be enough to split his chest. However, deciding I would kill him with my bare hands, I threw the spear near Sahadeva's feet.

We did not indulge in any formalities before the fight, nor did we conduct a puja or salute each other. Bare hands, man to man. His name was Jada. We learnt later that he had made several attempts to carry off women from hermitages.

While my brothers looked on, I endured the first few blows he dealt me, trying to assess the strength of his hands. Draupadi suppressed a lament filled with fear. Yes, I said to her silently, here is a fight for you to watch …

I moved quietly out of the way of the tribal when he charged at me again, then launched my attack. I aimed blow after blow at his chest and neck. Hitting out at him, I pushed him right up to the boundary of the hermitage. I took aim at his throat and heaved myself up. He lowered his hand to parry my blows. My left arm, that I had held ready, shot out at his right eye.

Agonised, he covered his face with his hands. I leapt onto his back, caught him by his neck, heaved him on my shoulders, then lifted him and flung him down in front of me.

Having fallen flat on his back, Jada was helpless. The next step was to kill him. It was the moment when, forgetting myself, I should have roared. Yudhishtira and Draupadi were watching me. But the impulse that should have spurred me to break his neck or his backbone refused to be awakened. An act of killing for spectators to watch … My arm dangled weakly. I could not do it.

I did not move even when Jada scrambled up with an effort. Looking into my eyes, he backed away slowly, then broke into a run.

His nail had scratched my face, and there was a blue patch on my ribs where his elbow had dug into me.

The inmates of the hermitage came running up to us. Some

of them found fault with me for having let Jada go free. They said he knew sorcery and that, disguised as a brahmin, he went to the hermitages pretending to seek alms and carried out atrocities.

Draupadi came towards me looking as if she had just woken from a nightmare. I thought she would ask me why I had not killed Jada, why I had let him go.

Yudhishtira said, 'There are tribals everywhere, to give us trouble.' He saw Ghatotkacha walking up and remarked to Nakula and Sahadeva, 'Who knows what this fellow will become when he grows up?'

Ghatotkacha spoke to Sahadeva. When he learnt what had happened, he said, 'Jada does not belong to our nishada tribe. He belongs to the asura clan. I'll see to him.'

An old brahmin said, 'You're just like him. You harass brahmins, prevent pujas from being conducted, steal women, kill cows – you're all the same.'

Someone voiced a fear: what if Jada returned with a band of companions? Others suggested that everyone move to Arshatishena's hermitage and offered to build two huts of grass there the next day.

The next day, there was a commotion. We heard people shouting that tribals had come to attack us. When we rushed out, there stood Ghatotkacha and his group. They carried axes, and ropes made of creepers and rings were slung over their shoulders. They came up to us, and Ghatotkacha said, 'We are going back to the Hidimba forest.'

He saluted Draupadi respectfully and placed a huge package wrapped in pandanus leaves before her. Then he turned to me, palms joined in obeisance, and left with his companions.

Sahadeva said, 'It must be a wild cucumber.' He bent down

and opened the package – and screamed. We saw Jada's head, blood still dripping from it.

※

There were more people in the new camp. We had to depend on the inmates of the hermitage for food. We were quite a distance from the forest, and there were not many birds we could hunt.

When I came back late one evening after wandering around, I found Draupadi in our hut with Nakula and Sahadeva, laughing about something.

My brothers made an excuse to go out as soon as I entered. I followed them.

Draupadi sniffed and said, 'There's a beautiful fragrance.'

I jested, 'Maybe you are perspiring, Draupadi.'

Happy with my quip, Draupadi looked at the peak in front of us. 'Do you know what there is on top of that peak?' she asked.

'Blue lotuses …?'

'No. Kubera's flowers. It's not a joke. I heard everyone in the hermitage talking about them. They said the flowers of this region are more beautiful than the santana flowers that grow in Heaven.'

The memory of the night I had spent with lances pointed at me when I went to pluck flowers from Kubera's garden for her was still fresh in my mind.

'We must climb that peak and look at the view. They say you can see the great Meru mountain from there,' she said.

I was at once ready to do so.

'Find out if there is a spot on top where we can sit down and rest.'

'I'll do that tomorrow.'

'Not tomorrow, the day after. The king's year ends tomorrow.'

The climb up the mountain the next day was not an easy one. I took my mace with me. I had wondered whether to take my bow and arrow as well, but decided against it. When I got to the top, I found four or five hearths, the ashes in them still warm. I presumed that foresters who had come to collect bitumen from the rocks had made the fires. I looked around, but saw no flowers. Nor did I glimpse the great Meru mountain. Still, the view from the peak was beautiful – valleys filled with mist and garlands of clouds circling the mountain ranges.

They were hiding behind the rocks. When I called out that I was not an enemy, they came out one by one. They were Kubera's servants – Maniman, a chief of the hunters and his band.

I requested them to stay away from the peak for a few days and offered them a reason: we Pandavas had to conduct some sacrificial rituals at the spot.

They hesitated and I changed my tone, 'I would not like to use force against Kubera's hunters. You have to help me make sure that will not be necessary.'

Maniman's stance continued to be challenging.

'Have you heard of Jada?' I asked.

They had.

'The vultures have not finished eating his body after I, Bhimasena, fought a duel with him.'

This challenge, highlighting a recent victory, that we normally use as a challenge during a duel, is often more useful than diplomatic words.

Maniman and his gang agreed to go away and leave the peak to us. They helped me prepare a place for Draupadi to rest. We spread wild grass over it, and hewed out steps with an axe so that she could climb to the top. By the time we finished, it had begun to grow dark.

Next morning, as I packed the food we were to take on our pleasure trip, I imagined us, Draupadi and me, together in the solitude of the mountaintop. This was not another of Draupadi's crazy dreams, for she herself had chosen the spot. When we reached the peak, Draupadi would forget about the flowers in Kubera's garden. As I wondered which war story I would tell her in order to transform the seductive enchantress in her into a lioness, she ran in like a wild dove, laughing.

'Arjuna is here! Didn't you know?' She looked thoughtfully at the packages I had made to take to the mountain. 'Tonight we can hear all about his travels.'

I undid the bundle of weapons I had left outside. By this time, Arjuna had reached the hut with Nakula and Sahadeva.

Arjuna touched my feet in obeisance. I kissed his head and welcomed him with a blessing. At night, we sat around the fire listening to Arjuna's news. He spoke first of new weapons. Arrows that had snake venom concealed in their tips or released blazing phosphorus as soon as they neared their target, powerful spear-like arrows that came back if they did not hit the opponents they were aimed at, arrows that could be used only at a specified moment, that could pierce armour crafted in iron …

Nakula wanted to see everything he had brought at once.

Yudhishtira said, 'We'll wait till tomorrow.'

Nakula threw fresh wood on the fire. What strange people inhabited the places Arjuna had seen! He said there were regions where women hunted and grew grain, while the men sat at home. There was a country where a swayamvara marriage was a game of chance – the bride would sit inside a hut and young men of marriageable age would thrust arrows through a screen. The bride would catch hold of one arrow and good luck would favour its owner.

We laughed.

Yudhishtira said, 'It could be bad luck as well!'

Draupadi asked, 'Do the lame and the blind stand in line to try their luck?'

We were astounded to hear about the ways in which people prayed in certain countries. There were places where Indra, Agni and Rudra were not worshipped. We were shocked to hear that there were people who worshipped the lingam and the yoni.

Arjuna had had no serious confrontations on the way. He fought a tribal chief named Kalakeya, that was all.

Draupadi moved. 'Tell us about it.'

Arjuna dismissed the matter lightly. 'There's nothing to tell. A tribal chief. I killed him.'

'Kalakeya ... tell us everything that happened.'

Heaping wood on the fire to make it burn brighter, Draupadi shifted so that she could see Arjuna's face more clearly.

Yudhishtira got up. He said, 'We have to go back to the Kamyaka forest.'

He explained that there were paths wide enough for chariots to move in Kamyaka, so people from Hastinapura and Panchala would find it easier to visit us. It would be more convenient for us to contact the Yadavas from there as well.

Once Yudhishtira left, Arjuna began to tell us stories about people who had hunted him. Tribals had hunted me wherever I went, but Arjuna had been chased by beautiful women. Draupadi got up, no longer interested, and went into the hut. It was my turn today to sleep with her.

Arjuna complained that he had not had any liquor. Only soma juice was available in hermitages, no rice-wine.

'What's been happening here?'

'We have been pilgrims, we visited all the sacred water-sources.'

Arjuna began to describe how liquor was made in certain regions.

Draupadi was waiting inside and almost half the night was gone, I thought. I had not noticed how quickly the hours had gone by.

Four years, and Draupadi was to be with me again.

I got up and went inside the hut. In the faint dark, I saw that she had fallen asleep. I bent down and looked at her face. There was a gentle smile on her lips.

I cleared my throat and was about to call her name when she murmured, without opening her eyes, 'The killing of Kalakeya. Tell me the story fully …'

I pulled myself up.

No, I did not desire her cold body tonight, as she lay dreaming of Arjuna.

I picked up a grass mat, went out and looked for a spot to spread it in the area around the fire where my younger brothers slept.

4

When we went back to the Kamyaka forest, sages and scholars who could predict the future came to see Yudhishtira. He found talking to them both entertainment and relaxation.

As we approached Hastinapura, memories of all the good things we had lost began to haunt us. A brahmin messenger brought us the news that all was well with Mother. Vidura had sent a servant woman for Draupadi through him and two attendants for us. Meanwhile, the messenger we had dispatched to Dwaraka returned and told us that Subhadra and Abhimanyu were well.

Vidura also sent word that he feared Duryodhana was going to perform the Rajasooya sacrifice and become more powerful.

'What should we do?'

'Our period of exile in the forest is nearly over. We have another year in which we have to live incognito somewhere.'

My beloved Sahadeva said innocently, as if plucking the thought from my mind, 'When it is over and we go back, what if Shakuni invites us once more for a game of dice, cheats and wins? It will be the forest again!'

Many days later, Krishna came. He embraced Arjuna and saluted Yudhishtira and me respectfully. Madri's sons paid him obeisance. Arjuna and he were meeting after a long interval; they held hands and went out.

Satyabhama had come with Krishna, which made Draupadi very happy. The two women stayed inside the hut and began to talk, or rather, murmur and giggle softly.

When Krishna and Arjuna came back, it was obvious they had been celebrating their reunion.

Krishna said, 'You have the full support of the Yadavas. I have told Arjuna where you should spend the year you must remain unrecognized.'

'Must we complete that year?'

'Yes. It was one of the conditions. The place is the kingdom of Virata. King Virata has wealth and a strong army, and by the time the year is over, I am sure he would have become your relation. I have explained it all to Arjuna in detail.'

When Krishna left with his retinue, the surroundings seemed silent and forlorn.

Messengers came again from Hastinapura. They said, 'King Dhritarashtra laments the fate of the Pandavas in the forest from time to time and scolds his evil-minded sons.'

I glanced at Arjuna. So the blind man was still playing his role. I had never forgotten how much he had enjoyed watching his sons win at the gambling sessions.

As royal custom demanded, Yudhishtira asked, 'Is my benevolent Uncle well? And my Aunt Gandhari?'

I could more or less guess the reason for the old man's grief. The Drupadas and the Yadavas had amassed greater armies. I hinted to my brothers that he was possibly even more upset by Arjuna's journeys. He must fear that Arjuna had learnt the secrets of divine weapons and military strategies that the people of Hastinapura knew nothing about. Arjuna agreed this might be true.

'I'll tell you why he doesn't have the courage to conduct a Rajasooya sacrifice,' said Sahadeva. 'No monarch will acknowledge a Rajasooya performed by a king who has not defeated the Pandavas.'

None of us had forgotten how Draupadi was dragged to the gambling hall while she was having her period and shamefully humiliated. It was like a dagger-wound dealt in war that would never heal, a wound that each of us nursed in solitude.

Yudhishtira consoled us, 'The great scholar and sage,

Markandeya, said recently that we are going to have better times. Here comes Dhoumya. He can see into the future as well.'

It was a habit of Yudhishtira's to ascribe all the misfortunes that had befallen us to an evil destiny, to the curse on the Kuru clan – a curse that I had often thought affected the whole land of Bharata. None of us argued with him, there was no point. He always cited some ancient tale involving a divine command to explain a death, a birth, defeat or victory. I would not be surprised if another gambling session were to take place …

All I said was, 'We have seen sacred spots, holy water sources, innumerable forests. It would be best now to ask Dhoumya what sort of good deeds we should perform over the next twelve years.'

Dhoumya remained silent.

Ignoring my ironic tone, Yudhishtira said, 'What is the aim of staying alive? To perform good deeds and attain Heaven. That is the ultimate and sole objective of every human being.'

Sahadeva said he did not know what Heaven was.

'Heaven is only for those who abide by righteousness, those who are in control of themselves and always calm, those who are charitable, those who give alms and the courageous – that is what I have heard our grandfather, Krishnadvaipayana, say. He codified the scriptures, after all, so no one knows these things better than he does.'

Dhoumya nodded in agreement.

Yudhishtira continued to enrich our knowledge, 'There are celestial gardens above Meru, spread over thousands and thousands of miles … Are you listening?'

'Yes, yes.'

Nakula and Sahadeva moved nearer. Arjuna stopped his task of tying feathers to arrows.

Draupadi, who was standing at the door, showed an unusual interest in what Yudhishtira was saying: 'Go on, tell us. I really want to hear.'

Yudhishtira was happy: for once, all the members of his family wanted to share his knowledge.

'In the celestial gardens, no one feels hunger or thirst; nothing wilts, there is no grief or cold or heat or fear. They are filled with beautiful fragrances and enchanting melodies. There is no fatigue, no tears, nothing wears out. There is no perspiration, no foul odour, no urine or faeces. The flowers there have a divine scent and never fade. Dust never settles on garments ...

'There are different worlds there, like the caste systems we have here. The sages attain the world of the brahmins and the world of the gods is above that. No one competes for wealth, women do not provoke trouble. The food served there is nectar. There are only celestial beings in that divine world, over which our thirty-three gods rule. There is no grief or delight or pleasure there. All intelligent people who attain Heaven reach the feet of the gods.

'Such are the qualities of Heaven. I will now tell you what the flaws are. Everyone has to endure the consequences of their deeds, even in Heaven. If the garlands they are wearing wither, they will have to return to Earth and be born again from a human womb.

'The world of Brahma is beyond that of the gods. All flaws continue to exist until this world is left behind. There is only one world where there are no flaws and that is where Vishnu's feet rest, beyond the world of Brahma. It is pure, radiant, eternal.

Those who are trapped in sensual desires will never attain it. Only those who renounce their senses and accept death while in deep meditation can attain it ...'

We listened to him attentively. I knew I would never reach the feet of Vishnu. I was bound in sensual desires. But when I thought of the other Heavens ...

A Heaven without hunger or perspiration ... I voiced a doubt. 'Has anyone ever renounced Heaven?'

Dhoumya answered my question. 'Yes, once. A great sage named Mulgala.'

'Why did he do so?'

Dhoumya did not know. Yudhishtira continued to speak of sinful deeds and good ones until we got up to go for evening prayers.

The next day, a messenger sent by Vidura came hurrying in a chariot drawn by a single horse. He talked to Yudhishtira.

Duryodhana knew we were in Kamyaka. He planned to come this way, leading a huge procession, with Karna, Shakuni, his brothers and his family. Cooks, musicians and prostitutes would accompany them. Once a year, kings generally organized a procession of this kind in order to round up and drive away the cattle in the forest.

'Vidura says we must be very careful,' said Yudhishtira.

'The Kauravas want go past us in procession, parading their pomp and prestige, while we live here like forest tribals, isn't it?' asked Nakula resentfully.

I was not sure that was all they wanted. If a confrontation took place here, no one outside would know. No one would bother about five dead bodies lying in the Kamyaka forest. Even if they were identified as the Pandavas, people would assume that dacoits or tribals had killed them.

Arjuna agreed with me. 'People often die after being hit by stray arrows while the forest is being agitated during such processions.'

Yudhishtira said, 'Let's go on with our routine as usual. If they come here, we will behave as if this exile in the forest has not affected us, and receive them with pleasure. The scriptures say that, no matter who he is, a guest should be welcomed with five gifts: first, their feet must be washed, then they must be given your eyes, ears, hearts and food. That is the rule.' He plucked out the little cottonseeds that clung to his ash-and-black deerskin garment and threw them away.

We decided that the four of us would stand at four different spots and keep track of the Kauravas' movements.

One day, we heard shouts, the clang of weapons and the clatter of horses' hooves in the distance. We listened attentively. No, they were not coming in this direction. The sounds faded away.

That night, however, we heard human voices. Half asleep, I scrambled awake hastily. Draupadi asked me something, but I picked up my mace and spear and rushed out without stopping to answer her. I saw Arjuna standing outside, stringing his bow. By the faint glow of the fire smouldering in a pit, we saw three soldiers walking towards us with their arms stretched out, to show that they were not coming to fight us. Nakula and Sahadeva arrived and stoked the fire till it blazed.

They were Duryodhana's soldiers. They knelt in front of Yudhishtira, who had arrived last, and saluted him.

'Save us!'

Our raised spears and strung bows kept watch over them.

They told us they were neither spies nor enemies. During the procession, Duryodhana and his band had encountered a soldier from some distant country. In the mood for some amusement, Duryodhana had ordered that he be tied up. The Kauravas had not realized that Chitrasena's followers had halted by the side of a lake nearby to rest. Before they could take out their weapons, the Kauravas were surrounded and taken prisoners.

Chitrasena and his followers would leave early morning with the Kauravas they had made prisoners. The soldiers had come with a request for help.

'This is a disgrace for Hastinapura and for the whole Kuru clan. We beseech the magnanimous Pandavas to come to our rescue.'

'Chitrasena made Duryodhana and his gang his prisoners even though Karna was with them? Incredible! Who is this Chitrasena?'

The soldiers were sure Chitrasena and his followers were sorcerers. Their military strategies were bizarre. They could even disappear at will.

The five of us moved aside to discuss the matter.

'Chitrasena did what we should have done. We should salute him, congratulate him, make an ally of him. What else can we do?' Arjuna laughed.

I too thought we should send the soldiers away now, go to sleep and meet Chitrasena in the morning.

But Yudhishtira would not take part in our rejoicing. 'We might quarrel or be enemies. But is it dharma if we stand and watch some lowdown rascal attack a clan related to us? That's what we should consider.'

Arjuna said, 'I know this Chitrasena. If my guess is correct, he is a close relative of Chitrangada's father. He is not a sorcerer or an outcaste or a tribal.'

Visibly uneasy, Yudhishtira ran his fingers through his long beard and stood looking at the ground. 'True, Duryodhana committed a grave sin against us. Still, I think we should help him.'

Madri's sons raised their voices together in protest.

My elder brother looked at me. 'You have to decide.'

I was in a dilemma. 'To me, this is not a question of dharma or mercy or family prestige.'

Clenching and unclenching his fists, Yudhishtira paced up and down. 'Which of us will look more powerful, they or us, when people learn that the Pandavas, who suffered so much at their hands, went to their aid when they were in danger? This is not just a matter of dharma, political strategy is also involved.'

It struck me suddenly that my elder brother was no weakling. He was not a coward either, wandering aimlessly in the forest, finding fault with fate after having lost everything through his own folly. He could still hold his head up proudly, like a king.

I said to Arjuna, 'He is right, what Yudhishtira says is right.'

Arjuna set out at once. He returned next evening, with Chitrasena and four soldiers. Duryodhana stood behind them, his hands bound with wild creepers, his head bent, a prisoner. He wore no ornaments, carried no weapons.

Chitrasena instructed his followers to untie the knots on Duryodhana's hands. They cut off the leather strap that bound his ankles. Duryodhana continued to stand with his head bent, rubbing the blue marks on his wrists.

Yudhishtira said, 'Duryodhana, never do anything so rash again. Go back quickly to Hastinapura.'

Duryodhana walked away hurriedly without thanking or saluting us.

Chitrasena smiled. 'I wanted to set him free in your presence. I have heard about his atrocities.'

We asked Chitrasena what he knew about Duryodhana's journey to this place. He told us that Chitravahana, Chitrangada's father, had suspected that the Kauravas would attack us during the procession, and had sent Chitransena to Kamyaka with soldiers and asked him to wait there, pretending he was on a pleasure trip.

We were filled with enthusiasm. We, the Pandavas, were not alone, our friends and relatives in various places were thinking of us, safeguarding us. Indraprastha was not just a village that had sprung up in the forest.

Chitrasena embraced Arjuna once more, saluted us, and declined to accept our offers of hospitality gently and affectionately. He went back with his soldiers.

I looked at Yudhishtira. He was trying to hide a smile.

5

Duryodhana had conducted an elaborate puja in which many kings took part, though it was not a Rajasooya. Karna had visited several countries and requested them to give the Kauravas armies and assistance if they should need them. He had been received everywhere as if he had won glorious victories. A brahmin who came from Hastinapura brought us this news.

'What he said must be correct. He is a paid spy appointed by our Uncle Vidura.' Yudhishtira smiled and added, 'We have spies now in several places.'

Once again, Yudhishtira surprised me. When he was seated with the sages, looking at the positions of the planets and predicting the future, when he spoke sadly of his unhappy circumstances, it seemed as if he had grown as old as a grandfather. His soft voice enunciated words slowly, thoughtfully. He often walked around muttering, as if he was talking to himself. But sometimes, when his face reddened and he raised his eyes to the sky, he looked invincible.

When a second incident occurred, we began to wonder whether the Kamyaka forest was turning into an abode for our enemies.

Yudhishtira had gone to see the sage Bhadra in his hermitage at the time, and the four of us were out hunting in the forest.

Draupadi had gone to the forest as well with her maid, to look for flowers with pollen so that they could be ground along with sandal paste. A king who had come to the forest to hunt thought she was some beautiful tribal girl and sent a soldier to fetch her. Draupadi scolded him roundly and sent him away. Then she did something silly: instead of going back to the hermitage quickly, the two women continued to wander around the forest. This time, the hunter came to fetch her himself.

Declaring she was no nishada woman, Draupadi told him who she was.

The king laughed. 'So much the better,' he said. 'Then you can stay in the women's quarters in my palace.'

A scuffle followed. The maid ran screaming to find one of us and tell us what had happened. Only Dhoumya was in the hermitage. I heard him cursing and the maid's lament. I was then chasing a wild rabbit the way Hidimbi had taught me, an exercise that helped me maintain strength and speed during this period of exile in the forest.

I climbed up some rocks and saw what had happened. Draupadi had just broken free of her captor's hands and was trying to jump out of his chariot, which had begun to move. Arjuna arrived at the same moment from another direction. He often used to say he could scent danger even before he saw or heard it.

I leapt down from the rocks. In minutes, I shouldered aside a soldier who had drawn his sword, gripped the whip lying around the charioteer's neck tight, lifted him high, flung him to the ground and vaulted into the chariot. The captor let go of Draupadi and jumped down. Grabbing a chariot that was rushing to his help, he managed to clamber into it. The charioteer turned the horses around skilfully and spurred them away, but fell prey to the single arrow Arjuna unerringly aimed at him. Draupadi had been saved, but we could not let the wicked fellow get away. He had no idea that, no matter what obscure trail he followed in the forest, I would be able to catch up with his chariot. I knew Dhoumya would take care of Draupadi. And Arjuna was more than a match for whatever supporters the fellow might have left behind.

No one could drive a chariot at great speed over the rough, winding trails in the forest. I ran faster than a boar, trampling the dense thickets. Arriving at a point ahead of them, I waited behind a huge ashwata tree. Before the horses could turn the bend and extend their necks, I sprang, shouting, into the middle of the path. The man caught the reins tight, but the horses reared, unable to hold their balance. He was confused, undecided whether to try and control the horses or confront me. Before he could let go of the reins and pick up his bow and arrow, I pulled him out and flung him on the ground. He scrambled up, but I dug my elbows into his chest. I could have stopped with that. But I caught hold of his leather belt, to which tiny golden bells were stitched, and dragged him to our camp. Arjuna too had arrived by then.

Upset that they had come too late, Nakula and Sahadeva took charge of the prisoner and bound his hands behind him.

What about his soldiers and helpers?

Arjuna said, 'I let them off and sent back both chariots with the charioteer's corpse.'

Yudhishtira joined us, saw the prisoner and exclaimed in surprise, 'The prince of Sindhu?'

Fuming with anger, Jayadratha looked at each of us in turn.

Jayadratha, the prince of Sindhu, who had married Dusshala, the sister of the Kauravas. It was the first time I was seeing him. Duryodhana's brother-in-law. To mark the joyous occasion, I boxed his ears over and over with the back of my hand. I would give him the five traditional gifts meant for a guest later.

Yudhishtira said, 'Don't, Bhimasena, don't …'

'This new incarnation of Ravana dared to carry Draupadi away in his chariot. Why show him mercy?'

Jayadratha's eyes were full of resentment.

I lunged to hit him again, and Yudhishtira commanded sharply: 'Don't!'

I was furious. 'I have killed brainless tribals for lesser reasons.'

Arjuna was troubled as well by Yudhishtira's attitude. He suggested we make the culprit admit his guilt, then let him go. Sahadeva wanted his head to be shaved. Nakula felt that five small tufts should be left on his head when he was shaven, to proclaim that he was a wrongdoer.

I said, 'We'll let him go once he arranges for a hundred horses and a thousand cows to be sent here to us. Send a messenger to the kingdom of Sindhu with a message clearly dictated by the fellow himself.'

Sahadeva thought it would be a bother to look after this man for the time it took to do this, and began to sharpen an arrow with a crescent shaped head on a stone, in order to shave off his hair. No one tried to stop him. The twins cut off his tuft. Jayadratha did not move.

Yudhishtira unbound his hands himself, then said to him, 'Tell Dusshala we asked after her welfare. I show you mercy because of her, not because I fear the prince of Sindhu.'

It would have been far better to kill him than show him mercy, but much time would pass before we realized that.

As the naga had said to me, no enemy deserves mercy. If he is shown mercy, he grows so strong that he becomes invincible, then attacks us again.

We forgot Jayadratha very soon, since another messenger arrived from Krishna. The same day, a soota who was one of Vidura's spies turned up as well.

Yudhishtira sent for all four of us after the evening prayers.

The period of exile in the forest would come to an end the fourth day after the next full moon. If we set out right away, we would reach the kingdom of Virata in time. The five of us had to arrive there separately, taking great care that we were not recognized, since innumerable monarchs had been witnesses to the verdict that we had to spend a year of exile incognito. We needed to be clear about what job each of us would ask for in Virata.

Yudhishtira said, 'The king likes playing dice. I will be an ideal attendant when he plays.'

Nakula and Sahadeva smiled.

Yudhishtira continued, 'Virata loves music and dance and has a huge dance hall. Arjuna can teach music and dance there. If he can play the role of a person who is neither a man nor a woman, so much the better.'

Seeing in this suggestion an opportunity to live peacefully in the women's quarters, Arjuna said, 'So I must take care to be clean shaven and use perfumes to keep my body fragrant. I will have to cover my head and be sure that my breath smells sweet when I speak. My hips must sway when I walk. Easy!'

I knew that eunuchs worked as guards in certain palaces. We had not had any in Hastinapura, but, as a child, I had heard the attendants in the elephant sheds crack obscene jokes about them.

Yudhishtira spoke of Nakula next. He was to ask for a job as a groom in the stables, as he could assess the qualities of horses and had learnt how to train them.

Sahadeva, who had no particular expertise, could work in the cattle sheds.

Draupadi joined us at that point. Yudhishtira continued to talk about Sahadeva. Virata would have countless workers in the cattle sheds, he said, no one would notice if one of them was inexperienced. 'All of us must say that we worked under Yudhishtira at Indraprastha. So it will be easy to answer if they ask questions about Hastinapura or Indraprastha. I can talk truthfully about Yudhishtira's likes and dislikes and even about his stupidities.'

Still looking very serious, Yudhishtira said, 'Krishna has already requested Virata to employ a group of people who left Yudhishtira's service when he fell upon evil days. So none of you need worry that you will be rejected.'

'What about Draupadi?' asked Nakula.

'She must say she was the servant woman of Draupadi, the wife of the Pandavas. She will grind smooth, sweet-scented sandal paste for Virata's wife and live as one of her serving women.'

Sahadeva reminded our elder brother that he had not mentioned me as yet.

Yudhishtira looked at Sahadeva seriously. 'Do I have to tell you what our blockhead, Vrikodara, will do? He'll be a cook, of course!'

All of us, except Yudhishtira, laughed. He went on in the same grave tone: 'During a game of dice, I might be given the remains of what the king ate. It would be useful for the cook to keep that in mind.'

When we all laughed again, Yudhishtira abandoned his mock-serious attitude and laughed with us.

It was not merely the thought that our exile in the forest was coming to an end that made us so light-hearted. We were going to live in a palace once more.

The day in Kamyaka had begun unpleasantly and, at one point, it had seemed as if the danger that lurked around us would end in calamity. However, it ended in laughter.

In spite of this, when I went to bed, I could not forget Jayadratha's eyes, full of snake venom. We had one more enemy to fear among the Kauravas – Duryodhana's brother-in-law, who had to flee with his five small tufts.

PART 6

THE KINGDOM OF VIRATA

1

During our sojourn in Virata, I realized once again that physical strength could be both a blessing and a curse.

I entered Virata as Vallava, who had once been the chief cook in Yudhishtira's palace.

A cook can move around the palace when he has no work, even as far as the immediate vicinity of the women's quarters. And no one would think it suspicious if Virata's wife's maid, Malini, talked to one of the cooks for a while. Nor would any of the other maids feel jealous if the lovely Malini spoke to Vallava, the cook with the uncouth body, dishevelled coppery hair and unkempt beard in his filthy black clothes. I could meet Sahadeva in the cattle sheds sometimes and Nakula in the stables. But it was difficult to meet Yudhishtira alone.

Virata, the king of the Matsya kingdom, was even more passionate about gambling than Yudhishtira had said he was. Kanka, his new attendant, enjoyed his job very much and often won more games than the king did. Once, when Yudhishtira and I had some time to ourselves, he told me that he sometimes allowed the king to win so as to not upset him.

Princess Uttara's mansion was adjacent to the main wing of the palace, and the dance hall was next to it. Quarters had been arranged just beyond the hall for Brihannala, who had come to teach music and dance.

In the beginning, Draupadi did not have too many complaints. She told me that Queen Sudeshna noticed how clean and discreet her new servant woman was and had begun to treat her like a companion. She added that the queen's brother, who often came to see his sister, looked at her maid meaningfully.

'That's not unusual when the maid is so beautiful,' I said, as if it was a trivial matter. 'In many places, servant women are meant for the queen's brothers or grown-up sons to enjoy.'

'Such a thing would never have been allowed in King Drupada's palace.'

But this was Virata's palace.

Draupadi said she had come to know that the maids were competing among themselves to please Nakula, and she felt sorry for Sahadeva.

Draupadi had told everyone that she had a husband, hoping that married women would not be called upon to entertain the men of the palace.

'Do you get news of Kanka?' I asked her.

'His private wealth has increased over these four months.'

I laughed, 'Do you think Virata will wager his country?'

Soon, it was time for the annual festival in the kingdom. A stage was built in the palace courtyard. Magicians, acrobats, singers and dancers arrived. There were wrestlers as well. All of them displayed their skills and competed for prizes.

Young men in Virata's army with brawn and muscle were sent to the arena to compete with the visiting athletes. One of the visitors, a fellow who wore bracelets on his arms and wrists, stood apart contemptuously and would not enter the arena. Apparently, he had said boastfully that he did not think he would find an opponent who would be a match for him here, and did not like the idea of claiming too easy a victim with the strength of his hands.

I was among the servants who went to watch the wrestling bouts.

The cross-eyed store-keeper needled me. 'This Vallava can fight him; he'll be a perfect match in brawn.'

The king too, wondering how he could arrange to witness the prowess of that aloof and defiant wrestler, thought for some reason of his cook.

I was summoned. I stood respectfully before the king, bowing low. I said I had learnt quite a bit about wrestling when I was a child, but had forgotten the moves when I became a cook.

The king looked at my massive frame and said, 'Just keep him at bay for a while, after that you can accept defeat and withdraw. From what I hear, even defeat at the hands of this Jeemootha will bring you fame.'

They saw that I was about to give in. Attendants crowded around me at once, removed my black kitchen clothes and fastened a tiger-skin around my waist. One of them helped me knot my hair. The kitchen workers and other servants came out to watch me get ready.

Nirathan, the oldest among them, tapped my chest and said, 'I wager five silver coins on Vallava. Anyone to better that?'

I stepped into the arena solely to please King Virata. Jeemootha looked at me approvingly and smiled in consent.

He began by dealing me a blow with his flat palm to gauge

my strength. Slowing down deliberately, I let him give me quite a few blows. Watching his stances and moves, I guessed that his style was yavana. Which meant that he could topple me over any moment, and I had to guard the calves of my legs. A wrestler assesses his opponent in the confrontations of head with head, hand with hand, shoulder with shoulder. Jeemootha's yavana style was the same as ours, performed with the ankles.

Out of the corner of my eye, I saw a group of women lining up on one side of the arena, Draupadi among them. I pretended to be defeated when Jeemootha first hit me on my chest with his hands, and again when he tried to pull me towards him. The kitchen workers began to chide and encourage Vallava by turns. I could distinguish Nirathan's voice clearly: he used words that showed he had forgotten it was a royal arena.

When we began a fist-fight, I invoked all my strength into my hands, and watched astonishment spread over Jeemootha's face. The onlookers were delighted. Nirathan began to shout. Before Jeemootha could overcome his surprise and change his strategy, I attacked his neck. My massive right hand caught him neatly below his left ear and he staggered.

'Kill him!' That must have been Nirathan shouting.

I held in my chest and neck and dealt him the next blow with my elbow; he bent over. He twisted his body, expecting another blow. I grasped his neck, threw him off balance, lifted him by the hips and twirled him rapidly. I dug my big toes into the ground, raised my feet, shook him by his shoulders, then flung him down. I wiped my hands as he landed in front of me. The spectators roared in appreciation.

Overjoyed, the king ordered that I be given a hundred coins. I was surrounded by a group of people who obviously did not believe I was just an old athlete who had once learnt these fighting skills and forgotten them. Murmuring that I owed my victory solely to the blessings of my ancestors, I walked quietly away.

Draupadi ran up to me. 'You should have killed him! Only then will everyone begin to fear Vallava.'

'This was only intended to entertain Virata, wasn't it? Besides, he is not my enemy, so why would I kill him? What I did was enough.'

I walked to the kitchen.

After this, the chief of the kitchen staff never found fault with anything I did, never complained that I was idle. I was served special dishes, and not scolded if I went out wandering for long periods.

A few more wrestlers who had heard of Jeemootha's defeat came looking for me. I evaded them, saying I was not prepared to try my luck again.

Unlike other capital cities, the houses in Virata were scattered, rather than built close together. The king's attendants told me he had 40,000 cows. There were several cow sheds in the forest, and a villager supervised the cowherds. Sahadeva worked in one of the five cowsheds between the low palace wall and the wall of the fort. I went looking for him there one day, but did not find him.

I went out through the door of the fort. The guards smiled affectionately at me and asked me how I was. Vallava had become famous. Before we had changed our garments and entered the palace under various names, we had tied our weapons to the branches of a tall tree that grew quite far from the highway. Sahadeva had hung a skeleton he found in the forest on one of the branches, so that shepherds, fearing the ghost of the man who had hanged himself on the tree, would avoid walking that way.

I made certain no one was around and climbed the tree. The skeleton still hung from a branch. I checked to see whether the weapons I had wrapped in an animal skin pouch and tucked into a cleft where three branches met were still there. I picked up my bow with the handle worked in gold, my dagger in its tiger-skin sheath and the iron mace Mayan had made for me and held them in my hands. I made sure the bundles containing my brothers' weapons were safe as well. When I returned to the kitchen, the servants there joked with one another, hinting that I must have gone to visit some woman who lived outside the palace.

I waited near the women's quarters at dusk to meet Draupadi. She told me that Sahadeva had come earlier to deliver some cows that were to be given to the brahmins as gifts. She looked upset.

'Sahadeva looks weak and tired. Mother had entrusted him to me when we started out for the forest, telling me I must look after him as if he were my son. What can I do now?'

She lamented the fate of Arjuna, who had to teach Virata's daughters. He was forced to wear silk and cover his head like a eunuch. How low Partha, who was the equal of Indra, had fallen!

'What amazes me is that the girls love this teacher who is neither a man nor a woman!'

Her complaint about Nakula was that he made no effort to find a chance to speak to her.

'What is Queen Sudeshna like?' I asked.

She showed me her hands. 'Can't you see? My hands are calloused because I'm eternally grinding sandal paste – what a job for the daughter of King Drupada! I wonder whether our dice player, Kanka, has any idea about all the miseries I endure.' She saw some servant women coming that way and quickly moved off.

I had realized why Krishna advised us to come to Virata's palace. The king was frank and open-minded. The army was not very well trained, but had the strength of numbers. Since the army chief treated his soldiers as if they were simple cowherds, many of them were not active or vigorous. But I saw they had fire in them and that all that had to be done was ignite that fire. Dwaraka and Virata were on very friendly terms. Virata was certainly the best place to prepare for a war.

One or two serving women came at night to find out whether I was comfortable. Neither of them evoked any emotion in me. I wondered whether they had asked each other afterwards whether the wrestler, Vallava, was impotent. After I sent the third one away as well without even touching her, no one came to bother me.

The queen's brother, Keechaka, the commander-in-chief of the army, was travelling during the time of the festival. He sent for me when he got back. I presented myself respectfully before him. Black as granite, Keechaka was a good five fingers taller than I was. His eyes were reddened by liquor, his eyelids puffy, his voice hoarse. He cast a glance over my body and nodded as if to express approval.

He said to the followers who stood behind him, 'He's enough to warm my hands with when they feel numb. Go along now. I'll call you when I need you.'

Over the next few days, I was so busy in the kitchen night and day that I had no time to meet Draupadi. We had to send food from the kitchen for about a hundred people who had come with Keechaka.

One day, as I was going back to the kitchen after having selected the goats to slaughter, a maid came and said to me, 'Malini wants to see you.'

Virata and the queen used to come at night to the dance hall to watch their daughters execute the dance steps Brihannala had taught them. I said I would wait outside the hall at that time.

I looked on as torches soaked in ghee and the small stone oil lamps on the walls of the hall were lighted. The veena and mridangam were being tuned. As soon as I heard the tinkle of ankle-bells and the sound of dancers' feet moving in time to the music, I went to the dimly lit yard at the back.

Draupadi was waiting there.

'Keechaka keeps pestering me. I can't bear it any more. He offers me enticements: a hundred gold coins, servants to attend on me, a chariot drawn by mares.'

'Tell the queen about him.'

'I don't trust her. I gave her several hints. She says it's disgraceful, unjust and so on. But every time he comes to see his sister, she insists I attend on her.'

'What about speaking to Yudhishtira? He could tell the king about it.'

Once Draupadi began to lament her misfortunes, there was no stopping her. She would recall her childhood in Drupada's capital, then go on to her humiliation in the gambling hall and the sojourn in the forest. So I quickly said to console her: 'I'll deal with it. I must go back now, I have work in the kitchen.'

Next day, I hung around the hall where the king played dice, hoping to find an opportunity to meet my elder brother and tell him about the matter. I saw Draupadi going by herself to the commander-in-chief's house carrying the big silver pot in which liquor was served. The pot was obviously empty. If she wanted to fill it with liquor, the store was nearer the kitchen.

I waited for her to come out. Meanwhile, I saw Kanka lose one game with the king and win two. The sound of the dice rattling in their case brought back a nightmare that had been lying dormant – the gambling hall in Hastinapura. The murmur of the spectators, the rattle of the dice, Dussasana dragging Draupadi by her hair. Drops of blood dripping on the cold white marble floor. Laughing eyes lengthening into bloody beaks that feasted on corpses ...

My thoughts whirled wildly as the lions I had laid to sleep raised their heads and the sound of their roars echoed within me. The muscles of my hands rippled.

Draupadi came running out, gasping, Keechaka close behind. He reached out and grabbed her hair. The same Draupadi, clutching her waist-cloth so it would not slip down. The same dice ...

Draupadi screamed. Keechaka kicked her as she fell. I could not hear what he said to her. Yudhishtira was in front of me, barring my way, as I ran up to her. I lunged forward to grab the long silver-handled hunting spear that hung on the wall as a decoration, and heard Yudhishtira's voice chiding me, 'Fool, that's not meant for the kitchen. Look elsewhere for firewood.'

The king had come up as well.

Draupadi scrambled up, weeping and said: 'The queen sent me to fetch liquor. This man ...'

Keechaka muttered something about the chastity of women servants, turned and walked away.

The king said, 'Find some other place for your bothersome activities. Let's go on with the game.'

His head bent, Yudhishtira walked to the hall behind the king. Draupadi glanced at him, then stared at me, her eyes wide. Then she walked to the other side of the courtyard and disappeared behind the pillars.

That night, Draupadi came to me as I lay in the kitchen wing. I did not hear her footsteps. It was her familiar perfume that woke me. She sat down near me.

'Didn't you see? Didn't all of you stand there and watch?'

She leant her head on my shoulder and hot tears flowed over my chest.

'There is no one else I can share my sorrow with. Even if the dice player sees something happen before his eyes, he pretends he has not seen it. As for our heroic warrior, he is so busy watching Virata's daughters giggle, he has no time to listen to me …'

I tried my best to comfort her. We were all helpless. I reminded her that if anyone recognized us in the course of this crucial year, we would be condemned again to exile in the forest. Even my massive arms, strong as iron pestles, were mortgaged now.

'What can I do?' I asked.

Draupadi got up and stood beside me, gasping. 'I'll tell you what you should do. Thrash that Keechaka, beat him up until he is shattered like an earthen pot broken to smithereens on a rock. I don't know when or how you can do it. If he is still alive at sunrise the day after tomorrow, I will consume poison and fall dead in this kitchen yard, I swear I will!'

I kept thinking. Distressed though I was, a ruse took shape in my mind.

'Smile at Keechaka when you see him tomorrow morning. Tell him you ran away because you were afraid people would go and tell your husband about him and you. Invite him to come to the deserted dance hall at night.'

She could not follow.

'The dance hall is the best place. No sound can be heard outside. Charm him and get him to come there alone. It is I who will welcome him when he arrives. Go now and don't worry.'

On her face blossomed a smile as radiant as the sun that comes out after rain. Next evening, at dusk, when the girls who had been dancing all day left the hall, I went in and took a look. There was an iron cot at one end, a convenient spot. When I came out, I saw Draupadi passing by with a flower basket. There were a few other servant women with her. She threw me a look that silently said: 'All is safe!'

Once the darkness of the new moon night spread through the yard, I entered the empty dance hall and extinguished one by one the little lamps that were still filled with oil. The iron cot protested softly as I laid my weight on it.

I felt very calm. I was going to enjoy this act of killing. In darkness like this, there was no need to abide by rules. I thought of the style which those who teach wrestling call paishachika, a fight in which even the teeth and nails are used.

It took what seemed like aeons for an hour to pass. Then I heard footsteps. He hesitated, then moved forward. I caught the perfume of musk mixed in sandal paste. He must have smeared it plentifully on himself to efface the stench of liquor. It was Keechaka all right. One of the talents I was proud of was being able to see in the dark. I saw the white of the flowers wound in his hair, the glint of the red stones in his earrings and the sheen of the gold bangles on his wrists.

He saw my shape like a shadow and called out softly, 'Malini …?'

I shifted my position on the cot. He laughed gently, happy that the beautiful servant girl had kept her word. He bent down and I grabbed his hair. I suddenly wished I could have spoken in Draupadi's voice. To round off the play-acting, I said in my gruff voice, 'I, a servant woman, have never seen a man as handsome as you!'

Instantly sensing danger, Keechaka caught hold of my hand and made an effort to free himself. His fists fell like sharp nails on my body, but I did not let go of his hair.

He tried then to hold me in a tight grip and squeeze the breath out of me. His teeth sank into my neck.

Keechaka was strong, stronger than Hidimba and Jata, but was nothing compared to Jarasandha. This knowledge gave me courage.

I let go of his hair and caught his mouth and nose together in a tight grip and the teeth embedded in the flesh of my neck slid out. I next caught hold of his waist. He kicked my ankles forcefully. I did not slacken my hold on him. Most unexpectedly, he attacked my chest with his head and I slumped down.

Keechaka was gasping and muttering to himself. When he saw that I had fallen, he bent down with a joyful grunt, in order to lift me up and fling me down again. This was exactly what I was waiting for. I gripped his neck and threw him backwards.

I leapt on his chest and used all my strength to pull away the arms that were trying to save his neck.

He asked, 'Who are you? I am Keechaka, the commander-in-chief of the army!'

'I am a gandharva, the servant woman's gandharva husband!' I growled.

Keechaka had an instant to remember the servant woman who had tricked him. In that instant, his arms weakened and mine descended on his throat. The blows he aimed at my chest and ribs grew weaker. As his tautened muscles slackened, my arms sank deeper on his throat, crushing his windpipe and shattering it. A faint sound like the cry of a wild bird was all that escaped him.

I stood up. I was gasping, but had not collapsed.

A gentle footfall, a tinkle of ankle-bells, a fragrance I knew.

'Draupadi,' I called out.

I picked up the almost extinguished wick of an oil lamp that I had hidden in a small opening high in the doorway, and threw it on the torn pieces of cloth left behind by the girls who had used them to wipe off the deep red dye that dancers use on their palms and feet. A long upper cloth lying among them caught fire at once.

Draupadi saw me in its glow. She looked at Keechaka lying on the floor. She came up to me and wiped the blood oozing from my shoulder. By the light of the fire that was now blazing, I saw her moist lips part.

Her nails dug into my wrists, then into my body.

I did not think about whose turn it was during this year when we had to live in exile unrecognized.

The rags were slowly burning out. But the fire in Draupadi's body had just started to blaze.

2

The servant women of the palace went around saying that Keechaka had been slain by a gandharva, but none of the men believed this. I felt that suspicious glances were being directed at me. Playing the role of dull-witted Vallava, I pretended to be as astonished as everyone else.

No one had heard the sounds of a duel. The commander-in-chief had gone to sleep in his own palace, and his corpse had been discovered next morning in the empty dance hall. Obviously, Keechaka could not have been easily vanquished. Eventually, people decided that only a gandharva who wanted to avenge some grievance carried over from a past life could have been the villain.

The palace calmed down. Kanka and the king went back to their gambling. The girls who were learning dancing flocked to the dance hall once more. Everything was as it had been.

Until a villager came running to the palace one day with the news that Trigartha had come with a band of people from a country in the north, broken the fence put up around a grazing ground and made off with 5,000 cows.

The king lamented the fact that Keechaka was no longer with them and said he had no idea what to do.

The dice player Kanka, made a suggestion, 'Ask the soldiers to come to the courtyard with their weapons. That fellow Vallava can lead the expedition.'

It was from the soldiers who came rushing into the kitchen that I learnt that Trigartha and his band had stolen cows. The first military expedition I was going to lead …

I went to the palace. Kanka was distributing weapons. The

king was there as well; his face brightened when he saw me. I selected a shield made of bull-hide, a sword and a bow with an iron handle. If only I could have had the mace Mayan had made for me and my own bow! I did not like any of the maces kept out for us.

The soldiers, bored and long denied an opportunity to demonstrate their strength and manliness, were energized by the thought of a fight. Sahadeva arrived from the cow shed, having heard that an army was setting out to retrieve the stolen cows. Nakula selected the swiftest horses to tether to the chariots. Chariots that could be driven over forest territory were of a special kind. They had small roofs, yokes measuring the length of eighty-six fingers and axles eighty-eight fingers long.

The guides who would clear our way took the lead.

As I climbed into a chariot, I jested with the soldiers, 'Remember, there's no place to accommodate prisoners here. If we bring them back, they'll only make more work for the kitchen staff!'

The young men shouted delightedly, they had found a leader after their own heart.

When the chariot that held Kanka and the king went out, I said, 'We have to lead.'

The horses reared impatiently and whips whirled. We sped out. We heard the cattle lowing as we left the grazing grounds behind. A cloud of dust moved around them like a whirlwind. Trigartha's soldiers were right behind the cows, pushing them ahead and controlling them from both sides. The earth quaked with the clatter of 20,000 hooves.

War cries arose from their group as they caught sight of us, the enemy. The first arrows flew through the air and I called out,

'Not yet. I'll tell you when.' The enemy was at twice the distance that our arrows could reach.

The enemy, who were moving with the herd of cattle, suddenly wheeled their chariots around, ready to fight. I was relieved when I saw the king and his group veer right to attack them. I was afraid that one line of the enemy would move in behind us, screened by the herd. To test the weight of my new bow and its feel in my hand, I aimed at the chest of an enemy archer who was standing up to take aim in a chariot drawn by three horses. I released an arrow, holding the bow close to my ear. The arrow, tipped with an eagle-feather, struck his neck. He fell all right, but I calculated that I had to lower my grip on the bow half a finger-length.

We drew nearer them. My soldiers cried out as arrow tips pierced their flesh. However, the enemy was weakening. Warriors jumped out of chariots that had lost their charioteers. Those among us who wielded spears dismounted from their chariots. Instructing a soldier to guard me from the rear, I commanded the charioteer, 'Go on, go ahead, hold the chariot low, close to the ground.'

The enemy had not expected my chariot to come upon them so suddenly. Scenting blood, the horses flew through the scattered lines of soldiers. The sword was the most useful weapon at that moment. I spun a half-circle and came back. The soldier who had guarded my rear asked, 'Who are you, Vallava? Tell me the truth.'

Virata and Yudhishtira were surrounded. I commanded the young man in the chariot next to mine not to spare anyone when the scattered soldiers tried to regroup, then directed my chariot to the spot where the king was.

I caught sight of the king seated with his elbow planted on the floor of his chariot. Yudhishtira was searching for a gap to break through the ring. Trigartha himself was leading his soldiers. He did not anticipate an attack from the back. As I advanced, sending arrow after arrow at him, he swung his chariot around. By this time, my soldiers arrived, having finished the task they had begun.

Trigartha tried to escape. His back presented a perfect target. But in accordance with the courtesies of war, I lowered the arrow I held between my fingertips and let it fly at the fast-retreating chariot. The horses Nakula had selected had not looked particularly impressive, but they astonished me now with their speed. Trigartha's black horses, though massive, were no match for ours. And I was an expert charioteer. I reached Trigartha's chariot and stopped it. If he had expected the usual challenges, if he had thought that he would be asked to take up weapons and fight in case he was not prepared to surrender, he was mistaken. I vaulted into his chariot, gathered him up in my arms and flung him out. Giving him no chance to get up, I pressed the handle of the bow onto his chest and saw the fear in his eyes.

The young man guarding my rear said, 'Cattle-stealers can be killed in any fashion.'

Yudhishtira's chariot arrived at that moment. The king was standing up, his temporary weakness forgotten.

Yudhishtira said, 'Don't kill him. Let the rascal go.' This was Virata's war and he had got back his cows. 'If he touches the king's feet and asks pardon for his crime, he can go.'

Trigartha had no option but to obey.

But when we returned to the palace, the intoxication of

victory suddenly faded. The king was exhausted. Knowing we had gone to confront Trigartha, Duryodhana and the Kauravas had made use of the opportunity to enter from the west and carry off 10,000 cows.

Yudhishtira said, 'Duryodhana planned it. Trigartha from the south and he himself from the west …'

When the king learnt that his young son, Uttaran, had gathered the few soldiers that were left and gone in search of Duryodhana and his band, he grew faint from shock.

'He's just a child. He's never taken part in a fight till now. All he knows about weapons is what he learnt when he was being trained to use them.'

We found out how many had gone with Uttaran. There were no experienced warriors in the group.

Someone said, 'That Brihannala, the dance teacher, claims to be an expert at manoeuvring a chariot and has gone along as his charioteer."

Yudhishtira heaved a sigh of relief: 'Do not fear, King. Uttaran will return absolutely unharmed. Brihannala is an extremely skilled charioteer, one who has learnt the ways of horses.'

I hid a smile when I heard that it was the maid Malini who had insisted that Brihannala accompany Uttaran.

Uttaran and his companions came back by dusk, as victors.

I waylaid Brihannala as he was about to join the girls. Arjuna's eyes were still bright with the excitement of the fight. He had a huge bundle in his hand.

'Who all were with Duryodhana?'

'Everyone. It was like a scene from the war that will take place one day between the Kauravas and the Pandavas. Drona was there and Kripa, Bhishma and Ashvathama. Karna as well.'

Stealing cows was a way for kings to display their prestige. I was truly surprised that all the teachers, including Bhishma, had taken part in the expedition.

'Those who assumed they had nothing to fear from Uttaran got what they deserved. Covered with wounds, Karna ran away, bleeding profusely. Dronacharya must have been wounded as well. But it was not they who tested my strength.'

'Bhishmacharya?'

I knew that Bhishmacharya, who had crossed ninety, was still a formidable warrior. No young man had the guts to confront him.

'No. Bhishmacharya stayed at the back. It was Kripacharya who really proved my match.'

In my heart I embraced Arjuna with admiration and affection.

'I saw the strength of their hands and weapons today. Remember, I was alone, with no support. We must prepare to fight now. Tell the gambling expert we should stop this game of hide-and-seek.'

I said Kanka had fought like a real warrior on my side in our attack on Trigartha.

Arjuna was about to walk away and I asked, pointing to the bundle in his hand, 'What is that?'

'My disciples had told me teasingly to grab whatever good clothes I could from those who surrendered. A wish the disciples expressed – I thought I should fulfil it.' He smiled and walked off.

Knowing that Duryodhana's side was so strong, who would believe that Uttaran and his army had defeated them and retrieved the cattle? The Kauravas were not that stupid either.

A Vallava in the group that defeated Trigartha and a charioteer who sent arrows flying from both hands with Uttaran!

For about three days, Uttaran pretended that he had led his army to victory, and then told the king the truth. That it was his charioteer who had really won the fight. The king was shocked. Brihannala, who was neither man nor woman, a warrior and an archer who could shoot arrows with both hands?

The guards at the gates ran up with news that another attack looked imminent. Kanka said, 'It's not an enemy. If my guess is correct, you will receive this guest with gold and flowers.'

As the guards watched anxiously, chariots stopped at the entrance to the fort. Krishna alighted with the Yadavas.

Before he accepted the king's salutations, Krishna embraced Brihannala. Then he received the king's courtesies and touched Kanka's feet respectfully. Satyaki went looking for Vallava the kitchen-worker.

Krishna told the stunned king our real names and introduced us. Amazed and delighted, Virata clapped his hands like a child. Attendants, who were given instructions to prepare a reception and a feast, began to run around wildly.

3

We sat in the audience hall, dressed in fine clothes.

Krishna said, 'The Kauravas know where you are. The teachers would have guessed at once when they saw the way Arjuna was shooting his arrows. That foolish disguise could never have deceived them.'

Calculating on his fingers, Yudhishtira looked distressed,

wondering whether the Kauravas would argue that the Pandavas had been recognized before the year was over.

Krishna said, 'I calculated the time before I came here. According to the lunar calendar, the year is over. The extra month has to be taken into account. Bhishmacharaya at least will be aware of this.'

'Ah, the extra month ... I had forgotten it.' Yudhishtira sounded relieved.

The days that followed were like a festival for the Virata kingdom. Krishna, Virata and Satyaki held many discussions with Yudhishtira, which included a proposal of marriage for Princess Uttara, Virata's daughter. Krishna told the Pandavas it would be a way to bond closer with Virata. Assuming that he was himself the prospective bridegroom, Arjuna gave me a secret smile.

Krishna said to him, 'You have not seen Abhimanyu after he grew up, have you? He's a young man now. Uttara will be the perfect bride for him in all aspects. Since you are her teacher, you are now like a father to her.'

Arjuna acknowledged that this was right.

Krishna said proudly, 'Abhimanyu is growing up stronger than his father and his uncles.'

Virata was happy to accept the marriage proposal, and the matter was fixed.

He then proclaimed that the Pandavas were welcome to use his palace, his army and his wealth in whatever way they pleased in order to retrieve the kingdom they were entitled to.

Drupada and Dhrishtadyumna arrived, completing the list of our close relatives. Dhrishtadyumna had changed beyond recognition. His frame was now as massive as mine, and his face had the seriousness of maturity. He and I lined up the entire Virata army in the courtyard and moved out those who lacked strength and those who were too old. We separated the rest into several rows and ordered that they begin their training. Satyaki appointed more workers in the weapon house, and flames and smoke began to rise from the new workshops.

Dhrishtadyumna sent messengers to various kings who would be able to offer us help, like Drishtaketu of Chedi and Jayasena of Magadha.

Satyaki and I watched the blacksmiths at work, while Drupada, Yudhishtira and Krishna held discussions in the audience hall.

Satyaki said, 'I came prepared. My army will arrive tomorrow at dawn and set up camp at the site of the elephant festival.' He saw Dhrishtadyumna coming towards us and asked, 'Are their deliberations not over yet?'

Dhrishtadyumna said, 'My father is going to dispatch a messenger to the Kauravas to say that if they will give half the kingdom to the Pandavas, we can effect a reconciliation. A courtesy.'

Satyaki said, 'It is a rule among kshatriyas that whoever asks a king for help first will receive his support and his army. By the time messages and replies to them are sent back and forth, the Kauravas would have commandeered all the strong armies. These people don't realize that. The first thing we have to do is gather and prepare the army. Courteous exchanges to effect a reconciliation can be made later.'

Dhristadyumna said all his friends had given him their word that they would help.

We knew the Kauravas would enlist many kings on their side.

In the force of weapons and numbers, they would certainly be superior to us. All the teachers who were familiar with military strategies were with them. We were convinced that Grandfather Bhishma and Dronacharya would remain neutral.

Satyaki voiced a doubt, 'But they were with the Kauravas who came to steal the cows.'

'Like hunting, stealing cows is an entertainment for kshatriyas. Moreover, these were Virata's cows. I see no reason why the teachers would feel any affection for Virata.'

Dhrishtadyumna thought Drona would fight for the Kauravas for the sole reason that Drupada was on the side of the Pandavas. However, his self-confidence did not waver. 'It is not teachers who are going to fight and win this war, it is we young men.'

I could not help thinking of Vidura. He would probably advise both Dhritarashtra and Duryodhana not to go to war. After Grandfather Bhishma and Dhritarashtra, it was Vidura who should have had the highest authority in the Kaurava kingdom. When Pandu died, he should have succeeded him as king by right. But no one had even remembered this. Was it because he was the son of a servant woman that no one had nominated him to the seat of power? But generally, the mother's family or caste was not taken into account. The fact that Vichitravirya's mother was a fisherwoman had not stood in the way of his coronation. I consoled myself with this answer: maybe expertise with weapons was considered greater than knowledge of the scriptures.

All of us went to the audience hall to hear what answer the brahmin messenger had brought back. These messengers were expert at repeating the messages they were given word for word.

'I went to Dhritarashtra's capital and saluted the great king and Bhishmacharya. I spoke the message: "All of you know what the dharma of a king is. In spite of that, I repeat it to you: Dhritarashtra and Pandu are sons of the same father. They have equal rights to their father's property. How did it happen that when Dhritarashtra's sons received their father's wealth, Pandu's sons did not? Not only did he not give them their due, Dhritarashtra also looked for ways to kill them. They are alive now only because they were destined to live. By your mean actions, you took over even the country they made prosperous. Now that they have fulfilled your conditions and lived outside your country for thirteen years, they are prepared to forget all that has happened if you are willing to give them what is their due."'

King Drupada asked impatiently, 'The answer? What reply did Dhritarashtra give?'

'They began to argue among themselves. Bhishmacharya said the request was just, so they did not allow him to speak any more. Karna, who was the most argumentative, sent me back saying they would dispatch Sanjaya with an answer. They gave me good food and a hundred coins.'

Drupada told the brahmin priest he could leave. Although he was grey with age, Drupada's every movement was eloquent with majesty and manliness. The Yadavas treated him with great respect.

He looked at us as we stood muttering and said, 'All this sending of messages and talks of truce can continue. But do not stop preparations for war.'

The next day, the minister Sanjaya, who functioned as Dhritarashtra's eyes, arrived. He ate, rested, then came to the audience hall, by which time everyone had flocked there. As protocol demanded, Yudhishtira asked for news of his uncle and all his children's families. Were the grandchildren well? Were the brahmins conducting the rituals regularly? Were the servants taking good care of all the older people?

Courteous questions of this kind were certainly part of the formalities, but I wondered whether it was really necessary to prolong them to include irrelevant details like whether the cows were yielding a good quantity of milk.

Satyaki said impatiently, 'Let us hear what the blind king said.'

I heard jewels clinking softly behind the carved screen of devadaru wood at the back of the hall, and recognized the tinkle of Draupadi's anklets. So she had come to listen to Sanjaya.

Sanjaya said, 'Son of Dharma, listen to Dhritarashtra's words. Pandavas, Krishna, Satyaki, son of Shini, and revered Drupada and Virata, you must listen as well. Dhritarashtra said: "You are all noble people, incapable of performing evil actions. Sin will look as conspicuous on you as a stain of lamp-black on white garments.

"'I will tell you what will happen if you are rash enough to start a war. You will be invincible if the Yadavas, the Panchalas and the Viratas come to your aid. But as long as they have Drona, Bhishma, Kripa and Shalya with them, and Karna to lead them, I do not see how anyone can defeat the Kauravas. I see no good in the success or defeat of either side. It is the Pandavas who must make peace. I pray that good may come to both sides."' Sanjaya stopped.

Then he added, as his own contribution, 'The great king spoke this message in the presence of Bhishmacharya.'

Maybe I was dull-witted, as Yudhishtira always said, for I did not fully understand this message. 'What does Uncle really mean? I don't understand.'

Dhristadyumna smiled. 'If you take away the coating of sweet phrases, this is the gist of what he says: lie and rot wherever you please, in some forest or other, but don't bother the Kauravas. That's what he means by telling us to make peace.'

I heard the sound of anklets and turned around. Draupadi was looking at me.

Sanjaya was waiting for a reply. As Yudhishtira walked up to Krishna to discuss the matter again, I said, 'There is no question of peace now. Tell him that the Pandavas are ready for war.'

Yudhishtira stared at me, shocked. Krishna, Arjuna, Nakula and Sahadeva were looking at me questioningly. I realized it was not I who should have answered, it was Yudhishtira. I had broken a rule.

4

King Drupada stood up. He came towards me, looking extremely dissatisfied. I thought he would find fault with me, the second brother, for having spoken out of turn.

He said, 'I am no expert at discussions. I'm leaving now. You can come and call me in the guest house when you need me. For the moment, I too make peace …'

Amusement glinted in the old man's eyes. In the centre of the hall, Sanjaya and Yudhishtira sat side-by-side, murmuring. Krishna stood silently by Arjuna. Finally, Sanjaya got up and went out.

I walked to the weapon house. Nakula caught up with me and said Yudhishtira wanted to see me. I went back to the hall.

Yudhishtira said, 'I am trying my best to avoid war. The ideal solution would be for us to get half the kingdom, Indraprastha included. Or at least five villages …'

I was roused to anger, 'Who decides that five villages will suffice?'

'I do. I have the authority to do so. If you doubt that, war will start at once, among the Pandavas themselves.'

Yudhishtira's words echoed in the empty audience hall. I saw the challenge in his eyes. Making a huge effort, I bent my head and walked away.

I lay down, listening to the sounds of iron sheets being flattened by the blacksmiths. Dhristadyumna came looking for me, and I got up. I did not speak to him of Yudhishtira's conditions. He seemed very happy.

He drank from the pot of liquor the attendant had filled and left near my cot and said, 'I had sent a spy to Hastinapura. He's come back.'

Now he had my interest. Long arguments were going on between Vidura and Dhritarashtra. Bhishmacharya was keeping aloof, neutral. Krishnadvaipayana and Gandhari, realizing that nothing they said had any effect, had withdrawn.

'What about Karna?'

'Karna and Bhishmacharya had a bitter argument, I don't know about what. Karna took offence, went away and did not return to the hall. He has not come out of his house since.'

He raised the pot of liquor once again.

'Dhritarashtra greatly fears one person on the Pandava side. Can you guess who it is?'

It was not difficult to guess. It had to be Arjuna, who had won new weapons, who could shoot arrows with both hands without missing a single target.

'No,' he said, giving me a genial blow on my chest. 'The one he fears is this Vrikodara. Do you know what the king's words were? "He will kill my sons. I think about it and stay awake all night, breathing hot sighs." What do you say?'

I grew thoughtful again. The leader of the Pandavas was a man who did not realize the physical strength of his own brothers or the strength of his relatives' armies ...

'Duryodhana keeps trying to comfort his father all the time, saying he can certainly finish Bhima off in a mace-fight all by himself.'

Dhrishtadyumna was like a war-horse that grows impatient the moment the charioteer reduces the speed of his chariot. He was extremely restless, and could not bring himself to sit still for even a second. He hurried out, saying he was going to look for Satyaki.

A messenger came again before evening. I was summoned to the audience hall.

My three younger brothers were there when I went in. Krishna, Dhristadyumna and Satyaki were seated in front of Yudhishtira. My younger brothers, standing apart from each other, looked at me. They were ill at ease. Neither Drupada nor Virata were in the hall.

'I have decided that we will make one more attempt to avoid a war.' Yudhishtira looked at me as he spoke. 'We will send a very important person as our messenger. Krishna has consented to go.'

I could tell from Krishna's face and his bent head that this role had been thrust upon him.

'I sent for you to find out what each one of you thinks. This is a crucial decision,' my brother said.

I bit down anger, tried to make myself as calm as possible and said, 'What means most to us at this time is that none of our royal lineages should be destroyed. I am willing to do whatever is needed for that, even to be a servant to Duryodhana.'

Having expected abuse from me, Krishna stared at me, incredulous, when he heard my cold and measured voice. He did not know that Yudhishtira had been furious with me earlier, that he had almost come to the point of throwing a challenge at me. I had not told anyone about it.

'The words of an impotent man! Are you becoming a coward, Bhimasena, as war approaches?' asked Krishna.

'If you expected more from the sons of the impotent Pandu, that's your fault.' I spoke without a trace of anger.

My brothers were shocked. Krishna calmed down at once, realizing that there was something he did not know underlying my words.

'I did not mean what I said. It was a harmless joke.'

It was Arjuna's turn to speak next. He looked at Nakula, then at Sahadeva, probably because he wanted to speak only after the others were done. They were silent, as if they awaited his decision.

'What do you say, Arjuna?' Yudhishtira asked again.

'I am upset because our teachers are on the opposing side. War is not the same as retrieving stolen cattle after all. If it is possible to make a treaty, it will be good for everyone.'

Nakula agreed with him.

Sahadeva came forward before he was called. His face was flushed. 'Bhima, Arjuna, Yudhishtira, they are all probably great followers of dharma. Nakula has no opinion he can call his own. But I do not think as they do.'

He stopped and turned to Krishna. 'I saw Draupadi offered as a wager and then dragged through the gambling hall, a sight no man can endure. I will not rest until I have destroyed them. I will kill Shakuni with my own hands. What I want is war. Krishna, if you wish, you can assume that Sahadeva is against dharma.'

Satyaki eagerly enfolded Sahadeva in a half-embrace. Sahadeva had been furious ever since he knew for certain that Shalya, Madri's brother and his maternal uncle, would side with the Kauravas.

Paying no attention to Sahadeva's words, Yudhishtira said, 'Let us all go now. Krishna can set out on his journey with our message.'

A faint voice was heard from behind the wooden screen. 'Wait. I have a word to say!'

Draupadi came out. Ignoring all of us, she went up to Krishna. 'I am aware that no one here has asked for my opinion. The object of a wager has no tongue to speak with, after all.'

Yudhishtira reminded Draupadi in a grave voice, 'This is a discussion about matters of state.'

'Women have to be blind or dumb to survive in the Kuru clan. All of yesterday and today, I have been listening to talk of reconciliation. Have a look at this before you go to beg for reconciliation.'

With her left hand, she drew her unbound hair over her shoulder.

'When Dussasana dragged me by my hair, it loosened around me and I have never tied it up since. These thirteen years, I kept alive the fire burning inside me, not allowing my tears to extinguish it. And now, even the one who swore he would kill all the Kauravas single-handed has become a votary of dharma!'

I had heard about Kritya, a guardian goddess who was invoked through occult mantras. Draupadi's stance, brandishing the seeds of curses in her hands and the flames of destruction in her eyes, was like that of Kritya.

Her anger suddenly cooled, Draupadi covered her face and wept.

Krishna walked towards her and said, 'Don't weep. Don't forget what I said to you earlier. In my mind's eye, I see your enemies destroyed, I see you reigning in prosperity with your husbands.'

Not looking at any of us, Draupadi walked away with a firm tread.

She must have singled me out in her accusation because I said I was prepared to even be a servant of our enemies. The mighty warrior who had forgotten his vow! Even Sahadeva's eyes held resentment as they looked at me. Did Satyaki and Dhrishtadyumna suspect that I was becoming a coward as war grew nearer? If Dhrishtadyumna of all people were to think that …

When King Drupada had declared it was not right to give away his daughter for five husbands to share, it was Dhrishtadyumna who had argued with him and overcome his objections. He had insisted that I was as desirable a son-in-law as Arjuna, perhaps even more desirable. Would Dhrishtadyumna, who adored me, feel now that I was a coward?

I walked until I reached the elephant sheds. I saw that a riot had broken out there. A tusker had run amok and attacked the mahout who came with a chain to bind its legs. The mahout was laid flat on the ground, and the animal was now trying to shatter the granite wall of the fort. A group of people stood apart, armed with long sticks and spears.

I walked towards the elephant and the mahouts barred my way. 'Don't go near it, it's run amok!'

I grabbed a spear from a mahout, thrust it into the ground so that its tip was blunted, held it by that end and walked on. The elephant swung around. I said to the animal in a language it would understand, 'Calm down, calm down.'

He curled his trunk and raised both his tusks to the sky. I threw the spear at the vital spot in the centre of his forehead; it found its mark. Standing like a madman before the elephant as it sank down on its bent foreleg, trumpeting loudly, I cried: 'Do you want a duel? Bhimasena is ready!'

Animals have a sure instinct. The half-mad elephant quailed before the completely insane man. I stood between his tusks, curled my fists, hit his forehead with them and asked him again, 'Do you want to fight?'

The mahouts came up with chains to bind the animal's feet. He had calmed down by then.

I turned and walked away, still furious, and saw Dhristadyumna among the crowd of people who had come running up hearing the clamour in the elephant sheds. Draupadi was with him. They caught up with me.

Dhristadyumna asked, 'Who are you angry with? Not with the elephant, I'm sure of that.'

I did not say anything.

Draupadi said, 'It's a blessing you didn't go so far as to fight a duel with your older brother this morning.'

She smiled at me. And the man in me calmed down.

All of us continued to feel uneasy until Krishna returned. The enthusiasm of the men in the army dwindled, although no one had told them anything. The manufacturing in the workshops slowed down. The young men in Virata's army, who had been breathing the scent of battle, were now filled with gloom. Several people came and asked me whether the matter of the treaty had been decided. I gave them all the same answer: let Krishna come and we'll decide.

Krishna came back looking satisfied, and we presumed that Duryodhana had agreed to give us half the kingdom. I stopped him on the way to ask for details, but he would not give me a clear answer.

'Matters of state can be discussed only in the audience hall,' he said evasively.

Drupada, Virata and Virata's son, Uttaran, were all in the hall when we gathered there again. Satyaki's three commanders-in-chief had been summoned as well, so that Yudhishtira himself could tell them in case the armies had to be disbanded.

Krishna did not drag out what he had to say, as the brahmin messenger and Sanjaya had done earlier.

'Duryodhana is not prepared to give you half the kingdom, or five villages, or even a house. Do you want to hear his words? He said he will not give the Pandavas even a needle-point of space in the kingdom!'

What did Mother say? It was the question that rose to everyone's lips: what did Mother say when you saw her?

'It was to listen to her words that I asked all of you to come to this hall. She said: "I can forget the fact that my sons lost their kingdom, that they endured innumerable agonies in the forest.

But I can never forget that my daughter-in-law had to stand like an orphan in the gambling hall, wearing a blood-stained cloth and suffering agony. Tell my sons the story of Vidula if they do not know it."'

Krishna stopped and looked at Draupadi, who was wiping tears of joy from her eyes.

He then related the story in his own words: 'Vidula was a kshatriya woman who sent her son back to the battlefield when he tried to run away and hide because he was afraid of war. Vidula told him that love without motive or courage was useful only to a she-donkey.'

We were silent, thinking of our mother. Everyone waited with bated breath, wondering what Yudhishtira was going to say.

Krishna continued, 'Your mother sent Bhima and Arjuna a special message. That they should win the war, make their elder brother king and perform his coronation.'

He turned to Yudhishtira, 'Now all that remains is what she asked me to tell you. This is the message she sent you: "Kings who do not know how to protect their kingdom and their subjects are destined not to a hero's Heaven but to Hell."'

Yudhishtira sank back into thought. Satyaki and Dhrishtadyumna got up and began to pace up and down. Drupada and Virata continued to stare at Yudhishtira.

The only sound that broke the complete silence in the hall was the tinkle of Draupadi's anklets when she moved.

Yudhishtira sighed and asked, 'What about Abhimanyu's wedding …?'

Krishna pretended he had not heard the question. The silence continued.

At the end of his patience, Krishna asked, 'So what have you decided we should do now?'

Yudhishtira raised his head and looked at us. With infinite calm, he answered in one word:

'War!'

PART 7

TATTERED CLOTHES

1

First of all, we set apart space for a burial ground. The site we chose, covered with rocks and thorny bushes, was on the banks of the Hiranvati river.

Military camps were then organized all over Kurukshetra. Tents were put up at once for the sages and priests. The huge royal tent, which had facilities for conducting sacrificial rituals, was constructed last, in the middle of army houses meant for the kings. Yudhishtira occupied it, and the discussions on military strategies were held there. Houses for the children were built near the brahmin dwellings. Grass and firewood were plentiful in Kurukshetra.

The armies, which had fought under seven kings, were split into seven groups. Seated around large fires, the soldiers sharpened their weapons. Satyaki took special care in attending to their welfare.

The horses and elephants were housed in a space on the riverbank, beyond the burial ground. The chariots of war stood between the main tents and in front of them. Dhrishtadyumna moved the chariots that would launch the second line of attack to a space behind the site for the sacrificial rituals.

The preparations and discussions took place in Virata's

capital. Opinions varied on who would be the best person to choose as the supreme commander-in-chief; he had to be capable of uniting all the soldiers in the fight for a single cause. Sahadeva mentioned Virata's name impulsively. Nakula's suggestion was more considered and there was good sense in what he said: that since older teachers like Bhishma, Drona and Kripa were ranged on the opposite side, it would be best for Drupada to lead our side.

I suggested a name no one had expected: Shikhandi. I saw this older son of Drupada for the first time when he came to Virata for Abhimanyu's wedding. He was aloof, speaking not even to Dhrishtadyumna. He had been wandering through several countries, hunting or fighting battles for anyone who requested his help. He was a slender man, with an unsmiling face and sunken eyes. Somehow, I had a feeling that killing was something he enjoyed. I had watched him at practice sessions and knew that he was equally skilful with all weapons.

I felt that when we came face-to-face with opponents who were our teachers and grandfathers, memories of the relationships we had had with them in the past, and of the debts we owed them, would trouble most of us. That was why I thought choosing Shikhandi to lead us would be wise military strategy.

Since Krishna had supervised all the arrangements, Yudhishtira felt that the final decision ought to be left to him.

'All three persons are equally worthy of the position in every way. However, the other side has more armies than we have, so we need someone who is young and forceful. I propose a man who will be aggressive when he attacks and know how to employ the right strategy to suit each occasion: Dhrishtadyumna.'

Everyone accepted this suggestion gladly. No one had proposed his name, fearing the accusation that the older leaders had been ignored. Brahmins performed sacrificial rituals and anointed Dhrishtadyumna our commander-in-chief.

The treasury and the mechanical weapons arrived the next day in carts drawn by donkeys. Yudhishtira ordered that dwellings be built for the physicians who followed. The last group to arrive were the magadha minstrels and musicians, who would sing heroic ballads to encourage our soldiers as they set out for battle and soothe their weariness when they came back at night.

It was decided that Draupadi would stay in a guest house beyond the river, situated on space that lay within the boundaries of Virata.

Standing on the roof of the watchtower, Yudhishtira supervised the preparations.

I concentrated on the elephants. I had the caretakers replace the decorative gear that covered their foreheads with spiked metal plates that would lend them greater force when they attacked – all the more useful for shattering chariots. Arjuna walked in and out of the weapon houses, giving instructions.

The spies brought news that the army had moved from Hastinapura.

When I came back to my tent from the battlefield, I saw someone waiting for me. The years had wrought no changes in Vishoka. He had the same soft laugh, a look of humility that veiled a streak of mischief. He had heard news of the war and come from Kashi.

I was relieved to see him. His presence made me feel stronger. The charioteer in charge of my huge chariot, which would be positioned in the centre, had to be an expert. Krishna was going to drive Arjuna's chariot.

Goaded by Duryodhana, the teachers had insisted that it was not right for Krishna – who, as mediator in the peace talks, had been a friend to both sides – to participate in the war. Dhritarashtra said the same thing. Krishna therefore made a vow not to take up weapons, knowing well that the expertise of a charioteer could determine victory or defeat in a war. Dhritarashtra was pleased by his vow. Krishna's own Yadava army was on the opponent's side, since Balarama had given his word earlier to that effect. However, Krishna himself had no great opinion about the Yadava army's capability. Balarama sent the enemy the army and stepped aside to show that he was neutral. Fearing that if he stayed on the spot, he might be drawn to one side or the other, he set out on a pilgrimage.

Two chariots drawn by single horses always accompanied a big chariot, one on each side to guard its wheels, and one went in front of it. When waging war from chariots, all four had to move as one. Their movements were controlled by the charioteer in the main chariot, who had to anticipate the commander's thoughts and act upon them.

Senesha had sent 300 horses and fifty-one chariots.

Vishoka, who was over forty, hinted to me that, at thirty-five, I looked older than him.

Two mahouts and the head cook came to see me.

Vishoka said, 'You're busy. I'll wait outside till you finish.'

The mahouts were unhappy about the food; it was not being properly supervised. I dealt with the problem and sent them away. I was examining some breastplates made of bull-hide one by one when a servant came and lit the oil lamps.

As he was going out, he said, 'A prince is waiting outside.'

I assumed it was one of the young recruits who had joined the army.

A strong, handsome young man walked in. Thick hair fell straight down beneath the hair ornament on his head, and his large eyes reflected the green of the forests. A tuft of coppery hair sprouted under his chin. I felt I had seen his face somewhere. He touched my feet in obeisance.

'I am Sarvada, your son. Balandhara is my mother.'

I embraced him, silently ashamed of my own callousness. We princes so often forgot our children who were growing up in other places. Even when Vishoka had said he had come from Kashi, I had not thought to ask him how Balandhara's son was. I wondered whether only we of the Kuru race were like this.

I had seen Sutasoma, the son I had by Draupadi, when he was a baby, and then again only when we were leaving Virata for Kurukshetra. And when Abhimanyu had arrived to wed Uttara, Arjuna had not recognized him.

Looking at Sarvada, I chastised myself. Bhima's courageous son was not yet old enough to fight a war; all the same, he had come. The son of Balandhara, for whom I had never spared a thought, whom I had abandoned as casually as a traveller leaves behind leftovers from a food packet on the wayside. But no, a kshatriya should never be weakened by blood ties: that is what the teachers who came to teach us in our childhood had instilled in us.

Sarvada said, 'My mother is waiting outside.'

Once again, I was taken aback. I went out and saw Balandhara, who bent down to touch my feet.

I gripped her shoulder and lifted her up, 'Come, come inside.'

She came in and looked in turn at Sarvada and me. Her smiling eyes were moist.

I had never asked after Balandhara while she was in Kashi, nor bothered to send a messenger there. Yet, she stood before me smiling brightly, as if we had parted company the previous day. The women who married into the Kuru race had to have great powers of endurance, as our Aunt Gandhari had once said to us. No, it was Draupadi who had said that, a few days ago. Draupadi, not Gandhari.

I asked a servant to take Sarvada to the tent where Prativindhya and Sutasoma lived.

'I've come to fight. Don't worry about me,' said Sarvada respectfully.

I told Balandhara about the quarters we had organized for women on the other side of the Hiranvati river. Women never slept in the warriors' tents.

'I'll stay with Mother, in Vidura's house.' She untied a knot in her upper cloth. 'We who are from the east usually perform sacrificial pujas for Rudra and Durga before a war.'

Red sindooram and white flower petals soaked in sacrificial blood lay on the fig leaf she gave me.

I noticed Vishoka lurking in the darkness, waiting for my orders.

I told him, 'Let's go to Vidura's house.'

Balandhara stopped me. 'The chariot I came in is waiting.'

Sarvada said he would walk beside her chariot and took leave of me.

Vishoka came up to me. 'I have three children now. When the woman I married from Hastinapura died, I married a woman from Kashi and had a son by her.'

I had not known he had two children earlier. No one ever asked charioteers about their families.

Vishoka asked, 'What news of your eldest son?'

My eldest son. That was Ghatotkacha. Charioteers were so predictable, they chose the same subjects to talk about, to ask questions about ...

The tribals of the forest, charioteers and the inferior castes set great value by family ties. I remembered Kirmeera, the tribal who had come seeking revenge because I had killed the brother of the woman he loved.

Mother had told us the story of Vidula to remind us that simple love, love that asked for no return, was only for a female donkey.

We had other dilemmas to deal with. The war we were getting ready to fight was between a king who had wagered a woman and a king who had accepted his wager. I said to myself angrily: women are either pawns in a game, or like packets of food to be eaten by the wayside and abandoned.

The more I thought about such things, the more distressed I felt and the more I despised myself. I asked Vishoka to bring me a pot of liquor quickly.

సా

At night, the sounds from the military camp sounded like the roar of the sea on a full moon night.

War would start in the morning. Dhrishtadyumna walked in and out of the encampment and the tents, looking calm and fully aware of his responsibilities. Krishna deserved to be congratulated for having chosen as commander-in-chief this young man who had the ability to issue commands in the gentlest of words.

On the first day, the military operations tend to be low-key. As in a duel, both sides would attempt to assess each other's weaknesses. Dhristadyumna gave orders that every soldier should select an opponent and attack him.

Nakula swore his target would be his uncle Shalya, who was on the opposing side.

Yudhishtira warned him, 'Don't take an oath like that. Shalya is a formidable man.'

Arjuna had no doubt that his target would be Karna. Sahadeva had chosen Shakuni much earlier. The Trigarthas were not great warriors, and younger men like Prativindhya, Sutasoma and Sarvada would be able to handle them. Jayadratha, the king of Sindhu, was an opponent to be feared. Satyaki would pursue him. Abhimanyu would attack Vrishasena, the son of Karna. Dhristadyumna asked us to leave Drona to him.

Everyone knew without being told that I would direct my attack at Duryodhana.

Warriors had been selected to confront all the important opponents, except one. The name that remained was Bhishma's. No one came forward offering to attack him.

'I will kill him.' Not attack but kill – Shikhandi, who had remained silent until then, spoke. All of us stared at him.

'Arrows do not recognize the breastplates of grandfathers or teachers,' Shikhandi said indifferently. The pupils of his eyes, unmoving as those of a dead man, reminded me of the messengers of death.

Arjuna, who was responsible for deciding the military strategies we would use, said it was best to organize the armies in a diamond-shaped formation for the attack. He sketched the formation on the sand with a finger. Who would stand in the front row of the attacking division and direct operations? Whoever it was would act as a shield for the whole army.

Yudhishtira asked anxiously, 'Who will it be? Who?'

Arjuna cried, 'Why even ask? My elder brother, Bhimasena!'

Yudhishtira heaved a sigh of relief.

I woke up before dawn. Yudhishtira had already left in a chariot drawn by a single horse for the Kaurava camp to pay obeisance to our teachers. Krishna had counselled us to pay obeisance to our gurus: Bhishma, Drona, Kripa and Shalya.

Bhishmacharya was the commander-in-chief of the Kaurava army. Our spies told us that there had been competition for the position. The dispute had provoked Karna's displeasure and he had withdrawn. Jayadratha and Bhagadatta, the king of Pragjyotisha, had been the competitors and it had looked as if a fight would break out within the camp itself. Duryodhana had then chosen Bhishmacharya, knowing that no one would object to his decision.

I put on my shoulder-guards and breastplate. Vishoka made marks with sandal paste and red sindooram on my chest. I went to Yudhishtira's tent to worship the sacrificial fire. The flames shone gold and there was no smoke.

Arjuna seemed very troubled. The look of exhaustion on his face showed that he had not slept all night.

Vishoka was ready with my chariot, which flew a flag that had a lion with diamond-bright eyes. We waited for Yudhishtira to return after having paid his respects to our teachers. Krishna went up to him anxiously when he came back.

'Every one of our teachers said to me: "If you had not come before the war started, I would have cursed you."'

Of all of us, Krishna was the happiest to hear this.

I made a few minor changes in the way Vishoka had arranged the weapons in my chariot. Everyone was ready. The armies grouped themselves in a diamond formation. The royal white umbrella above Yudhishtira's chariot was unfurled. Conches were blown, drums thudded. The magadha singers began to sing songs about the ancient warriors to encourage the men who were going to fight.

The representatives of both sides had together drawn up the rules of war the previous day. Though kshatriyas were well versed in the rules of righteous war, they were repeated once more. Words had to be confronted with words. If a soldier fought standing on the floor of his chariot, his opponent had to fight standing in the same position. Those who ran away from the battlefield could not be attacked. Weapons could not be used against the wounded, those whose limbs had been injured, those who had lost their weapons or breastplates, charioteers, drummers and spectators. We could fight only from dawn to dusk. Corpses could not be mutilated.

When we reached a point from where we could see the Kaurava army in the distance, Dhristadyumna instructed the army to halt. The drums changed their rhythm.

Arjuna looked extremely troubled. We exchanged glances.

The soldiers and their leaders roared as the army surged forward like a torrent of water that had breached its banks. I could make out the position of Duryodhana's chariot even at that distance. Vishoka steered our chariot towards it. The Kalinga army guarded Duryodhana in front and on his sides, serving as his armour. They were successful in preventing us from moving forward. Soldiers kept falling on both sides. We had no idea what was happening on the other fronts. As the fighting continued, it became clear to me that I would not get close to Duryodhana. Nevertheless, we managed to significantly wound the strong Kalinga force.

Fighting stopped at dusk and, as those who had fallen or were injured were lifted into the chariots to be taken away, three carts carrying corpses moved towards the burning ground.

I went straight to the council chamber. I knew there would be many mutual recriminations that day. Arjuna and Krishna were already there. Yudhishtira was full of grief.

Arjuna said, 'Virata's son, Uttaran, is dead.'

That was our most grievous loss that day. He had died in the attack on Shalya. A soldier who had been with Uttaran said he had died after fighting valiantly and inflicting severe losses on the enemy. I remembered the evening after the stolen cattle had been retrieved. He had stood by my side for a long time, stroking his moustache and describing Brihannala's valorous actions. The young man had expressed a hope that he too would learn military strategy and be a conqueror some day.

Dhrishtadyumna looked dissatisfied. He said that when Uttaran attacked Shalya, someone should have forced him back and pushed his way in front of him. Yudhishtira corrected him – it was Shalya who had attacked Uttaran, and the boy lunged towards him to counter-attack. Uttaran died a warrior's death.

Standing in front of the second line of soldiers as it ranged itself on the battlefield, I came to know that Arjuna had been deeply troubled when he caught sight of Grandfather Bhishma and his teachers in the distance. He confessed as much to Satyaki. He had even requested Krishna to turn his chariot back. Krishna had had to counsel him at length, in order to quieten his sudden fear and give him back the will to fight. Krishna had told Arjuna firmly that if one of his teachers or grandfathers fell in the war, it was only right and just. A person who performed an action that was part of his duty did not need to worry about the fruit of that action. Everyone who was born had to die; those who died would be reborn again. The killer and the slain: these were terms that had no meaning. The soul could never be destroyed. The soul discards a worn-out body for a new one as human beings discard old clothes for new, said Krishna, and there was nothing in this to grieve about.

Yudhamanyu, who guarded the left wheel of my chariot, had heard everything Krishna said. He said with reverence, 'Krishna advised Arjuna for a long time. He spoke of deep philosophical principles. I did not understand much of what he said.'

Death was like the body changing clothes! I looked at the grieving Virata's dull eyes and bowed head.

When I went out to the thorny thickets on the banks of the Hiranvati, all the tattered garments that souls had discarded that first day had caught fire.

2

That day, the army was organized in the shape of a krauncha bird in flight. My group and I were the beak. Dhrishtadyumna was on the left wing with Abhimanyu, Nakula and Sahadeva. Arjuna, Satyaki and Drupada were on the right wing. This was better than the diamond formation. Sarvada, Rukmi and Panchali's sons formed the legs of the bird, and Yudhishtira the neck.

The king of Kalinga and his sons fell that day. They were good warriors; it was their decision to send an elephant force before them that paved the way for their downfall. They had not expected that I would leap onto the neck of the tusker that led the force. I aimed a blow at a vital spot on the forehead – a technique that was part of the science of taming elephants. The animal spun wildly, crying out in pain. All the other elephants trumpeted and ran away. Many people were trampled to death. By the time I leapt back into my chariot, the Kalingas were completely shattered.

We gathered at night in the camp to count our losses and gains for the day, and found that it was the young Abhimanyu who had inflicted the worst destruction on the enemy.

Abhimanyu had Subhadra's eyes; you would think he was a girl when his eyelids fluttered. When the elders began to praise him, he slipped out quietly. I went out too.

Abhimanyu came up to me and said, 'Uncle, Sarvada is an amazing warrior! I was wonderstruck when I saw him shatter Trigartha's troops. I hope he will be sent to join Uncle Nakula – that is one of our weaker points.'

What self-confidence he had! Abhimanyu, Sarvada, Prativindhya, Sutasoma – we were nothing compared to them. I thought to myself: when these young boys of fifteen and sixteen grew up, the fame of the Kuru clan would spread throughout the whole land of Bharata. Maybe we would be remembered one day in the soota ballads as the fathers of these boys.

Abhimanyu walked along with me to my tent.

The next day, the army was organized in the form of a crescent. Neither side had any significant successes or losses. That night, there was a serious discussion. We had a bit of good news from our spies: the Kauravas had expected a swift victory, and Duryodhana was infuriated that it had not happened. Karna was still seated in his own tent like a man of leisure, declining to take up arms. Duryodhana had spoken of Bhishmacharya's inefficiency as a commander-in-chief in everyone's hearing. And unless Bhishmacharya relinquished his command, no one else could lead the army.

Arjuna remarked that Krishna, forgetting his vow, had stretched out his hand to pick up a weapon when he caught sight of Bhishmacharya standing unguarded, without a protective barrier of chariots around him or a line of soldiers in front.

Krishna said, 'Didn't I tell you at the very start – there are no gurus, no disciples in war. No blood ties. I felt at that moment that Arjuna was deliberately restraining himself from an attack on Bhishma.'

On the fourth day, I had a chance to confront Duryodhana directly. I had noticed him shooting arrow after arrow at Vishoka purposefully. Plucking each arrow out, Vishoka declared boldly that the wounds were not deep. I asked him to circle my chariot around Duryodhana. The movements of the guards shielding him grew slower and I was able to shoot three arrows at him in quick succession. They must have split his breastplate. I saw his chariot swing around and began to pursue him, but Bhagadatta's tusker planted itself in front of me like a huge fortress, blocking my view. I noticed Duryodhana's allies who were fighting on the flanks look at him with disgust as he turned his chariot to retreat.

Seated in my tent, I thought that neither side had achieved anything over the last three days. The attendants began to serve food.

Vishoka arrived, his arm bandaged, and said, 'Didn't you hear the commotion? One more person has arrived with an army to join us.'

I heard loud noises in the distance. 'They've come in bullock carts. Soldiers are flocking to watch them. An army of forest-dwellers.'

I got up and was about to go out when I heard a voice in the darkness.

'I have come. Ghatotkacha.'

I was astonished when he came in – the boy who had stood before me a few years ago with an axe and ropes had become a man. It seemed as if his head would touch the roof of the tent. A leopard skin covered his waist and chest. He prostrated himself at my feet, then rose and said, 'I am late. Forgive me. News takes time to reach the forest.'

I noted that his voice had become a man's and his language more refined. He had brought an adequate number of weapons and followers, as well as buffaloes and bulls to provide food.

I said we would put up tents for them in the camp, but he insisted: 'We are happier sleeping on the bare earth. Don't waste time looking after our comforts and conveniences.'

Saying they would be ready before dawn next morning, he went back into the darkness.

The next day, it was no archer or warrior who tested my strength and patience, it was an elephant. The tusker belonging to Bhagadatta, a man from Pragjyotisha.

As Bhagadatta rode towards me on his elephant, I realised it was an animal that was to be feared. How quickly it had screened Duryodhana from view the previous day ... The earth trembled beneath its feet. It was the biggest tusker I had ever seen.

I leapt out to protect the chariots. Vishoka threw me three spears, all of which I flung at the tusker, but they struck the iron plate on its forehead and glanced off. The elephant warded them off with greater expertise than a warrior fighting from a chariot would have done with his shield. My target was a spot just behind the elephant's ear.

The elephant charged, trying to crush me underfoot and I dived underneath to escape. Making my way between its legs, I took my stand under its belly. The lessons I had learnt as a child in the elephant stables stood me in good stead. When the elephant swung around to catch me, I turned with it. I was unarmed, so I knew I could not continue this game of hide-and-seek for long. With his arrows, Bhagadatta kept fending off those who came to help me. Three of the five soldiers who charged at him fell. Seated on the tusker, Bhagadatta took delight in my dangerous situation. It was then that I heard a roar loud enough to make the entire expanse of Kurukshetra tremble. A soldier seated on an elephant had come to my aid – Ghatotkacha. It seemed as if he and the elephant had trumpeted in unison.

Mountains clashed against each other. Bhagadatta's tusker was flung away. I stood stunned, like a person who, emerging from a cave, faces bright light.

Ghatotkacha cried, 'Here, here!'

Clinging to the tip of the spear he lowered, I clambered up and sat behind him. Leaving his own elephant to me, he leapt with great ease onto one of the two elephants that an aide who came to assist him had brought.

Bhagadatta's soldiers sent arrows and spears flying at him. Ghatotkacha was enjoying the fight. I saw three huge chariots coming at us from the distance, leapt down and vaulted into my own chariot. Bhishmacharya had arrived.

It was the first time we confronted each other. The initial shower of arrows that flew at me broke my flagstaff. The speed of the ninety-five-year-old Bhishmacharya's hands and the sharpness of his vision when he took aim amazed me. But Bhima had many debts left to settle – he had to win, no matter whether his adversary was his teacher or his grandfather.

I felt as if my bow had come alive. I gave my fingertips no respite, and they strung the throbbing bow continuously. I heard the war cries of Ghatotkacha and his forest-dwellers and found them sweeter than the magadha songs.

Grandfather Bhishma swung his chariot around and retreated, but my fury was unabated. Except for the seconds I had spent under Bhagadatta's tusker's feet, it proved, on the whole, to be a satisfying day for me.

Days passed, and we achieved no substantial victories. The discussions on military strategies turned into forums for finding fault with one another. Yudhishtira blamed Shikhandi for letting Bhishma escape, declaring that the first step towards the defeat of an army is the fall of its commander. Shikhandi listened without a trace of emotion in his dead-man eyes.

Abhimanyu was the only one among our sons who took part in the discussions. That evening too, he accompanied me to my tent.

Abhimanyu said, 'We suffered many losses these last seven days and many people fell. But we had one great achievement. We should not call it an achievement. It is a stroke of good fortune.'

I thought he was speaking of Karna, of how he had disagreed with the others and was standing aloof from the action.

'No, I meant the arrival of the forest-dwellers. Yes, of Ghatotkacha! The warrior who will not tremble even if Indra, armed with the legendary weapon with which he killed Vritra, confronts him. All weapons are the same to Ghatotkacha. His chariots are drawn by wild horses. How swiftly he moves! Compared to him, Uncle, all of us seem so insignificant.'

With a beautiful smile, he added softly, 'I will not say, all of *you*.'

Bhishmacharya saved Duryodhana from me on the eighth day. I was not afraid of going against righteousness, as Arjuna was, when I confronted my teacher. What I dreaded was that, any moment, he might smile and say, as he had often done in my childhood, while watching Kripacharya teach me, 'Not like that, blockhead, like this …'

From the distance I maintained to shoot my arrows, I could not clearly make out the expression on the face framed by that grey beard. However, I went forward, fighting fiercely. The younger Kaurava brothers attacked from both sides, anxious to earn fame by killing Vrikodara.

Vishoka steered the chariot sideways, to give the young men the impression that he was retreating from them. Scenting victory, they advanced, shouting in unison. I was waiting for this to happen. I felled the first three with my arrows. In their ignorance, they flocked towards me, ready to attack with their hands. In barely half an hour, twelve bodies crashed to the ground.

I plucked out the arrows from the bull-hide covering my back and chest. The only wound I had sustained was a bleeding tear on my left shoulder.

That day, when I got back, I did not attend the discussions on military strategy.

Abhimanyu came to enquire if I had any serious wounds. I assured him I had none. He told me then that Irava, the naga son Arjuna had had by Uloopi, was dead. He praised the young man, who had fallen after killing Shakuni's brothers.

Alambusha, one of a group of forest-dwellers on Duryodhana's side, had killed Irava. Later, Ghatotkacha had killed Alambusha and cut off his head. When he was about to offer the head to Arjuna, Abhimanyu had dissuaded him from doing so, and Ghatotkacha had thrown it into Duryodhana's chariot.

The next day, Ghatotkacha distinguished himself by sowing destruction in the battle lines, charging repeatedly into them like a rogue elephant trampling through a bamboo forest. On one occasion, I went to his help.

Krishna said, 'Grandfather Bhishma might be nearly ninety-five, but his strategy helps many people to escape. Arjuna wavered again today when he got Bhishma to himself. I even thought of taking up my whip to attack him, but Arjuna would not allow it. I vowed not to use weapons, but the whip, after all, is not a weapon.'

Arjuna changed his mode of attack. He placed Yudhamanyu on his left, Uthamaujav on his right and Shikhandi in front of him. Duryodhana's sons had been guarding Bhishmacharya until then like a coat of armour. Our spies told us that Dussasana had also been appointed to this task.

That day, as we walked back, Abhimanyu said, 'Tomorrow, Bhishmacharya will fall.'

'How are you so sure?'

'The new positions. I also saw the determination in my father's eyes. Our teacher will be felled by my father's arrows, but people will think it is Shikhandi who made him fall.' Abhimanyu explained, 'Father will confront Dussasana and Shikhandi will confront Bhishmacharya. But at some given moment, they will exchange targets. Wait and see.'

Abhimanyu's foresight amazed me.

On the tenth day, when the war had become frenzied, Yudhishtira himself confronted Bhishmacharya and fought with a courage that no one had expected of him. Then, when Shikhandi and Arjuna came charging up, he withdrew to make way for them. Duryodhana's chariot horses had no rest that day as he sped through the Kaurava troops, trying to infuse courage into them with reprimands and instructions.

The strength of my hands and weapons too were fully tested that day. If the Pandavas had come prepared to strike Bhishma down that day, it seemed now as if the Kauravas had sworn to fell me. Bhagadatta came at me with a war cry and I confronted him. Kripacharya, Shalya and Kritavarma joined him. Kritavarma was a distant relative of Krishna, and I had heard that he had wanted to marry Subhadra.

New groups joined the Kauravas to reinforce their strength – Jayadratha and warriors from Sindhu and Avanti.

When numerous adversaries join the action in their chariots, it becomes meaningless to adhere to the norms of righteous war. I knew Jayadratha would have no compunction about breaking rules. I struck down his chariot and horses, and he vaulted into the chariot belonging to Chandrasena, Duryodhana's brother.

The soldiers of Virata, fighting on both my flanks, challenged death. One of them saved me from a feathered spear that Jayadratha had aimed at my head.

Meanwhile, Bhagadatta and his group drew steadily closer. A chariot formation flew to my help, led by Abhimanyu.

I realised the difference between a sixteen-year-old warrior and a thirty-five-year-old one. If war was a profession and a duty for us, it was an adornment and entertainment for Abhimanyu. He ridiculed Kripacharya's weak marksmanship. Kritavarma turned tail and fled. Bhagadatta withdrew to the rear.

When he had a moment of respite, Abhimanyu said, 'People talk so much about Father's skill in archery. I had thought until now, Uncle, that you were skilled only with your mace and your hands. In truth, you astounded me!'

I knew I would cherish this praise from the younger generation within me, like a secret treasure. 'There were seven of them.'

'Not seven, ten, including Vinda, Anuvinda and Vikarna. Mighty men, all ten of them. Who is there here, Uncle, other than you, who can fight ten men single-handed?'

Delighted, I said, 'There's Arjuna. And then, you.'

I rushed to where Arjuna was fighting. Halfway there, I heard the Kaurava troops roar. I drew nearer. When the dust settled, my vision cleared and I saw that war at that spot had ended. I looked at the warrior lying on the ground. Bhishmacharya. His breastplate was split and his whole body pierced by arrows. Arjuna stood before him, overcome by guilt.

Drumbeats signifying the end of war echoed through the air. I saw the Kaurava chariots rushing towards their fallen commander-in-chief and turned back.

Members of the scavenger castes moved into the battlefield with carts drawn by donkeys, to take the corpses away.

3

We had assumed Karna would become the commander-in-chief when Grandfather Bhishma fell. But we heard that Drona had been chosen for the post.

Bhishma did not die on the battlefield. We came to know that he was very close to death, that it could happen at any moment. The spies told us that when Drona took charge, he gave his word that he would capture Yudhishtira alive. We therefore decided to guard Yudhishtira closely while we fought.

After fighting on three consecutive fronts, I clashed violently with Bhagadatta again in the afternoon. Knowing I was weak in a chariot, he came charging at me on his trumpeting tusker that was intoxicated with war. Several soldiers in the lower ranks were struck down dead. Fierce fighting took place on all fronts that day. Karna was on the battlefield; Drona in the front line.

Fearing that Yudhishtira would be isolated, Arjuna asked me to go to his aid and took over Bhagadatta himself. We could not allow Yudhishtira to be taken prisoner at any cost. Observing that Dhrishtadyumna was moving to the southern front, Arjuna insisted that I go to Yudhishtira's help.

When I got to him, Yudhishtira, intelligent enough to sense the danger he was in, was on his way back to the camp. I heard music as I neared the royal tent – a sign that he had returned – and went in, anxious to find out the news on other fronts. Suddenly, the conches, mridangams and veenas came to an abrupt stop, like an evil omen. I alighted from my chariot and walked towards Yudhishtira.

He was standing motionless as the soldiers from the northern front, who had given him the news, went away sorrowfully.

Abhimanyu was dead!

That was all the soldiers had said. That Abhimanyu was dead. It was only when Dhrishtadyumna and Satyaki arrived that we learnt the details of the battle. Dronacharya had been advancing with a wheel-shaped formation in order to capture Yudhishtira. It had soon become clear that the formation had to be broken. Abhimanyu had declared boldly that he would break in and fight from within it. As soon as Abhimanyu entered the formation, Jayadratha had moved forward in his chariot, drawn by a single horse, blocked those who came in on the flanks and trapped him. Drona, Kripa, Ashvathama, Karna and Shalya had then surrounded Abhimanyu, ignoring the fact that, according to the rules of war, the boy should have had soldiers to help him move forward or sideways. Several soldiers had come up to help the older Kaurava warriors. Abhimanyu had lost his chariot and horse and fought his adversaries standing on the bare ground. When his bow and arrows were taken from him, he had fought with his sword and his mace, then with the wheel of his chariot. Finally, he had fallen down unconscious, and someone had smashed his head and killed him.

Dhrishtadyumna told us that it was Lakshmana, Dussasana's son, a boy who was Abhimanyu's own age, who had killed him. I gave no thought to whoever had killed him. Six men, including Drona and Kripa, had attacked a boy who stood fighting on the bare ground.

Satyaki's commander remarked that even in the enemy camp the magadhas would sing about Abhimanyu's heroic deeds today.

Dhrishtadyumna reminded us that everyone had broken the rules of righteous war, even Drona and Kripa, that Jayadratha was a worse scoundrel than them. He had violated a basic rule that even a forest-dweller would have abided by.

I looked at Yudhishtira, who was silent, and said, 'That same Jayadratha once stood before me, a prisoner, guilty of a crime that deserved death as punishment. If I tell you what the crime was, none of you will forgive my elder brother. I let him go – my elder brother insisted I let him go, in the name of righteousness or the love of humanity or something like that ...'

Yudhishtira said nothing.

Krishna and Arjuna came in at that moment. Krishna's face was ashen-pale. I thought, when blood ties and family bonds are involved, we forget to compare bodies to tattered clothes we are ready to shed.

A magadha group who obviously had not heard the news began to play their instruments and Krishna said, 'Tell them to stop.'

I found it difficult to look at Arjuna's face. Standing with his back to us near the fireplace, he gazed at the burning embers. The defeat of Bhagadatta was not going to soften the loss of Abhimanyu.

No one had anything to say. Someone could have described the battle as one that the celestial beings must have watched, but no one did. There was no point praising Abhimanyu's courage or cursing the cruelty of the enemy.

Abhimanyu was dead.

I went out. Standing by myself in the stillness of the faint dark outside the tent, the memory of one who had died weighed upon me for the first time in my life – a burden my heart could not bear. I stood alone on the path we had always walked together to my tent. Abhimanyu's smiling eyes. His voice, calling me,

'Uncle …' My eyes filled. No, the mighty Bhima could not weep. Instead of turning towards my tent, I walked to the deserted battlefield. Jackals that had come down from the undergrowth on the riverside howled, delighted to have discovered a corpse that had not been taken away. There was an odour of rotting flesh and clotted blood. And a flapping of vultures' wings through the air.

I thought about death. I had felt deep sympathy for Virata when Uttaran died. Now, something had died within me. There was no denying that it was beyond me to look at this death as a soul changing its dwelling.

As a child, I had thought death was the coming of Yama, the God of Death. Then one of the teachers had told me about Mrityu, a girl whom Brahma had created in anger. She was born as a beautiful girl. But she had stood before him hesitantly, saying she did not know how to kill, and he had given her courage. The colour of her skin was a tawny red tinged with black. Covered with jewels, she had pale red eyes and dark red lips. Mrityu, the lovely virgin.

Wandering over Kurukshetra, this beautiful maiden had stolen a part of me.

The night grew darker. I woke up from my thoughts when the vultures began to hover around me.

Going back, I passed the tent occupied by Draupadi's sons and Sarvada, and went towards the river. I saw a huge chariot, flying a flag with a vulture on it. Someone was seated in it, his leg stretched out over the yoke. Ghatotkacha.

He came down when he saw me.

'Abhimanyu is gone.'

Death for him was an event that awoke an enthusiasm for revenge.

'I was closer to Abhimanyu than to anyone else. From now on, I will kill for his sake. Those teachers are worse than us forest-dwellers!'

I did not reply.

'From tomorrow, they are making preparations to fight at night. It's exactly what I want. For the nishadas, there is no better armour than darkness.' Ghatotkacha smiled.

I went back to my tent, without going on to the river.

Worse than forest-dwellers! I thought of Ghatotkacha's words. Today, the eighty-year-old Drona had supervised the killing of a young man who was barely seventeen, whose honeymoon had lasted only twenty-one days. The invisible beauty Brahma had created had watched it happen with pleasure.

Dhrishtadyumna was waiting for me when I got back, his eyes reddened by liquor. He was still untouched by the fatigue of war.

'I will kill Drona. Duryodhana will not come to the front ranks. Try to get Karna to fight a duel with you. He will certainly accept.'

I reminded him that Arjuna had vowed to kill Karna.

'Taking vows has become an everyday affair here. Only a fool takes a vow in the hearing of the soldiers saying that if he does not kill Jayadratha by sunset tomorrow, he will himself die. I just heard someone say that.'

'Who? Who?'

'Arjuna, who else? It's so easy to hide someone on a battlefield. And he takes a vow without thinking of that! The Kauravas must be laughing at him now.'

He stayed with me for quite a while, but said nothing. Then

he got up, took leave of me and went out. Although he had not shown it openly, I knew he was deeply troubled.

Vishoka had made it a habit to sit in a spot outside the door where I could see him until I went to bed. Besides the food that was sent for me from the kitchen, he had arranged with the hunters to send special meats, which he cooked for me himself.

Vishoka said everyone, right down to the workers in the kitchens, was deeply grieved by the death of Abhimanyu. Even the soldiers' camps were empty of laughter and fun.

I listened to him and thought: no one's death must shatter the morale in the camps.

Maybe to dispel my gloom, Vishoka asked, 'Do you know anything about Karna's lance?'

I said no.

'People say all sorts of things. Some say it is a divine weapon gifted to him personally by Indra. Others say that a craftsman of the Anga kingdom made it for him.'

We had spread the word that it was Indra who had given Arjuna all his weapons. People would believe that, since Indra was his father.

I had heard about Karna's lance when we were in Virata. It was said that it could not be recalled, as Krishna's discus could be.

'Is it a lance that can be used manually or a mechanical one?'

There were lances that could be gripped by hand, as well as those that did not need to be handled at all, said Vishoka. 'In all likelihood, Karna's can be fixed to the chariot. Any craftsman can make an ordinary lance. I've heard about this craftsman from Anga. The lance he made is probably released from a device fixed to the chariot.'

This was Vishoka's guess. I remembered Mayan having spoken of such a weapon.

There were weapons intended for use against the principal enemy, which never missed their mark. Like Krishna's discus, Ashvathama's Narayana arrow, Arjuna's Pashupati arrow that could be filled with serpent venom and many others.

Vishoka thought that if Karna's lance was designed to be used against one particular person, it would be fitted with a blade fashioned out of diamond and filled with poison. The blade would break as it entered the body and it would be impossible to extract it. Even if his wound was not deep, the opponent would die because of the power of the venom. If it penetrated deep through the breastplate, it was probably a mechanical device.

These were all Vishoka's surmises. He had a great quality: he would argue both for and against something, then come to a decision.

I said softly, 'He might have to take out the lance tomorrow.'

Everyone knew Karna intended to use this weapon against his arch enemy, Arjuna. But it was I who would confront Karna the next day. I did not need divine weapons, my bare hands would suffice.

Vishoka looked steadily at me for a while, then sighed and bowed his head.

The next day, the Kauravas kept Jayadratha covered while they fought. It happened as we had expected – while Dhrishtadyumna confronted Drona, Arjuna tried to penetrate Duryodhana's army formation. Seeing Karna drive his chariot from Duryodhana's rear right into Drona's line of action, we marched forward at once and lined up on the opposite side. Karna must have assumed that I was going to assist Arjuna.

He called out loudly, 'Vrikodara, you coward, are you running away?'

We heard the soldiers on his flanks laugh. Karna's arrows, which had peacock feathers as wings, fluttered around me like vultures. Arrows fitted with crescent-heads and snake-heads pierced my breastplate. I sent arrows fitted with eagle feathers at Karna, trying to overcome him. Vishoka kept filling my quiver as fast as it emptied. This charioteer's son must learn today that the science of archery flowed through the blood of a kshatriya, even if he did not regularly participated in archery contests. According to the rules of war, the aides on Karna's flanks requested time for him to change his bow on three occasions. I thought I would know for certain today who would tire first – the mighty charioteer Karna or Bhima, who was an expert at wielding the mace.

Karna looked surprised when the Kauravas who rushed to assist him as he began to tire fell to my arrows. I did not ridicule him. If he was better than me at a war with words, so be it, I thought. It was he who had triumphed in the gambling hall with words and explanations.

I confronted Karna as he took up his fourth bow, and said to him, 'Let's fight a duel, just the two of us. With whatever weapon you like.'

The answer he gave was to aim an arrow that grazed my neck, embedded itself in the chariot behind me and remained there, quivering.

The distance between us was growing narrower. I wished I had more than two hands. I yelled, convinced that this was my last fight in Kurukshetra. I strung the arrows held out to me by eight hands and heard them hum as they flew from my bow. I saw Karna begin to look exhausted and cling for support to a pillar in his chariot and asked myself: 'Now? Now? Now?'

If I could move ten paces forward, I would be able to shoot an arrow at his neck. My opponent was once again ready to fight. I would not break rules. I would kill him in the next few seconds. The long arrow tipped with a vulture's feather trembled at my fingertips. Now ...

Vishoka cried, 'Don't. You must not kill him!'

There was an unexpected note of pain in his voice. I looked at him, surprised and angry.

Vishoka said very softly, 'You must not kill him. It will be a great sin. He is your elder brother. He is not the soota's son, he is Kunti Devi's firstborn.'

I looked at him unbelievingly. Did he know the meaning of what he was saying?

'Karna is the eldest Pandava!'

My courage completely drained, I stood helplessly in my chariot, then slumped down.

Noticing that I had suddenly grown weak, Karna recovered his zeal and approached my chariot, hurling sharp words of mockery at me: 'You fool! You're neither man nor woman, the battlefield is no place for you!' Prodding my shoulder with the tip of his bow, he put his head out of the chariot and cried out, 'I gave your mother my word that I would kill only one of you. And that won't be you. Run away and hide somewhere, with your pot belly and scanty beard!'

I heard every word he spat out contemptuously and saw his face, distorted with mockery, for an instant.

On our way to help Arjuna, Vishoka said, as if in answer to my unspoken question, 'Before the war started, your mother begged the son she had by the Sun God, Surya, while she was still a virgin, to join the Pandavas. I had the misfortune to overhear her.'

'Mother ... Mother said this to Karna directly?'

Vishoka stopped the chariot. While coming from southern Kashi with the chariots and horses Senesha had sent, they had camped on the banks of the Ganga. Vishoka had seen Kunti Devi by the river at dawn and gone up to her to pay her obeisance, for he was seeing her after many years. But he stopped as he drew near. She was not alone. She was standing next to Karna, who was performing his morning salutations to the Sun God.

Karna had spoken with contempt, 'I do not wish to become a kshatriya now. The sootas brought me up. My wife and children belong to a soota clan.'

Vishoka had been upset at having heard what they said.

'My son, you should stand with the Pandavas. I concealed the truth all this while, fearing what people would say about me.' She sobbed.

Vishoka said that Karna had laughed.

'Since you came to plead with me, I will not send you back with nothing. I will kill only one of your sons: Arjuna.' He laughed louder, then controlled himself and said, 'Whether he dies or I, you will still have five sons. Isn't that enough?'

I heard all that Vishoka said, but did not say a word.

Vishoka loosened the reins and the horses broke into a run. When we went up to Arjuna, Yudhamanyu asked me what had happened. All I said was that Karna had defeated me.

Before dusk, Krishna instructed Arjuna to turn back despondently, pretending he had broken his vow to kill Jayadratha and had stopped fighting. Arjuna did as he was asked.

Krishna saw Jayadratha approach Duryodhana from the back with great fanfare. Astounding onlookers with the speed of the chariot, Krishna brought Arjuna before Jayadratha. Arjuna fulfilled the vow he had made.

But I did not see this. I could no longer see clearly. I heard even the sounds near me as if they were from afar. All I could see before me was Karna's face, mocking me. Karna, the soota's son. The Karna I had shamed on the day we displayed our skills, telling him that the weapon that suited him best was a whip. Kunti's eldest son. The son of the Sun God, the heir to the throne of Hastinapura!

How many more secrets were hidden in my mother's heart as she sat in Vidura's house?

4

The war continued even after sunset. Duryodhana accused Drona of not employing all the strategies he knew against his disciples, so Drona decided that they would go on fighting through the night.

I began the night by keeping company with Yudhishtira, who was attacking Ashvathama. The brahmin was trying to overcome Yudhishtira with a show of weapons that amazed Arjuna. Finally, I managed to make him retreat.

When he learnt that Satyaki had killed Somadutta, Yudhishtira set out to attack Drona. Krishna sent a messenger warning Yudhishtira not to expose himself, for it was possible that Drona's vow that he would take Yudhishtira prisoner may have influenced his decision to continue fighting at night.

Over the darkness of night, mist rose from the Hiranvati and it became impossible to see anything. A fierce war cry could be heard from time to time even in the dense darkness: Ghatotkacha's. For him and his companions, war by night was something to enjoy.

Dhrishtadyumna called out, 'Torches! Bring torches!'

The soldiers repeated the cry. As soon as the Pandava troops lighted torches, the opponents did so as well. Brightness spread over the battlefield as thousands of torches suddenly blazed.

At one point, when he felt that Kritavarma and Drona were going to encircle him jointly and capture him, Yudhishtira thought the most practical solution was to go back and turned his chariot towards the tents.

I met Duryodhana face-to-face briefly. Like me, he must have thought there was no point postponing the confrontation. Mace in hand, he jumped down from his chariot. That was what I wanted. A handful of people came between us and my blows shattered their heads. A carefully aimed blow landed on the outstretched head of Duryodhana's frightened horse. Duryodhana turned back and climbed into his chariot.

In the meantime, Ashvathama and Ghatotkacha were fighting each other. Ghatotkacha's band of forest-dwellers, numbering barely a hundred, turned into an unquenchable fire and destroyed an army of a thousand soldiers.

Sahadeva came up to me, his breastplate torn, bleeding in several spots where arrows had pierced him. Deeply distressed, he said resentfully, 'Karna ridiculed and shamed me. I escaped only because Satyaki came to my rescue.'

A much fiercer confrontation than the one between Ashvathama and Ghatotkacha was taking place on the western front, between Dhrishtadyumna and Drona. Sahadeva told me that Karna had joined this battle.

Seeing that Duryodhana had withdrawn, and I had nothing else to do that night, I ordered the chariot to be driven back to the camp. I found Arjuna resting there. He had not gone back to the battlefield after killing Jayadratha.

A soldier who came in to fill our quivers told us, 'Dhrishtadyumna is growing weaker in the fight against Karna.'

Krishna asked, 'Where is Ghatotkacha?'

I said, 'From what I know, he is destroying Ashvathama's army.'

Krishna stood up and said to Yudhishtira, 'Let Ghatotkacha go to the front line and confront Karna. Send soldiers immediately with the order.' Then he said to me, 'No one can match Ghatotkacha in fighting at night. He is the only one who can overcome Karna.'

The soldiers rushed away with the order and Krishna went out.

I stood in front of my own tent. Torches blazed in the distance. I could hear horses' hooves, the sounds of moving chariots and, from time to time, screams.

Vishoka said he would go in a chariot to enquire about the news and I agreed.

The battlefield was growing noisier. More chariots were participating in the action and the rolling of chariot wheels sounded like thunder sweeping through rain clouds. I saw balls of fire hurtling past – fighting with fire was an expertise that forest-dwellers had.

The darkness grew deeper when thick smoke began to spread from the burnt-out torches.

I saw that Vishoka had come back, and hurried to find out the news.

He smiled and said, 'Tonight is Ghatotkacha's. The Kaurava army will be finished today. He's fighting like a blazing fire, a whirlwind!'

'Who all are with him?'

'He is alone. From what I could see, he needs no companions.'

'And on the opposite side?'

'Alayudha, who would have been a match for Ghatotkacha and the rakshasas, is dead. Now there is Karna, and the Kaurava army that is too afraid of him to run away.'

Vishoka went back to the battlefield.

I wondered whether to go to Ghatotkacha's aid. I could guess the nature of the new taunts Karna would throw at him.

Suddenly, a question flashed through my mind like lightning. Who was I going to help? Ghatotkacha and his foresters, or Karna?

The roars of the warriors kept ringing in my ears.

Balls of fire rocketed upwards and splintered, scattering sparks. From a scream that rose from hundreds of voices, I distinguished Ghatotkacha's war cry.

And then suddenly, there was complete silence.

I heard drums thudding from the Kaurava front, like the heartbeats of the pitch-black night. Fighting had stopped for the time being …

I walked slowly towards Yudhishtira's tent, prepared to hear the news of Karna's death. Chariots were coming back from the battlefield.

Vishoka's chariot stopped in front of me. 'In the end, Karna had to take up his new lance, Vyjayanthi. It is a mechanical device. Ghatotkacha fell down dead.'

I noted that Vishoka's tone could barely conceal his secret relief.

The tawny-red beauty with glittering earrings and a smile on her bright red lips had singled out Ghatotkacha today. Ghatotkacha, for whom war had been a thrilling experience.

There was light in Yudhishtira's tent. I went in and found Nakula, Sahadeva and Dhrishtadyumna there. Messengers had brought them the news. Yudhishtira saw me and raised his head.

'I cannot bear the sorrow. The child who came to keep us company in Gandhamadana, the first son of the Pandavas ... Abhimanyu first, now Ghatotkacha ...'

I saw the shadow of grief on all their faces.

At that moment, Krishna hurried in with Arjuna. He looked at Yudhishtira, whose head was bowed in sorrow, and the stricken faces of the others.

'Why do you grieve?' he asked. 'Karna used the lance he had kept as a last resort against Arjuna on Ghatotkacha. Don't you understand? Arjuna escaped – so this is a time for celebration, not lamentation, in the Pandava camp.'

I do not know whether Krishna noticed me standing in the shadows, beyond the glow of the fire. I walked out quietly.

As I stood outside, I heard Krishna's voice again: 'We must celebrate. Where are the magadhas and the rhythm players? And those foolish soota paean singers?'

I could not make out what Yudhishtira said in reply.

Krishna said again, 'He may have been Bhima's son, but he was a forest-dweller, with the nature of a demon. An enemy of sacrificial rituals and brahmins. Someday we would have had to kill him. On both counts, it is convenient for us that he died.' I heard him laugh. 'It was not for nothing that I said to him, you are our only hope and sent him to face Karna.'

I walked away. I heard the musical instruments that had been silent until then start up. The celebration had begun. I waited by myself in the darkness. I knew from the drumbeats that both armies had stopped fighting and were going to sleep. The tents and camps fell silent. Soldiers rested their heads against the chariot floors and on the heads of elephants.

I kept walking.

Moonlight reached down to the dark space of Kurukshetra and the rogue elephants of darkness ran away from the tempest that was night. Moonlight as tender as the smile of a newly wedded bride and groom, as milky-white as Shiva's beautiful bull spread over the vast expanse.

I saw his dead body, a patch of darkness that had not been able to run away in time. The man-high iron handle of the lance that had pierced his breast rose sharply into the sky. A vulture had alighted on its tip and was gazing down greedily at the body beneath.

No pyre had to be built for a forest-dweller; he was not entitled to a warrior's Heaven. The donkey carts and chandalas were resting. The fluttering of vultures' wings grew louder.

I walked back.

As I neared the tents, the magadhas were changing the funereal rhythm of their songs to a happier mood in order to comfort the weary soldiers.

I did not sleep. The light of morning spread through the air, the beginning of another day. We offered prayers for victory at the sacrificial site. Yudhishtira gave gifts to the brahmins as usual.

As we set out, Dhrishtadyumna said, 'Drona ... Drona must fall.'

The Panchala army ranged itself to fight Drona. I attacked the other Kauravas, concentrating on shattering their chariots. The fourth battalion of the Kauravas, which had started out with more foot soldiers had now grown weak. It was Ghatotkacha that the Pandavas had to thank for this.

Yudhishtira stayed in the rear, watching the fight between Drona and Dhrishtadyumna.

We kept receiving news of the action. Dronacharya was a clever and skilful leader. It was significant that Dhrishtadyumna had looked upon him as his arch enemy from the very beginning, for, compared to Drona, Bhishmacharya had been a poor leader.

We had news of two successive deaths. King Drupada had been killed, so had King Virata. Both had been felled by Dronacharya. Yudhishtira kept riding around restlessly in his chariot, at the rear of the Panchala army and on its flanks.

Arjuna, who had been on the warpath against Ashvathama, turned his chariot around and approached us.

Krishna said, 'If we spread a rumour that Ashvathama is dead, the old man will lose heart and become helpless and weak.'

Arjuna said, 'Let our soldiers enter the Panchala ranks shouting that Ashvathama is dead.'

Yudhishtira was doubtful, 'Will our teacher believe them?'

'If you go yourself, proclaiming the news joyfully, he will.'

'Tell a lie ...?' Yudhishtira was worried.

Krishna managed to control his anger. 'This is war, not a game of dice. Drupada, Virata, all our warriors are falling one by one. We are collapsing before the old man like a herd of cattle before a tiger.'

Pointing to an elephant that my mace had wounded in a vital spot and brought down, Krishna said angrily, 'Look, that elephant that Bhima killed – I name it Ashvathama and say, "Ashvathama is dead". I am speaking the truth. Ashvathama is dead!'

As Arjuna's chariot and mine flew towards the flanks of the Panchala army along with Yudhishtira's, we shouted: 'Ashvathama is dead!'

Drona had just finished giving instructions to Dussasana and positioning his chariot when he heard us.

Yudhishtira shouted as well, 'Ashvathama is dead!', then spoke the truth softly to himself, to salve his conscience: 'The elephant, Ashvathama.'

The Panchalas shouted joyfully in unison and rushed forward. Utter chaos followed. War cries resounded and wails of lament. When the dust settled, I saw Drona lying on the floor of his chariot, his head severed from his body. Dhrishtadyumna stood over him, his sword dripping blood, a harsh expression on his face.

War ended with the fall of the commander-in-chief. Dhrishtadyumna mounted his chariot carrying the bloody sword and returned to his tent, and we followed.

Grabbing Krishna's shoulder for support, Arjuna vaulted out of his chariot in front of Dhrishtadyumna's tent and said, 'That was not right. It was not right to behead him.'

Satyaki came rushing up in another chariot and turned on Dhrishtadyumna angrily, 'You lowdown rascal! Drona was a brahmin, if nothing else. It was right to strike him down in battle, but how could you think of beheading him?' Then he said to himself, 'Yes, the Panchalas would think of doing so. Shikhandi and you are cruel sinners.'

I had not expected such rebukes, such anger, from Satyaki.

Dhrishtadyumna faced him without a trace of anger and said scornfully, 'Killing is always killing. I have never taken lessons on how to kill according to the rules of dharma.'

Satyaki muttered, 'He was on the enemy's side, but he was a teacher. And a brahmin.'

'And where was your dharma, Satyaki, when you beheaded Bhurishrava as he lay with his arm severed?'

But Satyaki only repeated, 'He was a brahmin. A guru.'

Dhrishtadyumna abandoned his contemptuous manner and turned on Satyaki with fury: 'Where was the old man's brahminic consciousness when he led six men to encircle the defenceless, sixteen-year-old Abhimanyu?'

Making an attempt to calm himself, he turned to Yudhishtira and said, 'I am not as wise as you. But I too have learnt that the duties of a brahmin are to seek alms, to teach, to perform sacrifices, to receive gifts and to study. Which one of these duties was the great brahmin immersed in at the moment when I killed him?'

He came up to me to gauge my reaction.

I said, 'My friend, I embrace and congratulate you.'

But Satyaki had not finished. 'For lifting up the brahmin guru by his hair and cutting off his head? Bhima, let him go. The rascal is no kshatriya!'

Satyaki lunged forward and Dhrishtadyumna responded likewise, deciding to end the argument with weapons.

Barring his way, Yudhishtira pleaded, 'Don't! I have only you Panchalas and the Yadavas to support me. If you start to fight among yourselves, what will I do?'

Yudhishtira drew Satyaki aside, I did the same with Dhrishtadyumna.

We went back to the battleground, our hearts troubled and our moves lacking coordination, and acquitted ourselves deplorably before an attack led by Ashvathama. To our relief, fighting ended for the day. I thought Kripa would be the next commander. Or that they would choose Ashvathama, who was thirsting to avenge Drona's death. But we came to know it was neither of them, it was Karna.

In that brief interval, we took stock once again of the number of people who had died. The Kaurava side had lost Bhishma, Drona, Jayadratha, Bhagadatta, Bhurishrava and several of Duryodhana's brothers, the most important being Vikarna and Chitrasena.

The magadhas had already composed songs about the people we had lost. Uttaran, Abhimanyu, Irava, Drupada, Virata. I could not help noticing that, when they strung the names together, they left out one. The death of a forest-dweller was not a fit subject for a heroic tale.

That night, we gathered in front of Yudhishtira to discuss a way to kill Karna. Arjuna drew the army positions on an expanse of sand, then erased them and redrew others.

I reminded them, 'In your hurry to strike down Karna, don't forget Drona's son, Ashvathama, who has sworn vengeance.'

'I know his strengths and weaknesses. First, Karna!'

I looked at Yudhishtira and Arjuna as they planned the killing of Karna and stayed silent, knowing I could not speak.

It was a secret that Mother had guarded until now. I must not reveal it. May I never have occasion to have to reveal it, I warned myself.

On the seventeenth day of the war, I challenged Ashvathama to a fight.

Ashvathama's war cry, intended to disarm his enemy, sounded like the neigh of a wild horse. Someone had nicknamed him Ashvathama when he was a child, because of this strange cry. He could move faster than Dronacharya, was more skilful than Karna. But I had Vishoka's expertise and good fortune on my side. As my opponent began to tire, Arjuna arrived.

'You can have him now. I've snuffed out half his courage.'

Sahadeva clashed with Dussasana. When Arjuna moved towards Ashvathama, Karna came forward, made a fool of Nakula and let him go. I saw Sutasoma fighting Shakuni courageously. Just behind them, Shikhandi had retreated after being defeated by Kritavarma.

Sarvada came to tell me that Yudhishtira was fighting Duryodhana. I rushed towards the spot in my chariot. Yudhishtira looked at me with relief, and I said, 'He is mine. Go back, I've come.'

As I advanced, Duryodhana swung to the right and joined the middle ranks. Satyaki saw Karna join Duryodhana, and vaulted forward to separate Arjuna from Ashvathama.

No one had much to say that evening. Someone praised me for the fight with Ashvathama. Thoughts of revenge smouldered in hearts that had been stricken by the deaths of several leaders.

The next day, Karna let loose a whirlwind on the Pandava army. Shalya was his charioteer – a strategic move on Duryodhana's part, for Shalya kept pace with the speed and control of Arjuna's charioteer, thereby adding to Karna's strength. Ashvathama attacked Dhrishtadyumna, tore his breastplate with sharp arrows and rendered him helpless. Meanwhile, Karna managed to get Yudhishtira to himself. Then he leapt forward when he saw Arjuna rushing to help Dhrishtadyumna.

I was attacking Duryodhana's front line at that moment.

It seemed as if Karna filled the entire battlefield. I discovered only later that he had almost killed Yudhishtira, and that a riot had resulted.

Yudhishtira was covered with wounds when he went back to his tent. Arjuna arrived as the servants and physicians were attending on him. Yudhishtira sat up, sure that Karna had been killed.

'I knew that only you could defeat Karna.'

Yudhishtira's face fell when Arjuna told him he was going back to put an end to Karna's atrocities.

'You left Bhima alone and came here? No, you must have run away, fearing Karna. Look, look at my body, lacerated by Karna's arrows. The Kaurava army laughed at me jeeringly.'

Yudhishtira chastised himself for having placed so much faith in Arjuna's boast that he could defeat Karna easily.

Then he said angrily, 'If you're afraid of Karna, give your Gandiva bow to Krishna here. I know for certain that Krishna will defeat him. All you need do is drive the chariot. Spend your time being a charioteer for the rest of the war!' He turned to the onlookers: 'I am a fool to have believed his boasts for thirteen years!'

Sweat beaded Arjuna's dark face. He loosened the knot of his quiver, and it fell to the ground with a clatter. He took off his bow with its golden handle and flung it at Krishna. Then he pulled out his sword, crying, 'Once your head is chopped off, this war will end!'

Krishna barred Arjuna's way as he leapt at Yudhishtira furiously, and cautioned him: 'Whatever he says to you in anger, he is your elder brother and the king. Do not forget that!'

Arjuna was still furious. 'A coward, who always stands at least half a mile from the battlefield! There's only one thing he knows, gambling, the profession of the lowborn! How is he worthy to be king? He's a coward who does not even have the right to share Draupadi's bed!' He turned on Krishna, who was still trying to deter him: 'I would accept it if my elder brother Bhima, who can take on a thousand opponents by himself, were to call me a coward. But what right has this man to do so? He is a curse on the Pandavas, he must be finished today!'

Krishna, the attendants and two old brahmins somehow managed to subdue Arjuna.

Later, Yudhishtira pleaded to be forgiven for having spoken thoughtlessly, impelled by his fear of defeat. Arjuna, who had calmed down by then, also asked Yudhishtira's pardon. Krishna prevailed upon Arjuna to go back to the battlefield.

While all this commotion took place in the camp, I saw that Karna had come forward again to help the Kauravas. I noticed Dussasana, who was guarding Karna's left flank, move into a bigger chariot and rush towards Satyaki, and asked Vishoka to bar his way with our chariot.

'Dussasana!' I shouted, 'I am coming!'

He halted, then turned his chariot towards me. We were by ourselves. I held my joy in check. I did not want to continue the fight standing on the floor of my chariot, waiting for him to make mistakes. What I hoped was that, true to his boast that he was as skilful as Duryodhana with a mace, he would put down his bow and pick up a mace.

The third time I attacked, his mace shot out of his hand. I threw my mace onto the floor.

'Bare hands, Dussasana, bare hands. For Draupadi's sake, for mine ... Let all those who remember that I vowed to tear open your chest and drink your blood come and see!'

I saw fear in his eyes.

He had only heard of the Bhima who had grown up among the nishadas, fighting with bare hands. In his first burst of enthusiasm, he rushed at me, using his legs, his hands, his head as maces. Then I began ...

Dussasana grew steadily weaker as I hit him repeatedly on his forehead, his head and his left ear. I parried his fists with my left hand and brought him down with a blow on his chest. I sprang on him, my foot on his neck, and as my fingers dug deep into his ribcage, his eyes protruded and I heard stifled moans.

Using all my strength, I pressed my hand down on his ribs and heard a sound like bark tearing. A stream of warm blood splashed onto my face, a garland of vengeance, red as ashoka flowers. Blood. The blood I had tasted over a thousand nights as I had bitten my lips in anger. The drink of celebration that is offered to a destroyer.

I stood up, feeling the gentle warmth of blood on my hands and face.

When the Kauravas who remained drew near, I said to them, 'Come. The massacre will take place only after the offering of a drink of blood. Today is the day Bhima will have a royal meal!'

They stopped. Some of them called out to me. I walked off,

picking my way among the fallen, immobile bodies. Someone's head ornament was crushed under my feet and blood-spattered pearls scattered over the ground.

I thought to myself, Death, the tawny-red beauty, is standing somewhere, watching …

It saddened me that another beautiful woman, who always thrilled to war stories, had not been there today to watch …

5

I saw seven chariots racing together into the camp and thought something important must have happened.

Vishoka was wiping the blood off my body.

I walked to Yudhishtira's tent. Catching sight of me, Arjuna jumped down from his chariot and ran up to me.

'I killed Karna, I killed him!' Full of happiness, he held out his arms to me, waiting for my embrace.

I sighed and closed my eyes as he moved into the circle of my arms.

All those who had come with him were congratulating one another joyfully.

Arjuna called out, 'Where is the music? Where are the sootas and the magadhas? Karna is dead!'

Yudhishtira ran up to take part in the celebration.

In the distance, songs of lament began to waft towards us from the Kaurava camp. They faded away into the medley of instruments that accompanied the paeans that suddenly rose from the Pandavas' singers.

Yudhishtira ran around, spurring on the musicians: 'Sing,

magadhas, that Karna is dead! Arjuna, the expert archer, the victorious warrior, equal of Indra, killed him. Sing full-throatedly!'

Yudhishtira reminded Arjuna that it was the blessing of Indra and all the other gods that had gifted him the crucial moment when the wheel of Karna's chariot sank into the earth, rendering him helpless.

They kept describing Karna's end.

In the name of the rules of dharmic war, Karna had requested for time to change his wheel before he continued to fight. Arjuna said to us, 'I told him that dharmic war ended with the fall of Bhishmacharya. I asked him what rules they had abided by in Kurukshetra when they attacked Abhimanyu.'

Yudhishtira said, as he walked towards his chariot, 'For my own comfort, I need to see the body of the soota's son lying in his chariot. Drive on!'

I stood by myself, watching Yudhishtira's chariot melt into the distance as he sped to see Karna's body.

The stench of the bodies that had not yet been removed from the battlefield lay heavy in the air. Jackals howled without a pause even in the daytime. The breeze from the Hiranvati blew waves of heat towards us from the continuously burning pyres.

Shalya continued to fight with the few soldiers that remained, merely to maintain the dharma of the kshatriyas, not with any hope of victory. Shakuni was his main support. Dejected by Karna's death, Ashvathama did not come to the front line at all.

An enthusiasm they had not felt before possessed the Pandavas. Sahadeva carried out his vow: Shakuni died at his hands, proving an insignificant enemy before the young and manly Sahadeva. Yudhishtira seemed to have suddenly grown mighty after Karna's death. He sent Nakula away and confronted Shalya himself, probably because he wanted to slay at least one great charioteer. Yudhishtira had never fought a war that merited a ballad of victory. I struck down Shalya's charioteer and horse from the left and quickly withdrew, so that Yudhishtira would not feel that I had gone to his help.

My principal enemy was still far away. I kept searching for Duryodhana.

Vishoka thought that he was probably making a final effort to gather all the soldiers who were fleeing, to form them into an army. He was right. Soon after Shalya fell, Duryodhana arrived with a small army. The fact that Sanjaya, who had been keeping Dhritarashtra company, constantly reporting the progress of the war to him, was part of this army was enough to assess its strength.

Duryodhana resisted for a very short while, then stopped fighting and ran away. Our soldiers shouted: 'The Pandavas have finally won!'

The women, who were in the temporary shelter beyond the river, had to be taken to Hastinapura in boats. Yudhishtira entrusted this task to Yuyutsu, who was born to a servant woman as Dhritarashtra's son, but had come and joined Yudhishtira's servants when he realized that war was inevitable.

I had no wish to participate in the celebrations. My war was not yet over. One of Dhritarashtra's sons was still alive. The soldiers and spies who had gone in search of Duryodhana said that he was not in Hastinapura.

Meanwhile, the pots of liquor opened in the tents and camps to mark the celebration frothed and overflowed.

Seeing me seated alone, Vishoka said, 'Duryodhana could

not have gone very far. When we last saw him, he was running away without a chariot or a horse.'

There was nothing I needed, so I gave Vishoka permission to go and join the celebration.

But I discovered that he had not gone to celebrate when he came back with two hunters. One of them looked familiar. I had seen him when he once came with meat that he had hunted on the bank of the river. He was a middle-aged man and the other was a youth who looked like his son.

They said they had seen three men talking to one another near the deep part of the river while they were hunting on the banks. One man was armed, although he was a brahmin. From the hunter's description, I knew it was Ashvathama. It became clear that the others were Kripa and Kritavarma.

Vishoka took the hunters aside and questioned them again. Then, with my permission, he gave them a hundred coins each and sent them away.

There was nothing astonishing in three men standing by the river and conversing. What was surprising was they were talking to an invisible person. Who else could the fourth have been but Duryodhana in hiding? Vishoka said it was clear now where our enemy's lair was located.

Arjuna came looking for me since he had not seen me at the celebration.

I said to him, 'One person still remains. I will celebrate after I finish with him.'

Dhrishtadyumna came in, intoxicated both with liquor and victory, and pulled me up from my seat affectionately.

'Duryodhana has not left the country. He's hiding by the deep part of the river,' I said.

Dhrishtadyumna's manner changed when he heard this. He ran out. Krishna, Yudhishtira and Satyaki climbed into a chariot, which Arjuna drove. Nakula and Sahadeva got into my chariot. I took up the reins myself and sent Vishoka in front, in a small chariot, to show us the way.

The river was calm and very deep at the spot called the Dvaipayana. There was no one in sight. There were caves at the mouth of the river, amidst the aattuvanji trees that stretched into the water. Vishoka said Duryodhana was probably in one of them.

Yudhishtira decided on a plan. We would entice him to come out by hurling abuses at him and humiliating him: 'Duryodhana, we are Yudhishtira and the Pandavas!'

There was no reply.

'Are you hiding, coward? Destroyer of the clan, come out, fight like a kshatriya. Either win and become a hero, or sleep your last sleep.'

At first we heard the soft sound of the water from the depths of the Ganga circling the cave.

After that, Duryodhana's voice, 'I don't want the kingdom. Why should I want a country where all my relatives and friends are dead and only their widows are left? I have decided to put on a deerskin, go to the forest and do penance for the rest of my life. Let me go free!'

Yudhishtira called out, 'I will not take over the kingdom without defeating you first. You lowdown rascal, come out like a man and fight.'

'Is it manly to challenge me, exhausted as I am with fighting, and weaponless as well?'

Duryodhana's words infuriated Yudhishtira. He shouted, 'If

you have the guts, if you are a man, come out! You can fight any one of us, with any weapon you choose. If you win, you will be king!'

Krishna shuddered when he heard Yudhishtira speak so rashly. I concealed my unease. Pointing to Yudhishtira, Krishna was about to say something, then he checked himself.

The trees moved as Duryodhana crawled through the bushes and came out. His grimy body was covered with wounds. He had lied when he said he had no weapons. The gold-studded mace that he never parted from was in his hand. He said, 'I accept your conditions.'

Unable to control his anger, Krishna turned to Yudhishtira.

'What a stupid thing to have said! That he can fight with whomever he chooses and have the kingdom if he defeats him! What if he asks you to fight? What if he challenges Nakula or Sahadeva or Arjuna to fight him with a mace?' He added disconsolately, 'I doubt even Bhima would be a match for him.'

Yudhishtira was distressed. He could not now withdraw the arrogant words he had uttered in a moment of weakness.

Krishna continued to mutter angrily, 'It must be the destiny of Kunti's sons to spend their entire lives in the forest.'

I went up to Duryodhana. 'You and I have many accounts to settle, starting with Pramanakoti. We had vowed to kill all Dhritarashtra's sons, you are the only one left.'

His eyes held mine in a look that reminded me of that first moment when wrestlers grip each other's fists tight and do not let go.

'He who can defeat me in direct combat is yet to be born!' declared Duryodhana arrogantly. 'Don't stand there roaring at me, Vrikodara, like a cloud empty of rain.'

Spectators had arrived to watch us, even at Dvaipayana. They took their places in two separate camps.

Duryodhana's voice grew louder, now that he saw he had listeners. 'It's true, I defeated you at dice, sent you to the forest, made you work in strangers' houses. I even made you dress up as clowns. All because I was stronger than you. Both sides suffered loss and destruction in equal measure. Now muster your might and do battle with me! I promise you a duel fit for the gods to watch.'

We should have begun to fight at that moment. But Duryodhana hesitated when he caught sight of the man who came rushing up to the riverbank in his chariot and leapt out. A look of welcome spread over his face. Balarama was walking towards us.

Krishna received him warmly. 'You've come at the right moment. They are both your disciples, after all.'

Balarama said he would be the referee. He instructed us to shift the arena to the other bank of the river. I was not pleased that Balarama had intervened. I was fighting this duel for my life, for the kingdom. My last duel. As Balarama lay down the rules and defined the boundaries, I wondered: did he think his disciples were entering the arena merely to entertain the onlookers, as if they were competing for a king's golden casket?

Duryodhana curled tightly into himself, then straightened and drew himself erect. I felt as if my enemy had grown half an arm's length taller as he stood before me.

I thought his mace was very light as I parried the first blow he dealt me with it. That might help him to move faster. I kept trying to find gaps to attack him as I withdrew, then leapt forward and circled him. A blow I aimed, without turning my face as I drew back, struck his shoulder. He came at me, roaring, swinging his mace right and left by turns; I escaped each time, only by a hair's breadth. He kept changing his stance. As he moved in from the left, I parried him from the right. One of his blows struck my left shoulder.

Sparks scattered as our maces clashed. His dexterity and the speed of his hands astounded me. I managed to parry a blow he aimed at my head, but my own mace dashed against my forehead. I was afraid I was tiring. Where is the mighty one, I rebuked myself – the Bhima who had killed Baka, Hidimba, Jarasandha, Keechaka? Here was the enemy I had been waiting for, the enemy who had nurtured my strength. With every blow I dealt, I reminded myself of my enemy's crime and the strength of wild horses leapt through the roots of my arms, through my bones and nerves.

Before he could lower the hand he had raised, I changed direction, veered right and hit him. All my strength was behind that blow. It hit him below the armpit, on his ribs, and I felt his bones crack beneath my fist. Duryodhana fell.

Planting myself in front of him as he struggled to get up, I taunted him, 'Ridicule me once more, there's time for you to laugh one more time.'

I was gasping for breath.

I heard Yudhishtira say, 'Stop, Bhimasena. You have won.'

I looked at Duryodhana's virile thigh and remembered how, in the gambling hall, he had moved his garment and drummed his fingers over its bare expanse, watching Draupadi.

My mace rose and fell.

'Don't, that's unfair!'

I heard many voices. Duryodhana attempted to say

something, then his head touched the ground. He was still alive. I looked once more into his eyes and walked towards those who were waiting for me.

I was exhausted. No duel had ever tired me out like this. I felt as if all the strength had flowed out of me.

Balarama said, 'That is against dharma!'

Yudhishtira said, 'It was wrong to hit his thigh after he fell. Adharma!'

I said to Yudhishtira, 'I had vowed I would kill him. A kshatriya who does not fulfil his vow acts against dharma and will be condemned to Hell. It was you who taught me this, Elder Brother. I am going to hit him on the head and finish him off. If anyone wants to prevent me from doing so, he can.'

I looked at Balarama. I thought he would get up. I saw Dhrishtadyumna, Satyaki and Krishna consoling him. But no one stopped me as I walked back to my enemy one last time.

I flung away my mace. I needed it no more, my war was over.

Vishoka was waiting for me.

I still did not understand what dharma and adharma really meant. Everyone stared at me, their eyes tearing into me and accusing me, the victor, of being their enemy. I walked some distance and peered into my chariot. I saw the mace I had flung away, the one Mayan had gifted me, lying on the floor there.

I looked at Vishoka.

He said, 'It is a good mace, I did not throw it away. A mace does not differentiate between dharma and adharma.'

I gazed at the great river, where the waves were still quiet. The wind was asleep that night.

Krishna and my brothers had gone away from Kurukshetra to celebrate victory. Satyaki had gone with them. I had excused myself. Dhrishtadyumna had stayed behind, he wanted to enjoy a long sleep. We went our separate ways.

I remembered how I had stood and prayed at dusk as a child on the bank of this river, the bathing ghats where I had waited for a message from the God of the Wind. I thought of the child who had prayed that he would become a mighty man. I could still see him in the distance of time past, the Vrikodara who had played and swaggered there …

He had grown into a mighty man. He had won a battle.

The last enemy I had was lying now on the soil of Samantapanchaka, drawing his dying breath. I was a kshatriya who had fulfilled all his vows.

Mighty Bhima. I had fought in the forests, in the palace courtyards, finally here in Kurukshetra and subdued my enemies. Ordinary human being that I was, it was not my own strength that had made me mighty. Someone had lent force to my voice when I roared a war cry, sent strength coursing through my arms when they had grown tired. Let me not be arrogant in these moments of victory. Let me bend my head in humility.

O God who chains hurricanes, who hunts above the clouds, the God who is my father, I give you thanks today. Believing these rocks to be your feet, I lay my head on them.

I felt as if my mind had cleared after I prayed. I did not want to go back to the deserted battlefield. The tents slept in darkness and the songs of praise in the camps had stilled. Only my brothers were somewhere, celebrating.

I continued to sit on the steps of the bathing ghat.

Night had ended and Venus had risen. Blood-red streaks of light streamed from the peak of the mountain where the sun rose. I started to walk back.

At the confluence of the Drishadvati river I saw smoke rising from the burning ground.

Instead of the music of the Kaishika raga that usually heralded the dawn, a lament rose unexpectedly from the deserted expanse of Kurukshetra – the screams of a mass of people. I shuddered.

Vishoka ran up to me and said, between sobs, 'Ashvathama and his men set fire to the camp at night.'

Nakula and Sahadeva arrived as well. 'They hacked all the people who were asleep to death. No one was able to run away and escape.'

What I had thought was smoke from the burning ground had been smouldering tents.

A question hung frozen on my lips, unable to frame itself. Who all? Who?

Dhrishtadyumna who had lain down to enjoy his sleep; Panchali's sons: Prativindhya, Sutasoma, Shrutakeerti, Shatanika and Shrutakarma; and Sarvada who had fallen asleep with them.

Ashvathama had hacked all of them to death.

Kripa and Kritavarma had come with him and mounted guard to prevent anyone running away. They had helped Ashvathama kill the soldiers and servants who attempted to escape.

Fresh blood still flowed over the battlefield. One of the sootas who was describing the dreadful scene said, 'You would never believe the atrocities those despicable men committed unless you saw them with your own eyes.'

I had no wish to see them.

We had laughed when we had heard that, before he died,

Duryodhana had made Ashvathama the commander-in-chief of an army that had no soldiers.

All around me, I continued to hear descriptions of the terrible night. Ashvathama had used the sword that Rudra had blessed and gifted him to hack his victims to death. Rudra himself had appeared in front of the tent. When our children had said their prayers at dusk that day, Rudra would have been one of the four gods they invoked, as they had been taught to do as children. And now Rudra's sword had fallen on their necks.

Enough of these descriptions, I thought. There were many things I did not understand. But I did understand that my children, the children of the Pandavas, were no longer alive to perform our funeral rites. Yes, I did realize that.

The enemy had not died. Would never die.

PART 8

THE INHERITANCE

1

Child widows with white cloths covering their heads led the way. Behind them came the older women whose widowhood had erased the auspicious vermilion mark in the parting of their hair. Aunt Gandhari came next. Mother and Balandhara were among those who followed Vidura. Subhadra came next, her hand on Uttara's shoulder. The last to arrive at the banks of the Ganga was Draupadi.

We brothers took off our head ornaments and upper cloths and immersed ourselves completely in the water. We made offerings of water in our cupped hands to those who had died.

To a son.

To a brother.

To a husband.

To relatives and friends.

We lined up in our wet garments in front of the priest, our palms joined in prayer. Mother came towards us, her eyes dry, tearless. Uttara, pale as a crescent moon at dawn, was the only one who had unshed tears in her eyes. I had been told that she was pregnant.

Mother said to Yudhishtira in a calm voice, 'There is a name you must not forget when you make the funeral offerings. A great warrior who died, on the Kaurava side. The eldest of all of you brothers.'

Arjuna was stunned, not knowing what she meant. Yudhishtira moved closer to Mother and bowed his head.

She said to him, 'Your elder brother as well. Karna, whom you knew as Radheya, the son of Radha.'

Words hung on Arjuna's trembling lips, unable to find a voice. But I could hear them: Karna, the Karna I killed?

'Karna,' Mother said, her voice as calm as before. 'My eldest son, born to me when I was still unmarried and whom I abandoned in the river because I feared disgrace.'

I did not raise my head.

Mother said to her children, who were still in a state of shock: 'The Karna whom Radha and Adhiratha brought up. A handful of water for him as well.'

Mother went back to join the group of women.

After a long silence, Yudhishtira sighed deeply, completely in control of himself. 'Let Karna's wife and daughters-in-law come and stand with our women.'

Sahadeva went to find them.

The river Ganga, who had many years ago received a newborn baby from her sister, the Charmannvati, now received the offering of water in a silence full of meaning. Ganga who had seen and knew all.

We went back again to Hastinapura. We were the owners of the palace now, but each of us sat in corners, like wayfarers in resting places on the roadside. The sobbing of widows floated through the dark corridors for days together.

When the wheel of his chariot had sunk into the soil, Karna had asked Arjuna to stop fighting in deference to the rules of dharma. Not heeding him, Arjuna had released an arrow from his bow. The look in Karna's eyes as he did so haunted him incessantly, robbing him of sleep.

I could not sleep either.

Not because of the memory of those who had died at my hands, but because the man whom Krishna and Krishnadvaipayana had allowed to escape was still alive. I imagined that face in the glow of the burning tents. Ashvathama, holding the sword of Rudra, stained with the blood of those who were still asleep and those who had just woken up ...

The night Duryodhana had fallen, a sense of emptiness, of knowing that everything had ended, had filled my mind. Now I waited for the dust of war to settle again, so that I could target the form of my enemy. The thought of Ashvathama, his head bleeding, fleeing to the forest with the vestiges of life Krishnadvaipayana had granted him, tormented me at night.

We brothers did not meet one another for days. One day, Yudhishtira came looking for me.

'Karna! I still cannot believe it. I gazed at his corpse, knowing I would be satisfied only if I saw him lying dead with my own eyes. That woman is the cause of all this destruction.' He wandered around the palace lamenting Mother's crime.

Mother never came out of the women's quarters. Even when we had thought that we could avoid war and make a treaty, she had fanned awake the feelings of vengeance lying dormant in us. Arjuna and Nakula cursed her too. Sahadeva said nothing.

I could not bring myself to curse her. But I could not forgive her either.

I thought of my mother's life as Shoorasena's daughter and the younger sister of Vasudevar – the child her father had loaned to Kuntibhoja, who had no children of his own. In order to please the sages, her foster father had sent her to work for them as a servant. Misfortune followed her when she came to the palace of Hastinapura as a bride. A co-wife who became more and more beautiful with each day that passed had arrived to share her position. It shocked her to discover that her husband was impotent. Later, she had had to leave the palace and live in the forest. For her husband's sake, she had slept with gods and by the time she bore three children, she had become a widow.

Although she had grown-up sons, she had to leave them, stay in Vidura's small house and accept the generosity of his family for thirteen years.

No, I could not curse her.

I thought of Karna. On the day when we had displayed our skills, it was I who had shamed him the worst in front of all those spectators. He should have vowed to kill me, had a lance made for that purpose.

I stopped when I reached Duryodhana's deserted palace. The metal statue I had heard about, the one he had had made in my image to wrestle with, grinned foolishly at me. It had a huge stomach and massive arms. Below its rounded head, the gaping mouth grinned. The day Duryodhana had died, Dhritarashtra had hurled himself at it like a madman, to fight with it.

A servant came looking for me to say that my elder brother wanted to see me.

Dhritarashtra was still seated in the great hall. As I passed by, he heard my footsteps and asked, 'Who is it?'

'I, Bhimasena.'

He did not say anything more.

If anyone were to be blamed for transforming Hastinapura into a country of widows, it was this blind man. I wanted to cry out that he, this sightless man, whom death had passed by, was the reason for all the tragedies that had befallen us. This old man, who had not been able to conceal his delight when he heard the score being called out as his son cheated at the game of dice and won.

Yudhishtira was in the old gambling hall. Arjuna, Nakula and Sahadeva were there as well. I greeted him.

He said, 'I have been thinking things over for several days and have finally come to a decision.' He stopped and was plunged in thought again. Then: 'This kingdom that has come to me is like a widowed girl's dowry. We have no children, no relatives. Wherever I look, I see widows with tears streaming from their eyes. I cannot govern this country, I cannot.'

All of us remained silent.

'The stench of blood clings to this place, refusing to leave it. At night, I dream of skeletons and cannot sleep. I have decided to go to the forest and live as an ascetic. I do not want Hastinapura.'

He gazed at the white marble floor, then raised his head and looked at Sahadeva, as if asking for his opinion.

Sahadeva said, 'You must govern the kingdom, Elder Brother. All of us have waited to see you become king. We suffered the rigours of war for it.'

Nakula did not say anything. From his expression, it was clear that he did not think the decision was a right one.

Arjuna tried to lighten the atmosphere. 'It's often happened that a kshatriya feels detached from the world at the end of a war. But we have a responsibility to the subjects, don't we? Elder

Brother, you have endured so many hardships, accepting them as our evil destiny.'

Yudhishtira's expression did not change.

Arjuna went on, 'Let Krishna come back from Dwaraka. You can discuss the matter with him before taking a decision.'

'I have already decided. I never say things I do not mean.' He looked at me. 'Let Bhimasena govern the kingdom.'

I held my breath.

'The Kauravas died by Bhima's hand. According to the kshatriya law, the throne is for him who wins the war. Bhimasena is worthy of governing in every aspect.'

I felt I had to speak. 'It is the king who wins a war. You were king even when we were in the forest. This great war was fought so that you could reclaim your right to the kingdom, Elder Brother, not to avenge Panchali's unbound hair, as I heard the magadha minstrels sing so wittily.'

His answer was that if I gave my consent, he would ask Vidura to start preparations for the coronation. He got up and went away.

We stayed on in the hall.

Arjuna said, 'The great King Pandu sat on the throne that Dhritarashtra abdicated. What our elder brother said is in keeping with tradition. You must become the king.'

Sahadeva cried joyfully, 'Say it! Say that you are willing.'

Nakula said the same thing.

'What more is there to think about now?' asked Arjuna.

I said, 'Give me some time. Let my mind grow calm.'

Assuming I wanted to be alone, they left. I went out, and walked through the corridor into the courtyard. The plants in the garden had grown shrivelled and dry. I passed by the buildings where we had slept as children and reached the elephant sheds. I halted.

Vrikodara, the boy with the hungry stomach of a wolf, the king of Hastinapura? I wanted to laugh. None of those who would have made a joke of the matter were alive now. I walked back the way I had come. Looking at the withered plants, I thought about the coronation. There were not many of my friends left to come. I would have to quickly decide where special messengers should be sent. To Satyaki, Senesha …

I saw the blurred form of a woman in the shadows at the door to the women's quarters and drew back, startled. The tawny-red beauty …? When she came out, I was relieved. I smiled. It was Draupadi.

She came up to me and, unusually for her, made an obeisance to me. She observed such customs only in Yudhishtira's presence.

The silence of a blue lotus as it watches the sun set was on her face.

'The date of the coronation will soon be decided,' I said.

'Have you decided?'

'My elder brother took the decision. I have not yet given my word,' I said in a casual manner, hiding my pleasure.

'I came because I knew that.'

I had expected a secret smile and words of congratulation, but what I saw were her tear-filled eyes.

'When I lived in the forest, when I worked as a servant, I hoped I would come back here one day. Will that hope too be denied to Draupadi?'

I was transfixed.

'I am not yet old enough to retire to the forest. Nor have I achieved the state of mind to do so.'

I thought ... when Yudhishtira goes to the forest to become an ascetic, Draupadi ... But I would still be here, wouldn't I?

'I may not be a scholar, but I know the rules. Either I have to follow him, or I have to live on Balandhara's generosity in some corner of the women's quarters here.'

I was surprised to suddenly hear Balandhara's name.

'Balandhara?'

'Yes, Balandhara. When you are crowned king, who will become queen? Balandhara of course!'

Dabbing at her tear-filled eyes, she spoke to the earth beneath her feet. 'Maybe Panchali was born to be an eternal servant woman!'

She went back.

Dusk picked up the slivers of light in the shadows. I continued to stand by myself in the courtyard. From somewhere, I heard evening prayers being chanted. I walked to my mansion.

Two people awaited me there. At first, I did not notice the woman whose head was covered. Vidura was in front. The woman who stood behind him was Mother.

Mother said, 'I too heard about the retreat to the forest, the decision to become an ascetic. Your uncle gave him some good advice, but he does not seem inclined to change his mind.'

What were they saying I should do? Vidura helped to make things clear.

'All the people of the kingdom are waiting for the auspicious day when the follower of dharma, Yudhishtira, will become king. After all, they know that he was born to rule Hastinapura.'

At last I heard my voice. 'What must I do? Command me, Mother.'

She said, 'Your elder brother must become king. You are not worthy enough, you know nothing about the codes of dharma or about political strategy. Therefore, you must say firmly that you are not prepared to be king. This is your uncle's opinion as well.'

I remained silent for a while, in order to calm the secret furies within me. Then I laughed. First, Draupadi. And now, another woman – my mother!

'I, a king? Vrikodara, the king of Hastinapura? What foolishness!' I laughed louder. 'A joke my elder brother made … he's always made jokes about me. The blockhead, a king!'

My laughter spread to Vidura's face. He sighed with relief.

After they left, I sank down on my bed, weighed down by the burden of thought. I forgot to laugh.

I had governed Hastinapura for a moment, just a single moment. I was a king who had abdicated. I laughed again, in the dark. A mighty man should not weep, after all.

2

Yudhishtira's coronation was conducted simply, without any pomp. Nominal sums were given as gifts to the brahmins. The granaries in Hastinapura had been depleted by the war. We were all given small responsibilities to carry out during the royal procession around the city, in which Vidura, the brahmin priests and family members took part. Gifts were distributed according to custom: gold for the commander of the army; a white-backed bull for the king's chief priest; a milch cow for the queen; a horse for the principal soota story-teller in the palace;

bulls for the ministers and for the caretaker of the palace and its grounds; two bulls for the king's charioteer; a chess board and chessmen carved in ivory for the chess master; a curved knife for the chief of the hunt; a bow and arrow and a red head-dress for the chief messenger. (If the king had abandoned a wife, she had to be given a black cow that had run dry.) At the end of the ritual, the king presented himself with a white bull.

I thought to myself as I watched the ritual that there was no end to the lessons a kshatriya had to learn.

In the hall, Yudhishtira gifted all four of us swords that had been sanctified by the priests. The senior members of the family had to anoint him first, starting with Dhritarashtra and Gandhari, then Mother and Vidura. The brahmin sages came next, then we brothers, followed by relatives, the army commanders and friends.

I occupied the raised seat next to the king's, the one reserved for the second in line, the crown prince. Only Yudhishtira and one of the priests had to anoint me.

Draupadi was on the other side, on the seat meant for the king's consort. I noted the fragrance of the sandal paste she wore and the glitter of her silk garments. She looked contented. The memory of her dead sons did not seem to trouble her.

Of the guests who had come to watch the coronation, only Krishna and Satyaki could be described as important. We had thought Senesha would come, but he did not. He sent his minister with gifts.

Citizens of importance lined the courtyard to watch and servants were ranged behind them.

The king's proclamations followed the coronation. He ordered that the loads animals had to carry be lightened. He did not issue the customary proclamation that all prisoners be released and that death sentences be revoked, since Duryodhana had already given the prisoners weapons on the last day of the war and sent them to the battlefield to fight. We had begun to forget the war. I had stopped thinking about the enemy who still remained as well.

When Yudhishtira began to reign, Dhritarashtra moved to the seat in the gambling hall.

Yudhishtira summoned us to discuss ways and means to refill the depleted granaries, and Sahadeva described the state of the country to us. The fields were dry because there had been no rain, markets did very little trade, the cowsheds were empty. He suggested several ways to increase the levies and fill the granaries. Yudhishtira listened to everything and sat silent for a long time.

'Uncle Dhritarashtra and Aunt Gandhari want to conduct the rituals necessary for the peace of the souls of the dead and distribute the gifts they are expected to give. We have to find a way to fulfil their wishes.'

Uncle wanted to gift cows to a thousand brahmins. We would need gold and money for the sacrificial rituals. Sahadeva made calculations.

Everyone was full of resentment.

I voiced mine openly. 'Hastinapura is poverty-stricken after the war. Doesn't Uncle know that?'

But Uncle wished to complete these rituals before he retired to the forest.

Yudhishtira said, 'He says he will have no peace if he remains here. Moreover, he told me he caught people making fun of him.'

Everyone stared at me. I did not try to explain further. Only once had Dhritarashtra and I exchanged words.

'It is usual to kill in war, Son. But does anyone drink blood?' he had asked me. 'I could not believe what I heard.'

Aunt Gandhari had been seated next to him.

I had answered respectfully, 'When Dussasana's blood wet my lips, Uncle, I did not like its taste, so I did not drink it!'

That was all that had happened. I had told the truth, I had only wet my lips.

As long as he remained in the palace, we would remember the horrors of the war. Therefore, I decided to give in to the last request of the old couple.

So the gifts were distributed and the rituals performed. As the old couple were about to start on the journey to the forest, we heard that Vidura had decided to go with them. He had given up the householder's life long ago. Now that he had supervised the coronation, he had nothing left to do in the palace.

We decided that Dhritarashtra would be accompanied by a grand group of followers. Many of the servants who had worked for them and several old brahmins gathered at the palace doors to witness the old king's departure.

When the chariots drew up in the courtyard, Yudhishtira ran up looking very upset and said, 'Mother is going with them to the forest! What does this mean?'

Sahadeva rushed to Mother, then came back. 'I said everything I could. Mother seems absolutely determined. Imagine, she wants to go to the forest when she should be staying here as the Queen Mother. She says Uncle and Aunt are her parents now. She has made up her mind to stay in the forest and look after them.'

'Mother seems to take the greatest pleasure in giving us surprises from time to time,' said Arjuna with a cruel smile. He was not prepared to plead with her or dissuade her from going.

Nakula tried to plead with Mother, but met with no success.

I went to her last. 'You think of doing this at a moment when you should have stayed in the palace enjoying all its comforts and pleasures,' I lamented. 'When we were too distressed to take a decision, wasn't it you, Mother, who prevailed upon us to wage war? If you wanted to stay in the forest, you could have spent all those years with us there. Why did we fight and shed so much blood? Why did we make so many women widows?'

'What I wanted was radiance and glory for all of you. If you die maintaining your dharma, you will achieve renown. Your dharma now is governing the country, mine is to look after these old people. There is no need for anyone to grieve.'

There was no point in arguing with her.

Vidura took Dhritarashtra's hand and helped him into the chariot, then he climbed in as well. Mother climbed into the second chariot with Aunt Gandhari. We walked ahead of and behind the chariots, keeping pace with them.

The chariots stopped in the middle of the forest. Everyone alighted.

Mother came up to us. 'Live by your dharma. May you prosper!' Saying nothing more, she walked away and caught up with our uncle and aunt.

I could not believe that Mother was leaving for the forest, it seemed like some crazy trick of my imagination.

When we got back to the palace we were even more silent than we had been on the night the war had ended. Yudhishtira was the most troubled of us.

After days, an ascetic arrived from the forest. We asked him anxiously for news of our people. They were well, at peace, living as guests of the sages, listening to their wise counsel. Vidura was going to renounce food, perform penance and give up his life to fall into a yogic sleep – the end that all ascetics accept with happiness.

Yudhishtira asked, 'Shall we go there and find out how Mother and all the others are?'

Sahadeva felt that we could beg Mother once more to come back.

Yudhishtira said sadly, 'I found fault with her, said so many cruel things. I want to ask her forgiveness again.'

I was certain that Mother would not come back. Still, I followed my elder brother.

Our guide told us that all of them were in the hermitage of Shatayupa. We reached there after noon. Grandfather Krishnadvaipayana was with the sages. He was explicating a text from the Vedas.

Dhritarashtra expressed his gratitude and happiness that we had gone to ask about their welfare. Mother was seated next to Gandhari. She smiled at us, but did not say anything.

Yudhishtira asked, 'Where is Uncle Vidura?'

The sages told us that he was wandering in the forest, wearing strange attire, his body smeared with ashes. Yudhishtira decided to go to the forest and pay his respects to him. I walked in front, clearing the way for him.

A young sage we met on the way told us, 'I saw him two days ago, under that ashvata tree.' He pointed to a treetop in the distance.

Vidura was lying under the tree. His body, smeared with

ashes, had shrunk to a skeleton. He was motionless, but he opened his eyes slowly when he heard our footfalls on the leaves. He gave Yudhishtira a weak smile. It was clear to us that he was very near death.

He tried to say something but the words were not clear.

Yudhishtira said, 'I think his time has come. Bring me some water.'

I hurried away to find a pond. I rushed back as quickly as I could with some water in a leaf cup and saw Yudhishtira standing beside Vidura. He did not take the water from me, there was no need for it. Vidura had stopped breathing.

Yudhishtira walked away silently and I followed. When we came within sight of the hermitage, he stopped and sighed.

'He must be at Vishnu's feet now. Do you know something, Bhimasena?'

I saw the conflict on Yudhishtira's gaunt face. He said, 'He was my real father!'

I was astounded by one more of Mother's secrets. Yudhishtira saw my confusion and said, 'Do not blame Mother for this. It has always been customary for kshatriyas to have children by a brother's wife. Vidura was a part of Lord Dharma.'

I listened to him in silence.

We entered the hermitage and Yudhishtira said to Krishnadvaipayana, 'The great Vidura has slipped into a yogic sleep.'

Even at that moment, Dhritarashtra did not forget to lament, as custom demanded.

I looked at Mother with fear and anxiety, and saw no change of expression on her face.

When Yudhishtira finally mustered the courage to ask about

the funeral rites, our grandfather said, 'They are not necessary. Vidura is at Vishnu's feet. Great yogis do not need funeral rites. Although he was born as my son, he was a part of Dharma. Before he departed for the other world, he gave you his entire consciousness.'

Krishnadvaipayana watched Dhritarashtra lamenting and said: 'Vidura was Dharma himself. And this Pandava, Yudhishtira, is that Vidura. When Yudhishtira stands before you as your servant, why do you grieve?'

I stayed with Yudhishtira until he climbed into the chariot. Then I went back to the forest. Catching sight of Krishnadvaipayana and the sages walking towards me, I turned into another path in order to avoid seeing them.

It was Krishnadvaipayana who had prevailed upon Arjuna not to kill Ashvathama, to let him go free. I could not see his plea for mercy to the murderer of the last seeds of his race as a great action. Every time I met him, I remembered the incident.

The code of justice the Kuru race followed was beyond my comprehension.

I wandered around the forest, keeping away from the hermitage. Vidura was Dharma, the Pandava was Vidura – Grandfather had said so.

Then who was I?

Kusha grass rustled beneath my feet. Shorn of leaves, the bare branches trembled in the wind. Did the wind have anything to say to me?

Who was I?

I sat down near a pond that had almost dried up. Then I lay down and looked up through the leafless branches at a sky through which autumn clouds floated. A deer that had come to drink water thought there was no one around and came very near me, then fled into the forest, its hooves clattering, and disappeared. Once again, there was utter silence.

I heard footfalls on the dry leaves. It was Mother, with a bundle of chamata twigs in her hand.

She saw my troubled face and said, 'Go back.'

I stood before her. For some reason, my voice grew harsh.

'Who am I? Please tell me, at least now. So that I should not do wrong again. The sorrow of having derided my own elder brother, calling him the son of a charioteer, still weighs on my mind.'

Mother looked steadily at me. Then she said softly, 'Karna was the son of a charioteer. Kuntibhoja's charioteer was a handsome man. And very courageous as well. When I worked as a servant of the sages, that charioteer was the only person who showed me kindness.'

Mother's face darkened. I saw perspiration beading her forehead.

I asked her again, 'Who am I?'

I saw weakness on her face, helplessness. I waited for her to gather enough strength to look at me directly.

'I accepted Vidura in order to have a son who would have great spiritual knowledge. For kshatriyas, wives are only wombs to receive their seed. So, Vidura, to have a man with spiritual knowledge as a son.'

I thought Mother was beginning to smile. But she had not answered my question. She knew that.

'Then my husband, the king, needed a strong man. As strong as the God of the Wind. A man of might. I prayed, obediently.'

'And then …?'

Mother looked at the dry blades of grass, her head bowed.

'And he was?'

Mother raised her head and looked at me as if my voice had startled her. I saw reddish flames of anger spread over her face.

She murmured, 'He came out of the dense forest. Like an unchained tempest. A forest-dweller whose name I did not know.'

I have no idea when Mother went back, or when darkness came down, and began to wander through the emptiness of the forest.

A forceful wind that the god had unloosed from its chains passed by me, making the dark treetops tremble violently. I waited eagerly for a message. The wind burst into laughter.

I walked on, keeping my eyes on the light at the boundary of the forest.

༺༻

My friends, it is time for the great journey. You know that all the old people perished in a forest fire.

Yuyutsu has been entrusted with the supervision of a palace, where the only inhabitants are Subhadra and Parikshit, the son born to Uttara by Abhimanyu. The Khandava forest, which had been burnt, has grown again and begun to envelop Indraprastha. Uloopi and Chitrangada have left for their fathers' houses. Last of all, I said goodbye to Balandhara, and what you heard now was the sound of her chariot leaving for Kashi.

I said goodbye to Vishoka as well. My friends, your grandchildren and later their grandchildren will sit around the fire and sing the stories of Kurukshetra for the generations that follow Parikshit. I do not know who I will be in their alluring narration. Maybe they will laugh as an image takes shape before them of a man with a huge belly and a wide mouth, just like the statue in Duryodhana's hall. Or maybe they will shudder when they see the frightening form of a man with the might of 10,000 elephants in rut, standing with his head in the sky and his feet on the earth ... Whatever it be, let them go on singing.

The four of them who were getting ready for the great journey have fallen asleep. So has Draupadi. Bhimasena's story does not end here. Like you say, sootas, stories never end.

All good wishes for the journey, my friends, for you and for me!

3

Bhima smiled. Then he stroked Draupadi's forehead gently.

Draupadi opened her eyes once more and closed them. Her body became motionless. He laid her head, drenched in perspiration, on the ground. There was no fragrance of lotus flowers now, only the odour of human sweat.

Bhima got up.

Those who had gone in front of him were far ahead. Somewhere on the mountain of Meru, a divine chariot would be standing ready to welcome those who did not fall down on the way.

Bhima hesitated, looking at the mountain ranges. He saw below him, on the slopes, the green treetops of the forest.

The souls of those who fall down reach the Heaven of the heroes as well. A Heaven where there is no hunger or perspiration, where flowers never wither. A world meant for those who no longer feel passion or anger.

The second throne lies empty now.

Do I aspire to sit on it?

No, for I have not subdued my senses.

As I move from one deserted area to the next, my eyes search incessantly for the enemy who wanders in the unknown forests. Ashvathama.

No, I have not conquered my senses.

A Bhima who thinks that Draupadi, who fell by the wayside, is still beautiful even though she is middle-aged, has not conquered his senses.

It was no kshatriya who dwelt in me when I let the anger of selfishness smoulder inside me while sharing a woman. The man within me, roaring loud enough to make a forest quake, was a forest-dweller.

As I gazed at the green of the distant forests, I felt as if the strength I had lost was flowing back into me.

The forest which was the playground of the forest-dwellers, with its date-palm groves where elephants grazed, its rock peaks which scattered sparks when wild goats sharpened their horns on them, the cries of its hunters.

Somewhere inside it, a black-skinned beauty was wandering around, the flames of her passion still unslaked …

Somewhere there, an enemy was wandering around with an open wound on his wounded scalp.

While those two people lived, he would not be worthy of the second throne.

Planting his feet firmly on the precipitous path, Bhimasena

walked towards the forest that lay like a fallen black cloud below him.

White-winged birds came down from the clouds at that moment in perfect formation and flew into the valley as if to show him the way.

EPILOGUE

They roamed around, singing ballads. In all the places where people gathered, particularly in centres of pilgrimage and sacrificial sites. They turned old histories as well as recent events into ballads and sang them. In the hierarchy of castes, the position they were allotted was immediately below the vaishyas. The sootas. Storytellers who enchanted their listeners with words.

They must have been a small community. Historical texts may not have descriptions of them that would warrant calling them a society, although many renowned sootas have been spoken of from time to time in an individual capacity.

Just as they were excellent charioteers, they were also gifted storytellers. In the Karna Parva of the *Mahabharata,* there is an incident where Shalya tells Duryodhana about a soota who feels resentful when he has to become a charioteer and serve the brahmins and the kshatriyas. Although the sootas occupied a position below the vaishyas, even people of high status respected the soota who could sing a ballad. It was true that sootas were often scolded, but the one who could spin a good tale was given an important seat anywhere and accorded great respect.

The *Mahabharata* is structured around an incident involving a soota who was an excellent storyteller. Fed up with a lengthy ritual that he was conducting in the Naimishya forest, the ascetic Shaunaka asked a gifted soota to sing to him in order to relieve his boredom. The story the soota sang was composed by Krishnadvaipayana, who is the poet-sage Vyasa himself, and narrated by Vaishambayana. The soota had heard this story at the time when King Janamejaya was conducting a great ritual. Janamejaya's father, King Parikshit, had died of a snakebite when his son was still a baby. When Janamejaya grew up and became king, he decided to conduct a very elaborate ritual called a sarpasatra and kill all the serpents in the world, to avenge his father.

The sage Vyasa came to this ritual and Janamejaya requested him to sing. On Vyasa's instructions, his disciple Vaishambayana sang the story of the *Mahabharata*, which the soota who later attended Shaunaka's ritual in the Naimishya forest heard and committed to memory. The soota's story dealt with people who had lived three generations before him and was one in which the author, Krishnadvaipayana, who later became the sage Vyasa, transforms into a character. Because the author appears in an unimportant role in the epic, and because of the way the story is crafted, we tend to look at him from a distance, although he is actually very close to us.

In its initial form, the *Mahabharata*, which was initially called *Jaya*, was a heroic tale and researchers say that is all it was. There are scholars who think it took on its present form after several people added philosophical tenets and sub-stories to the original tale. The conclusion that it is a text to which many Vyasas contributed, Vyasas who were compilers, editors and publishers, infuriates those who revere the halo of divinity that lies over the *Mahabharata*. But, in general, everyone admits that there was a main body of work to which many additions were made later.

There is no doubt that there is a great genius at work behind this rare oeuvre. Whatever differences of opinion there might be about the period or authorship of this poem that Krishnadvaipayana 'created' after editing the Vedas, all historians and researchers of later periods have had the utmost respect for it.

It is said that everything that exists is in the *Mahabharata* and this is no idle boast. History, Geography, Botany, Zoology: they are all part of it. Do you want to know about the movements of the wind? There is a whole chapter on the subject. Do you want to learn Anatomy, or the symptoms of diseases? They are there for you. It is a great and rare work and a most poignant human story. The *Iliad* of the Greeks would pale in comparison. The *Shahnama* of the Persians cannot be reckoned as anywhere near it.

Many years ago – during a period of my life when I imagined that I too had read the *Mahabharata*, having gone through Thunchath Ezhuthachan's *Kilipattu* and C. Rajagopalachari's *Bharatasangraha* – the great Malayalam poet Akkitham advised me to read the Malayalam translation of the full-length version of the epic done by Kunjukuttan Thampuran, the poet and scholar who belonged to the royal family of Kodungalloor. Later, the well-known Malayalam writer P.C. Kuttikrishnan insisted, 'You must read the entire *Mahabharata* once. It will stand you in good stead. It was because I read it that I wrote the novel, *Ummachoo*.'

It took me a few more years to take up Kunjukuttan Thampuran's translation. I read through it initially as if fulfilling a duty, then realized what I had missed. My sense of responsibility towards it turned into a passion. Once I had read the great work, I could not put it aside. Thampuran's translation is obscure in many places, even displeasing in some. Nevertheless, it helped me discover a great poet, a storyteller par excellence. I paid obeisance to Thampuran in my mind. Kisari Mohan Ganguli's prose translation in English, which has tried to be as just as possible to Vyasa's great oeuvre, came to my help later. Ganguli's *Mahabharata* is the result of another extraordinary human effort.

At the end of the nineteenth century, Dr Reynold Ross of the India Office Library wrote to Pratap Chandra Roy, a leading publisher in Calcutta, pointing out the necessity for an authoritative prose translation of the *Mahabharata* in English. Roy agreed with him. But whom could he find to take on the responsibility? Several people discouraged him, saying the project might be considered against the Hindu religion. Roy discussed the question with Ishvar Chandra Vidyasagar. Vidyasagar was of the opinion that the translation would have a unified form only if one person did the entire work. He advised Roy to first find the necessary funds, then look for a suitable translator.

He found a person who declared he was ready to take it on: Kisari Mohan Ganguli. Working diligently on it from 1883 to 1896, Ganguli completed the translation. He was insistent that his name should not be revealed. When the work began to come out in serial form in 1904, the translator's name was not mentioned. Pratap Chandra Roy started the publication and his wife, Sundari Bala Roy, completed it after his death. People from Kerala knew the translation under Pratap Chandra Roy's name. The British government even gave Roy various awards for the translation. The first edition was sold out during Ganguli's lifetime. The edition that came out immediately after he died did not carry his name either. It was only in 1974, when the numerous printing errors were corrected and a new edition issued, that we discovered that Ganguli was behind this great achievement.

Ganguli's *Mahabharata* retains the lyricism of the original poem. Whenever doubts arise, he points out the differences between the Poona and Calcutta editions. There is also a Kumbakonam edition. Several studies based on these three editions have been of great help to me.

When the epoch of the *Mahabharata* becomes the setting for a novel, innumerable doubts arise to confuse the author. He has to acquaint himself with countless details: the landscapes of that era, its agricultural patterns and lifestyle, the architecture of the houses, dress, ornaments, food habits, objects used in everyday living and so on. He has to study the codes of war and weapons. English translations of Sanskrit works were very helpful in these areas, particularly *Vedic India*, *Vedic Index* by A.A. McDonald and A.B. Keith, Ralph Griffith's study of the Yajur Veda, Georg Buhler's *Sacred Laws of the East*, Julius Eggerling's *Shata Patha Brahmanam*, Pandit Rajaram's *Dhanurveda Sankalanam*, Pandit Ajaya Mitra Sastri's *India in the Brihad Samhita* and Yohann J. Meyer's *Sexual Life in Ancient Bharatha*. Other works that helped me to study the culture of that epoch are too numerous to be mentioned and I will not list them here.

There are two characters in the epics that children all over India have always loved and admired: Hanuman of the *Ramayana* and Bhima of the *Mahabharata*. Both are personifications of strength. In Kerala, many warnings are handed out to children in Bhima's name. 'Don't let your legs hang out of the bed when you sleep, it will rob you of your strength. Duryodhana always gave Bhima a small mat to sleep on, in order to lessen his strength.'

'And what happened?'

'Bhima kept both his legs on the mat and let his head be outside it!'

The child laughs, amazed at Bhima.

There are so many stories of this kind.

Anyone who reads the *Mahabharata* attentively will realize that the real Bhima is not the Bhima presented to the young minds that devour children's literature and illustrated classics. Bhima has not only a huge body, but also a great mind. The Bhima of the *Mahabharata* is a human being, an archetypal image with human weaknesses and strengths. Several scholars who have done studies of the human story that is the *Mahabharata* have cursed those who added childish stories and inconsistencies to it to satisfy the whims of priesthood.

I have not made any changes to the framework of the story that Krishnadvaipayana, the first Vyasa, codified. The parts where I have taken liberties are those in which he maintained a silence that those who came later were to find meaningful. There are moments when, between the lines, he gives us hints. For example, Vyasa himself hints clearly that Yudhishtira is Vidura's son. In the Ashramavasa Parva, when Vidura has sacrificed his life after renouncing food and going into meditation, Krishnadvaipayana points to Yudhishtira and says:

Dharma is Vidura and Vidura himself is the Pandava
That Pandava stands before you as your servant.

(Kunjukuttan Thampuran's Malayalam translation)

It is significant that, at the moment of Vidura's death, the entire radiance of his consciousness enters Yudhishtira.

There are occasions when the poet changes the subject after a few moments of silence. Yudhishtira clearly says 'Let Bhima be king' after the Kurukshetra war has ended. Later, he gets ready to be crowned himself. What happens in the interval between these two moments? The storyteller has to find out what might be the natural sequence of events. Yudhishtira, who had grown detached from worldly affairs after the war, suddenly sets aside his initial idea of retiring to the forest and prepares himself for the coronation. He must have had a reason for this. Kunti Devi, who had taken control of events at many decisive moments, both overtly and covertly, could not have stayed idle during these days. Vidura could not be king because he was the son of a servant, so he would have wished for his son at least to become king. And on such an occasion, Draupadi, always talented at discovering arguments in favour of a just cause, would surely have considered the risk to her own position and spoken her mind.

Another scene: Abhimanyu has been killed. The whole camp is plunged in grief. Almost immediately, Ghatotkacha is killed as well. Krishna says:

I should have killed him, Bhima's son, Ghatotkacha.
Knowing all of you loved him, I did not do so earlier

(Kunjukuttan Thampuran's Malayalam translation)

Would not Bhima have heard him?

I have not added any new characters. Vishoka, Balandhara are all in the *Mahabharata*. All I did was to look a little more closely at people whose image remains blurred in the general perspective.

Bhima was a warrior who never knew fatigue. The heroes of wars in those days were not sportspersons who alternated between being in form or out of form on the playing field. Bhima was capable of attacking Karna from head to toe and making him tremble with fear. The same Bhima collapses when Karna comes up to him, slings his bow around his neck and drags him, insulting his scanty beard and pot-belly and demoralizing him. It is common for warriors to collapse on hearing of tragic events that have just taken place. That is how Drona perished, after all. The only valid reason the mighty Bhima would have had to collapse so pathetically when he confronted Karna, to lose his courage and valour, to almost die while he listens helplessly to insults to his manhood is that he had heard news that had dealt him a terrible blow. And what news could have shaken him as deeply as the truth of Karna's identity?

There is an endless list of stories in the *Mahabharata* where events that we could accept or understand as human are invested with the halo of a destiny that has been divinely ordained. These are certainly later additions. Karna was an excellent warrior and archer, but he was not invincible. He was not successful at Draupadi's swayamvara, or in the episode of Virata stealing the cows, or during Duryodhana's procession: he ran away from all of them. Though there is a story to illustrate that Karna too was superhuman: it says he endured the bite of a worm so that his guru, who was asleep on his lap, should not wake up. The guru, Parashurama, guessed at once that his disciple was not a brahmin and cursed him, saying his weapon would become useless to him at a critical juncture.

The wedding of Draupadi is another such story. Polyandry was considered uncultured even among the tribes of that time. Drupada was against it. Later, in the gambling hall, insults were hurled at Draupadi's chastity, since she had five husbands and such a marriage was not in keeping with local customs. Kunti must have devised a solution to ensure that her sons did not quarrel over a beautiful girl and go their separate ways. She knew that Yudhishtira, as the eldest, had a special right over his wife. Whatever people might have said, Kunti knew for certain that her sons had to stay together. She was, after all, a woman who had exceptional strength of mind: she recognized the forest woman and her five sons who came to the house of lac as suitable victims whose charred skeletons would replace her sons and herself.

However, there is a story that treats the wedding of Draupadi as a divine decision. It says that she was an ascetic maiden in her previous birth. She performed penance and Shiva appeared before her. Without meaning to, she chanted the words 'Give me a good husband' five times. This meant that she was therefore destined to have five husbands. This argument is put forward by no less a person than Krishnadvaipayana himself! Who could imagine that great man telling such a silly story? No wonder fine scholars of the *Mahabharata*, including the Malayalam critic Kuttikrishna Marar, find fault with additions like these that flaunt divine haloes that mar the strength and beauty of the poem.

Studies and research projects that deal with these interpolations continue to be popular. Many things that Bhishmacharya was supposed to have said during the long period when he lay on a bed of arrows are considered to have been added later. There are scholars who argue that even the *Bhagavad Gita* was a later addition. Dr Phulgendu Sinha, a scholar of Vedanta, said recently that the *Gita* of today was put together in 800 AD, that the real *Gita*, Vyasa's *Gita*, which took shape 600 years earlier was another work altogether and that he was going to dedicate his entire life to discovering this original *Gita*.

Enough of all that. The *Mahabharata* is an immensely powerful family saga, a ballad of war, and a history of tribal culture. It is easy to surmise that a story that took shape orally must have sustained many changes as it was passed down from generation to generation. Most of the descriptions of war scenes are similar, as happens in folk literature everywhere. All the images of handsome men and beautiful women are similar. 'Many' may mean a hundred; 'very many' may run into thousands. When a thousand arrows were sent from a bow, 10,000 came back. A huge army becomes an immense formation, an akshouhini, which, according to the rules, should contain 21,870 elephants, as many chariots, three times as many horses and five times as many foot soldiers. When the poet says that eighteen such formations fought in the war, we can only conclude that he used poetic licence to describe a mighty war that had no eye-witnesses.

Gandhara in the north-west; Kekaya, Madra and Vahleeka in

the basin of the Sindhu; Indraprastha, Hastinapura, Ahichhatra, Mathura, Kambilya and Chedi in the area contained in the Sindhu–Ganga basin; Magadha in the north-east and Anga just beyond; Kamaroopa at the top: these were the most important countries in North India during the period of the *Mahabharata*. They were all small countries. Cattle was their main wealth, and it was usual to wage wars for them. We come across cattle wars in the ancient history of all countries. Kurus, gandharas, chedis, nishadas, magadhas, madras, vangas, vidarbhas, panchalas, salwas are all mentioned among the tribes of Vedic times. The people in the countries mentioned in the *Mahabharata* war were all great tribals.

Chariots were vehicles meant for journeys. Although horses were plentiful, horse-riding was not popular and horses were used only to drive chariots. The main crops grown were paddy and barley. Artisans making handicrafts were found everywhere. There were large orchards and gardens for medicinal plants on the slopes of the Himalayas. Even now there are gardens supplying huge medical institutions in parts of Kumaon and Garhwal, and the Valley of Flowers still attracts visitors to the Himalayas.

Since messengers were illiterate, the practice was for them to learn messages by heart and repeat them in full.

The people of that epoch worshipped Agni and Varuna, Indra and Rudra. Vishnu became a god only later.

This is the setting for the novel.

Bhima was the centre-point of the Mahabharata war. No matter how many leaders there are, victory and defeat depend on the astuteness of the warrior who commands the spot that bears the entire brunt of the enemy's onslaught. Bhima was chosen unanimously for this position. Dhritarashtra spent sleepless nights worrying only that Bhima was fighting on the opposing side.

Bhima won the war and yet achieved nothing. That is why I adopted his perspective for the novel. Kunti and Draupadi were the characters who controlled the movements of Bhima's life. Vidura wielded an influence as well, in a very covert manner. Bhima was a man who did not expect much in the way of blessings to be reaped in another world. And because of this, he made a vow in the gambling hall. It was not Arjuna or Karna who displayed the greatest courage in the war, it was Bhima. He killed all the Kauravas in direct combat. He who kills the enemy becomes the supreme leader and, according to the law of the times, he had the right to the kingdom.

When we follow Bhima, for whom strength was both a curse and a burden, through the universe of the *Mahabharata*, it becomes clear that he is not just a man with a scanty beard and a pot-belly, wielding a huge mace. He is a savage warrior who does not find it necessary to conceal the emotions of passion and desire, a man uncluttered with the baggage of philosophical thoughts or the code of the Aryas. His relationship with Draupadi illustrates his simplicity and innocence at many points. There is the incident of the stealing of the Sougandhika flower, made famous in our country by storytellers. Bhima sets out on an expedition because Draupadi is obsessed by a flower. After numerous adventures, he plucks the flower from Kubera's garden. But in the *Mahabharata*, he does not place the flower in Draupadi's hair, or indulge in amorous dalliance with her, as the stories say. Draupadi arrives with his brothers, who have come to look for him. When she reaches the garden, Draupadi seems to forget about the flower she wanted so much. Bhima is scolded by his elder brother for having been so rash:

> *If you care for me, do not do things like this,*
> *Said Kunti's son as he took the lotus flowers*
>
> (Kunjukuttan Thampuran's Malayalam translation)

This is all the *Mahabharata* says.

Soon after this, Draupadi becomes obsessed with another dream: she wants to scale the mountain peaks. Bhima goes up the mountain, chases away the demons who are there, beats some of them to death. And did Draupadi enjoy looking down at the world from the peaks, as she had wanted to? Vyasa does not tell us. Why did Draupadi change her mind after having said to Bhima: 'I want to see the mountain peaks, standing within the protection of your arms ...?'

When this novel was serialised in the *Kalakaumudi*, many people, particularly women readers, wrote to me voicing their doubts on Krishna's role. What they were thinking of was the Krishna who was first a little child in Ambady, then Radha's lover. The eternal lover with his flute, wearing a crown with a peacock feather, is shaped from the beautiful imagination of another poet. It is unlikely that the divine baby that every mother wishes to see in her own child, the Radhamadhavan every young girl longs to see in her lover, will be found in the *Mahabharata*. Neither is the story of the endless sari that flows out at her waist at the moment when Draupadi is disrobed found in Vyasa's *Mahabharata*.

The Krishna of the *Mahabharata* is the prince of a small and not very powerful country. The Yadavas were defeated in many wars. They had to leave Mathura and move to Dwaraka because they feared Jarasandha. The Krishna of the *Mahabharata* is an excellent charioteer, a warrior without equal in war with the discus, an expert on diplomatic relationships with other countries (non-alignment starts with him). He has an unerring eye for a vital flaw in an enemy, a talent that is of great use in a war. He tried to establish friendly relations with other countries and win back the prestige that the Yadavas had lost. It was not only the bond between him and the Pandavas, who were his father's sister's sons that led to his closeness with them – he would have also thought it wise to have a mighty warrior like Bhimasena, capable of attacking Jarasandha, on his side. He was loved both by the brahmins and the kshatriyas. One of the best proofs of his expertise in forging diplomatic relations with the Pandavas is, of course, the episode where he favours the abduction of Subhadra by Arjuna.

The role of Krishna in the *Mahabharata* is a much debated one.

He has been constantly criticized by several scholars, including Professor Meyer, as a good-for-nothing fellow, an upstart and a man without traditions. I have only dealt here with the Krishna who is involved with Bhima, from Bhima's perspective. Bhima never attempted to get too close to Krishna. He liked him, but kept his distance from him, probably because Krishna was his younger brother's closest friend. And Krishna always accorded Bhima the respect he merited.

My theme in the novel is certain human crises in the *Mahabharata*. My salutations to Krishnadvaipayana (Vyasa), who set apart for me the meaningful silences that spurred me to take this direction.

Weak family relationships and human beings who become entangled in them: these are themes that have always been available to me in my own village. The only difference is that I am dealing here with a family story set in a more ancient era.

In November 1977, after death came very close to me and then withdrew, I longed to complete at least this novel in the time left to me. I started to write it in my mind, to read and gather information. But I finished it only in 1983. For the days that time in its infinite mercy allowed me, my gratitude.

I consider the reading and study that I did as part of the preparation for writing this novel as a valuable achievement. I am deeply indebted to the books that made it possible, to the friends in the Nagpur, Kozhikode and Bombay universities and in other establishments who helped me find these books. My friends, I thank you.

I believe that what really spurred me to write this novel was the inner strength I garnered from having been born and having lived in a village in India, and having grown up listening to epics and histories.

Let us salute Krishnadvaipayana (Vyasa) once more.

Translator's Note
Gita Krishnankutty

A Family Tree

Travelling with MT
Anoop Ramakrishnan

Major Works

P.S.

Insights
Interviews
& More...

Translator's Note
Gita Krishnankutty

Randamoozham, the Malalayam original of *Bhima: Lone Warrior*, was published in 1984 and went into its thirty-eighth edition in March 2013. What explains the continued success of this novel? A retelling of the *Mahabharata*, of course, never fails to enchant. The magic of this particular retelling has probably remained untarnished because M.T. Vasudevan Nair chooses to narrate it from Bhima's perspective, looking at him not merely as a mighty warrior, but as a human being beset with unfulfilled longings, haunted by doubts and fears, and often ridiculed and misunderstood by the people around him. 'The human being,' says MT, 'is a writer's sole theme.'[1] His Bhima is lonely, often helpless, constantly aware that his physical strength is both a boon and a curse. So intimate is this portrayal that, across the gulf of space and time, the reader sees Bhima up close.

In fact, MT's Bhima is of a piece with the protagonists of his other novels – Sethu of *Kalam*, Appunni of *Nalukettu* and many characters in his short stories, all of whom are alienated individuals caught in the family feuds stemming from the disintegration of the matrilineal joint family in Malabar. Bhima shares their 'outsider' consciousness, their tendency to introspect, their desperate desire to succeed. Whether he fails completely because of the choice he makes on the family's final journey together, or whether MT has in fact freed him from the pain and humiliation he was subjected to throughout his life, is for the reader to decide.

Randamoozham is a departure from MT's usual style. The paraphernalia of the royal courts and of war, the moves in gambling and wrestling, the rituals and customs of the period, the historical and mythological references, demand an idiom that is different from the one he uses in the majority of his novels and short stories. He takes meticulous care not to fall into the trap of adopting a language that is overwhelmingly classical. The characters speak as ordinary human beings do, and are as susceptible as anyone else to jealousy or arrogance or meanness. However, the novel is enveloped in the aura of the epic that inspired it. Not only does this influence both form and content, it also presents a continual challenge to the translator.

There are several Malayalam as well as Sanskrit words in the text that have no satisfactory equivalent in English. In certain cases, it was possible to add a brief explanation, but on many occasions, I had to resort to a longer phrase that would convey the meaning. To quote a few examples: the word 'rathaveeran' stretches into the somewhat clunky 'a warrior who masters fighting from a chariot', 'panchavarnapookkal' became 'the flowers in Kubera's garden' and 'rajasvala' had to be explained as 'she was having her period'. I was aware that the new phrase lacked the beauty and precision of the original word, but hoped that the storytelling would not be overly hampered by it.

Whether the characters in the novel are placed in a sombre audience hall or a secluded forest retreat, the rhythms of

Malayalam speech used in the village backgrounds familiar to the readers of MT's novels are woven seamlessly into the settings. This quality, which P.P. Raveendran terms a 'thematic ambience' in MT's writings,[2] linking his fiction effortlessly to facets of his own personality and to the life of the village he grew up in, is not easy to capture in English and is a daunting task for the translator.

Despite these problems, I am grateful to have had the opportunity to read and work on this novel. While studying it, I was repeatedly encouraged to go to Malayalam and English translations of the *Mahabharata*, not only to check references, but also to seek out fascinating details and little-known incidents. Like the fact that the Ashvanadi is a river that flows through Kuntibhoja's country, that Kunti set afloat the infant Karna on this river, that the Asvanadi joins the Charmannvati, which flows into the Yamuna, which in turn flows into the Ganga, where the Pandava brothers made a funeral offering to their brother, Karna. And that the quest for the sougandhika flower during which Bhima is said to have met Hanuman – made unforgettable in Kerala by kathakali artistes – did not happen quite that way!

I would like to express my profound gratitude to Sri Vasudevan Nair for the time he gave me so generously to discuss the framework of the novel, to explain the nuances of language and expression, and to patiently answer the innumerable queries I beleaguered him with.

I would also like to thank V.K. Karthika for her unfailing support and encouragement, and my editor, Ajitha, for the infinite patience and kindness she extended to me when we worked on the manuscript.

Chennai, 2013　　　　　　　　　　　　　　　　**Gita Krishnankutty**

Notes

1. M.T. Vasudevan Nair in 'The Travails of a Writer', in *Vakkukalute Vismayam*, ed. M.N. Karassery (Kozhikode: Pappiyon, 1999), p. 85.
2. P.P. Raveendran, Introduction to the *Writings of M.T. Vasudevan Nair* (New Delhi: Orient BlackSwan, 2010), p. xi.

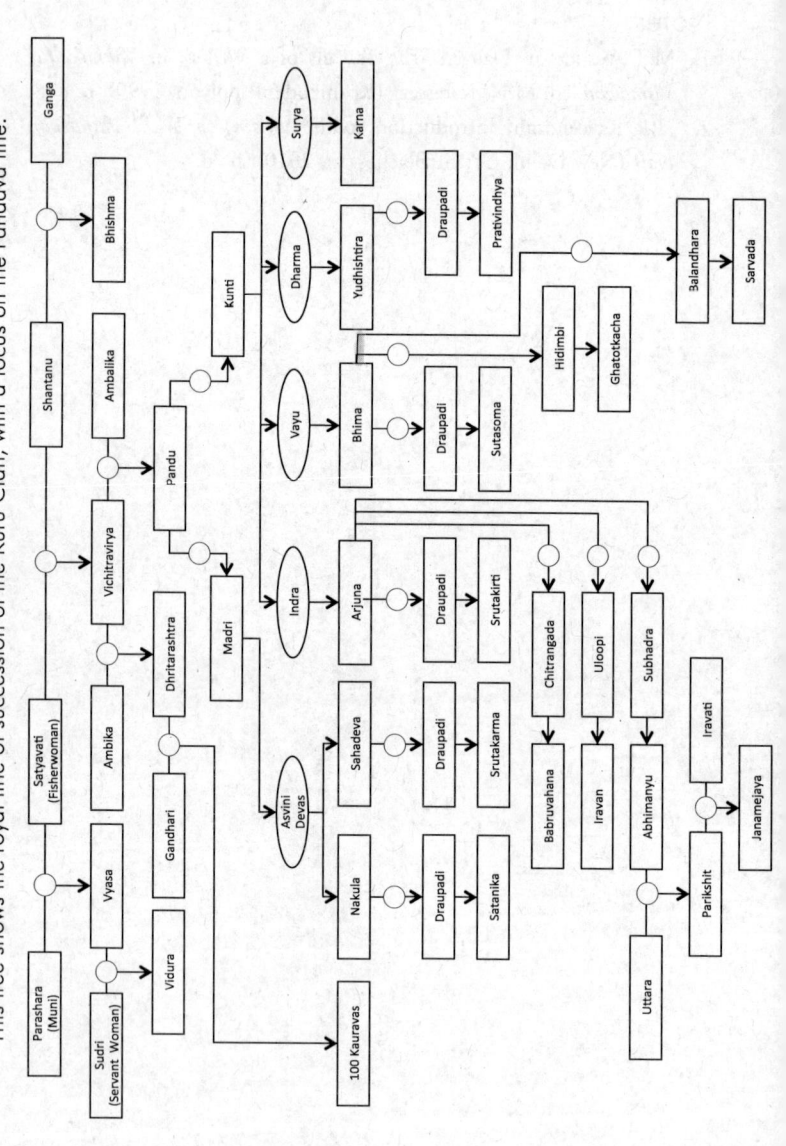

Travelling with MT
Anoop Ramakrishnan

I've read, loved and admired MT since I was a very young man, which is not remarkable in Kerala, where he is an integral part of the Malayali's literary consciousness. But a few years ago, at the *Malayala Manorama* in Kottayam, I got the opportunity to helm a unique project that allowed me to get to know MT, the writer and the person. The two are complementary entities, I realized.

We had decided to try and recreate MT's personal and artistic genius with the help of new technology. My team and I eventually documented his major literary works and films in fourteen DVDs and released them with the title *MT's Worlds*. There are video interviews, documentaries, audio books and interactive presentations in there. Our objective was to try and create as complete a picture as possible of a creative life spanning fifty-odd years. The *Limca Book of Records* awarded our multimedia project a World Record in 2010 as 'the first and the largest digital compilation of a writer's work'.

As I began to walk the researcher's path, I was amazed by the distances MT had covered. We interviewed over 300 people who had been associated with MT as a person and as an artist. The image that we uncovered was of a giant who straddled several creative worlds.

There is Mani Ratnam, who eagerly awaits an opportunity to direct a script written by MT. Govind Nihalani speaks at length about the explosive climax of *Nirmalyam*. The actress Sarada feels overwhelmed even now when she recalls the scene in *Iruttinte Atmavu*, where the madman Velayudhan pleads with her to let him touch the tip of her finger. Bombay Ravi wants to produce a Malayalam film that MT has scripted. U.R. Ananthamoorthy says, 'MT represents the best in the liberal, democratic, humanist tradition of Indian writing.' Adoor Gopalakrishnan dwells on the similarities between MT's childhood and youth, and his own. Vairamuthu describes MT's rare, measured smile as a 'centimetre sirippu' (a centimetre-long smile). M. Mukundan speaks of how he felt like taking a quiet walk by a river after he read a story by MT. The actress Srividya declares that if there is any scriptwriter who has the ability to hold an entire film unit, including the director, captive, it is MT. Vishal Bharadwaj says, 'MT says only what is absolutely necessary. And that too he would rather not say, if he can convince you with his eyes.' O.N.V. Kurup insists that MT may write in prose, but his works are poetry. Kamala Das says that his stories 'wring women's hearts like hands wringing water from a wet towel'.

We met characters who peopled MT's stories, observed the background they belonged to and investigated the changes that the passage of time had wrought on them. For instance, we went to Shukapuram, the village where the film *Nirmalyam* was shot. Ratheesh, the grandson of Gopalan Nair – who taught P.J. Antony, the principal actor of *Nirmalyam*, how to perform the role of the velichappadu dancer – is now the velichappadu of the temple and still has the sacred sword that was used in the film.

The house where the movie was shot has not changed much. We captured MT in a pensive mood as he stood silently in the room where *Nirmalyam*'s velichappadu realized that his wife and the mother of his four children has betrayed him.

For the documentary *Vanaprastham: A Relook*, MT came with us to the Mookambika temple, which is the setting for the original story. He told us that Karunan Master, the protagonist, resembles him in some ways, that MT himself had a student who used to send him a greeting card every New Year and that he met her once after many years.

We journeyed through the corridors of history looking for the characters in his film *Parinayam*, which tells the story of Kuriedathu Tatri of Kalpakaserry Illam, the namboodiri woman who broke all social norms to wreak revenge. The spot where the illam stood is a ruin now, covered in thick undergrowth. No one seems to have visited it for years. We met Kavungal Chathunni Panikker, the last link in the family of Kavungal Sankara Panikker, the unfortunate kathakali artist who was expelled from the Namboodiri community and his art for consorting with Tatri.

The Tale of a Ferry is based on the film, *Kadavu*, the ferry that linked two separate worlds. MT came with us on a ferry to meet Santosh Antony, the young man who played the role of a child in the film twenty-five years ago.

Appunni's Quest, the documentary based on the novel, *Nalukettu*, has MT talking of his own tharavad, of the flood waters that once came up to the yard and of the people who came asking for shelter. Of the goddess who came one stormy night with a pot of rice for the starving children, walked into the house, her ankle bells tinkling, and made the machu, the small room on the western side of the nalukettu, her permanent abode…

We saw the pond in the Malamakkavu Devi temple as well, where the blue lotuses of *Neelatamara* bloom. The popular belief is that they bloom only if someone with faith makes an offering at the temple. When we reached the spot, there were four or five lotuses in the pond, perhaps to greet the writer who gave them fame – and a new name (they are called chengazheer flowers by the locals).

At some point during our travels, MT told us that even the trees and palms that swayed in the breeze were characters to him. There were moments when, in the midst of introducing his characters to us, he became silent and thoughtful. At other times, he spoke excitedly... Many of the characters he loved and wrote about are no more, only their children and grandchildren came to answer our questions.

MT is an ardent devotee of Kodikkunnathu Kavilamma, the deity of the temple in his village. As he climbed the steep steps to the temple energetically, MT transformed into a genial grandfather and told us old legends about the temple.

Throughout this quest, the stories we had read and the films we had seen returned to us as new experiences. I thank the destiny that allowed me to wander with MT through the landscapes of his stories and films. I am grateful for those moments.

My salutations to the storyteller.

Major Works

Novels
- *Nalukettu* (The House Around the Courtyard), Current Books, Trissur, 1958
- *Patiravum Pakalvelichavum* (Midnight and Daylight), P.K. Brothers, Calicut, 1958
- *Arabipponnu* (Arab Gold, written with N.P. Mohammed), Current Books, Trissur, 1960
- *Asuravittu* (Demon Seed), Current Books, Trissur, 1962
- *Manju* (Mist), Current Books, Trissur, 1964
- *Kalam* (Time), Current Books, Trissur, 1969
- *Vilapayatra* (The Funeral Procession), SPCS Kottayam, 1978
- *Randamoozham* (Bhima: Lone Warrior), SPCS Kottayam, 1984
- *Varanasi* (Benares), Current Books, Trissur, 2002

Stories (Anthologies)

Raktam Puranda Mantarikal (Blood-soaked Sand), Kalaradhana Sangam Palakkad, 1952

- *Veyilum Nilavum* (Sunlight and Moonlight), Janata Printing & Publishing House Madras, 1954
- *Vedanayude Pookkal* (Flowers of Sorrow), Samadharsi, Palakkad, 1955
- *Ninte Ormaykku* (In Your Memory), Current Books, Trissur, 1956
- *Iruttinte Atmavu* (The Soul of Darkness), Current Books, Trissur, 1957
- *Olavum Teeravum* (Ripple and Shore), Janata Books, Thiruvananthapuram, 1957
- *Kuttyedatti*, Current Books, Trissur, 1959
- *Nashtappetta Dinangal* (The Lost Days), Current Books, Trissur, 1960
- *Bandhanam* (The Binding), Current Books, Trissur, 1963
- *Patanam* (The Fall), Current Books, Trissur, 1966
- *Kaliveedu* (Playhouse), Current Books, Trissur, 1966
- *Varikkuzhi* (The Trap), Current Books, Trissur, 1967
- *Tiranjedutta Kadhakal* (Selected Stories), Current Books, Trissur, 1968
- *Dar-es-salam*, Current Books, Trissur, 1972
- *Ajnatante Uyarata Smarakam*, Current Books, Trissur, 1973
- *Abhayam Tedi Veendum*, SPCS, Kottayam, 1978
- *Swargavattil Turakkunna Samayam* (When the Gates of Heaven Open), Poorna Publications, Calicut, 1980
- *Vanaprastham* (Into the Forest), Current Books, Trissur, 1992
- *Sherlock*, Current Books, Trissur, 1998

Literary Studies
- *Kadhikante Panippura*, Current Books, Trissur, 1963
- *Hemingway Oru Mughavura*, Current Books, Trissur, 1968
- *Kadhikante Kala*, DC Books, Kottayam, 1984

Children's Literature
- *Manikyakallu*, Current Books, Trissur, 1957
- *Daya Enna Penkutty*, Malayalam Publications, Calicut, 1987
- *Tantrakari*, Guru Publications, Calicut, 1993
- *Manikyakallum Kuttikkadhakalum Chithrangalum*, DC Books, Kottayam, 2009

Travelogues
- *Manushyar Nizhalukal*, Poorna Publications, Calicut, 1960
- *Alkoottatil Taniye*, Current Books, Trissur, 1972
- *Vankadalile Tuzhavallakkar*, SPCS, Kottayam, 1998
- *MTyude Yatrakal*, H&C Books, Trissur, 2010

Essays
- *Kilivatililoode*, August Books, Valappadu, 1992
- *Ekakikalude Shabdham*, DC Books, Kottayam, 1994
- *Ramaneeyam Oru Kalam*, Olive Publications, Calicut, 1998
- *Kannantali Pookalude Kalam*, Green Books, Trissur, 2003
- *Ammayku*, Current Books, Trissur, 2005
- *Chitrateruvukal*, Current Books, Trissur, 2010

Screenplays
- *Pazhassiraja*, Current Books, Trissur, 2010
- *MTyude Tirakkadhakal* (6 volumes), DC Books, Kottayam, 2011